THE GIRL IN THE SPRINGS

ELLE GRAY
& K.S. GRAY

The Girl in the Springs
Copyright © 2024 by Elle Gray & K.S. Gray

All rights reserved. Without limiting the rights under copyright reserved above, no part of this publication may be reproduced, stored in or intro-duced into retrieval system, or transmitted, in any form, or by any means (electronic, mechanical, photocopying, recording, or otherwise) without the prior written permission of both the copyright owner and the above publisher of this book.

This is a work of fiction. Names, characters, places, brands, media, and in-cidents are either the products of the author's imagination or are used fic-titiously. The author acknowledges the trademarked status and trademark owners of various products referenced in this work of fiction, which have been used without permission. The publication/use of these trademarks is not authorized, associated with, or sponsored by the trademark owners.

CHAPTER ONE

"Birdie!"

MY NAME CUTS THROUGH THE WATER THAT CASCADES from the edges of my umbrella, forming an eight-pointed waterfall. I am literally veiled by water to the point of blindness and deafness, but the person who is calling for me is loud—very loud—and they are using my nickname, which means we're close, perhaps even friends. This only rules out about half of the town. I know most people around here to a nickname-level degree. The fact that the voice is male rules out another half again, but disorientated by the downpour, I'm still clueless.

I swivel on my heel and tilt my umbrella back so that I might see better and fill the backs of my Wellington boots with water. Not wanting the recipient of my attention to mistake my discomfort for irritation, I resist the instinctual grimace and smile politely. When I see Archie Whitman waving at me—his upper body peeking out of Curio's warped, emerald-green door—my eyes crinkle, and I forget all about my soggy socks. Archie Whitman is a good friend of mine. Curio is the best antique shop in town, at least in my opinion. It's hard to be unhappy when seeing either of them.

Archie's grey hair is slicked back, and the tiny silver hoop that dangles from his left ear catches the light. My dad affectionately calls him Daniel Night Lewis because of his resemblance to the actor and his eclectic fashion taste. I'd be lying if I didn't think the comparison was apt.

The persistent downfall eases for a moment, and Archie steps out onto the cobblestones of Heritage Lane, better known as 'The Knobbles' by the locals. Not all of Serenity Springs is so uneven; most of the sidewalk is brand new, but this section of the center of town, home to our oldest boutiques, is still as it was when it was built in 1898.

Archie has outdone himself in the fashion department today. On the top half, he's wearing a Fair Isle sweater in a lovely creamy color that reminds me of cheesecake, and on the lower portions, he is wearing a green tartan kilt with white knee socks and hunter-green Wellington boots that are identical to the pair on my own feet. I know this because we bought them together during the last blue moon occasion when he left his lair.

It's odd seeing someone's legs for the first time, and I resist the giggle that further curls my lips. Not that the sight is unpleasant; his calves are surprisingly muscular for someone who spends all day sitting in the corner reading or whittling. Maybe he gets out more than I think, or perhaps he has a Peloton stashed away in that mysterious upstairs apartment of his.

"Hi, Archie!" I yell out, too loudly, considering the lull. "The roses look good," I add, gesturing to the blooming bushes of crimson 'Mr. Lincoln' that grows on the road verge. I can tell he appreciates the compliment, but our eyes wander across the street to the parallel road verge outside of The Petal Parlor. Rosie's display—which all shop owners are permitted to curate upon their designated section of dirt—is magnificent, but it's an unfair comparison. Rosie is a florist, after all.

"I've got some things I think George would like," Archie replies, referring to my dad, his gaze still fixated on the perfectly spherical topiaries.

Archie doesn't bother with the basic conventions of conversation. He doesn't ask how you are; he'll tell you that you look sad. I appreciate that he doesn't mince words, especially today, considering the weather and that I have somewhere to be. Yet, I feel that something is going unsaid. Something important. I pause, waiting for him to elaborate, but he never does.

"Great, I'll swing by after work!" I chirp.

He nods, still not looking in my direction, and reverses back inside the slightly wonky two-story building. I chuckle, turn, and continue my journey toward Sproutville, the local preschool. After maybe twenty steps, my lingering smile falters as I rehash Archie's cryptic statement. He always has things my dad would like—my dad's office is basically a shrine dedicated to Curio—but he's never said so before. So what's different? What's new? Is he lonely or struggling to pay the bills? I suppose I haven't stopped by in a while, and March isn't exactly a booming sales period in a tourist town.

It clicks, and I stop dead. If I had a free hand, I'd smack my forehead. Something has been niggling at me all day, and now I know what. My parent's thirty-fifth anniversary is tomorrow, and whenever a special occasion involving my dad arises, I always buy him something from Curio.

With that remembrance comes another. We always have lunch together the day before their anniversary, as they spend their anniversary itself as just the two of them. It's my opportunity to hand over presents, and this year, I haven't even gotten them a card. Not yet, anyway. Thanks to Archie, the disaster may still be averted. Maybe he should take my place and become their child instead. He'd surely do a better job.

I hope whatever Maisy needs help with at Sproutville won't take too long, but considering I don't work there on Mondays, I have the feeling that there is a problem to solve. She would never call me in on a morning off if it wasn't important.

I arrive at Sproutville, the local preschool, and look it up and down, checking for open windows as I shake off my umbrella. Fortunately, it seems that Maisy has remembered to shut them all this time. Sproutville—adorably named by Dolly Abel, our boss—is like most of the buildings in the center of town. It's another porchless Victorian-era two-story with bow windows crammed into a row with no alleys or gaps. The only thing that sets it apart, aside from a couple of modern tweaks, is that it's painted a gleaming white instead of a bold color like the emerald Curio or mauve Petal Parlor.

I close my umbrella, balance it against the pot of waterlogged primroses, type in the security code, and rush inside as soon as the buzz sounds. The noise of children grows as I meander up the cubby-lined hallway, and I think to go back and tip out my boots when I see Maisy Jenkins, my best friend and co-worker, glance at me, her face consumed with pure panic.

"Miss Hartley!" the children cry out as I emerge, but my greeting is quieter than usual. This, I soon realize, is because half of the children are crying.

As I move to Maisy, who is half-standing, half-kneeling, I put a hand on her shoulder and hear relief whistle out of her nose. Even her hair—coily, blue-tinted, and slicked into a high puff—seems to deflate as the exhale continues.

I'm about to ask her what's going on when Ethan, the loudest boy in the class of twenty-three kids, asks, "What if Rex ate Snowball?"

The kids who were already crying, cry harder, and a few that had remained strong break down with them. I look at Maisy, who doesn't look back. So, I look around instead, and my eyes land on a remarkably pristine squoval patch of wooden countertop. That's where the hamster cage is usually located. A cage currently inhabited by a giant, male Syrian hamster—with even bigger nuts—named Snowball—and both animal and cage are, unfortunately, nowhere in sight

"Rex could've eaten him!" Ethan reiterates, seemingly enjoying the screams this remark issues from his classmates.

"Yes, honey, you've said that," Maisy says kindly before muttering in my direction, "Several times."

Rex is a grey tomcat who basically owns Serenity Springs. If Rex were a human, he'd be Vito Corleone in *The Godfather*. Last year, I saw that cat give a raccoon a dirty look for playing in my neighbor's trashcan, and I swear to God, I've never seen a raccoon in this town again. So, I suppose it's not too far-fetched that he'd kill the preschool hamster, but much to Rex's annoyance, I have something in my arsenal that he doesn't—the ability to open and shut doors. We also have security cameras because what kind of preschool doesn't in this day and age?

Furthermore, thanks to my morning shift co-worker Maisy Jenkins and her technological prowess, we even have our own app that the parents can tune into. I think they and I would be aware if a twenty-pound grey tabby with one eye and a perpetual scowl had broken in. Which, to say the least, is good news for Snowball.

"Rex hasn't eaten anybody," I reassure the kids, lowering myself into a squat on the floor so as not to be imposing.

"I saw him eat a squirrel yesterday," Talulah protests.

Maisy muffles a snort, and I resist the twitches at the corners of my mouth. "Okay, but Snowball lives inside, and his cage is also missing. I don't think Rex could've eaten that, could he?"

Daisy, another tear-streaked little girl, shakes her head. "Because he doesn't have hands."

"That's exactly right," I say, though I don't exactly understand her meaning. "Now, did anybody see a grownup or a kid take Snowball and his cage out of Sproutville? I know he goes home with you for sleepovers if you get a lot of gold stars in a row."

The kids look at each other blankly, and though no one admits to having taken Snowball, this case is not a lost cause yet. Children of this age are easily preoccupied, distracted, and even more forgetful, which makes them poor witnesses. As a grownup,

I need to focus on the evidence, which in this case is gold stars. If I find out who got five gold stars last week, Monday to Friday, I'll know who had Snowball for the weekend.

I straighten and help Maisy to her feet. She gives me a half hug and whispers, "Thank God you came. I was considering pulling the fire alarm."

"This might just be my greatest case yet," I mutter in response.

Maisy titters and leads me away to the welcome desk. "That's not how I'd put it."

"You wouldn't?" I ask, semi-surprised. Tracking down a beloved pet feels like a highlight in my career thus far. Especially considering I've only been a fully-fledged PI for the past six months.

"What about Jerry Ruger and the missing snow tires? Or Pam Brown and her long-lost sister?" Maisy asks, and I open my mouth to interrupt, but she holds up a hand. "What about the 'Welcome to Serenity Springs' sign vandal? Or that traveling psychic guy who was scamming all the old folks? Not to mention all that online armchair investigating stuff."

"Alright. You're right, I've had a very illustrious career," I admit sarcastically.

"Oh my God, you're so modest," Maisy grumbles, rolling her eyes dramatically. "If I was also a world-famous detective—"

"Local private investigator," I correct.

"And I looked like Miss America meets a Victoria's Angel," she continues, ignoring me, "I would be the opposite of modest. Seriously, I'd be a nightmare. I don't know how you do it. I guess that's why you're America's Sweetheart and I'm not."

"*America's* Sweetheart?" I laugh in disbelief, though the compliment still makes me blush. "A handful of articles, a true crime Reddit following, and few small-time cases does not a celebrity make."

She rolls her eyes. "Fine. Serenity's Sweetheart. But you'll get there one day."

"I hope not."

"Alright, Miss Hermit. Do you have any leads?"

It's not as catchy as Miss Marple, but it is apt, so I don't request a rebrand. "Do we keep copies of the star charts?" I ask, knowing that the parents take them home on Fridays and neither Maisy nor I work that day. Dolly is also on vacation and has made it explicitly clear that she is not to be contacted unless it's an emergency, and I don't think this constitutes one, not yet.

Maisy shakes her head. "Nah, I scan in written reports, but I've never bothered with star charts."

"What about the app? Can you watch previous streams?"

Maisy's eyes light up. "Yeah. You can watch up to a week's worth."

"Then consider this case as good as solved, my dear Jenkins," I say, affecting a terrible British accent as I open the app on my phone and flick back to Friday.

I skim through the day to pick up time and see Cole Cabrera and his mother, Jennifer. She—towering, tan, and dressed in a power suit—holds Cole's star report in one of her hands, and in the other, she grips the handle of Snowball's cage. I tilt the screen toward Maisy, and she exhales once again. This explains where Snowball is and why none of the kids owned up to having Snowball at their house. Cole is selectively mute, especially at preschool.

"I'll call Jennifer," she says.

"Let me. She lives next to Curio, and I'm going that way anyway. I'll pick Snowball up once I'm done with my errands, and I'll be back way before closing."

"I owe you a coffee in the morning," Maisy replies.

"No reward needed," I reply, turning into a bastardized version of Columbo. "I love that little fluffball."

Maisy scoffs. "I like your Holmes better. And he is cute for being such a bastard."

"Cute but a bastard... Isn't that your type?" I tease.

Maisy shoves me gently. "Get going and bring my boyfriend back."

I laugh as I leave, and though my doing so causes further distress, Maisy loudly announcing that I'm on a Snowball rescue mission triggers a return to form for the usually happy children of Serenity Springs. Their giggles remind me of how much I love what I do, both as an assistant childminder and a private investigator. I want people to be happy.

I open my umbrella again and step out onto the sidewalk when something catches my eye. It's a laminated poster stapled to the nearest telephone pole, black and white and unaffected by the weather. At the center is a smiling photo of eighteen-year-old Mia Ramsey. They've raised the reward. It makes sense. She's been missing for five days now.

CHAPTER TWO

Mia Ramsey, daughter of Lloyd and Kate Ramsey, has been missing for nearly five days. Last Thursday, she left the house at 7:13pm on the dot. Kate knows this because she was making dinner—salmon and boiled potatoes—at the time, and was in the middle of setting a timer on her phone when Mia kissed her on the cheek and headed out the front door. I know this not because I'm nosy—which I can be—but because the Ramseys are long-time family friends. They might as well be my aunt, uncle, and cousin, respectively. To say the least, I've been climbing the walls since Mia disappeared. Which might explain my recent forgetfulness.

Mia did not say where she was going but did say that she was getting a ride and would be back by ten. Neither Lloyd nor Kate questioned this. For one thing, she'd never been out past curfew and had never shown signs of drunkenness or drug use. I get it. Mia is an angel. More than that, Mia has proved herself to be a trustworthy, sensible girl not only in manner but hard evidence. She graduated from school with honors and a 3.8 GPA. She was on the track team, debate team, and any other team you could think of. She has every Girl Scout badge on offer. She plays the flute, picks up trash on weekday evenings, and volunteers on Sundays at Sunny Side, the local retirement home. She is not the type of girl a parent worries about. Especially as she has a scholarship and will be, God willing, starting at Oregon University in the fall.

Even without the posters, her image is etched into my brain. She is five foot nine, lanky, with freckles, green eyes, and coarse brown hair, often worn in French braids. She has braces, and I told her I envied her the last time I saw her. My teeth are straight, for the most part, without the help of metal brackets, but I begged my parents every day as a teenager to pay to make them perfect.

That isn't my only source of envy where Mia is concerned. In the summer, Mia's skin turns to a rich tan color, whereas I just burn. I know this because I've spent at least one week every summer for the past seventeen years with her, her parents, and my parents at the Ramseys' lake cabin in Medina. One might think it strange to go on a vacation that's only two hours away, but Serenity is more of a mountains and rivers type of town. So, if you like fishing and boating, you have to go elsewhere, and Lloyd Ramsey really likes both of those things.

I digress. Mia is a very trustworthy girl, which is why neither of her parents, who were busy with other things—Lloyd in his office and Kate in the kitchen—looked out the window at the car that was picking her up. They assumed she was hanging out with friends, trying to make the most of her family-orientated gap year before moving to Oregon. Even when the clock ticked past ten, they still weren't concerned. Only when it hit eleven, and she hadn't answered their numerous attempts at contacting her, did they begin to fear for their daughter.

THE GIRL IN THE SPRINGS

They then called Mia's friends, the local hospital, and then the police. There had been no road accidents. There were no young women in the hospital. Their neighbors, who had been busy with their own 7:00pm dinners, hadn't looked outside. And in Serenity Springs, nobody has Ring doorbells or security cameras. People pretend to, with signs and dummy cams. Nobody wants to be the first to get one and look as if they're paranoid and distrusting of their neighbors. After all, Serenity Springs is a safe haven. Bad things don't happen here.

Which is why Mia is fine, I'm sure. Or, at the very least, alive. She ran off with a boy or is getting cold feet about college. Perhaps she's having a mental health episode. It happens, especially with high achievers like Mia. She'd be the type of person to hide it well.

Yeah, it's probably something like that. Still, when I pass yet another poster, I avoid eye contact and then feel guilty for doing so. I shouldn't be ignoring Mia; I should be looking for her. I am a private investigator, after all. Her parents have indicated on more than one occasion that they'd like my help. The problem is, I've never handled anything this serious before. Maybe Maisy is right. Maybe I am too modest and riddled with self-doubt, but at the same time, I think I'm right to be nervous. I know I'm letting the Ramseys down, but they'd be all the more disappointed if I started investigating and turned up nothing. That's probably selfish. No, not probably. It *is* selfish. I'm more concerned with my own failure than the possibility of success. I'm worried about what they'll think of me if I say yes and fail to bring their daughter home.

I shake my head at myself in shame as I trot across the road. I nod at the driver, who stops for me, but their headlights bore into me like a sign from above. I should do this. I need to look into this. So I tell myself, at the very least, I'll write up all the information I have and see if anything jumps out at me. I won't tell her parents that I'm taking on their daughter's case. I don't want to get their hopes up any more than the local police already have. I'll dip my toe in and see if it leads to swimming.

I approach The Petal Parlor to get my mom's gift and see Rosie watching today's tenth bout of rain from the doorway with a steaming cup of tea. She's dressed in layers of finely knitted gold and mustard, her envious rainboots are yellow with an adorable chicken print, and her pixie cut is a wonderful shade of flamingo pink. She looks as if she was born with that color, even though I've previously known her to be pink and purple. I envy her funkiness, as well as the boots, even though I know I could never pull any of it off. My naturally platinum blonde locks are all I'll ever have until I go shock-white like Mom.

"Hi, Birdie," she says dreamily. "Fabulous weather we're having."

She's not being sarcastic. She says this rain or shine, and though I consider myself a positive person, I have nothing on Rosie Sheen's optimism.

"It certainly is relaxing," I reply, not happy about being wet but looking forward to curling up next to the window in my apartment later and listening to the pitter-patter as I read.

"Mm," Rosie agrees. "Here for Eleanor?"

"Yep," I chirp.

My mother loves flowers more than she loves most things. I think in order of preference, it's family, the dogs, then the garden in Eleanor Hartley's list of loves. I must admit I love these things, too, and envy my mother and sister's gardens. When I can afford to stop renting and buy a house, a large yard for ducks and vegetables will be high on my list. I'll need their help, though. I know my peonies from my dahlias, but I'm lost when it comes to germinating and cutting. All I can hope is that I've inherited their green thumbs.

The old bell above the door dings as we enter the mauve-colored store with its gold filagree cursive sign, and Rex meows at me as he laps from his water bowl in the corner. He isn't Rosie's cat; no one could 'own' Rex, but they are companions of sorts. She also got him fixed, which I suspect every female cat owner in the area thanks her for.

Rosie removes her spectacles as she moves behind her desk. "So it's your parents thirty... third?"

"Thirty-five," I correct.

"How time flies. I remember their wedding day well. Much nicer than mine, to say the least."

"I didn't know you were married," I reply, just trying to make small talk, but I can tell it's a misstep when her gaze turns vacant.

"As nice as it could be, considering I married a man with a secret family on the side."

"Ah," I say, words failing me.

"Anyway. The color for thirty-five years is..." she trails off, humming, looking at a chalkboard behind the desk. "Coral. And the stone is jade. So I'm thinking coral and a light, yellowy green. Perfect for Spring."

"Sounds great."

"You sure?" she questions skeptically as if she hasn't been doing this for longer than I've been alive.

"You're the master," I laugh. "I'll happily defer to you."

"Well, if you're anything like your mother, I daresay you know a thing or two, too."

"I think I need a few more years under my belt before I even consider myself a novice. Let alone a master."

"Calling me old?" Rosie teased.

"Not old, wise," I reply quickly and bat my lashes for good measure.

"You charmer," she says with a blue-lidded wink, pushing past me as she rounds the desk.

As if in a trance, she begins to put the flowers together on a large sheet of thick, pink paper. I love watching her work. I barely know what ASMR is, but I think this must be akin to it. It's how the colors come together and how she deftly arranges them. It's the sound of the paper and scissors snipping. It's the ambrosial smell. I could watch her for hours, and I have. What's funny is that I always think it's already perfect, but then she'll swap or add something, and I realize how little I know. Watching a genius at work is always nice, even if it fills me with envy. I'm a jill of all trades and a master of none. I always want to add more to my hobby repertoire, as if I don't have drawers filled with half-finished craft projects.

She adds a bow to the bouquet, and I pay up. She gives me a hug that smells like cinnamon, and then I'm 180 degrees and heading back across the road toward Curio. As I cross, Maisy sends a text telling me that Jennifer isn't home, but I'll find the front door key underneath a pot of geraniums in the front 'yard' of her 'redstone' home. We call them redstones as they're reminiscent of New York brownstones, but instead of brown, they're red brick and have a significantly more Victorian look to them. Curio is the last store at the end of the row, then there's a crossroad to the right, then the houses.

I text back with a thumbs up to reassure her that I will retrieve Snowball and step inside Curio. This door also jingles when opened, but it's lazier and lower-pitched than the Petal Parlor's high-pitched ding. Archie looks up from his usual spot in the corner. There's a small desk beside him with an ancient cash register, an even older typewriter, and several mugs of coffee whose contents are another form of fusty. There's a glass ashtray, too, even though Archie hasn't smoked for five years. Not that he ever did so inside, but on his breaks, he'd pick it up and hold it in hand in the street or in the small backyard while puffing away.

"Birdie," he states bluntly in neither a greeting nor a question. His thick reading glasses are on, and his gaze is downcast, focused on some hefty-looking tome.

"Archie," I reply in a similar cadence.

He looks up, amused at my mimicry. "I like the outfit. Vintage?"

"The cardigan was my great aunt Mary's, but my Grandma June made me the dress," I say, glancing down at the knee-length, white, linen, shirred dress with its elegant square neckline. The spaghetti straps beneath my baby blue cardigan are a secret just for me. They're a sexy secret, just for me, much like my matching bra and underwear.

Though obviously platonic, I'm glad that Archie appreciates my outfits. Few men do. My ex-boyfriend Gavin—who I was with for most of my ten years spent in New York—always wanted me to be sexier rather than appreciating how much effort I put in or how my clothes suit *me* and make *me* happy. I think he was embarrassed to be with me sometimes, as he used to call me a grandma.

"The boots don't match," Archie critiques.

I acknowledge this sagely. "I know. I need these in more colors."

"As do I. Thank you for them, by the way. I don't know how I lived before these came into my life."

"No problem. They suit you. And they match your outfit."

"They do," Archie replies, standing and moving to a nearby shelf dedicated to paperweights. I follow him, and he, as usual, umms and ahhs, plucks things from shelves, and puts them in my arms. I then move these items to the small desk, where I will then sit, have a coffee, and decide which item is best suited for my father. And by 'I decide,' I, of course, mean Archie will tell me what to buy and make it seem like it's my idea. In my opinion, it's a perfect system, and he's not steered me wrong so far.

Usually, we don't speak during the initial stages of this ritual—aside from his under-the-breath muttering as he curates the selection—but today, he sparks conversation. "So, Mia Ramsey is still missing," he says.

"Yeah, she is," I say sadly, staring a cat-shaped piggy bank in its big blue eyes.

"Hmm," he hums.

"Five days now," I add.

"That's not good, is it?"

"I guess not."

"Are you going to investigate?" he questions, his tone implying that I should.

"I'm thinking about it."

"Good. It's about time someone around here did their job," he retorts, his tone unusually cold.

"Well, I think Sheriff Mercer—"

"Oh, I'm not talking about Sheriff Mercer," he says, returning to his usual flat tone. "She's a smart woman. I'm sure she'll find Mia. I'm sure she'll attend to anything presently pressing."

"Presently?" I push, sensing more things unspoken.

"The missing teenagers," he states, glancing at me sharply before returning to his duty. This is something he expects me to know about; this is my hometown, after all.

"Missing teenagers?" I inquire, holding a glass paperweight in each hand like juggling balls.

"How many was there?" he asks himself. "Six? Seven? I can't remember. But every few years, another pair disappears. The first couple was, oh, twenty years ago now, I think. The prior sheriff did nothing. God rest his soul," he adds dryly.

Something unlocks in my head, and I remember Lucia Nunez, one of the girls in my sister's friendship group, going missing. It must have been about fifteen years ago now. Regarding twenty years ago, I'm clueless, considering I would've been only ten, and regarding anything more recent, I was in New York from 2011 to 2021. A waste of a decade spent on a man who didn't love me, but that's a story I rarely have the mental capacity to recount.

"And none of them have ever been found?" I question, confused.

"Nope."

"And their cars?"

"Left behind along with their belongings."

"Why..." I trail off, flabbergasted, a state of being I'm rarely in. "If their cars were left behind, that means they were taken. Surely. Why doesn't anyone ever talk about this?"

"Well, when it comes to couples, people assume they've run away together. And then there's the gap between the crimes. People forget. Police get lazy. Families move away." Archie shrugs, but it's sharper and higher than usual. This bothers him.

"Mia doesn't fit the pattern. Of being in a couple," I say.

"Didn't somebody pick her up?"

"I guess. But her boyfriend—Samuel, I think—isn't missing."

"Can one not have more than one boyfriend?"

"That's true."

Archie shrugs again, softer this time, steps off a stool, and hands me a whiskey decanter. "Milk and two sugars?"

The topic of Mia has come to a close, and I know better than to poke and prod. "Always," I answer.

He shakes his head in disappointment at my order, puts the last of the items on the desk, and hurries off to the little kitchenette in the back to start up the coffee. I sit in my usual spot, and on any other day, I'd use this time to go through the objects on the table, but today, I stare blankly at them, my mind in other places. I have added another item to today's agenda after retrieving Snowball and having lunch with my parents—research.

CHAPTER THREE

USING THE WOBBLY OLD STILE, I HOP THE FENCE AND succeed in neither snagging my dress nor dropping my parents' gifts. Hardly surprising considering I've used this stile a million times before, but I've seen my fair share of accidents on its account. Before encountering this one, most locals have no idea what a stile is. They're uncommon, if not nonexistent, in North America. My parents, George and Eleanor, might very well be the owners of the only one. Probably not, but I've never seen another one.

A stile is typically a plank placed perpendicular to a fence, which allows you to climb said fence easily. It's a leg up, basically, and they're popular in the UK, allowing citizens and their

'Right to Roam' to cross paddock boundaries while keeping livestock contained.

Similarly—to contain livestock but not ruin the scenic view—the UK also has something called a 'Ha-ha,' which is a trench that's invisible until you're standing on the very edge of it. Or until you fall in. Thus, the name.

Fortunately, my parents' property doesn't have a Ha-ha, and the only 'livestock' they have is an abundance of dogs and a handful of ducks. However, there is a stile because when my English great-great-grandmother married my great-great-grandfather and moved to America to be with him, he decided that the preexisting houses weren't good enough for her and handed her the reins to have a new one built.

Inspired by what she had seen thus far in Serenity Springs, she opted for a Queen Anne Revival style in baby blue with white lattice and trim. However, an English likeness wasn't enough; she wanted authenticity, or at least touches of it. She wanted what she'd grown up with in the beautiful Avon countryside. I don't consider myself English—don't tell my dad—so I'm not the best judge of these things, but I think she did a pretty good job considering the pine tree surroundings.

I wander up the hill, and the three-story house comes into view. At over a century old, it's looking good for its age. Really good. Breathtaking even. Much like my great-great grandmother herself. Winifred Hartley made it to an impressive 101 before passing away in 1989, which was sadly before my time. Luckily, I did get to meet her daughter, Lydia, before her peaceful departure in 2001, and her daughter, my Grandma June, is still alive and kicking. I'm going to visit her at Sunny Side—the best retirement home in the county—later in the week. I am not overexaggerating when I say that place is fit for a queen, which is probably why she was so eager to move in after my grandfather Gerald's passing. Frankly, I'd give my left hand to move in tomorrow. Well, maybe half a pinkie.

Piper, Seamus, and Murphy—my parents' border collie, Irish wolfhound, and golden retriever, respectively—bound down the hillside to meet me in the middle. Unfortunately, due to the slickness of the terrain, I know that we're doomed to collide before it even happens. Soon, my white dress resembles a dirt-brown and grass-green Jackson Pollock painting with finishing touches in three shades of hair. Ironically, this is what I love about white dresses. If they stain, you can always bleach them back to ivory. If this was pastel yellow, then I'd be screwed.

"Hello, hello, stinky one, two, and three," I coo, stooping to their level while skillfully keeping the flowers out of chaos's reach. Not that Mom would mind a couple of missing petals. As I said, dogs rank above flowers.

I'm also a dog lover and can't wait to have one of my own. Something pocket-sized that can endure apartment living and is less of a bull in a china shop than this bunch of bruisers. Maybe a dainty Italian greyhound. I need something other than my sister Ada's unborn baby to knit outfits for, or else that poor kid's wardrobe will be overflowing.

"Hello, darling!" Dad calls from the top of the hill, sounding—and looking—much like Richard E. Grant despite the fact that Grandma June doesn't have a trace of her grandmother's posh accent. I'm not sure whether to blame his time spent at Cambridge University or his anglophilia for that.

"Oh, God, your dress," Mom follows up in dismay, her strong Tennessee accent starkly contrasting my father's gentle English tone. "Honey, don't let them jump all over you like that!"

I laugh as I stand up, and the dogs run toward my mother's commands. "It's fine!" I insist.

"You're filthy," Mom counters.

I look down. I am. I shrug.

She tuts. "You're not coming inside like that."

I look past them at the paved patio and see that the outdoor table is set with nibbles and, as predicted, champagne. She's joking, in her dry, haughty way. We were always going to eat outside. "That's brave," I say, pointing at the spread.

"We trust in Bruce," my father says, faux-sternly, referring to our local weatherman.

"Far be it from me to question Bruce," I reply, out of breath as I finish my ascent. It's a long walk to my parents' house, and Dad's present—an ivory carving of a beluga whale mounted to a slab of driftwood—is heavier than I thought. The bouquet is heavier still.

Mom shrieks as I reveal the poorly hidden flowers from behind my back. "Are these for me?" she asks, even though she knows they are, and I know she saw them before now.

"Happy Anniversary! And, Dad, this is for you."

"Thank you, darling," Dad murmurs, his glee apparent but subdued. As Mom hugs me half to death, he nimbly takes the brown paper-wrapped gift from my outstretched hand and puts it to his ear as if it will reveal its secrets verbally. Meanwhile, Mom keeps hugging me, and I happily let her. If I was breathless before, now I am suffocating. Mom doesn't look like a hugger. She's tall, thin, poised, with a 'resting bitch face' that can hurt the feelings of even the most steeled individual, but despite appearances, she's a major softy. I'm actually the prickly one when it comes to physical intimacy. 'My little cactus,' Dad likes to call me. It's not that I never give out hugs. I hug my family and Maisy on occasion. I'm just not big on being touched. My ex-boyfriend Gavin hated that. He wanted constant access to intimacy. I actually think I was cuddlier before I met him. His constant haranguing wore on me, and it didn't help that he was often shower-averse.

My mind wanders to Patrick Donovan, my sister's perfect husband, who definitely is not shower or grooming averse and has never forced me to hug him. "Is Ada coming?" I ask. They only live three towns away, but I feel like I barely see them anymore.

"No. We might stop by at their house tomorrow morning on our way to Seattle. But we do want to talk to you about her." My dad's expression is mischievous, and he glances at Mom, who smirks at him.

"You two have a secret," I say, hands on my hips.

They laugh, and without answering me, Mom herds us to the white, wrought iron table with Piper's help. There's a vase ready on the table filled with water, and she rips the paper off in a deft singular movement and plunges the bouquet into it. She knows me well. Maybe I should change things up.

Dad, on the other hand, won't open his gift until he's alone in his office later. I think he worries that he won't like something I give him, and it'll show on his face. Based on the shelves in his office filled with my presents, I haven't disappointed him yet, but I guess there's always room for unlikelihood.

I settle into my seat, reach for a carrot stick, and dunk it into the bowl of creamy ranch dressing, which is here solely for my benefit. My gaze lingers on the array of tiny triangular sandwiches and the world's best potato salad. I adore lunches at my parents' place. While my mom may shy away from spice and foreign flavors, her culinary skills and presentation are undeniable.

"So, what's the deal with Ada?" I inquire, trying to sound blasé, even though my heart rate has increased to 'brisk walk' levels.

"Well," Dad begins. "As you know, we sold the businesses and the hardware store last year in order to retire comfortably and set aside money for your inheritance."

"Except for Hartbeats Playhouse," Mom adds quickly, referring to her community theater. She was a reasonably successful TV actress in the eighties, but her real love was always the theater, so when she met my dad and moved out here, he bought the local playhouse for her to renovate and run. It's been quite the hit.

"Yes," Dad continues with a nod. "You'll be inheriting that one."

"Please stop talking like you're going to die soon," I say, half-joking, half-nervous.

"Well, that's exactly the point. We're not—God willing—going to die soon. Ideally, we'll both live to see triple digits. And we'd rather see you girls thrive while we're alive instead of making you wait around until we're dead to get a leg up in life."

"Okay," I say slowly, shifting from nervous to excited. I make okay money doing what I do, but I'd be lying if the idea of a 'leg up' didn't thrill me. I mean, what apartment-renting millennial doesn't want that?

Dad suddenly looks sheepish, and I realize I'm grinning uncontrollably. "Now, we don't know what we'll do for you yet. But we do have an idea for Ada."

"Oh, that sounds terrible," Mom says remorsefully. "I hope you don't think we're picking favorites! I promise you'll get something of equal value, and we're open to suggestions. Perhaps we could buy your apartment outright? Get you on the proper ladder."

"It's fine," I laugh. "And I'll think about it. So, what's the plan for Ada?"

Mom exhales and fills her glass with champagne. "Well, what with the baby on the way, and because we own some land on the edge of Salish Pines Forest, we thought we'd build her and Patrick a surprise house. They've already been looking in the area."

"Really?" I question in genuine disbelief. Ada's never shown much interest in moving back to our hometown or even visiting it.

"Isn't it wonderful?" Mom responds dreamily.

"Yeah," I say, retaining my shocked expression. It really is. I've missed my sister.

"They've asked us to join them on the house viewings," Dad interjects. "We'll hold them off by poo-pooing everything while you design their dream home. We've already hired a crew."

I raise my eyebrows and point inwardly. "Me? You want me to design the house?"

"Of course you, darling. You two have always had the same taste. You have that, you know, sibling telepathy thing. Like identical twins have."

We're not identical twins; Ada is four years older than me, but he's not wrong. We often have silent conversations, and not one thing passes the other by despite the lack of audio. He's also definitely not wrong about our taste. Every thrifting adventure together ends in us gravitating toward the same items and having to decide who goes home with the prize via an endless game of "You take it," "No, you take it."

"Okay, and when do we tell her?" I inquire, completely on board now, a vision board blooming in my mind.

"At the baby shower in two months," Mom replies. "The guys are going to head over tomorrow to take a look at the land, so can you swing by the day after that to get the ball rolling?"

I nod enthusiastically, mouth full of sandwich and champagne. Though a little stressed, I am overjoyed to have been designated this incredibly important task. I'm already co-hosting the baby shower, but this is an even greater honor. This will be the house my niece or nephew grows up in. This could be my sister's forever home.

"And you're not jealous at all?" Mom checks, scrutinizing my beaming expression.

"God, no. Ada and the baby are the priority. Of course, they are."

She looks satisfied and takes a sip. "Well, we haven't forgotten about you. Just one thing at a time."

We continue to chit-chat, and snack, and when the conversation wanes, I change subjects. For whatever reason, I land on Mia, even though today is a day of celebration. "Have the Ramseys heard anything yet?" I ask.

My parents' expressions darken just a touch. Dad shakes his head, and Mom chews her lip. "Not yet," the latter states, coldness tinging her words.

"The traffic cams haven't shown anything?"

"They must've taken the back roads. Easy to avoid cameras in this town," Mom replies, irritation replaced by frustration and sadness, white knuckles emerging as she grips the condensation-coated bottle.

"Yeah, of course," I murmur distantly, staring at nothing, lost in thought.

"You're not considering taking on the case, are you, darling?" Dad asks airily as if he doesn't have an opinion on the matter, even though I know he does.

I focus and see that both of my parents are staring at me. "Maybe."

"Honey, don't you think this is a police matter?" Mom asks.

Her tone is nonchalant, breezy, as if she doesn't have an opinion on the matter even though she most certainly does. She just doesn't want to sound rude or condescending, but with a question like that, both are unavoidable. I know what they think of what I do, even though they've never said it outright. Working part-time at the preschool is barely a real job in their eyes, but amateur turned professional sleuth? That's a hobby at best.

Dad clears his throat. "You are very good at what you do, Birdie, darling. Finding pets, long-lost relatives, stolen tires. But this is serious. Poor Mia might've been trafficked. Or worse. I just don't think you should get in the investigator's way. Sheriff Mercer knows what she's doing."

I nod and smile, but the corners of my eyes crinkle. I reach for a sandwich if only to occupy myself with something. "Yeah," I say at last, after several dry-mouthed bites to occupy myself. "You're right. It's just hard not doing anything. I want to help."

"Send them some flowers," Mom says kindly, reaching out and patting my hand. "That's all any of us can do. But don't send them too soon. They're away."

"Away?"

Mom purses her lips, then sighs and relents. "They're on a road trip to somewhere in the middle of Idaho. They think that Mia might've been in touch with Lloyd's family and that one of them might've come to pick her up."

My face must ask further questions because Mom impatiently adds. "Lloyd is not in contact with his family. It's been that way for as long as we've been close to the pair of them."

"Do you know why?" I ask.

"We've heard whispers," Dad replies, but I can tell that that is a complete sentence and no more information is coming.

"Why do they think she was in touch with them?"

"Who knows?" Mom says. "Maybe she misses her grandmother. They've been trying to log in to her Facebook and all of that, but to no avail. Apparently, that's only permissible if foul play is suspected and at the request of the authorities. Hopefully, it ends up being as simple as family drama."

"Yeah, hopefully," I reply, and feeling the tension lay over me as thick as the post-rain humidity, I change the subject once again and regale my parents with the somewhat anticlimatic tale of Snowball, the hamster. This delights them, and I allow them to think that they've won, that they've convinced me, but that couldn't be further from the truth.

CHAPTER FOUR

I OPEN MY EYES AT 5:00AM, AND IMMEDIATELY, I AM WIDE awake, fueled by last night's failure. I'd gotten home much later than expected, damp, muddy, and tipsier than I'd been in months. So, I showered, ate some of the luncheon leftovers for dinner, sat down in front of my laptop, and promptly fell asleep on the couch. I didn't get any research done. So, I am dedicating today to making a start on the case. I can't believe it's taken me this long. Mia has been missing for six days. I guess that's fear for you—or faith in the local police—but I refuse to be a coward any longer.

First on the agenda is coffee with Maisy, which is not as frivolous an activity as it sounds. In order to do research, I need to be able to focus, which requires caffeine and lots of it. I also require peace and quiet, which I won't get if I don't appease Maisy by taking her up on her 'IOU.'

I examine my outfit in the full-length ornate mirror: a pale, spring-green tiered dress, Birkenstock sandals, and cable-knit cream tights. I narrow my eyes and decide that the green doesn't wash me out as I had feared. It's easily done when you're as pale as I am with white-blonde hair and icy blue eyes. I add a matching cream cardigan to the mix, sling my crochet daisy purse over my shoulder, and I'm ready to go.

I walk through my apartment and consider my parents' offer to buy it outright. I do love it here. It's the first place that's ever been all mine, and it's the perfect size for me and in an ideal location. Not to mention, it's beautiful with its bay window seat, high ceilings, and glossy wooden floors. Yet, maybe something bigger and more rural would be better. I want at least two children before I'm forty, and a garden to tend would be a dream come true. Maybe some livestock, too. A pony, perhaps. For the kids. I laugh at the thought. I'm getting way ahead of myself. Before any of that, I need to meet a man, and it seems good ones are hard to come by. And as Maisy likes to remind me, you can't meet men if you don't leave the house. So, off I go.

Though chillier than expected, it isn't raining today, which means that Maisy and I might stand a chance at snagging a seat inside Cobblestone Cafe. Most people around here prefer being outside if it's an option, flocking to the park benches and picnic tables of Secret Garden or Willow Walkway. I enjoy being outside, too, but there's something magical about the cafe itself, and it's nice to do something different for once. I've seen the gardens a million times. Though, in saying that, I've heard that Secret Garden—our not-so-secret 'central park'—has joined forces with local bar and brewery, The Homestead, by erecting a pavilion-slash-beer garden. As a borderline teetotaler, I rarely go to the Homestead, but I might make an exception if only to admire the locals' efforts to keep this town fresh. I just hope that the idea doesn't result in cigarette butt litter or broken glass.

THE GIRL IN THE SPRINGS

I warm up as I walk, and catching the eyes of a group of young male tourists, I feel good as I do so. You can look, but you can't touch, gentlemen. Remember, this is *my* kingdom.

When I see the sign for Cobblestone Cafe—a wall-mounted teapot that hangs over the white picket gate—I pick up the pace, enter the brick floor courtyard, and swerve right. Immediately, I see Maisy sitting inside by the window, and she excitedly gestures at the empty seat beside her, her mouth open in a silent scream. I laugh as I jog toward the door, and as soon as I'm inside, warmth washes over me, as does the rich scent of freshly ground coffee and vanilla tea candles. It's dark and moody, and I am hurtled back through time to an era of corsets and hoop skirts. I could spend all day in here, and I would if I could afford to do so. It's not cheap, so I make my drinks and occasional sweet treats last as long as I can without getting side-eyed by the baristas.

I approach Maisy and hook my cardigan over the back of the seat, and Maisy rises to hug me before we join the waiting line, which is more of a vague assembly of people who step up to the counter in order of arrival. Glancing around, it appears that we'll get our turn after the blonde lady with the pug in her purse and the old man in the bright red sweater. They order a flat white and Earl Grey tea, respectively, and I take a step forward once they're waiting in the wings.

I gasp as a very tall man dressed in flannel, dirty jeans, and muddy boots enters the building, steps in front of us, and ambles up to the counter, pocketing his ancient flip phone and swapping it for a deteriorating wallet. I scoff, but he mustn't hear me because of the hustle and bustle because he doesn't turn or acknowledge me in any way. Surely, no one is that rude. *Surely*, this must be a mistake. He orders an espresso, and I don't recognize him or his voice. He's a tourist, I realize. Figures.

I move to tap his shoulder at the same time as he turns, which ends up with me nearly jabbing his chest. I drop my hand sheepishly before straightening and resuming my indignation. "You cut us off," I loudly inform him.

He looks down at me with raised brows. Then he then looks at Maisy, who offers a small wave and a dimpled smile. She doesn't look annoyed at all. If anything, she seems apologetic for my behavior. I resist rolling my eyes. He's her type, and she's probably his. The tall lumberjack with thick, brooding brows, slicked back yet artfully tousled medium-length chocolate-colored hair, and intentional stubble. Beyond his rugged 'look,' he's annoyingly naturally handsome, too, with a strong jaw, big arms, and dark green eyes. With nothing more than a look, he has immediately disarmed one of his opponents, and I am alone in this battle.

The man smiles, though I detect a note of falseness. "Sorry, didn't see you," he says in a deep husky voice that sounds decidedly east coast. Definitely a tourist. A New Yorker playing dress up while glamping in his fifty-thousand-dollar van, complete with a Wi-Fi satellite and all the modern conveniences.

"Well, maybe you should be more aware of your surroundings," I retort, unimpressed.

"I'll look before I leap next time," he assures me, crossing his heart with a wink.

I push past him—not literally, I'm not an animal—and take my turn at the counter. We order our usual, a spiced chai latte for Maisy and a vanilla latte for myself, and while we wait, I occasionally glance at the man whose attention has returned to his phone once again. What could he possibly be doing on that thing? I bet it can't even connect to the internet.

It takes the girl at the counter two attempts to get his attention before I loudly call across the room, informing him, "Your espresso is ready."

He looks up, salutes me with a smirk, and grabs his drink before leaving. Even his walk and the way he opens the door are cocky, and I have the distinct feeling he is mocking me when he offers a faux apologetic wave through the window, as Maisy and I, with our drinks in hand, take our seats at the table.

"Can you believe that guy?" I ask.

"Mm," Maisy says dreamily.

"Maisy," I scold.

"What? He was dreamy."

"I don't think jerks can be dreamy."

"That, my friend, you are completely wrong about. Sometimes jerks are the dreamiest."

THE GIRL IN THE SPRINGS

I want to tell her this is why all of her relationships always end in tears because she dates cocky, good-looking bad boys who ride motorcycles and can't keep it in their pants. I, of course, don't say this because she already knows, and I don't want to sour the morning further. Nor do I want to hurt my best friend's feelings for no reason. She's been single for five months now, and the last guy, Lionel, wasn't *that* bad. Maybe she's on the road to improvement.

"He was good-looking," I admit because he was. He looked like a model turned farmer or a farmer that should be a model. That is to say, he looked like he could chop wood to perfection, but he definitely uses sunscreen, moisturizer, and chapstick. He's not my type, but I can admit beauty when I see it.

"What's your type?" Maisy asks as if she can read my mind. "I don't think I've ever asked you that before."

I hum thoughtfully. She definitely hasn't asked me that before because I've never thought about it before. Gavin was a slightly weedy software developer with a penchant for puffer jackets and sportswear, and though he's been my only serious, long-term relationship, I don't know if I'd say he was 'my type.'

"I don't know if I have one," I say eventually. "But that guy was not it. I think I'd prefer someone more... elegant."

Maisy shakes her head as if I'm a lost cause. "You read too many old romance novels."

"Maybe you don't read enough," I tease.

Luckily, she laughs. "Slim pickings around here. You might want to lower your standards."

"Well, if that's the best the dating pool has to offer, I'll stick with my books and my trusty bedside drawer buddy. Thank you very much."

"Birdie!" Maisy exclaims, clutching imaginary pearls before falling into a fit of giggles.

"It hasn't let me down so far," I reply with a sly smile.

"Whatever you say. But I'm telling you, if you had five minutes with Lionel—"

"Ew, Maisy," I scold before the giggles take me, too.

After we finish our drinks and split a slice of chocolate cake, we amble along The Knobbles, thinking we might do a little thrifting before parting ways. After all, it's only 7:00am, which gives me at least fourteen hours to start my investigation. Then, a car pulls up near the small police station, and when I recognize it as Lloyd Ramsey's Ford pickup, I know that the investigation has come to me rather than the other way around.

Both of us instinctively slow, not quite to a halt, but enough to watch as Lloyd and Kate Ramsey emerge from the vehicle. They're back much earlier than expected, but what shocks me is that Lloyd is sporting an impressive bruise on his left eye. Maisy notices this, too—it would be impossible not to—and looks at me with wide brown eyes.

As the Ramseys enter the station, we continue walking, and I murmur, "My parents told me he went to see his family. He believes they might have taken Mia, but he couldn't reach them because they're in a zero-contact situation. So, they had to go all the way to Idaho to talk with them directly."

"I can see why," Maisy mutters, glancing over her shoulder. "Mia isn't with them."

"That's not good," I whisper.

"No," Maisy agrees. "Because if she's not with them..."

"Yeah. I know. Hey, can we take a rain check on the thrifting? I have some stuff to do."

"Of course, but what kind of stuff?" she asks, nudging me. "Oh my God, are you taking on Mia's case?"

I take a breath and then nod. "I think I'll go crazy if I don't."

Maisy looks at me as if a holy figure has appeared before her. "You're amazing," she says. "You're going to solve this. I just know it."

I groan. "Don't say that. I'm terrified of disappointing everyone. Which is why this has to stay between us."

"Yeah, of course, but seriously, Birdie, you've got this."

I hum, internally cringing at all the undeserved praise. "I should've started sooner, but I didn't really take it seriously at first, you know?"

"Probably because nobody else did," Maisy replies kindly. "I mean, her parents have been freaking out, but for the first couple of days, it kinda just seemed like... I don't know, a teenager being a teenager. I can't count the amount of times I went 'missing' when I was eighteen just because I was passed out on someone's couch."

I nod. She has a point. Mia isn't exactly the partying type, but people still make assumptions about teenagers. Even me. "Archie told me about some missing teenagers," I say. "They vanished a while back. You don't know anything about that, do you?"

Maisy shakes her head. "Nah, I only moved to town like a year and a half before you did. How many missing teenagers?"

"Six, I think."

Maisy toys with the M pendant by her clavicle and frowns. "Really? In Serenity? I mean, I believe you. It just seems so... weird. This place is safe as houses."

"So we thought. Admittedly, they went missing over the course of twenty years, which I guess is why no one makes a big deal out of it, but Mia is definitely not the first kid to go out and not come back."

"You don't think it's connected, do you?"

"I have no idea," I answer honestly. "But I think it's worth looking into. I mean, I'm sure Sheriff Mercer is already on it, but I guess you can't have too much help with this sort of thing."

"No, you definitely can't, and if Snowball is anything to go by, I'm sure you'll find Mia in no time."

I smirk. "I don't know if Snowball is a great testament to my abilities, but here's hoping."

"Well, raincheck approved, so long as you keep me updated about those teenagers. Leave me a voice message. I'll listen to it like a true crime podcast." She stops herself. "Oh, God, that's so insensitive. Sorry. I just meant—"

"It's fine, seriously. And I can do that. It saves me from talking to myself."

"Well, good luck. I love you."

"I love you, too, and say hi to the kids for me."

"I always do," she replies and wraps me up in a hug before heading in the opposite direction.

Once she's gone, anxiety settles in. Now that I've told somebody that I'm investigating, I really have to do it. I have to believe in myself. I have to bring Mia home.

CHAPTER FIVE

GOOGLING 'SERENITY SPRINGS' ITSELF ONLY BRINGS UP the town's website, Facebook page, and the respective websites for all our local businesses. Whoever is in charge of the SEO has done a great job because unless you tack 'missing teenager' on the end—something that doesn't come up in the predicted searches—you won't find anything dark for pages and pages. However, when you do tack those two words on, it yields a *lot* of results. A horrifying amount, in fact, and I'm dumbfounded as to how I've never been aware of this before. Not really. Not enough to really sink in and stay in my hippocampus.

Sadly, the amateur sleuths on Reddit haven't caught wind of this yet, so there's no cheat sheet of compiled information to piggyback off of. There will be no painting by numbers here. All I have is a blank canvas and a primitive knowledge of color theory. I have to learn on the job, but I'm not completely useless. I have some experience in the craft and a definitive starting point—the year 2004.

In 2004, on the 30th of October, Carrie Olson and Gina Martin headed off on a date to Ridgeway Farm to pick out some pumpkins to carve. According to several eyewitnesses, they left the farm after having their photo taken against the sunset at roughly ten past 7:00pm. They told friends where they were heading via text, Lovebird's Nest—Serenity Spring's most popular and remote makeout point—and left in Gina's blue Kia Rio.

The mention of Lovebird's Nest brings back memories, even though I never went as a teenager. Not that I wasn't invited, but I understood the implications. I heard plenty of stories. *Plenty.* Nowadays, it's fenced off by a ten-foot chain link topped with barbed wire. It's been like that for the three years I've been back, and according to my parents, it's because of vandals and an uptick in underage drinking. Though reading through articles about Carrie and Gina, I have a feeling that there's more to it than that.

When the girls, eighteen and nineteen, did not arrive back at Gina's house by ten, Gina's mother, Carol, began to worry and called both of the girls repeatedly. They, like Mia, were good girls with straight A's and, aside from a handful of detentions, had never been in trouble of any kind. They were even seen as a bit 'square' by their peers, preferring to spend time together: reading, going on walks, and doing arts and crafts. They, like I do, had an affinity for historical romances and even crafted their own lesbian-themed illustrated novel version of *Pride and Prejudice* in which Carrie was Mr. Darcy, and Gina was Elizabeth. They sound like my kind of girls, and my heart aches as I read more and more about them, flick through old pictures, and laugh at the things we used to wear back in the early aughts. They'd be older than I am now, nearly by a decade. They'd probably be married, maybe with kids. Carrie wanted to be an author, and Gina wanted to be an illustrator of children's books. Neither even got close to fulfilling their dreams.

Their parents searched for them all night, but nobody checked Lovebird's Nest because it wasn't a place the girls ever went to. At least as far as they knew. However, in the morning, upon contacting the girls' friends, they discovered that they were wrong. That's exactly where the girls had been. Two police officers went to Lovebird's Nest shortly after and found the Kia Rio parked facing the view. Almost immediately, they knew they were looking at a crime scene. The driver's side window had been smashed. All of their possessions had been left behind, including phones and wallets. There was blood on the upholstery that was later identified as Gina's. Unfortunately, the blood didn't end there. There was also a ten-foot trail of blood leading from the car that abruptly ended, implying Gina had been wrapped up or put into a vehicle of some kind.

The investigators, including Sheriff Donald Phillips, gained some hope when other teenagers who had also been at Lovebird's Nest that Saturday night came forward. Yet these hopes were quickly dashed when all teens—and their respective parents—confirmed they were back by midnight and that when they left Lovebird's Nest, neither Gina nor Carrie seemed close to leaving. They were in their own world, in their car, talking, laughing, listening to music, and ignoring everyone else.

Beyond this, I can't find much about the investigation, but considering that there are no more articles by the end of December 2005, it lost steam pretty quickly. I continue to scroll, hoping for more, and stumble across an old, basic HTML website called carrieandgina.com. At the top of the page, in massive font, is, '*Help us catch The Willow Wraith.*' This sends a chill through me. There's a killer at large in my town, complete with a name, and I've never even heard whispers of them. I suppose they really are a wraith, a ghost, a wisp, in that sense.

The title is followed by a number, email address, and a plea for information. Then comes a photo of Gina and Carrie. Gina has mousy blonde hair and is short, curvy, feminine, and clad in purple. Carrie is androgynous, tall with short ginger hair, and is dressed in a black suit and purple tie. Gina has a lavender corsage, and Carrie has several sprigs in her breast pocket. They're so adorable and so clearly besotted that I find myself beaming. Especially as they were so accepted by their school, community, and peers even as far back as 2004. My face falls when I remember how awful the ending to their story is.

I keep scrolling, and another large header asks, 'Have you seen this couple?' followed by a different phone number, email address, and a photo of a couple. This pair is straight, the photo and fashion are newer, and they're standing in front of the Serenity High football field. The boy is broad, blond, tall, and tan. He's wearing a football uniform, which figures because he's a stereotypical jock. Not that that's a bad thing. He looks sweet, with a smile that's warm and unusually pale blond hair not unlike my own. He looks like he could be my brother, and I think, *What if he was?* and put myself in his family's shoes. It makes a knot form in my throat, and I look to the girl next to him to clear my head. She's beautiful, like a model or a famous actress, possessing that type of symmetry that makes you believe in God picking favorites. She's wearing a crop top, low-rise skinny jeans, and high-heeled boots, and though it takes me a second, I recognize her.

Lucia Nunez. She was in my sister's circle of friends. Being more artsy than sportsy, Ada wasn't as close to her as some of the other girls, but I've met Lucia on a few occasions. She came over for lunch a handful of times. We enthused about volleyball, our sport of choice, and she encouraged me to join the cheer squad, which I did in my junior year. I miss volleyball and cheering. I'm more of a tennis girl nowadays just because it's more accessible to adults, but if a volleyball match crops up at the Y, I might sign up in her honor.

Though it pains me to do so, I scroll, and 2010 comes rushing back to me when I read, 'Chad Bennett and Lucia Nunez went missing on the September 5th, 2010, six years after Carrie and Gina.' I knew this was coming. I was sixteen that year, so I vividly remember Lucia going missing and my sister's distress. Yet, for the past fourteen years, it seems I've locked that information away, and I'm dismayed by the resurfacing. More than dismayed, I'm horrified. It feels like picking up a pretty shell at the beach and finding an Irukandji jellyfish inside. I thought Serenity Springs was safe. Maybe that's naive, or perhaps my parents' ability to shield me is more effective than I thought.

I open a new tab and do some further digging on Chad and Lucia, and it soon makes sense why they are also featured on carrieandgina.com. It's not just that they were teenagers who went missing in Serenity Springs; it's that they also went to Lovebird's Nest, and their car was also found there. Mercifully, there was no blood, but both unlocked doors were open. Weirdly, it seems their case was written off as a case of lovesick teenagers running away together, but riddle me this: how could they run off together without a car, phones, cash, or cards? Unless they were in witness protection—which is ludicrous—this reeks of a miscarriage of justice and downright neglect.

I make some green tea to quell my fury, but my break doesn't last long. Soon, I'm back on carrieandgina.com, staring at Chad Bennett and Lucia Nunez, and then I'm scrolling. Just as I thought—based on Archie's information and the size of my scrollbar—I'm staring at yet another photo of a teenage couple, and I'm typing up more notes on my split screen as I read 'Sanya Gupta and Jayden Nelson.' I've never heard of this pair who went missing in 2016 while I was still in New York. This time, they were taken in November, and like the others, their car was also found at Lovebird's Nest. Similarly to Chad and Lucia's, their vehicle was undamaged, likely because they also didn't lock the doors because they didn't need to. They were amongst peers, even if they stayed until after the other kids departed. I'm noticing a pattern, and I'm baffled by the fact that only I and the immediate families seem to see it.

Jayden has perfect cornrows and dimples that remind me of Maisy. Sanya is tiny and adorable, with the biggest smile I've ever seen. Supposedly, they snuck out and went to Lovebird's Nest in his car once their parents were asleep. Neither the Nelson nor Gupta families noticed anything until they woke in the morning and called their children down for breakfast. This case, like all the others, went cold way too quickly, and Lovebird's Nest was fenced off two months later. This means the police and the council knew something bad was happening there. So why isn't this an ongoing investigation? Why are these cold cases? We have a pattern. A location. Blood. Eyewitnesses. Not to mention that eight years isn't even a long time ago. Maybe if this happened in the 1950s, I could understand, but all of these teenagers' parents, siblings, and friends are still alive. All of this happened in my lifetime.

I'm getting mad again, and I'm almost never mad. I uncoil my fists and see that I have red crescent moons in my palm. They're bordering on bloody. I breathe in and out repeatedly until I can think and see straight. After fifteen minutes of forced meditation, I achieve clarity and think of Mia. I had assumed she didn't fit the 'pattern' when I spoke to Archie, but knowing what I know now, I'd say there's a very good chance that whoever took those couples took Mia and whomever was with her. Or whoever was with her took all of them. Yes, some things don't fit. It's not autumn, it's been eight years instead of six, and there's no car or belongings left behind that we know of. However, I have the distinct feeling that despite it being fenced off, I'll find something of interest at Lovebird's Nest.

On my way over, I call my sister Ada, and she picks up instantly. Her voice surrounds me through my speakers, and it feels like a hug—one that I actually enjoy. This also immediately makes me feel guilty because Ada is pregnant, and I'm sure the last thing she wants to think about is her missing and presumed dead friend, Lucia Nunez.

"Hi, Birdie! I was just thinking about you," she coos, her voice like a melody.

"Oh yeah?" I ask, unable to tamp my smile despite my bleak morning.

"Yeah. There's a hummingbird that keeps flitting past the window."

"Oh, yeah, my name," I hum happily, nodding along.

"No, silly," Ada laughs. "Your whole birdwatching thing."

"Oh yeah!" I laugh, having honestly forgotten about my latest hobby. "I saw a barn owl on Sunday when I went for a night walk."

"Patrick has been so excited ever since I told him. Apparently, his dad was a birdwatcher, and he's got tons of binoculars you can borr— Wait, did you say night walk?"

"Yeah, you know me. I'm one of those freak people who's a morning person and a night owl. I'm like a vampire. I never sleep." I throw in a vampiric laugh for good measure, but Ada doesn't reciprocate.

"No, I know that," my sister responds, putting on her 'mom' voice. "But, Birdie, you're a young woman; you shouldn't walk alone at night."

I stop laughing, hearing the sincerity and seeing the articles I've read flash before my eyes. "Before today, I might've disagreed with you, but consider my night walks on indefinite hold."

"Why? What happened today? Are you okay?" She sounds panicked, and I recoil at the sound. She's had trouble conceiving and is considered medium risk. I don't want to do anything to escalate that risk to high.

"I'm fine," I reply confidently. "Seriously. Don't worry. I've just been looking into Mia Ramsey's case... You know she's missing, right?"

"I do. Poor thing. Hope she's found safe and sound soon." I hear her kiss the crucifix that she's always wearing. She wasn't really religious before she met Patrick, but he's Catholic and devout, so she converted. It seems to make her happy.

"Yeah, well, I started digging after Archie mentioned some missing teenagers and found some pretty horrifying stuff."

"Oh?" Ada asks, much coarser than usual. She knows where this is going, and from that, I can infer that she's also been holding out on me. So, I press forward as sensitively as I can. Besides, I need all the help I can get.

"Over the past twenty years, three couples have vanished from Lovebird's Nest, all of them presumed victims of foul play. Lucia Nunez and Chad Bennett were one of the couples."

"I know," Ada says softly.

"You told me that they ran away together."

"I know. I'm sorry. Mom and Dad told me to tell you that. You already struggled with night terrors, and they thought you might freak out your friends. You know what you were like, telling everyone about messed up true crime stuff."

"She was your friend," I say, not really sure why I'm saying it.

"I know," Ada laments, sounding frustrated with herself and me. "That's why I moved in with Patrick as soon as we were ready. I couldn't live in Serenity after that. I didn't feel safe."

"That's why you moved?" I ask in disbelief. Ada moved in with Patrick shortly before I went to NYU when she was only twenty and he was twenty-three. Eighteen at the time, I thought that was very young to settle down, but my parents always flouted the subject. Now, I see it for what it was—an escape. Luckily, it's worked out for her and Patrick, but I can't help but feel bitter over the lifetime of lies. I feel like I have whiplash despite driving below the speed limit.

"Yeah, that's why I moved," Ada sniffled. "I was paranoid. If my friend could be taken, why not me?"

"I'm surprised you want to move back," I say, softening my approach. I doubt she knows more than the articles can tell me. "Mom and Dad said you're looking at houses around here."

Ada hesitates, and I worry that her 'desire' to move back to Serenity isn't as strong as my parents think. Then she says, "Yeah, well, it's been a long time. Fourteen years. Wow." She exhales. "And obviously, I want you guys to get as much baby time as possible."

"You mean you want us to babysit," I tease.

"What else is family for?" she retorts, and I can hear her smile. "So, you're looking into Mia's disappearance?"

"And the rest, if I can," I answer. "Gina, Carrie, Chad, Lucia, Sanya, and Jayden. Their families deserve closure."

"You think they're dead?" Ada asks, matter of fact.

"Yeah," I admit. "After twenty, fourteen, and eight years, yeah. But there's still hope for Mia," I say, and for the first time, I doubt myself. Six days is a long time in regards to a missing person. What if the 'Willow Wraith' has claimed her, too?

"I'm sure you're right," Ada replies, though she doesn't sound convinced. After all, her friend never showed up again. "And I'm glad somebody is paying attention to the cases, but be careful. Chad was a linebacker. If somebody could take him down, they can take you down."

I try not to be offended, even though I know she's right. A linebacker would break my arm in an arm wrestle, and someone that could take one of them down is foe worth avoiding. "I'll be fine," I assure her.

"You better be. This baby needs an auntie."

She's joking, but I can hear the warning and the worry, so I reassure her as best I can, and I choose not to tell her that I'm heading to Lovebird's Nest so close to sundown. Instead, I tell her I'm going to get Thai food, and that shifts the subject to more pleasant places. She's not the only one who's good at lying, apparently.

"I love you," she says as the small talk comes to a close.

"I love you soooo much," I say in a sickly voice, which makes her laugh again. "I love you more than coffee," I add.

"I love you more than banana bread."

"I love you more than pad thai."

"I love you more than you love Jane Austen," she retorts.

"Wow, you win," I say. "I guess you love me the most today."

"I love you the most every day."

"Your baby is going to be jealous."

"Yeah, she will," Ada laughs.

"She?" I ask, tearing up almost instantly.

"I still don't know for sure. I just have a feeling."

"Well, you're basically psychic, so I'm sure you're right."

She laughs, and it might be the cherry on top of a rancid cake of a day, but it's still a cherry, glistening, red, and delicious. I feel sugar high as I bite into it and enthuse with her. When we finally hang up, the feeling is still there, at least until the steep road leading to Lovebird's Nest comes into view. Then, the cherry is forgotten, and the only red in sight is the phantom splatter of Gina Martin's blood.

CHAPTER SIX

L OVEBIRD'S NEST, LIKE SO MANY MAKEOUT LOCATIONS, IS also a lookout point. At the top of the steep road is a large dirt clearing, and if you reach it, turn right in an arch, you'll find yourself at the edge of a cliff facing the town with the Salish Pines Forest behind you. Before the chainlink fence, there was a hip-height steel pipe railing at the edge of the cliff to stop cars from rolling off the edge. That was ugly, but this is menacing like a prison courtyard. Yet, I look past the chain-link and barbed wire to the back of the sandy dirt clearing that leads out into the woods. On that side, there is no fencing. I'm sure this is because driving a car through the densely populated trees would be impossible, but it would be no trouble for a human to pass through. And considering the broken glass, cans, and graffiti, humans haven't had any problems accessing this supposedly prohibited zone.

I park on the dirt slope—praying my car doesn't roll back onto the highway—and hop out. I leave it here because I have no choice. If there's evidence to be had, I'd hate to accidentally run it over, but more than that, with a closed gate, there's nowhere else to go.

I glance back at my car nervously as I step toward the gate. Yet I border on forgetting my car entirely and even my own name when the left gate panel blows open in the breeze, and the chain and padlock slip through a link and fall to the ground. As I move tentatively closer, I can see a bright silver slash among the dull, weather-worn exterior of the chains. Somebody has cut this with a bolt cutter, and it's not hard to figure out why as my gaze drifts downward toward tire tracks. They're deep, and there's splatter where they've clearly struggled on some of the muddier sections of the track. This was no four-wheel drive.

Somebody drove up here, cut the chain, drove inside, and then, for whatever reason, put the chain and bolt back in haphazardly, giving the illusion that the gate was still locked. Why? To throw the police off? To not draw attention? And why bother coming here? Why all the effort? There are so many beautiful sightseeing spots in Serenity Springs, and this is the only one that requires breaking and entering to visit. It doesn't make sense to me. I know teenagers are drawn to rebellion, and maybe Mia was breaking free from her goodie-two-shoes typecast, but still, something is wrong here.

Maybe whoever picked her up is a copycat? Perhaps they wanted to murder her where all the others were murdered. That would explain why the car is no longer here. Somebody picked her up, took her out here under the guise of romance or rebellion, killed her, and then drove away undetected.

I stop and think about this theory, and in realizing it ends with a dead Mia, I second guess myself. I have no proof that these tire tracks belonged to the mystery person who picked her up. These tracks could belong to anyone. And as far as I'm aware, you don't need an ID to purchase bolt cutters.

I'm going to tell the police about this, but first, I want to take the opportunity to snoop. I've never broken into anywhere before, but there are no cameras here, and the gate is already open. As I enter the clearing, I'm careful not to leave footprints, but considering how many others there are—partial, well-defined, and overlapping—my leaping and tiptoeing feels a little silly. I do it anyway. I don't want to make the police's job any harder, and I definitely don't want to get caught.

I follow the circle of tire tracks to where it seems that the car was likely parked, facing the view of the town. The view is the whole point of coming here, and I take it in briefly before lowering my gaze and scouring for evidence. I hope that I'll find something definitive, linking Mia to this place, like a wallet or her favorite initialed bracelet. Instead, all I discover—after crouching and wading through the muck like a gold miner—is a brown wooden button with a dark grain. It looks like a shirt button. It's probably nothing, and even if it is something, it would be almost impossible to link to anyone. But you never know, and I slide it into the right pocket of my cardigan anyway.

I straighten, turn around, and look back at the dark, dense forest and all the footprints that lead from and into it. I decide to pick a set and follow them; if they lead nowhere, I'll go back and pick another. I close my eyes, spin around, and point, picking one at random. I open my eyes and see a well-defined set of hiking boot tracks, and I begin to follow through on my idea before acknowledging that this is a ridiculous and dangerous plan. For one thing, there are at least twenty sets of footprints, and for another, Salish Pines Forest is very easy to get lost in. I also consider what my sister said about Chad and his being a linebacker, and I think that if I did stumble across the person who abducted six, maybe seven, teenagers, what could I do about it? I'd probably just end up 'missing,' too.

I wander to the edge of the forest line, arms wrapped around myself, and peer into its endless depths. I wonder how many people live out here. How many rural properties? How many sheds, barns, and hunting cabins? How many places that the council, the police, or even the locals don't know exist? Plenty, I'll bet.

The gate bangs shut behind me, causing me to start and turn. I'm alone. It's just the wind. I exhale. I mutter quiet reassurances. Yet, with the forest now at my back, I find I don't want to look at it. I glance around, from side to side, and seeing only trash, I allow myself to leave. I walk back to my Rugiada Green Fiat 500 at a hasty pace and reverse even faster.

Once I'm halfway home, I call the local tipline, and a female officer answers. "Hello. Serenity Springs police department. Officer Alexis Winter speaking."

"Hi, Officer Winter," I reply. "This is Bridget Hartley. I'm a local."

"Oh, Miss Hartley," Alexis replies warmly. "I know your parents. How can I help?"

"Well, I was up at Lovebird's Nest," I begin.

"Oh?" Officer Winter questions, using the same tone of voice my mom employs prior to a lecture.

"I'm a private investigator," I explain, and not wanting to overstep into police territory regarding Mia, I continue with, "I'm investigating the Gina Martin and Carrie Olson case."

"Ah. That one is a bit before my time, I'm afraid."

"Well, I came up here just to look through the fence and get a better scope of where they were taken from, and I found that someone has cut the padlock from the gate with bolt cutters. There are tire tracks, too, and they look recent."

"Okay," Officer Winter says slowly, her interest obviously piqued.

"And I was thinking about Mia Ramsey and how someone picked her up and took her somewhere. I was thinking that maybe they came here."

"Mm." It's the muffled reply of someone concentrating on note-making, and I can hear the mechanical keyboard clacking.

"I thought I should let you know so that somebody could come and have a look and repair the lock."

"Yes, we will get right on that. Thank you so much for letting us know. Any information is appreciated."

I'm tempted, but I don't tell her about the button or that I entered the premises. I also want to ask her if she thinks this is anything, but I don't because she probably can't tell me either way. Not without being certain. Misinformed, unsubstantiated opinions are how you start mass panics and create sketchy, untrue articles. I want to be helpful, not burdensome. I want to be on good terms with the local police.

"You're welcome," I say. "And if I come across anything else, I'll be sure to let you know."

"Please do," Officer Winter replies a little curtly. As long as I'm not doing anything illegal, there's not much she can say or do to stop me. "Have a nice day, Miss Hartley," she adds.

"You, too," I reply, hoping she's telling the truth about further investigating my findings. That's the problem with something being 'out of your hands'; all you can do is hope.

I arrive back at my apartment and double-check the locks when I close the door. All of the research I've done and the eerie energy of Lovebird's Nest has admittedly gotten under my skin. I'm no chicken, nor am I a sensitive person like the rest of my family. Not that there's anything wrong with being soft-hearted or quick to cry; I'm just not. I can watch horror movies—though I rarely do—in the dark without flinching. However, this isn't a movie. Six people have been murdered on my doorstep, and a young girl is missing. This has rattled me, to say the least.

I make myself a cup of Earl Grey, and just as I pour hot water into my favorite Beatrix Potter-themed mug, my phone rings. I don't recognize the number, but I answer anyway. It could be my boss, Dolly, calling me from her hotel, but after the day I've had, I half expect a terrifying threat coming from a killer with a voice changer.

Instead, a woman with a velvety voice asks, "Hello, is this Bridget?"

"This is she," I reply, overly formal. "I mean, yeah, I'm Bridget."

"Oh, hi! This is Sheriff Donna Mercer."

"Oh, hello, Sheriff Mercer," I reply, blinking rapidly.

"Please, call me Donna."

"Okay, Donna, how can I help you?" I ask, matching her sunniness.

"Officer Winter just informed me about the tip you called in, and I wanted to assure you personally that I've sent a squad car to Lovebird's Nest to further investigate. I think this is a very hopeful lead."

"So you haven't been there yet?" I ask, and then cringe at how judgmental my question comes across.

"No, we haven't," she replies, sounding surprisingly apologetic. "Officers check it frequently for vandals and drunken teenagers, but I'll admit, it didn't cross my mind regarding Mia Ramsey. I don't know this town as well as I should, having only lived here for two years, and I was unaware of its previous 'popularity.' Officer Winters mentioned that you're looking into the Gina Martin and Carrie Olson case?"

"I am. Along with the other missing teenagers," I admit, truth rolling off my tongue with ease. Donna doesn't sound like she's likely to lecture. She seems genuinely grateful. "And I did go there for them, but I also thought, well, Mia Ramsey was in a car with someone else. Maybe she fits the pattern."

"The pattern?"

"Three couples have gone missing from Lovebird's Nest over the past twenty years. One second," I say as I hastily reach my laptop. "Carrie and Gina in 2004, Chad Bennett and Lucia Nunez in 2010, and Sanya Gupta and Jayden Nelson in 2016. All of them were in relationships, and all of them were taken from Lovebird's Nest. Their cars and belongings were left behind."

Donna is quiet for a moment. "Was there a car at Lovebird's Nest when you visited?"

"No. Just tracks going in a circle."

"Thank you for this, Bridget."

"You didn't know? About the teenagers?"

"No." Her tone is terse, but I can tell her annoyance isn't aimed at me. "As I said, I've only worked in Serenity Springs for two years. My predecessor, Sheriff Donald Phillips, would have handled these cases, and he, along with the other officers, failed to mention them. I asked if there were any cases I should be aware of..." She trails off and clicks her tongue. "It's my fault, really. I should've done my research."

"Well, if it makes you feel any better, I didn't know about any of this until yesterday, and I was born here."

Donna chuckles. "It does. A bit. Small towns and their secrets, huh?"

"Tell me about it. And you couldn't have done much for Carrie, Gina, and the others, anyway. They're not, you know..." Now it's my turn to trail off.

"Alive?" Donna asks. "No, I expect they're not, but I could've been searching for their bodies."

I like Donna. She's an elected town official, but she doesn't beat around the bush and can admit to her mistakes, even to a total stranger.

"Anyway," she continues. "Thank you for bringing this to my attention. I promise to do my due diligence and research these cases and see if I agree about Mia fitting in with this pattern you speak of."

"They call him the Willow Wraith," I blurt out.

"Sorry, what was that?"

"The killer. The families call him or her the Willow Wraith."

"Oh, because of the forest."

I flush. The information is useless. "I have some notes I can send over from articles. I mean, you probably don't—"

"Please," she insists. "My email is on the Serenity Springs PD website. Your information, I'm sure, is invaluable. You're a PI, correct?"

"I am," I reply, embarrassment lifting.

"Well, there we go then. I trust your research as much as I'd trust my own. It's not easy getting a license."

I blush and don't know what to say. I land on, "No, it isn't. And I'll get everything I have to you right away."

"Thank you, and should you find out anything else, please contact me directly. I'll reply with my personal number when you email me."

"Okay, great," I chirp, refreshed by the whole exchange. Sheriff Phillips certainly would not have listened to me. I doubt he would've even sent a car to Lovebird's Nest. I can now see why Donna's career has been so illustrious. She's intelligent and capable but not afraid to ask for help.

"I hope to continue working with you, Bridget. And I hope that, together, we can bring Mia home."

"Yeah," I say, a little breathless.

"Well, I'll let you go," she says kindly. "Talk soon."

"Talk soon," I parrot, and she hangs up.

I'm stunned momentarily, but quickly, I round up links and all of my notes and send them to the email she provided. I'm surprised I can even remember it, considering how star-struck I am. Once I re-read my email three times and settled on 'kind regards,' I press send. Then, out of curiosity, I google Donna Mercer, and gradually, my jaw drops. I knew she had impressive credentials, but I didn't know the half of it. During her time as a homicide detective in Seattle, she took down not two but three serial killers. Including the infamous Silence Seeker, who used to glue his victims' lips shut to keep them silent. It's been a long time since I've looked at this case, and though it still turns my stomach, watching Donna Mercer's press conference brings me hope. She's the best ally I could ask for, and I believe that, together, we can bring Mia home.

CHAPTER SEVEN

It's Wednesday morning, and despite the shining sun, all I want to do is draw the blinds, open up my laptop, and continue my 'paperwork.' I know I've unearthed everything the internet has to offer, but there is more to working from home than just Googling. And it's particularly frustrating when I remember I have somewhere to be this morning, and it's not just Sproutville for my regular, after-lunch Wednesday shift. I also need to meet with the team in charge of building my sister's house.

I try to force excitement as I drive to my destination, but it's difficult. I couldn't even drum up a smile as I printed and compiled all of my inspiration into a binder this morning. It's going to be beautiful, that's for sure. I just wish I could put it all on hold until Mia is home. Thinking about her, those tire tracks, the dark woods makes my skin feel hot and tight. I'm sure I'll be fine once I get there and start talking through it all, but this fifteen minutes of interim is excruciating. It's day seven, and this teenage girl is still out there somewhere. She could be being abused or tortured. She could be dead or close to it. And what am I doing? Helping my parents to build a million-dollar present.

I don't have to drive often, and I don't enjoy doing so. I like walking. I like the smell of the crisp country air, the sound of the gurgling brooks and birdsong, and the breeze, which is cool year-round. Actually enjoyable cardio? Count me in. Technically, I could walk to my parents' plot in just shy of an hour, and on another day, I'd happily do so, but I don't want to risk being late for my shift.

Glancing at the forest that flanks the road, a shiver runs through me, and I'm ultimately happy with my decision. Sure, my paranoid powerwalk would've burnt off the chocolate bar I inhaled last night, but I don't think it would've done my nerves any good. And while I highly doubt that the person who took all those teenagers knows I'm looking into them—not yet, anyway—I know every snapping branch or crunching leaf would have me looking over my shoulder.

I've never been a fan of guns, and I've never carried any sort of self-defense item more extreme than mace, but all of this has me rethinking my safety and that of those I love. I used to think Maisy's sketchy boyfriends were merely annoying, but now her affinity for meeting with dating app strangers is worrisome. I might be overthinking it, but with a probable serial killer on the loose, it's better to be safe than sorry. Even the knowledge that this team I'm going to meet is all male gives me momentary pause.

The clearing isn't easy to find. GPS, as it turns out, isn't very good at finding places with no addresses, and neither of my parents is tech-savvy enough to drop me a pin. So, I have to use my muscle memory to find it despite never having driven here before. It takes a couple of U-turns and a lot of angry muttering, but finally, I spot the almost invisible dirt road and veer onto it. After a few minutes of seriously bumpy and muddy terrain, I emerge into a large clearing. It's lush, green, and much larger than I remember it being. You could build at least three houses bigger than my sister's current home and still have room to spare. Obviously, I won't do that, nor will I make her some sort of tacky mega-mansion that she'll hate. No, this land will be used for gardening and animals, and for the first time, I feel a prickle of envy.

The two dozen men stop and stare as I park before resuming their half-assed attempts at looking busy, even though there's clearly nothing to do. I chuckle and shake my head as I open the door. They might as well crack a beer and relax until the boss starts drawing up blueprints.

I continue to laugh, watching as a man closely inspects a port-a-potty for faults when I catch sight of a man approaching and compose myself. He's enormous with a barrel chest and tree-trunk limbs. His hair is red, and his beard is one of the most impressive I've ever seen. He looks as if a youthful Santa Claus was an Olympic shotputter and also a Viking. He sticks out a hand at least twice the size of my own, and I accept the shake. His hands are rough but warm, and his shockingly blue eyes twinkle. I like him already.

"You must be Bridget Hartley," he says, in an accent I'd wager he obtained in West Virginia or maybe one of the Carolinas. "Name's Keith Hicks."

"Nice to meet you, Keith. Are you in charge of the project?" I ask hopefully.

"No, not me. You want Noah for all that. I'm sort of a jack of all trades. Whatever he wants me to do, I do it. I'm mainly security. I'll be staying over there in that trailer at night to protect your assets." He cocks and phantom shotgun and 'fires' it into the tree line.

"Wow. You won't get, I don't know, creeped out?"

"Nah."

"That trailer looks kind of flimsy," I add. "And there are bears around here."

"Good. I've always wanted to wrestle one."

I bark a laugh as he flexes his muscles. "If you keep leaving food out, you might get your wish," I tease, nodding toward the stack of sandwiches on one of the nearby tables. Not that I'm actually concerned. I genuinely believe he could take a bear or cougar bare-handed.

Keith snorts. "Don't worry, ma'am. Those will be packed away at night." He looks away, shielding his eyes from the sun, and points into the middle distance. "Ah, there he is. Our esteemed leader."

I follow his finger, and my jaw drops. It's *him*. The rude man from the coffee shop. He's the one in charge. Great. That's just perfect.

'Noah' comes to an immediate halt as I turn to face him, and my sunny disposition darkens. Keith notices and looks back and forth between us as if at a tennis match. "You two know each other?" he asks.

"You could say that," I reply tersely as Noah slaps on a smile and jogs in our direction.

My arms are folded as he sticks out his hand, and accepting the gesture takes a lot of mental effort. "Noah, is it?" I ask coolly.

"Noah Fletcher," he confirms. "And you are?" he inquires as if he doesn't already know my name. Keith knew it, so surely the leader of this project does.

"Bridget Hartley. Daughter of George and Eleanor."

"Of course," he says with a broad smile. "Nice to meet you."

"We've already met," I retort. "At the cafe."

"Oh yeah. The girl who hates line cutters."

Girl. He's really trying his luck. I stiffen, straightening my posture, and gain two inches of height in the process. "I wasn't aware that anyone liked line cutters."

"Well, some people might forgive those who accidentally cut lines."

"It depends on whether it was truly accidental."

"It was," he replies earnestly, meeting my reluctant gaze. "And I'm sorry."

"Well, then, I guess all is forgiven," I say dryly, even though it is.

He scrutinizes my expression with a smirk. "I'll make it up to you."

"Oh yeah? And how do you plan on doing that?" I inquire, still behaving like an ice queen. I almost can't believe what's coming out of my mouth, and a quiet voice of reason tells me to knock it off. I'm never like this.

"By building your sister the house of her dreams," Noah retorts matter-of-factly.

My mouth pulls upward on the left side before falling. He's got me there. "That seems like a good deal," I say.

"Friends?" he asks.

"Acquaintances," I correct, but this time, I let the smirk take hold and hope that I don't seem like a complete cow.

"I can do acquaintances."

I relax a little and thrust my binder toward him. "I've compiled some ideas."

"Perfect. I love a client with vision. Let's take a lap of the property, and we can look through this afterward over a coffee. Though if you want something sugary, you're out of luck."

"I can drink it black," I reply, knowing that he's mocking me for my vanilla latte.

"If only everyone was like you. Then we wouldn't need lines."

I purse my lips and stride past him. "Come on then," I call over my shoulder. "I'm a busy woman."

He laughs as he catches up to me. "I'm sure you are."

At least he's a good sport, I think. Most men aren't. Most men that I've met take a joke like a bullet and retaliate accordingly. A play tap is met with a punch, and though I've never been physically hit, Gavin's mouth could deal blows harder than most fists. Mind you, I still don't like Noah, but if he continues being this amiable, we might just be able to get along for the duration without strangling each other.

After wandering around the grassy bank and talking about square footage and the basic possibilities, we sit at one of the folding plastic tables, coffee steaming before us, and Noah flips through my book. The more he looks, the more surprised he becomes.

"What?" I demand.

"Is your sister much older than you? Like fifty years older than you?"

"She's thirty-two," I retort. "What's wrong with my ideas?"

"Nothing. It's just... A red and white colonial-style farmhouse? I thought someone so young might want something more modern."

"We like classic things in my family."

"Well, it's certainly different from what we usually do."

"And what you usually do are big, square eyesores that belong in a sci-fi movie," I reply, taking a swing. His expression tells me that I've hit it out of the park.

"Correct. Though I have to say, even though this isn't my thing, I think it could be cool. I never get to do anything unique."

I almost tell him I don't care about his 'thing,' but I see the joy in his eyes as he flicks through my inspiration—clotheslines, flowers, chickens, vegetable patches, vintage-inspired interiors—so I keep my vitriol to myself. "I'm glad you approve," I say dryly.

He looks up at me and flashes that now signature smirk, and something lurches within me, and to my surprise, it's not disgust. In fact, it's the opposite of disgust, though the feeling does rhyme with that word. Oh no. Maisy is right. He is sexy.

Luckily, it's not hard to tamp that feeling down. He's far too annoying to be attractive beyond his appearance, and he's also clearly been told he's good-looking far too often, which has made him cocky. I don't smile back.

"I'm excited about this, really," he says, earnest again.

"I am, too," I admit, avoiding eye contact and acting aloof, hoping this might annoy him into being a jerk again.

"She's going to have her first baby here, so it has to be perfect," I continue.

"Are you two close?" he asks, and I detect something strange in his tone. Hesitancy, maybe? It's as if he's only asking to be polite, but he doesn't really want to know.

"Very. So expect to see a lot of me. I need to make sure you're not cutting any corners."

He crosses his heart like he did at the cafe. "I promise to make all your wildest dreams come true. Just so long as your folks don't run out of money."

"They won't. Not for Ada."

"Ada," he repeats, and there it is again—that note of discomfort.

I steer the subject away from Ada. "Where do you live? Are you local?"

"I'm new to town. Built myself a tiny house on a patch of land not too far from here. It only takes me five minutes to get here on my dirt bike."

Of course, he rides a dirt bike. I'm starting to think Maisy made this man in a lab. "Did you move here for the project?"

"No, lucky coincidence. I was looking for affordable land in Washington and stumbled across my patch about eight months back. Then I put an ad in the paper when I was settled, and your parents called me."

"And what does your place look like?"

He chuckles and shakes his head. "A square eyesore that looks like it belongs in a sci-fi movie."

"You're so predictable."

"It's off-grid," he says as if trying to impress me.

It's not working. Well, maybe it is a bit. Most men can't build their own houses. "Do you chop your own wood?" I tease. "Forage for your own food?"

"Yep."

"Solar panels?"

"And a compost toilet."

I snort. "Glamorous."

He shrugs. "I don't get many visitors."

"And why might that be?" I ask wryly.

Then he gets this distant look in his eye, and I genuinely think I've offended him until he says, "I think I might have a ghost for a neighbor, though."

"Why do you say that?

"My dog barks at the door every night, and I hear these weird screams."

"Where are you from?" I inquire.

"Chicago."

"Ah, a city boy. Well, what you're hearing is probably a fox. Maybe a cougar. Keep your dog inside, and you'll be fine."

He looks relieved, and for a second, I glimpse somebody I haven't met yet. Somebody who isn't a cocky jerk. Somebody who is new to town and doesn't know anyone except for his co-workers. Somebody who I'm quite happy to have as an acquaintance. Somebody I can have another coffee with.

CHAPTER EIGHT

Every Wednesday night for the past three years, I have taken myself out on a date. I can't remember how it started now. Maybe I wanted to reacquaint myself with the town I'd grown up in, or, more likely, I was tired of being disappointed by men. Gavin never took me on dates. He didn't see the point, but I do. These date nights are the highlight of my week, and despite having been run ragged by a day filled with house designing, kid herding, and email sending, I have no intention of staying home.

In the beginning, I visited every location in town that served food in alphabetical order. When I reached the end of that list, I started again. When that got boring, I began drawing names from a hat. Nowadays, I'm a lot less adventurous. Ninety percent of the time, I go to Notte Stellata, a beautiful, family-run, formal dining ristorante. It's one of the only places in town that encourages you to dress up, and the atmosphere is something special—especially for me. Every Wednesday, on a private balcony, a table is prepared for me, complete with a place card, a long taper candle, and a singular red rose in a vase. I don't even need to make a reservation.

It all started in 2010 when I was sixteen and a volunteer lifeguard at the local pool. Antonio and Isabella Rossi were new to town and were often busy establishing their restaurant. They had a menu to create, walls to paint, a name to come up with, staff to hire, and so much more. Seeing how bored their son Marco was, I offered to look after him if they dropped him off during my shifts at the pool. He was only eight at the time and very sad about leaving all his friends behind, so I thought it would also give him the opportunity to socialize. His parents enthusiastically agreed. I mean, who would say no to free child care?

Unfortunately, the pool can be a dangerous place for a kid who can't swim, and one day, even though I had warned him repeatedly about running, Marco fell into the pool's deep end. I dived in after him, performed CPR, and, to put it simply, saved his life. Aside from the trauma, he was fine, but I was terrified that I was going to be in trouble with his parents. Luckily, the opposite happened, and ever since that incident, they've treated me not only like family but royalty. Marco's actually off to college now, which is great, if a little unsettling. Nothing will make you feel older at thirty than bumping into adults you used to babysit.

From my second-story balcony vantage point, I stare out at the glittering lights of town and suburbia and sip my weekly glass of wine; I'm not a big drinker, but a large glass of Tuscan Chianti Classico goes down very smoothly. I suppose I treat wine like I treat cake—perfect in moderation.

They're playing Giuseppe Verdi's "La Traviata" over the speaker, and I put my feet up on the chair beside me. There are always four seats, despite me always coming alone, and I use them accordingly. I sigh as I slip down further into my seat. When I get home, there is more house planning to be done and more crime to research, but for the next two hours, I'm in Italy in a romantic movie. I'm sipping wine in my favorite white silk dress. My hair is perfectly set into Hollywood waves, and bruschetta is on the way. I look and feel good. This is a suffering-free space.

The door behind me opens, and I turn, expecting to see one of the servers holding a plate of food. Instead, I find myself beaming at a complete stranger. I quickly turn back to face my table and sit up straight, an embarrassed flush creeping up my neck. I take a sip of wine and watch out of the corner of my eye as he sits at another table and reaches for the champagne flute that is waiting for him.

I hadn't even noticed the other table. I'm usually the only one out here. It isn't a large balcony. However, it is jam-packed inside for a Wednesday, so they must've had to make do. I don't mind, not really. It's not like he takes up a lot of room. He's clearly alone, after all. I guess this is where we go, the people who dine by ourselves. We're cast outside, so nobody has to witness our freakishness. I smirk. As if these aren't the best seats in the house.

"Hi, sorry," the man says abruptly, and I'm flustered all over again. I thought and hoped he was intent on ignoring me. I had been considering putting my feet back up.

"Hello," I reply, with one of those awkward, straight-lined smiles.

"Sorry," he says again. "You probably don't want to talk, considering you're out here alone. And I thought I would be fine with that when Isabella told me, but now that I'm out here... Well, it feels rude to not introduce myself. So, hello, I'm Stanley. Now, I'll leave you alone."

I swivel in my seat to get a better look at him and feel my face burn hot once again. This time, for a different reason. *This* man *is* my type. I couldn't answer Maisy when she asked because I don't think I've ever seen my type in the flesh before now. Not so up close, anyway. Now I know exactly what to say, and I plan to call her on the way home to deliver the news.

My type is a slender yet toned man wearing a soft-looking black sweater, dark grey slacks, and polished black brogues. My type is a man wearing browline glasses that make him look like a sexy English teacher. My type is a man with black, wavy hair that reminds me of Clark Kent's 'do. My type is a clean-shaven man with a pretty face, full lips, and blue eyes, who is simultaneously very masculine. My type smells warm, spicy, woody, with a pinch of pepper.

I realize I still haven't said anything. "Bridget," I say. "And it's fine. I always come here on my own. I wouldn't mind some company for a change."

He smiles, and it sucker-punches me. "I also come here on my own. On Friday, though, not Wednesday. Apparently, Wednesday is your day."

"It is."

"So, Bridget, why do you like to dine alone? If you don't mind my asking. Not a fan of people?"

"Actually, the total opposite," I laugh. "I love people so much that I spend all of my time with them."

"So you come here to have a break?"

"I work at Sproutville, the local preschool," I explain, giving him a meaningful look.

"Wow. Gotcha." He looks thoughtful. "I went to Sproutville when I was a kid. Is Dolly still in charge?"

"Oh yeah. Dolly isn't going anywhere."

"I'm glad to hear it."

"So you're a long-time local?" I ask.

"I am. We actually went to school together," Stanley says with a sheepish smile.

I clap a hand to my mouth. "Oh, God. I'm sorry, I—"

"Oh no, don't be!" he insists. "I was the year below you, so you wouldn't have known me. I just knew you because you were on the cheer team, which made you a bit of a celebrity."

"What's your last name?" I ask, sounding hopeful as if something might click into place if I have more information.

"Crawford."

I grimace.

"No cigar?" he asks.

"Yeah, sorry. Doesn't ring any bells. I guess high school was a long time ago now. Not that that's any excuse. It's not exactly a big school." I feel like I'm putting my foot in it, considering how it sounds.

"No. You're right. It was a long time ago," he replies kindly.

"So, what about you?" I ask, desperately wanting to change the subject. "Why are you here alone?"

"Well, I like fine dining, but it's not really my friends' scene."

"They prefer getting drunk at The Homestead?" I ask.

He nods. "Yeah, especially on barn dancing Fridays."

"Okay, so why are you here tonight?"

"I don't know, honestly. I think I just needed to get out of the house." He smiles again, shyly this time. There's the tiniest of gaps between the front two teeth that I find incredibly charming. The same goes for the beauty mark on his right cheekbone.

"I'm glad you did," I reply and cringe again, hoping I'm not being too forward.

"I am, too," he replies. "The only thing that beats being alone is good company." He clears his throat. "Would you like to join me for dinner, officially? My treat."

My heart palpates, and I grin. "I suppose that would save us from shouting across the balcony."

"May I?" he asks, gesturing to my table.

"Yeah, of course," I reply, sliding the vase and candle to one side as he sits opposite me.

"I—" we both start in unison. He holds out his palm to me, gesturing for me to go first. Annoyingly, this reminds me of Noah and his lack of manners or respect for turn-taking. I don't want to think about Noah right now, but once he's there, it's hard not to, and I find myself comparing the two. Noah has freckles instead of a beauty mark. Noah's eyes are green, not dark brown. Noah is much taller and much stronger than Stanley. Not that any of these things make Noah superior. I love brown eyes. I'm indifferent to height. Yet, he remains, smirking at me, his phantom competitive.

"What do you do?" I ask, throwing a blanket over Noah's head in my imagination, muffling his goading and hiding his face.

"I'm a librarian," Stanley replies casually as if that's not the sexiest job a man could have.

"Seriously? That's like my dream job."

"It's not as fun as you might think."

"Still, being surrounded by all those books," I say dreamily.

"You read?"

"A lot," I answer giddily. "Neoclassical mostly at the moment, but I like all sorts."

Stanley looks at me as if I've just performed a magic trick. As if *I* am magic. I feel that blush creeping back and realize it's here to stay. Hopefully, the vivid pink can be blamed on the heat lamp and the unseasonably warm evening.

"And you said that you're a preschool worker?" he asks.

"I am, but I also recently became a private investigator."

His eyes widen. "That's quite the combo. Do those worlds ever collide?"

"Well, actually," I begin, giggling as I regale him with the tale of Snowball. By the end, I realize I've already finished my glass of wine, and when the bruschetta arrives, he orders me another of the same, and I don't protest.

We order the same thing simultaneously and talk about the cases I've solved, the books he's read, and our time in high school. I tell him about my sister and the house I'm building, and he tells me about his deceased mother and the time he spent in Northern California after her death. He tells me that his father is also dead, and he inherited his home in Serenity Springs, which is why he's back here.

I have a third glass, and I savor it until closing, and we reluctantly shuffle out of the front doors and say our goodbyes. It's only when he's out of sight that I realize I didn't get his phone number. I don't let it get me down as I call Maisy while practically skipping home. Fate brought us together tonight. I'm sure it will do so again.

CHAPTER NINE

'M WOKEN TWO HOURS BEFORE MY 7:00AM ALARM BY THE feeling of my phone vibrating on the pillow next to me. I groan, and then I panic. A call this early typically spells disaster. Or death.

My fears aren't exactly alleviated when I flip my phone over and see that the caller is Grandma June, though it does rule out a grim possibility considering her recent health struggles.

"Hi!" I chirp, answering quickly. Grandma June is also struggling with some mental decline, which can make her prickly and prone to hurt feelings. I have enough stress right now without getting the cold shoulder from my grandma.

"Birdie, my love," she coos, her voice soft like down. "How are you?"

"I'm great," I lie. There may be a lot to be happy about in my life right now, but missing teenagers, serial killers, and murder pretty much trump all.

"I'm so glad to hear it," Grandma June enthuses. Then she begins to hum and mutter, and I can tell she's forgotten all about me and her reason for calling.

"How are you?" I prompt.

"Well," she starts, and I can immediately tell all is not well. I hold my breath, waiting for the worst. Grandma June had two older sisters who both died of breast cancer, and I know she goes for very regular checks because of it.

I cross my fingers and my toes. I selfishly can't deal with the idea of her being sick on top of everything else right now. When Grandpa Ken died five years ago due to heart complications, I was completely destroyed. I'm not ready to go through something like that again.

I stay like that, contorted, waiting for her to continue, but she doesn't. I unfurl. "Are you alright?"

"Oh, yes. It's just... Oh, it's so silly, and I don't want to bother you."

I exhale, hoping that it really is something 'silly.' "You could never bother me. I promise."

"I think somebody is stealing my jewelry."

A weight lifts, and then anger descends, hot and heavy. I clench my jaw, and my sleep retainer begs for mercy. I relent, but I am still furious. Sunny Side is supposed to be safe. It certainly costs enough that that should be a guarantee. Grandma June's 'rent' is double my own, for God's sake. No one should be breaking in and robbing her. They shouldn't be able to.

"That's not silly at all, Gigi," I say, using her preferred pet name. We came up with it together about half a decade ago when she admitted that 'Grandma June' was too ostentatious and frumpy for her liking. I was inclined to agree, so now she's only Grandma June on paper or in my head. In-person, she's something much more glamorous than that.

"Well, I checked my jewelry box this morning and found that my pearls were missing. Normally, I'd think I'd just misplaced them—I do that a lot these days—but on Monday, my tennis bracelet also disappeared."

"The diamond one from Gramps?"

"Yes, that one," Grandma June replies, and I can hear her cup of tea clatter against her saucer. She's shaking, and my fury is so great that I'm actually on the verge of tears.

"I thought you locked your door at night," I counter.

"I do, but the staff are all equipped with skeleton keys in case of an emergency. After I told Tanya about my jewelry, she confiscated all of the keys."

"Did she say if any were missing?"

"No, dear. They don't tell me much around here," Grandma June laments.

"And you didn't see anyone come into your room?" I question, opening my laptop and noting all of this down.

"No, not with the sleep medication they have me on. I could sleep through a hurricane."

"I'm jealous," I half-joke, though I should grab some melatonin from the store before heading home. These fitful nights are burning me out, and I need my wits about me.

"You can have some if you like," she offers.

I swallow my laughter. Grandma June tries to hand her medication out like other grandmas do with hard candy. I guess it must be working if all of her pills and potions come so highly recommended. "No, that's okay," I reassure her, glad that she can't see my amused expression. "I'll be at Sunny Side in half an hour."

"No, Birdie, you don't have to do that," she protests, always very anxious over the idea of inconveniencing anyone. I suspect that was partly the reason for her moving into a retirement home in the first place.

"Yes, I do, Gigi. It's my job to solve things like this."

"I know, but you have work today."

"Not today, I don't. Well, not at the preschool. Apparently, I do have work to do at Sunny Side."

Grandma June sighs. "I suppose if you must. It will be nice to see you."

I try not to laugh again. As if she didn't call for exactly this reason. She's one of the only people in the family who truly believes in my work as a private investigator. She knows what she's doing.

"Some of the other ladies and gents have complained about the same thing," Grandma June adds, and I prickle, my metaphorical hackles rising.

"And have they also complained to Tanya?"

"Yes, and she said they're looking into it, but…"

The 'but' is weighted, politely irritated, and I know all that I need to know to march down there and raise hell. "I'll figure it out," I promise. "See you soon. I love you."

"I love you, too, little bird."

Half an hour later, I arrive at Sunny Side and I am as blown away as I was the first time I came to visit. The residents call it The Palace, but aside from the English-inspired walled gardens, bowling greens, and hedge maze, it doesn't really resemble Buckingham or Windsor. It's more like the White House. Stately, and, well, white. Almost blindingly so.

It's busy for a Thursday, but maybe it just seems that way because I never come this early, before everyone else's nine-to-five begin. Everyone looks so happy, and it's a good day for it. Last night hinted at a warm day, but this is unprecedented in March. I spot Bert, Enid, and Ida, some of Grandma June's best friends, playing bocce on the lawn with their grandchildren. I wave, and the group responds enthusiastically, but they don't part from their families, and who would blame them? They know they'll see me soon anyway. I'm always hanging around after my Sproutville shifts and have been known to attend a knitting club or two. My parents also come by often, even though they wish Grandma June still lived at home with them. But like me, she enjoys her independence, and she also has the bonuses of a built-in social circle and endless classes, clubs, and activities at her doorstep.

In fact, she's become quite the chess champ, and her pottery improves with each bowl she gives me.

I enter through the front door, and my demeanor shifts when I see only staff occupy the space. I'm stiff, my expression cool and stride determined. Julia, the receptionist, smiles at me, falters when I give her a knowing look and stands behind the desk to match my height.

"Birdie! How can I help you?" she inquires, even though I can tell from her engagement ring fiddling that she knows exactly why I'm here.

"Is Tanya here?" I ask. Tanya is the big boss at Sunny Side. She has been since before I was born, and she's a commanding presence that can be a little intimidating. Considering the occasional ne'er-do-well who stops by to ask for money or request inclusions in wills, I suppose she has to be. However, today, she's the one who should be nervous.

"She is," Julia replies, eyeing Tanya's office door.

"Good. May I speak with her?"

The door opens with a creak. "Birdie!" Tanya exclaims, and I focus my laser beams on her instead. She's standing in the doorway, dressed in culottes and a flowy blouse and wearing her signature turquoise statement necklace and earrings. Her dyed black bob is tucked behind her ear, and she looks at me fondly through her bright red horn-rimmed glasses. If she's nervous, she doesn't show it.

"Hi, Tanya," I say, terse but polite. "Do you have a minute?"

"Of course. Come on in."

She steps aside as I enter, and though I resent how obviously angry I appear, I do nothing to shuck my mannerisms as I sit opposite down and place my hands in my lap. Tanya shuts the door slowly and takes her time to sit down on the other side of the desk. She takes so long that I have a moment to scan her desk for new holiday trinkets from the cruise-obsessed residents. They all love her here, as do the families. I, myself, adore Tanya and have always thought she was great at her job, but that won't stop me from criticising.

She sits, her chair squeaks, and she looks over her glasses at me. "So, how can I help you, Birdie?" Tanya inquires calmly, using her signature 'therapist' voice.

"Somebody has been stealing from my grandma."

Tanya nods. "Yes. I'm aware. Somebody has been stealing from a few of the residents."

I want to throw my hands up, but I keep them firmly in my lap. "And what is being done about it?"

Tanya laughs, but I don't join her. She clears her throat and explains. "Sorry. It's just that I was actually just about to call you and inquire about your services."

"Oh," I say, taken aback.

"We're having some issues tracking down the perpetrator. I rounded up all the skeleton keys, and there hasn't been a 'hit' since, but we still need to find who did this and return the items to their owners."

"Of course," I say, even though I mean 'no kidding.' "So none of the keys were missing?"

"No. We had a full count. Which, of course, led me to suspect the staff. But the thing is, we actually search the staff when they leave each day, and, as you know, everyone has to pass through a metal detector beyond the lobby. And considering the lack of gun crime around here, those are primarily in place to stop exactly this from happening."

"And no one set them off?"

"No. Staff does not wear jewelry aside from simple wedding bands or piercings studs, and visitors are required to leave large jewelry items at the desk."

"So, the jewelry is still inside the building?"

Tanya nods. "I imagine there's a stash somewhere, and someone is just trying to figure out how to shift it."

"Or you have a kleptomaniac on your hands."

"That," Tanya sighs, "Would actually be a relief. I'd hate to think I hired some sort of larcenist."

"And the cameras haven't picked anything up?" I ask, my eyes flicking to the CCTV in the corner of the room.

"Unfortunately, there are a lot of blindspots in the building, and they simply don't exist in any private quarters, including the bathrooms and changing facilities."

"That makes sense."

"We'll pay you, of course," Tanya hastily insists. "And—"

"I'll do it," I say, and finally give her a smile. "Of course I will."

"Great. How would you like to begin?"

"Do you have a list of victims?"

"I do."

"I'd like to question them together. See what I can find out through their testimony."

"That can be arranged."

"Great. I look forward to working with you."

As I move through the building, I take note of the cameras or lack thereof. Despite the metal detectors, a serious crime could happen here, and no one would see it until it was too late. Especially considering that the 'security detail,' Luis and John, are as old as most residents and spend a lot of their time playing bridge.

This lack of security is starting to feel like a trend. We've taken this town's supposed safety at face value and failed to protect ourselves from the evil that clearly runs rampant in the crevices. When something does happen, we blame bad apples and newcomers. We say things like, 'We could have never predicted this,' but we could have and should have. We've failed to reinforce the coop and let the snakes in. And the chickens—or locals—aren't to blame for getting eaten; the ones in charge are. The authorities knew that teenagers were going missing. Worse still, they knew that there was a killer on the loose, and they did nothing. No patrol, no curfew, not even a warning in the local paper. I know that this jewelry thief is not at the same threat level, but I still feel like this was preventable with a watchful eye, digital or otherwise.

I continue to rant and rave in my head as I walk up the stairs to the first floor before rapping on my grandmother's apartment door. She opens it quickly as if she is waiting on the other side, but I soon realize that's not the case when I see a pot of tea steeping on the nearby kitchenette counter.

Grandma June—an elegant, slender woman much like my mother with a short, chic silver haircut and a penchant for vivid silk scarves—lights up as she looks at me and pulls me in for an embrace. She kisses my face over and over again, and her Chanel No. 1 fills my nostrils.

I let her do this for as long as she likes, giggling like a child, and when she releases me, she physically pulls me into the room by my jacket, and I kick the door shut behind me as I topple forward. I don't fall; my balance is too good for that, but every encounter runs the risk. Luckily, I know she could take the hit. It's not only chess and ceramics that she spends her time perfecting; she also leads the Monday Zumba classes in the downstairs assembly hall.

"Go on, sit," she instructs, and I do as I'm told, opting for the two-seater set by the window. Her room has a view of the twelve-foot-tall hedge maze, and I love solving it with my eyes. Not that it poses much of a challenge after all of these years. I could probably walk through with my eyes closed.

She waltzes over—her hips displaying flexibility that mine dream about—the hot teapot in hand, and I see that there are already two cups and saucers waiting on the table. First Mom's vase, now this. I'm becoming predictable. Maybe next time, I'll go for the padded bench on the balcony with its rattan accompaniments.

"Ugh. You are so beautiful," she says, shaking her head. "How did you and your sister get to be such beauties? I suppose I have your mom to thank for such gorgeous grandbabies."

"As if we don't have you to thank."

She tuts. "You flatter me. Half of my bunions stand a better chance of winning Miss America than my side of the family."

I laugh. "Come on."

"I'm serious! Have you ever seen a photo of your great-great-uncle? The man looked like a radish."

THE GIRL IN THE SPRINGS

She's right about that. He did have a very root vegetable look to him, which is hard to explain to people until I show them a photo. Maybe it was the haircut. "You don't look like a radish, though," I insist.

"I do if I do this," she replies, pulling her hair into a top knot with the tie around her wrist. I shake my head but can't stop laughing long enough to argue. She hates phone calls and has her moments in general, but she's often a riot. And she knows it. "I love your laugh."

"I love that hairdo," I choke out.

"Speaking of hairdos. What did Mia Wallace tell you?" she asks, referring to Tanya and her signature bob.

"She hired me to solve this case."

"As she should."

"I'm going to get everyone who's been affected together to ask some questions later in the week. But, for now, do you have any suspects for me?"

Grandma June chuckles. "I'm afraid not. But I do have tea and biscuits."

Close enough. I reach for a chocolate bourbon and dunk it into my perfect cup of English Breakfast tea. She copies me, and for whatever reason, we fall into another fit of hysterics that ends in tears rolling down my cheeks. Just when I think a reprieve has come, and I reach for my tea, she regales me with the events of her latest life drawing class, and I'm hunched over and pink-faced once again. These are the moments, amongst all the horror, that keep me sane. May they never stop happening.

CHAPTER TEN

"**B**RIDGET," A MALE VOICE CALLS FROM BEHIND ME AS I enter Cobblestone Cafe. I turn, and for a joyful moment, I think that the voice belongs to the lovely Stanley and that I'll be saved from the degrading mission of internet stalking him and 'hitting him up.' Instead, I see Noah standing in the corner, and as he bounds over like a labrador, I try very hard not to let my disappointment show. I must pull it off because he grins at me as if we're old friends rather than—as previously stated—firm acquaintances.

After my brain finishes grinding and manages to change gears, I notice that he's shaved his head. Not to the skin, but it's short, and annoyingly, he really pulls it off. It adds to the tough mountain man thing that he's got going on but doesn't harden him to the point of being unapproachable. In fact, he looks sweeter than he did before.

He notices me looking and rubs his velvety skull. "Long hair just gets too sweaty," he explains. "And with building work starting up, I'm going to be sweating a lot."

"Thanks for the visual."

He flashes a smile. "You're very welcome. Touch it. If feels amazing."

"Mm. I'll pass."

"Your loss."

I hum thoughtfully, still staring. "Must be nice to be a man and be able to shave it all off."

"I think you could pull it off." He stares at me, clearly trying to imagine me with a buzzcut. "Actually, on second thought—" he begins.

"Hey!"

He shrugs. "Your hair is too pale. You'd look bald."

"I could dye it. Maybe bright pink."

"I don't know," he says skeptically.

"What?"

"You just don't strike me as the kind of girl who dyes her hair. And bright pink is very..."

"What?"

"Punk rock."

"I could be punk rock," I protest as if I'm not currently wearing mittens and an embroidered sweater.

Before he can argue with me, the girl behind the counter yells, "Next!"

Noah holds out his arm and sweeps it dramatically toward the counter as if guiding a celebrity onto the red carpet or a princess up the castle steps. "After you," he says, and I half expect him to tack a 'my lady' onto the end.

"You were here first," I counter. "And I don't cut lines."

"Come on," he replies, eyeing the girl behind the counter and the other people waiting.

"Fine. Thank you," I say tersely, jaw clenched to the point I'm surprised any sound passed through my teeth. At least I'm not wearing my retainer, but if I have to keep hanging out with Noah, I might actually need braces.

I order and stand by the window, and soon after, Noah joins me and chows down messily on a blueberry muffin. "That was cute," he says, lazily making an effort to cover his full mouth.

"Excuse me?"

"The whole 'you go,' 'no, you go' back and forth. Like a chick flick."

"Was that what that was?" I ask. "Is this you hitting on me?"

"Oh, God, no," he replies in earnest disgust.

I scoff, amazed at his obvious repulsion. "Wow. Tell me how you really feel."

He takes an oversized bite, his brow crease deepening. "Do you want me to hit on you?"

"Definitely not," I reply with the same amount of disgust, and I get his point. I can't be offended if the feeling is mutual.

"Well, there you go." He laughs as he shakes his head. "I can't win with you. Either I'm rude, or I'm trying to get in your pants."

"The two need not be mutually exclusive. I get hit on a lot by jerks." He looks surprised again, and I roll my eyes. "What now?"

"Nothing, nothing. It's just as a jerk..."

"What?" I snap.

"Us jerks just tend to like our women a little less... granny-like."

I immediately see red, remembering how Gavin used to call me a 'granny,' but Noah doesn't know that.

I give him a sardonic smile. "No. I imagine you don't. I can just picture your girlfriend now. Sharleen. Late forties. Barfly. Missing a few teeth but that just gives her character. Five kids. All boys with mullets. Am I close?"

"Now you be nice about Sharleen; what we have is real."

"I bet," I reply dryly.

"We're getting married in September."

"Shotgun?"

"Is there any other kind?"

"Tuxedo t-shirt?"

"Cheaper than a rental."

I snort. "Am I invited?"

"Jerks only, I'm afraid," he says somberly.

"Darn."

"But if you shave your head and dye it bright pink, I might make an exception."

"I can make no promises."

Our coffees are placed on the counter, and I copy his sweeping gesture from earlier. Laughing, he dutifully retrieves them, and when he returns, he hands mine over gently, drops his shoulders, and says, "I'm sorry for the other day, Bridget. Honest mistake. I swear. I might be a jerk, but I don't make a habit of being a dick."

Oddly touched by this moment of sincerity, I reply with, "It's fine. And it's Birdie."

"Huh?"

"People call me Birdie, not Bridget."

He shakes his head and opens the door. "Such a grandma."

And just like that, he's ruined it, and I purse my lips and push past him. Unlike the first time, we collide, and my coffee splashes out of the mouth hole, which only ensues more laughter on his part. "Wanna give me a lift?" I ask, not even looking his way. "I was heading your way anyway."

"Only if you promise not to backseat drive."

I glance at him. "I'm sure you know that I can't do that."

He internally debates, tipping his head from side to side. "Fine, but I pick the music."

"Country?"

"Dad rock," he corrects.

"Great," I mutter and walk toward the dirty pickup truck parked badly beside the curb. He doesn't even ask how I know it's his car. We both know it's obvious. And, for the first time, as he struggles with the rusty door, he looks a little sheepish. I count this as a win.

When we arrive at the clearing—after a lot of me backseat driving and a lot of him turning up the volume—I see that Noah and his crew have been busy during the past twenty-four hours.

There's an excavator, and I can see that they've made a decent start on the distant foundations.

I accidentally make my surprise known with a loud "Huh."

"What is it now?" Noah groans, teasing me but also genuinely annoyed after our unpleasant journey.

"You've gotten a lot done."

"And?"

"Nothing, nothing. It's just from what I've seen of building sites, your line of work seems to involve a lot of sitting around. And considering there's nobody here... I'm just surprised, that's all."

I worry for a second that I'm being too rude, but, luckily, he chuckles as he opens the door. "They start at eight," he explains. "I'm just an early bird."

"What does Sharleen think of that? You must have to poop on a lot of late-night parties."

"She's too busy dancing on the bar Coyote Ugly-style to care."

"Good ol' Sharleen," I reply, opening the passenger door. "Okay, so walk me through all of this."

We start walking toward the nearest trench, and I think of a Ha-ha again and how it would be hard to see until it's too late. The only indicator that it's even there is the dirt piled on either side.

"Well, the front wall is going to go there," he says, gesturing to our destination. "With big double doors and two windows on either side. Classic colonial style. Double hung. Then, to the right, there will be a matching, attached two-door garage."

"Okay, and the first-floor layout. Walk me through it."

He walks me through it, and I like what I envision. He's listened to me. And he's clearly willing to keep listening to me as he's pulled out a notepad and flipped to a blank page. He pulls a pencil out from behind his ear that I hadn't seen before, and involuntarily, I bite my lip. I don't know why that turns me on, but it does.

"I think sliding barn doors for the two in the living room," I tell him. "The one that joins it to the foyer and the kitchen. That way, she can opt between cozy and an open plan feel."

"Noted, we'll make a wider gap to incorporate that."

"And then four bedrooms upstairs. A big bathroom, and in the master, an ensuite and a walk-in."

"Agreed. What do you think your parents would think about hiring a landscaper? I know a few. I was thinking we could plant some privacy hedges instead of fences or set up some raised beds for gardening."

I hum. "I think a mix of white picket and hedges would work, yeah. And definitely some beds in the front for flowers and a lot of big ones in the back for vegetables. Can we add a shed?"

"We could add a cowshed on this square footage. So, yeah."

"Awesome," I reply. It's a word I rarely say, but I'm feeling this. Despite the rocky start, Noah and I are on the same page.

Noah charges ahead to the trench and turns around, holding out his arm, this time like he's unveiling a statue. He's so excited, and honestly, it's infectious and downright charming. I chuckle, holding back, waiting for a speech, as he turns to face the ditch.

Even though he's wearing three layers on top—undershirt, flannel, and denim jacket—I can see his muscles tense. His shoulders rise and then fall as if a shiver ran through him. When he does it again, I frown. Is he having some sort of episode? A heart attack? Then I hear it, the awful panicked breathing.

"Noah?" I ask.

He doesn't reply, and I don't move. I don't like this. It feels weird. It only feels worse when he takes a step backward and stumbles, landing hard on his rear.

I don't know what to do, so I call out to him again, my voice catching. I try again, and I'm almost sobbing this time. Something is wrong. Something is so, so wrong. And yet I can't help myself, so tentatively, I take a step.

He turns to me sharply, hands buried in the dirt. His eyes are wide, manic. "Don't," he says firmly.

For whatever reason, I crouch into a squat and wrap my arms around my knees. "What is it?" I moan.

"Seriously. Birdie. Don't."

I am crying now, hard. There's something in there. Something he doesn't want me to see. "Noah," I plead. "What is it?"

"Birdie, just stay there, I'm going to..." He trails off, getting awkwardly to his feet, patting his pockets for his phone. "Do you have your phone?" he asks.

"Yeah," I croak.

"Can I borrow it?"

I nod, unblinking, and hold it out. He doesn't ask for my passcode as he walks away, which means he can only be calling one number—911. While the phone rings loudly on speakerphone, he tells me over and over again, like a child, not to move, but I can't help it. I have to see. I think I already know what's down there, but I have to know for sure.

I crawl through the wet grass and the dirt and head toward the trench. Noah is either distracted or knows he can't stop me. Or maybe he is calling out, and I can't hear him for all the blood rushing past my ears.

She comes into sight before my hands are on the ledge, but I keep going anyway and lean over, nearly toppling onto her body before Noah scoops me up by my middle. I bray like an injured animal. It's a noise I've never made before, and it scares me, as well as Noah, who drops me. As soon as he does, I scurry forward again, reaching out but not touching.

Mia Ramsey's body is in the trench.

CHAPTER ELEVEN

"**O**H, GOD," I BURP, ON THE VERGE OF PUKING. "IT'S her."

"I'm on the phone with the police right now," Noah says, trying to be reassuring, even though he looks as green as I feel. "Yes, ma'am," he says, addressing someone other than me. "Yes, that is the location."

"No," I whisper. "No, no, no. This isn't..."

But it is. And she is. She's pale, bordering on blue. Her skin is bruised and battered, the trickle of blood coming from her slightly parted lips is already congealed and dry.

Once he's hung up the phone, Noah sits beside me and lays my phone out in the grass. He doesn't touch me, and I'm thankful for that. My skin feels sore, like I'm running a fever. "I think she ran here," I choke out before spitting to my left, gesturing to her bare, raw feet and the leaves in her wiry locks.

"Birdie, don't look. Leave it for the police."

I shake my head and crawl back, getting closer, leaning over. Noah readies himself to catch me again, but I'm steady, my nails embedded with dirt as I grip the ninety-degree drop. "What the fuck is on her chest?" I ask. I haven't said that word in years. I don't swear. Not ever. But it's all that comes to mind through the disgust and outrage as I look at the card pinned to her bony chest.

Noah kneels at the edge, looks down, and repeats after me. "What the fuck *is* on her chest?"

Clarity comes, but the answer still doesn't make sense. "It's a tarot card. I think."

"What the hell does it mean?" he sniffs, wiping his face. I don't look to see if it's his eyes or nose that are running.

"I don't know," I reply. From the look of the card—with its shattered tower and the man being run through with what seems to be some sort of golden appendage—nothing good, and when pinned to a dead body, something even worse.

"Jesus."

I retreat. "She didn't do that to herself. And she didn't position herself like... that. Like she's in a coffin."

"No," Noah says, agreeing with me, though his voice is hoarse and his mind seems distant.

"Somebody killed her, and—" I can't finish the sentence.

"Hey, the cops are here," he says, lightly patting me on the back as he gets to his feet. "I'm going to go find Keith and guide them over. You stay with her."

I nod and stay by Mia's side until an EMT wraps a shock blanket around my shoulders and helps me to my feet. I don't want to leave her. She must be so cold and lonely. But I know I'm in the way, so I go willingly, my neck turned painfully to stare at the trench.

After maybe half an hour—I don't know, time is moving strangely—Donna Mercer approaches me, and when she smiles, I momentarily forget about everything. Her statuesque beauty is something to behold, especially in the flesh. Her headshots were one thing, but now I see how tall and athletic she is. I bet that, under that uniform, she's muscle-bound like a cage fighter. Even her asymmetric bob is unflappable, even in the wind, and her dark brown skin makes her already blinding smile glow. Then the awfulness comes flooding back, and I curl in on myself, feeling very much like a child and hating myself for it.

"Bridget," Donna says gently. "Can I call you Bridget?"

"I prefer Birdie," I murmur and try to straighten in her presence, but my spine won't allow it.

Even though Donna isn't my friend, I'd like her to be. Her energy is positive and warm, and she makes me feel safe despite the crime scene being erected in my periphery. I finally unfurl somewhat, my muscles tight and aching, and shrug off the blanket.

Donna reaches out and puts the blanket back on, which annoyingly makes me start crying again. Donna's expression becomes soft and she squats to be on my level. "Hey, it's okay. You don't need to be a hardass right now, even though I'm sure you can be. Is this your first body?"

"Yes."

Donna nods. "I cried when I saw my first body, too. And I didn't even know her."

"Really?" I ask, assuming she's just saying that to be nice.

"Oh yeah. Not at the scene, but as soon as I got home and locked the door behind me, I crumpled. You can train as much as you like, but nothing prepares you for that first time. Especially when it's a homicide. She was a young girl, too, like Mia, and maybe it shouldn't be, but it's always more painful when they're young. So much life they'll never get to live."

"Was that the Silence Seeker case?" I ask, miming my lips being glued together and then immediately regretting doing so.

Donna nods again, unphased. "It was. Minnie Fisher."

"Wow, you got thrown in the deep end."

"I could say the same about you," Donna replies. "This is your case, too."

"You really know what to say," I joke weakly.

"I'm not just saying it. You were looking, and you found her."

"By accident."

"Still. This is your case, Birdie. And if you want to, I'd like you to help me finish solving it."

I nod gently, not wanting to move too quickly in case my stomach turns again. "Do you think the killer put her here as a warning? I mean, none of the other missing people ever showed up. Why now?"

Donna's happy expression twists into something dark. "That's an excellent point. See, you're the investigator here. You're the brains. But I won't lie, that concerns me. I'll get someone to watch your house, just in case."

"That sounds expensive."

Donna smiles again. "Please. We're under budget, and if we don't hit it, we get defunded. You'll be doing us a favor."

The sentiment is nice, but considering there's now a homicide on the department's hands, I doubt they'll be under budget even by the end of the week.

"Thanks," I mutter.

"Now, do you mind if I take your statement and ask you a few questions?"

I shake my head. "So, I got up at around 6:15 and headed to Cobblestone Cafe. I bumped into Noah there, and because I was going to come here later anyway, he gave me a ride. That's his truck over there. Then we walked up to the trench and discovered her body. Then he called you. I... I didn't check for a pulse because—"

"It's okay. You know your stuff, I'm sure, and she was dead long before..." Donna trails off. "Was there anyone else around?" she continues, pressing her clipboard against the floor of the ambulance next to me.

"No. I mean, Keith Hicks should be here. He's security."

"Yeah, Noah told us about Keith, but he's not in his trailer. Do you know much about him?"

"Nothing, really. Other than that he's working for Noah."

"And what was your impression of him?"

"That he was really nice. Super sweet. Reminded me of a teddy bear." I pause. "Is he a suspect?"

"Or a victim," Donna replies honestly, pausing to look me in the eye. "I don't like to assume."

"It doesn't make sense," I say. "Sorry," I add, pawing at my pounding forehead.

"No, go on."

"Well, if he's the killer, where would he have hidden her if he's living onsite? She's been missing for seven, eight days, and her body..." I swallow that persistently rising bile down. "Her body is fresh. Surely, someone would've heard her if she was being held onsite. And I think Keith only arrived when they set up camp. He's not local. He doesn't know the area or have a house or cabin here."

"Uh huh," Donna says, opening a leather notebook and making a different set of notes.

"Even if she was being held here, escaped, and ran into the woods, why would she come back? I guess she could've been disorientated." I take a breath, winded by the entire experience and my ramblings, but I don't stop. "And she was a track star. Best in this county. And Keith is... well, he's heavyset. Also, if he was the one who picked her up, why would she get into a car with him? He's at least twice her age and, as far as I know, a total stranger."

Donna gives me this look. It's hard to describe, but I think it means that we're on the same page. "So what do you think happened if you had to guess?" she asks.

"I think her boyfriend, or somebody else, picked her up, took her to Lovebird's Nest, and then, I don't know, locked her up somewhere, and she busted out. She must've fallen into the trench and broken her ankle or something, which allowed them to catch up with her."

"You know what, Birdie, I agree. Now, we've spoken to Mia's boyfriend, Samuel Henderson, already, and he told us that he and Mia had actually broken up before she went missing, and his parents say that he was home with them the night she disappeared. But if you can talk to him and you manage to get anything out of him, let me know. He might trust you more, considering you're a local and the fact that you can't arrest him."

"Did he say who did the dumping?"

"Mia did. She didn't want to be long distance."

"Did he seem cut up about it?" I inquire.

A corner of Donna's mouth quirks. "You're good, Birdie. Really. I also have my suspicions about the jilted lover."

"But then, what about all the other missing couples?" I ask rhetorically.

"Exactly," she says, gesticulating with her pen. "Samuel's only eighteen. Keith isn't from around here. It's all very... interesting. So what say you that we both investigate and come together when we have more information? Obviously, some stuff on my end will be confidential, but I can point you in the right direction if it's going to end with a killer, or killers, behind bars."

"Yeah, okay," I say, a little breathlessly.

"Do you have a card?" Donna asks. "I know I already have your information, but for the sake of professionalism."

"Yeah, I do, um..." I rummage around in my cardigan pocket and hold out my own card. It's white with cursive font and little flowers on it. Donna smiles and pockets it.

"Now, I just have a couple more questions. Is that okay?"

"Sure."

"Great. Then you can go home and rest. You deserve it."

"I think I'll need someone to knock me out."

"I'm sure that can be arranged," Donna jokes. "Drugs or a punch?"

I muster a weak smile, even though I'd usually laugh. "Drugs, I think."

"Yeah, that's my pick, too. Ambien in particular." She lowers her voice. "Do you need one?"

This time, I actually muster a laugh. "You sound like my grandma."

Donna, fortunately, doesn't look offended as I cough before I can explain. "She loves giving people drugs."

"I'll have to keep an eye on her." Donna winks. "Anyway. Noah Fletcher. Do you know him well? He's new to town, lives out here in the woods, he's young and handsome."

"He fits my theory," I whisper, hearing Donna's implication loud and clear.

She shrugs. "Can't leave any stones unturned."

"I've only met him twice," I say. "And he seems normal enough. No red flags. And he was really, really upset when he found Mia."

"He also led you straight to her."

"Oh," I say. "*Oh,*" I repeat. "I could be his alibi."

THE GIRL IN THE SPRINGS

Donna shrugs again. None of this is official, and I didn't hear it from her. This is speculation; I get it. We're just two investigators 'shooting the shit.' "It would be a convenient way to get rid of a body without running the risk of burying her," Donna says.

"And it would be easy to kill Keith. They're friends. He'd never see it coming. They have a few drinks and bang."

"Does Noah carry a firearm?" Donna asks, brows lowered.

"Not that I know of," I clarify. "I'm just saying. He could've also paid Keith off." My stomach roils, and I'm unsure if it's because of Mia or what I'm saying. Noah and I just endured the same trauma, and here I am, throwing him under the bus.

"Of course, this is all conjecture," Donna says as if to quell my worries. "But maybe keep your distance from Noah until we know more."

I nod, but guilt continues to twist my stomach into knots. Noah and Keith don't seem like evil people, and certainly not murderers. I doubt we'd ever be close friends, but casting such aspersions on them feels wrong even though I'm doing so with legitimate, thoughtful, logical intent.

Another officer walks past, an older man with thinning grey hair, and Donna stops him. "Miller. Find anything in Keith's trailer?"

The man looks at me and hesitates until Donna gives him a nonverbal go-ahead. Officer Miller clears his throat. "No. The guy lived like a monk. No booze, no guns, no porn. There are some photos of a woman Fletcher identified as being his mom, and there are plenty of porcelain figures. Guy's a softie."

"Does he have a car?"

"Yeah, it's still here."

"Huh," Donna says and turns back to me as Miller continues on his way. "How long does it take to walk to town from here?"

"An hour," I reply. "So it's doable. But there are plenty of structures out in the woods. Unoccupied hunting cabins and stuff."

"Yeah, there are," Donna says slowly. "Alright, while we wait for the dogs to get here, would you mind running me through the other missing people again? I've got notes at the office, but just for the sake of right now."

"Yeah, sure. Wait...dogs?"

"Cadaver dogs."

"Cadaver..." My voice fades away. "Wait, are you looking for the other teenagers?"

"Consider the cases of Carrie, Gina, Chad, Lucia, Jayden, and Sonya reopened. Are you up for joining us?"

"Of course," I say, jumping to my feet despite my body's protests.

Donna holds out a hand and grips my biceps, steadying me. "See, you're tougher than you think. Let's find this freak."

CHAPTER TWELVE

Noah and I are following Donna, Donna is following a row of officers, and the row of officers are following the cadaver dogs. The arrangement makes me feel as if we're heading into battle, and I should be carrying a bow and arrow and looking for higher ground. Maybe that's just the recent *Lord of the Rings* marathon speaking. Or, more likely, it's the shock. I want to cry, I want to laugh, but my face is frozen, eyes unblinking and sore from all the crying.

The group reaches the edge of the clearing, stops, parts for Donna and myself, and Mia's path reveals itself. There are broken branches and footprints, and a piece of her shredded outfit dangles from a small tree. There is only one set of footprints, which are small and clearly made barefoot. Whoever caught up with her must've come from a different direction or the clearing itself. Maybe Keith didn't take her but saw the opportunity when she fell. It's hard to say, but I'm right about her coming from the woods, which is a good lead so long as the trail remains clear.

"Alright, everybody, spread out and mind where you tread!" Donna thunders, commanding the group like a goddess on the warpath. "Keep your eyes peeled for evidence, and for God's sake, don't touch anything. I'm talking to you, Pete."

I give her a split-second smile, and she shoots me a wink that says, 'You got this,' and despite myself, I believe her. I think I might be forming a little girl crush on her, and who could blame me? She makes me feel smart, heard, and necessary, which is exactly what I need on a day like today. It's also what the town needs, this knight in tan armor.

"Let's move out, people!" she says and steps into the woods, avoiding but staying parallel to Mia's tracks.

And I'm moving, switching my brain back on, ducking and diving through the forest, keeping an eye out for anything of interest, and listening to the persistent sniffs of the Belgian Malinois and German Shepherds.

Noah jogs up to my side, and I tense as he enters my touching distance radius. "You doing okay?" he asks.

"Not really. Mia Ramsey was a family friend. Basically, my cousin. I used to go on vacation with her and her parents. Which means I don't just get to go home and process my feelings. I also need to comfort her parents, my parents, my... Oh, God, I'm probably going to have to tell my family."

"I'm sorry, Bridget," he says, returning to formality now that the crying has stopped. "And you're also... investigating? I overheard something about you being a PI."

"Yeah. I'll go crazy if I don't. I need to feel like..." I trail off, gesticulating in frustration. My brain is still malfunctioning, and I don't expect it to stop any time soon.

"Like you're in control?"

"Something like that."

THE GIRL IN THE SPRINGS

"I get it. Better than feeling useless. Now that the building site is a crime scene, all I can do is sit around and think about— Where the hell are you?" he asks, interrupting himself.

I see that he's holding out his phone and typing rapidly on the old T9 keyboard. "Are you trying to get ahold of Keith?"

"Yup."

"Have you known him for long?"

"Oh yeah, Keith and I go way back. We ran a carpentry business together back in Chicago, and when I moved out here and got this gig, I called him and asked him to come out."

"And he's never given you any reason to be, I don't know, suspicious?"

"No," Noah replies firmly before faltering. "Sorry, it's just that Keith is the nicest guy I know. He can be unreliable, especially back in the day before he got sober. But unreliable meant showing up for work late, not anything like… terrible. He'd never hurt a fly. Seriously. Which is why I need him to show up and explain himself, and then everyone will see. Once the sheriff just talks to him…" He curls his hands into fists and sets his jaw, the muscles ticking. "I'm telling you, it's a misunderstanding."

I don't want to be Noah's enemy, even if I am suspicious of him and his friend. It won't do me any good. I can't arrest him and grill him in an interrogation room. I soften and say, "We don't have any reason to believe that Keith is her killer. It's conjecture. A theory based on the fact that we can't find him and he was living at the place where her body was found. He's just as likely to be a victim." I see Noah pale at that and almost trip over my tongue, trying to reassure him. "Not that those are the only two options. He could have taken off. It can be eerie out here, as you've said yourself. Maybe he couldn't take it. Was he showing any signs of relapse?"

"No. At least, I don't think so. He just celebrated his two-year sober anniversary in February."

"Alcohol?"

"And other stuff."

"What other stuff?" I ask.

Noah narrows his eyes. "I want a lawyer, Officer Hartley."

"Come on, Noah. You know the cops are going to ask the same questions."

"Then let them ask. I don't want you feeding them information and misquoting me."

I think I've overstepped the line. "Was that your first dead body?" I ask.

"No."

"Sorry," I say, not expecting that answer.

His lips are parted, about to speak, when a dog starts barking loudly, borderline aggressively. That seems odd, considering how well-trained these animals are. My heart pounds when I realize they might've stumbled across a bear, and I take a step back. Noah, however, picks up the pace, cursing under his breath as he goes. I stop reversing and accelerate, catching up to him quickly.

"What's going on?" I ask.

He shakes his head and charges ahead, and soon, we're in another clearing, and at the center is a tiny, black, ultra-modern house complete with huge windows, a herb garden, and solar panels. This must be Noah's house, and that—banging at the door and snarling—must be his dog.

Donna hears Noah swearing and turns to him. "Is this your residence, Mr. Fletcher?"

"It is," he confirms.

"Okay, and would you like to explain why the victim's footprints are on your property?" she asks, gesturing to a straight line of Mia's footprints that cut through the clearing, about thirty feet to the right of Noah's house. They don't veer, nor do they come from his home, but they are here, and they are close.

"I, uh..." Noah clams up, pawing at his neck until it turns red.

Donna looks impatient, so I prompt Noah with, "You said you heard noises at night."

Noah drops his hand and nods. "Yeah. Weird ass noises. Sounded like screaming. I thought it was foxes or mountain lions or something. It always sets Buckaroo off," he says, gesturing to the dog, who is still, understandably, going crazy behind the front door. He's another Malinois, and I assume it's the fellow dogs setting him off today, considering how much he's wagging. He just wants to play, but Noah's coat and shoe racks are paying the price.

"Foxes do sound pretty awful," I say, trying to balance the scales somewhat.

"Yeah, they do," Donna says, and though I sense some skepticism, Noah doesn't seem to pick up on it and slumps like he's in the clear. "Does your dog play nice with others?" Donna asks.

"Yeah. He's ex-K9. Well, failed K9, but he's a good dog. Just excitable."

"Good. Bring him along, but keep him on a leash. And don't worry about him distracting these guys. They passed their exams," she teases, and there, beyond the hardness and the suspicion, is a glimmer of kindness. Which, again, is exactly why I like Donna.

"Thanks," Noah says, looking like a six-foot little boy as he nervously jogs to his front door and apologetically struggles with his keys. It's electric. He just needs to press a button, but he must be more shaken up than I think because it takes a painfully long time. Then, Buckaroo tries to slip through the gap, and Noah holds him back by the collar while simultaneously reaching for a harness and leash. I decide to lend a helping hand, and chuckling quietly, I take Buckaroo and allow him to lick, jump, and wiggle while Noah clips him in. Then, we're ready to go, and Buckaroo is dragging Noah along on a mission to sniff butts and lick hands.

Once the greetings are done, the professionals continue on ahead, and Noah, me, and Buckaroo hang back. It's nice to have something else to talk about. Buckaroo is eleven years old. Noah's grandfather, whom he lived with in Chicago, named him. And he was rehomed twice for being a serial humper. This makes me laugh loudly for the first time since finding Mia, and when I acknowledge this, I quickly stop. It feels wrong, hearing my own merriment ring out through the forest while on a literal corpse hunt, but no one seems to care. Donna even looks back at me and smiles, which makes me feel less guilty. I guess even murder investigators are allowed levity. If we weren't, I suppose we'd all lose our minds.

We keep walking, and at a certain point, both Noah and I check our phones. It's been at least twenty minutes since we passed by his house, and I'm surprised that the dogs are still so focused. I know it's their job, but still. I guess I'm used to my parents' spoiled pack, whose skills involve giving up on walks, hunting for treats, and barking at the mailman.

Then something changes. People start to mutter and congregate, and I stand on my tiptoes and see that those at the front line are bottlenecking into yet another clearing. I hear Donna saying something that sounds like instructions, but a sudden gust of wind whips her voice away. Wherever we have ended up, I don't know this place. Nor should I. The forest of Salish Pines is vast and seemingly endless, and you don't venture out this deep unless you want to get lost. I look at Noah, and he seems as clueless as I am.

"We never come this way," he says, referring to himself and Buckaroo as we clamber over a fallen tree. "It always seemed—"

"Hazardous?" I ask, as my skirt catches on some kind of bramble and tears loudly, giving the calf-length garment a new sultry thigh split makeover.

"Yeah," Noah replies, politely averting his eyes. "There's plenty of beaten tracks, you know. I figured coming this way was just asking to be eaten by a bear."

It's finally our turn to enter the clearing, but I have to work my way through the crowd to figure out what everyone's looking at. I'm slightly annoyed by their dawdling until I see it and stop dead, too. This is a cemetery. It's makeshift with wonky wooden crosses, but its purpose is unmistakable. There are seven in total—one for each of the missing teenagers and an extra—and even though the dug earth is grown over with grass, there's a hillock in front of each marker of roughly seven by three feet.

Donna hangs up the phone and wanders over to me. Very quietly, even though it's obvious to all involved, she says, "I think we just found those missing teens."

I barely hear her. Not because she's quiet but because I'm too busy staring. There are no names on the crosses, but pinned to each one is a tarot card.

CHAPTER THIRTEEN

I WASN'T ALLOWED TO STICK AROUND WHEN THE BODIES WERE exhumed. Donna was very apologetic about leaving me in the lurch, especially when she wouldn't have even been looking for the teens without me, but I was understanding, and I do understand. This type of thing is official, confidential, and way above my pay grade. However, this—my grasp of the situation—doesn't make sitting around and waiting any easier. Especially as these 'long' moments of quiet are never long enough to allow me to get in touch with my feelings or process what happened and what I've seen. They're constantly punctuated by calls and texts from my family and friends, who are either in distress, want to know more, or a bit of both.

When my phone buzzes for the fiftieth time in twenty hours, I assume it's Mom, Dad, or Ada again, and I'll have to listen to another frankly ridiculous theory or disheartening update on the Ramseys. Except, when I flip my phone over, I don't recognize this number. Tentatively, staring at the police car parked outside of my apartment, I answer.

"Hello. This is Bridget Hartley," I say, annoyed by the nervous waver in my voice.

"Hi, Bridget. It's Donna Mercer," Donna replies, her voice quiet and conspiratorial. "I'm calling you from my husband's phone. How are you holding up?"

"Well, my parents are in pieces, and I'm sure you know the Ramseys are distraught. Kate's in the hospital because Lloyd is worried she'll hurt herself."

"I know. It's a very hard time for them. But what I asked is how *you* are holding up."

I haven't really thought about myself that much. I've spent most of my time listening, comforting, and sympathizing. "I'm... bad," I say, as if that word even covers the half of it.

"Me, too," Donna admits. "I don't think a single soul in town is having a good day. But you were there, so I wanted to reach out to you personally to check in and ask if you want to continue investigating. I understand if you're not—"

"Yes," I reply firmly. "Sorry. It's just... Yes. I want to be a part of this. After finding Mia and seeing that graveyard, I need to find out who did this. *We* need to find out who did this. I can't stay cooped up in this apartment, not knowing, not doing anything."

"I'm so glad you're onboard. I know this is all a lot to take on, but at this point, I'll take all the help I can get. You have a very keen mind, and frankly, I need someone to bounce ideas off of. And because we're partners of sorts, I think I owe you an update," Donna continues. "But you didn't hear this from me, which is why I'd appreciate it if you kept this to yourself and deleted the call from your log once we've finished talking."

"Of course," I say, lowering my voice despite being alone in my home.

"We've identified six of the bodies," Donna informs me, and I hear that coldness seeping in again. She's mad that it's taken this long to find them, and I'm in the same boat. If the previous sheriff hadn't died last year, I think we'd both be on his case. "They were wearing the same clothes that they went missing in, which made things easier. The families came in this morning and made it official. Carrie Olson, Gina Martin, Chad Bennett, Lucia Nunez, Sanya Gupta, and Jayden Nelson."

"Wow," I reply slowly. I knew this was coming, but it still takes me aback to hear out loud. I'd been ridiculously holding out hope that at least some of them were out there somewhere. "And the seventh body?"

"A Jane Doe, as of yet. Not as decomposed as the first four victims. She was likely murdered more around the time that Sanya Gupta and Jayden Nelson were."

"What about dental records?" I ask before hastily following up with, "sorry, I'm sure you're already looking into that."

"We are, but no matches yet. She might've been from somewhere else. Overseas even. There are a lot of factors at play, but hopefully, we can identify her soon. I have two people looking at missing person reports from that time period from Washington State in general. Hopefully, what she's wearing, her clothes and jewelry, will mean something to somebody when we can make the information available to the public."

"Is there a cause of death? For any of them?"

"Nothing official at this point, but preliminary findings suggest that the injuries are consistent with both blunt force trauma and strangulation. The male victims exhibit significantly more severe skull injuries."

"Maybe they put up more of a fight," I suggest.

"That's what I think, too. Take out the men and then toy with the women."

"I know we can't assume, but are we looking for a man?"

"I would say so," Donna replies.

"So," I begin, looking at my notes. "We're looking for a male serial killer—"

"The Willow Wraith," Donna adds, remembering what I said.

"Yes. Exactly. An established killer who is still alive and in his forties at the least. He's likely local because of the location of the bodies and where they were taken from. Possibly lives out in the woods." I pause. "Did you find anything out there? A hunting shed, maybe?"

"We've found some cabins, yes, and we're working on tracing them to owners. We haven't found anything suspicious, however. No footprints, no Keith, no blood. Nothing like that. But don't worry, I'm not done looking."

"And how can I best help you?" I ask, rewriting the question over and over in my head before asking it. I don't want her to feel like she needs to give me assignments like I'm a toddler or an employee, but at the same time, I want to be useful. There's no point in me looking for something that she's already assigned a team to.

"I want you to ask around town. You know these people, and they trust you. I want you to talk to Samuel Henderson, I want you to keep an eye on Noah Fletcher, and I want you to turn over rocks, no matter how small or insignificant. And you're invited to the funeral?"

"Yes."

"Great. No cops allowed because of Lloyd Ramsey's vendetta. But, as I'm sure you're aware, killers sometimes turn up at funerals, vigils, or graves. Keep your eyes peeled for anyone acting strange or anyone you don't recognize. It might be someone you know or someone you don't. You know this town better than I do, and I will defer to your judgment, Birdie."

"I can do that." I hesitate. "I know we're pressed for time, but I'd like to speak to Mia's family and Samuel Henderson after the funeral. I think they might be more open to talking then."

"As I said, I will defer to your judgment. And don't worry about the other victims' families. I'm going to talk to them personally if they'll let me. But cold cases are tricky, and there's a reason they're cold. Not to be crass, but Mia is fresh, and I think if we find her killer..."

"Yeah," I say, understanding completely. Mia is the key to solving the backlog of crimes.

"I just hope her killer wasn't a copycat," Donna murmurs, sipping on something, and for once, despite it being the morning, I wish I had some alcohol in the house.

"I've thought about this," I reply, a little hesitantly. After all, Donna took down the Silence Seeker. If she thinks this could be a copycat, maybe it is.

"Go on."

"Well, it's just... How would the copycat know about the tarot cards? It's not public knowledge now, and it never has been. I mean, nobody except the killer even knew the missing teens were dead. Yeah, people suspected, but no one knew for sure. It seems unusual for copycats, considering most do it for 'fame' or 'glory.' It would be like a serial confessor confessing to a crime nobody cares about."

"Excellent point. See, this is why I need you, Birdie. Now, I won't keep you any longer, but please, call if you need me, and if I have any more sensitive information, I will call you from this number."

"Thank you for keeping me in the loop, Donna."

"No, thank *you*. We're going to get him, Birdie. I know it."

"Yeah," I say a little tentatively. "Yeah, we will."

When the call ends, I begin to squirm. I already know this to be the case, but there's nothing more that I can find on the internet. No theories, no suspects, and nothing to do with tarot cards. The frustrating thing about a lot of serial killers is that they don't know their victims. They're opportunistic. Their motive is simply to kill rather than anything more personal. That's why they can become serial killers. They're untraceable versus someone who murders their wife or their ex-boyfriend.

However, it's strange. Mia's death seems different, personal. I think the car is throwing me off, along with where her body was found. Maybe the killer really is threatening me, or maybe there's more to it than that. Perhaps she knew something. Maybe whoever she was on a 'date' with was a jerk, and she ran off into the woods, got lost, and met someone even more unsavory. However, surviving for a week in the woods seems unlikely.

My knee is bobbing, my head is swimming, and my jaw is clenched. Not knowing what else to do, I decide to head into town. The funeral is on Sunday. I need to find something to give Lloyd and Kate, and I need to buy something black. Hopefully, I'll unturn some rocks along the way.

At Curio, Archie watches me with fascination as I aimlessly browse the overstocked shelves. I want to get the Ramseys something thoughtful, something meaningful. Of course, I'll get them cards and flowers, too, and I'll bring a bouquet to the funeral, but we're basically family, and neither of those things feel like they're enough.

Then I worry that whatever I get them will forever remind them of their dead daughter. I suppose they can always throw it away; though wouldn't that render what I'm doing right now pointless? Is it better to try or obey the status quo about grief gifts? I guess they might throw Mia's clothes and belongings away, too. Or perhaps they'll lock it all away in her bedroom like some sort of crypt. There's also the possibility of their home becoming a museum or shrine to her life. I'm honestly not sure which is worse.

I'm on the verge of tears thinking about her belongings going dusty like the things in the store when Archie asks, "Birdie. Are you okay?"

I turn and nod, managing to reabsorb the brimming saline. "Just trying to find something for Lloyd and Kate."

"Ah," he says softly, twisting off the top of a cheap bottle of red. I look at the selection of clocks, which are always accurate, and give him a pass. It's five after five. "Well, Lloyd likes ships in bottles, and Kate likes ceramics."

I hum thoughtfully, facing the ceramic section in the far corner. "Have you sold any of these to a Keith Hicks by any chance?"

"Doesn't ring a bell."

"Big guy. Beard," I say, turning back to him.

"No. Sorry, Birdie."

"Don't be, I'm just..." I sigh and pinch my nose. "He's missing, and he was staying at the worksite where Mia..." I trail off, failing again.

Archie pulls another smaller glass out from under the desk and fills it halfway. It's much smaller than his own. Like everyone else, it seems he knows me well. I venture up to the desk, pull up a purple poof, and collapse.

"And do you think it's related to those missing teenagers I mentioned?" he questions.

"Yeah. I do."

Archie frowns and scratches his stubble. "They found some bodies, didn't they?"

"Yeah, but I'm not privy to that information."

He eyes me skeptically but doesn't push. "Seven," he says. "There's an extra."

I wonder how he knows this, but then I remember that it's a small town, and I'm sure some of the cops get loose-lipped with their partners, and their partners get even looser at The Homestead.

"Yeah. There's an extra," I answer, careful to repeat after him and not provide any new information.

"I wonder..." he begins but then stops himself and clamps down. I know, even if I ask, he'll dodge the question. I don't think he's withholding information so much as not wanting to put unfounded ideas in my head. "Is it a woman?" he asks at last.

"I... Yes." I promise myself that that's the last tidbit I'll reveal. "How did you know?"

"It almost always is, isn't it? It's just common sense."

"Yeah. You're right about that."

"Hm. But with Mia... I wonder if the mystery woman and her had someone in common. Considering neither of them have been found with a partner."

It's a good point, and I jot it down mentally. "Yes. Maybe."

"Maybe they knew too much." He sips and looks at me furtively. "You should mind yourself; single female who knows too much."

It's a warning, and it chills me more than the officer who basically lives outside of my house. "I'll be careful," I promise.

"Do you need any help deciding? Regarding the gifts," he says, changing the subject again.

"Yeah," I exhale. "I really do."

"Not a problem. You stay there, and I'll pick something for Lloyd and Kate. It'll be our little secret."

Archie stands and begins to peruse, and I sip my room-temperature wine. I watch in fascination as he deftly plucks options from shelves, piles them before me, and silently deliberates. I think he's a genius, but I also know that genius, and its process, takes time, so I swivel back again and take the opportunity to look at the world behind the desk. Two doors, nearly touching, form a corner. One leads to the staff room and then the backyard, and the other leads to the apartment. Next to that one is a glass-fronted shelving unit where he keeps the good stuff.

I gasp and glance over my shoulder to check that he hasn't heard me. He hasn't, but as I turn back, I smack my glass on the table's edge, nearly knocking it out of my hand.

"Careful," he warns.

I laugh, but it's false. Every fiber of my being is focused on the third shelf down and the collection of vintage tarot cards that inhabit it.

"These are beautiful," I say, gesturing to the cards as he meanders over with ceramic salt and pepper shakers.

"Ah, yes. Tarot. I collect them," he informs me without hesitation. He must not know about that detail regarding the murders, or else I'm sure he'd not be so forthcoming. "My mother was a very magical person. Used to scry and dowse and all that. I suppose she got me into all of this."

"Do you use them?" I ask.

"Occasionally. When I feel I need some supernatural guidance."

"And what do the spirits say?"

"They mostly encourage me to sell Curio and travel the world, but I've never been a good listener."

I smile. "I don't know about that. Do you sell them often?"

"Occasionally. The cheaper sets, the reproductions, sell well with teenagers. The Rider Waite, for example. The classic one people always think of. Kind of cliché."

"Do you have a favorite?"

"The Sola Busca," he replies, walking up to the glass and pointing at a particularly ancient-looking set. "Those are original. But I've sold some of the replicas over the years."

I stare at the card, pulled from the pack for display purposes, and know without a doubt that these are the cards I saw at the graveyard and pinned to Mia's chest.

"Do you have a record of who you've sold them to?" I inquire.

He looks at me curiously. "Why do you ask? Something to do with the murders?" I don't answer him, but he gleans my answer from my silence and expression. "I'll have a look, but I make no promises."

"Thank you," I say. "Seriously. This could be everything."

"$156," he says abruptly, gesturing to the two items before me—a particularly large ship in a bottle for Lloyd and a teapot set for Kate. This is all the information I'm going to get out of him today.

I drain my drink, pull my wallet out, pay him in cash, and leave him to close up. We say little to each other as I depart, but my tongue is twitching, eager to talk. Once a few minutes down the road, I call Donna's personal number and say, "I unturned a stone."

"Oh yeah?" she asks, her excitement evident.

"Archie Whitman, the owner of Curio, the local antique store. He sells tarot cards. Actually, he collects them. One of the sets was the same as the ones on the graves and Mia. I'm sure of it. Sola Busca."

"Thank you, Birdie," Donna replies. "We'll talk to Mr. Whitman and see what we can find."

We have a brief back and forth about a job well done, and then her husband calls for her, and she excuses herself. I feel pleased. I failed to get my dress, but I have my gifts ready for the Ramseys and, better still, a promising lead. I just hope that Archie can find what we need in his unorganized desk and that he's as cooperative with the cops as he is with me.

CHAPTER FOURTEEN

"They've arrested Archie!" Mom cries down the phone. She's loud enough that I can hear what she said before the receiver reaches my ear. My mom never yells or skips 'hellos' or 'how do you dos,' and her doing both sends me so off-kilter that it takes me a moment to process what she's said. "Birdie! Are you there? Did you hear me?"

"Yeah, I'm here," I say, sitting up in bed, the comforter slipping down and exposing my bare shoulders to the cold. "What do you mean they've arrested Archie?"

"Rosie called me. The police turned up at Curio about an hour ago and took him away in the back of a squad car."

I blink rapidly. Surely Rosie is mistaken, or my mom misheard. Donna said she was going to talk to Archie about the cards. They probably just gave him a ride to the station to make an official statement. Maybe he looked through his records and found the name of whoever bought a pack of the Sola Busca twenty years ago.

"Was he in handcuffs?" I ask.

"I don't think so, but he looked very upset, according to Rosie." Mom tuts, and I can hear her heels clicking across the tiled kitchen floor. "This is just outrageous."

"Are you sure he was being arrested?"

"Yes, Birdie," she replies, exasperated. "I'm not some busybody gossip, you know?"

"I know."

"Rosie spoke to the officers who stayed behind, and they told her that they had a search warrant. Why would they have a warrant if he wasn't in trouble?"

She's right, and my forehead creases. Why would Donna arrest him? I told her that he might know something. I didn't say that he was a suspect. Because he's not. Why would a guilty man tell me, a private investigator no less, about his murders? No one ever talks about them; he could've just kept his mouth shut, and we would've never found the bodies. Not to mention, he didn't seem to know anything about the tarot cards playing a part. I suppose Donna doesn't know about these aspects, and I intend to tell her right away.

"That's weird," I say as if that covers even the half of it.

"It's a disgrace, is what it is. Half of these officers aren't even from here. They have no idea what they're talking about or the enemies they've made today. For God's sake, we've known Archie for all of our lives. He and your father went to school together. He babysat you girls when you were small. I'm sure we would know if he was a serial killer." She pauses, and I can hear that she's still pacing. "What it is is discrimination. Just because a man lives alone and has poor family relationships doesn't mean he's... Ugh! I'm sickened, Birdie. Really sickened."

"What's the deal with his family?"

"Oh, not you, too," she scolds.

"I'm just curious!" I protest. "I'm not investigating him."

"If you must know, his parents disowned him when he was seventeen and then moved away because of the backlash. He would've been homeless if Grandma June and Grandpa Ken hadn't set him up in an apartment and given him a job at the hardware store. You know they actually paid the deposit for Curio?"

"I had no idea."

"He's practically family. I'm sure we'll get a call from him shortly. Dad's already on the phone with the family lawyer."

"And why did his parents disown him?"

Mom clucks her tongue. "You're the investigator, Birdie. You put it together. A single man who loves antiques, flowers, and fashion? Come on, honey."

"Oh."

"As I said, discrimination."

"I'll head down to the station. I've gotten to know Donna. Maybe I can sort this out."

"Maybe I was wrong about you investigating," she says, though her tone is far from anything akin to pride. "Maybe you can keep this bunch of idiots above board. Or, at the very least, bring them the right person."

I begin to speak, but she cuts me off. "I have a dress picked out for you. It's very elegant and black. I thought you might not own anything black, so I went through my wardrobe and found this amazing but casual dress. Knee length, v-neck, puff sleeves. Adorable. We'll pick you up bright and early tomorrow morning, and we can all get ready together."

I don't tell her I've already borrowed a suitable dress from Maisy, who swung by last night on her way home from The Homestead. Mom does this when she's in crisis mode or feeling helpless; she looks for something to control. In this case, it's how we'll all look at the funeral, but often, it's renovating the house for the millionth time.

"Sounds good. Is Ada coming?"

"Yes, and Pat. It'll be lovely to see them. I've washed some old baby clothes for them to look through." Mom inhales sharply, suddenly stricken. "Oh, God, they'll never be grandparents. Lloyd and Kate. I suppose they're not even parents anymore, and they're much too old to try again. Promise me you won't wait until you're forty to have a child."

I promise, but I'm glad no one else will ever hear what she just said. I know she's in shock and babbling because of it, but it's a cruel implication all the same. Lloyd and Kate are not to blame for their bleak future by having only one baby and having her so late. Yet, I know what she means, and it's not that Mia is replaceable by another conception. It's that when you have a child, you must have an idea of what your life must look like. You raise them, they fly the nest, they bring back babies of their own, and then they look after you when you get old.

Lloyd and Kate will never have any of that now. Only an empty void where a daughter used to be. It's only made worse by the fact that Kate is also an only child with deceased parents, and Lloyd isn't in contact with his family. All of their eggs were in one basket, and that damned snake got into the coop and ate them all up.

"I know," I say softly. "I'm going to call the sheriff now and see what I can find out."

"Okay, honey. I love you. Be safe."

"I love you, too. And you, too."

I hang up, but I'll call her again later. I'm as worried about her and Dad as I am about the Ramseys.

I call Donna without even getting out of bed, and to my surprise, she picks up after only two rings. "Birdie!" she exclaims. "How are you?"

"I'm okay," I reply, suddenly nervous about what I have to say. "I heard that you've arrested Archie Whitman."

"We have, yes."

I exhale and close my eyes. I was still hoping this was all a misunderstanding or, at the very least, he had only been brought in for questioning. However, an arrest implies that charges have been pressed and they are holding him in a cell until further notice.

"Is something wrong?" Donna inquires.

"It's just... I think you got the wrong end of the stick. I thought he might be able to tell us who bought the cards, not that he's the killer."

Donna sighs. "I take it you're close with Mr. Whitman?"

"I am."

"I thought so. Which is going to make what I have to say very painful for you, but I want you to bear with me."

"Okay."

"We had intended to just talk to Mr. Whitman, but when he took us upstairs to his apartment, I noticed something very interesting. A bracelet with the initials 'MR.'"

I freeze. "Is it gold? With a t-bar clasp?"

"It is. Do you know it?"

I want to scream but hold it together as I say, "Yes. That was Mia's favorite bracelet. Her parents gave it to her on her thirteenth birthday."

"Thank you for that information. Mia's parents are on their way to the station to make an official identification. It's personalized, which makes this easier, in some ways."

"So you found the bracelet and obtained a search and arrest warrant?" I ask, my eyes scrunched closed.

"Yes, I did. I'm sure you can understand why."

"Yeah," I squeak, drawing my knees to my chest.

"I'm sorry, Birdie. I know this must be painful."

"It can't be him," I weakly protest, no longer one hundred percent sure.

"And why do you say that?"

"Because he was the one who told me about all the missing teenagers. We would never have found them if he hadn't. And he had no idea about the tarot cards and their relation to the case. He just seemed to think I was interested in them."

Donna hums. "Perhaps with Mia missing, he was trying to throw you off the scent. Make himself out to be the good guy. He certainly seems intelligent enough."

"Would you be willing to let me go through his files?" I ask. "To see who he's sold cards to?"

"I'm sure that could be arranged, but Birdie, if you're going to be an investigator, you need to be unbiased. Even when it comes to people you know and love."

"I know," I sigh. "I know."

"I'm sorry, Birdie."

"He's gay," I blurt out. "And maybe asexual."

"Okay."

"It's just... Aren't serial killers usually sexually motivated? Bundy, Dahmer, Gacy."

"Surprisingly, only 27 percent," Donna responds, not at all condescending, but I still feel like an idiot. "Consider the Son of Sam and the Zodiac Killer, for example. I understand what you're getting at completely, and if Mia had been sexually violated, I would give credence to Mr. Whitman's sexuality as an alibi."

"So she wasn't..."

"No. She was not."

I breathe a sigh of relief. It might not get Archie off the hook, but at least Mia didn't have to suffer that. "Good."

"Thank you for the information, regardless. I'll keep it to myself for now to avoid offending Mr. Whitman, but it does raise some interesting questions."

"Like why he had a teenage girl in his apartment if he didn't want to sleep with her."

"And why he might've picked her up and taken her to Lovebird's Nest. Yes. Mr. Whitman is handsome and charming, and Mia wouldn't be the first girl to fall for an older man, but clearly, that doesn't apply in this case."

"They were probably just friends," I say. "Like Archie and me. Though, he's never taken me up to his apartment. I don't know why she..."

"Maybe she dropped her bracelet in the scuffle, and he brought it home."

"Then why leave it out in the open? Doesn't that seem weird?"

"It does," Donna admits. "And I'm glad you're asking these questions. It forces me to think about the answers."

"You don't sound convinced that it's him."

I can practically hear Donna's gentle smile as she replies. "That's because I'm not. A good investigator should never throw in the towel at the first sign of success. Sure, another sheriff might coax Archie into confessing just to call it a day. They might intimidate, manipulate, and ask leading questions. But I'm not most sheriffs, and I do not intend to fight dirty. Nor do I have any intention of letting a killer run rampant while an innocent man spends his life behind bars."

I unfurl, somewhat comforted by her words. Yet I can't help but pity Archie. He might be innocent, but his arrest will cause jaws to flap. He's undeniably weird, local, single, and in his fifties, which makes him a match as far as profiling goes, and he'll forever be tainted by this. Though, maybe I am being biased. Maybe I'm too close. Maybe Donna is right. Maybe that's why I never see her around town—she can't afford to get close to the locals.

"I'll find a way to get you into Curio once it's no longer a crime scene," Donna promises. "Now, unfortunately, I have to go, but it's been very enlightening speaking to you. I'll be in touch. Bye, Birdie."

After the call ends I finish my morning routine and make my way to Curio, wanting to see the scene for myself. When I arrive, two police officers—one I recognize as Miller—are standing guard, and there's police tape stretched across the open doorway. It's garnered a lot of attention, but I suppose that's the way of things when you work for law enforcement. You can't be subtle like me; you have to go by the book. Even if it attracts the media like flies to manure.

I'm standing on the opposite side of the street by The Petal Parlor—which is closed for business on account of Rosie's distress—and watch on with an expression I know must be disapproving, drawn, and bitter like an old lady snooping on her neighbors behind curtains. I can't help it. This feels like an injustice, and their manhandling of Archie's collection sickens me. I hold my breath, waiting for somebody to drop some invaluable antique, when somebody calls my name, and I let go of my phone. It clatters to the ground and I internally scold myself for being such a butterfingers.

"Oh, God, I'm so sorry," the somebody says, and I swivel to see Stanley, stooping to pick up my phone. He picks it up from the damp sidewalk and hands it over, his expression sheepish.

"Hi!" I explain, taking my well-protected phone from his elegant, long-fingered hand and pocketing it.

"Hi," he responds, straightening, his expression warming rapidly. "You hear to watch 'the show'?"

"Yeah, kind of. The sheriff called me earlier and—"

"Oh, of course. You're a PI. You must be looking into all of this."

"Yeah, I am."

"Well, Miss Marple, can you tell me what's going on?"

"Not really. I think they found something in Archie's apartment," I say, keeping it vague even though Stanley seems more trustworthy than most.

Stanley tuts. "I can't believe this. They've got the wrong man."

"What makes you say that?"

"Well... I don't know. It's Archie. The man wouldn't hurt a fly."

I've been hearing a lot of that going around—men who wouldn't hurt flies—and doubt grows inside of me like a malignant tumor. Am I just a poor judge of character, or are the police the ones who are misguided? Keith seemed like a hairy angel, Noah appears troubled but otherwise normal, and Archie is, as my mom said, practically family. Before now, I wouldn't cast any sort of aspersion on them, but now they're all suspects in a brutal homicide. I worry that I've put myself in dangerous situations without realizing it.

"Were you close with Archie?" I inquire.

"As close as you can be, I suppose. We like a lot of the same things. History, antiques, old movies. We had some wine on Friday and watched *Casablanca* in the basement. You wouldn't believe the collection he has."

"Oh, I can believe it. I've seen it, too," I answer with a sorrowful chuckle.

"He's an amazing man. You know I trust him so much I'm tempted to pay for his defense if it comes to that."

"I know the feeling, but at the same time—"

"You never really know anyone," Stanley finishes.

I nod. "Unfortunately."

"I'm sorry if this is weird or bad timing," Stanley begins, looking away with his hands in his pockets. "But I had a really nice time the other night, and I meant to ask for your number."

"I'm actually more of an email type of girl," I reply, blushing and smiling.

"I am, too! An email man, I mean. It's like writing a letter."

"Yes, exactly!" I enthuse. "I'm Bridget Hartley at gmail. No dots or numbers or anything. Just my name, all one word."

"That's a very sexy email address."

"My dad made it for me when I was twelve. I got in early."

Stanley laughs; it's melodic and beautiful. "Well, don't judge me for mine. I made my own when I was fifteen."

"I can't make any promises," I tease. "Let me guess, it's something to do with Edgar Allen Poe."

He looks aghast. "How did you know?"

"You just look like the kind of guy who spent a lot of time in cemeteries as a teenager, brooding and listening to Mozart."

"Try Radiohead, but close enough." He pauses. "It's Quoth The Stanley, also gmail."

I laugh. "That's actually pretty good."

"I'm glad you think so." He kicks a rock into the drain, looking around. "It seems like our favorite restaurant has just opened for brunch. Fancy some food and a commiseration drink?"

"That honestly sounds amazing," I say, even though I have a rule against drinking before noon.

"Come on then. Before the vultures pick us to pieces," he says, referring to the vans that are beginning to pull up beside Curio. Journalists and reporters. I was one of them once, but I think the nickname is apt, considering how much they prey on the weak.

To my surprise, Stanley hooks his arm around mine, and I find that I don't mind being so entwined. In fact, I relish in it. He smells just as good as the day I met him, and I lean into him as if he's a crutch. I didn't realize how much my body ached until now. With his spare hand, he pats my arm, and drags me down the road and then across it to Notte Stellata. With Archie in jail, Mia dead, and the whole world feeling miserable and revolting, I could do with some beauty, and his will do nicely.

CHAPTER FIFTEEN

POST YESTERDAY'S BRUNCH IS A BLUR, AND TODAY IS blurrier still. I don't remember the last time I was hungover, and today feels like an awful day to be in this condition. Still, I'm here, dressed in black, and no one seems to suspect that I'm worse for wear. Though, I really, really am.

"I'm so sorry for your loss," I say, leaning toward Kate for the kind of hug that is more of a forearm grab and air kiss.

"Thank you, sweetie," Kate Ramsey replies, gripping me so tight I'll be surprised if she hasn't left a mark. She's repeated this same line over and over to at least a dozen women before me as the line shifts into the church, but with me, she makes eye contact, and for a moment, I feel every ounce of her pain.

I'm glad when the embrace is over—that transference of grief—but then it's my turn to speak to Lloyd, and he pulls me in for a tight hug, and I feel it all over again, mostly in his stifled sobs.

"I'm sorry," I say again as if I'm responsible for all of this horror. In a way, I suppose I am. I found the body and took their hope away.

I decided not to give them the gifts from Curio. They're still sitting in their brown paper wrapping underneath my coffee table. Nobody wants a gift from a store belonging to a suspected murderer, especially if that suspected murderer is being investigated for the killing of your eighteen-year-old daughter. So, I opted for flowers instead. White roses. They were all out of lilies at The Petal Parlor.

Once Lloyd frees me apologetically, I reassure him with a rub of his upper arm and trail after my family. We walk up the aisle, the other four in pairs, and me holding up the rear. It's silly, but I envy them. I wish I had someone's hand to hold right now, and though Stanley pops into my head, I quickly stamp out the daydream. It's not the time nor the place for romantic fantasies, and this is hammered home by the photos of Mia beside the coffin at the front of the room. Her coffin—shiny wood and satin lined—doesn't have a lid. I didn't know this was an open-casket funeral, and it takes me by surprise, but I don't look away. Seeing her body once again, dressed in the elegant dress she wore to prom, is almost soothing. I thought the last time I saw her would be the last time. This is better than that. She looks pretty. Peaceful, even. They've managed to hide the cuts and bruises well. You can't heal injuries once you're dead, but the physical trauma she sustained is invisible.

Her dress—which I remember from her prom photos on Facebook—is silky and peach-colored, which complements her pale skin. It's simple and elegant with spaghetti straps and has none of the bells and whistles—or rather, bows and frills—of the prom dresses from my era. She looks like an angel, a sleeping beauty, snow white in her glass casket. If you buried me looking as I had at prom with stiff hair-sprayed curls, clumpy mascara, and aquamarine satin, I'd prefer my casket closed. The thought is

THE GIRL IN THE SPRINGS

dark, but it amuses me, in a way, for long enough to hold back the flood until I sit down.

Then I start to cry, and I'm not the only one. Half of the attendees, the ones who knew Mia, have joined me. My sister Ada—who looks as strange as I do dressed in black—reaches for my hand and massages it. With her other hand, she fiddles with her crucifix before drifting to her petite four-month baby bump. The thought of meeting my niece or nephew later this year soothes me until it doesn't. As my mom said, Mia will never get to have children, should she have wanted them. She'll never get married. She'll never go to college, get a job, or buy her own home. She's permanently eighteen, on the cusp of everything but unable to seize it.

I've been to a lot of funerals before, but never for someone under the age of seventy-five. This feels very different. They'd gotten to live long and happy lives. They'd done most of what they'd wanted to do. They'd traveled, fallen in love, and built families, careers, and homes. They'd had adventures of varying sorts, and those who spoke at their funerals regaled the audience with joyful stories and happy memories. Their lives were novels, whereas Mia's is a short story, and I've never been a fan of short stories. They can be beautiful and rich in their own right, but they always leave me wanting more.

I feel sick, and I flinch when I hear Kate sob from the front row. I hadn't even noticed her and Lloyd come in, but their presence indicates the beginning, and soon enough, the priest takes the stage. He doesn't smile like he has previously, even when he says that we've gathered to celebrate Mia's life. I understand. This doesn't feel like a celebration, and anger pulses underneath the outpouring of grief. Mia was a blessing to all who met her, and she did amazing things in her short time here on earth, but despite the turnout, there's nothing to be happy about today.

The stories are equally somber, and though they elicit the odd smile and rarer laugh, they always end in tears. When I see another person stand to speak, I'm torn between wanting it to stop and wanting it to never end. I know that talking about her is the only way to keep her alive, but every story about the child lying before us cuts like a knife.

Once their bodies are released to their families, Carrie, Gina, Brad, Lucia, Sanya, and Jayden's funerals will be happening soon. I intend to go to them all, even though a few will be happening far away where the families live now. It seems the right thing to do, and there is the possibility that the killer might show up at their 'celebrations,' allowing me to spot a trend. I'm sure it will be a harrowing couple of weeks, and I'm trying not to be selfish, but even one funeral feels like too much to bear.

After everyone has spoken, one of Mia's favorite songs begins to play. I don't recognize it, but it's beautiful, and I close my eyes, moved by the lyrics. Then, the church door opens, and I am ripped from my trance. I look behind me instinctually and watch as a man—who is mostly hidden by one-half of the large wooden door—whisper-argues with an usher. He's not allowed inside, which strikes me as odd. Usually, people can come and go at funerals—people with screaming newborns, for example—but this man is not welcome here. That much is clear.

People begin to titter as Lloyd rises, and the song's volume is raised. He yanks his jacket sleeve from Kate's grasp and marches to the back of the church. I should stop looking; I know it's rude to stare, but I can't help myself. This could be important.

It's over as soon as it begins when Lloyd shoves the man hard in the chest, the door closes behind them, and another song starts up. Kate is weeping again, and slowly, one by one, the crowd faces the front again. I need to find whoever that was. Based on Lloyd's reaction, I assume the man is a family member, but I need to know for sure.

I remember what Donna said about lurking killers, and I look around the room. I don't see anyone suspicious. Not in the stereotypical sense, anyway. There are no lone, creepy-looking men lurking in corners—that would be too easy, wouldn't it? No, instead, I see families, family members, and sobbing high schoolers. I see people who loved Mia. The only people who really catch my eye are Stanley and Noah because I know them, and a young man—a boy, really—who is crying almost as hard as Mia's parents. I assume he must be the ex-boyfriend, Samuel Henderson, and despite him being a potential POI, it's hard not to pity him.

He's wearing an all-black suit with shiny black buttons. Stanley is wearing something similar, though his suit is clearly tailored and custom-made. Noah has opted for something more casual—a dark grey shirt with wooden buttons and a navy sports jacket. Apparently, like me, he's not a fan of black. I narrow my eyes, looking at the buttons, but I am forced to stop when he sees me staring. All of the buttons were there anyway, but, like Archie, he might have a wardrobe worth looking through.

The funeral ends, the close family heads to the cemetery for Mia's burial, and the rest of us mill about, chatting and consoling. Most of the group is heading home now, but a select few are going to the wake at the local country club. I'm invited to the latter, but I know Noah isn't, so I take the opportunity to talk to him before he leaves. I jog over to him, my family's eyes locked on me as I do so, and I recoil as he lights a cigarette. My family abhors smoking. However, I'm not concerned that they'll say something to him. They're much too polite for that. No, it'll be me who gets the lecture about secondhand smoke and shaving precious minutes off of my life.

"Nasty habit," I say.

Noah looks up at me, and I can tell I've startled him. His eyes are wide, and he begins to cough as he shoots smoke out in a thin wisp from the corner of his mouth. He fans it away with his hand, trying not to get the smell on me, but we both know it's hopeless. Gavin was also a smoker, and despite only doing so outdoors, our apartment always smelled faintly of cigarettes. I hated it, and I'm glad that my attraction to Noah is nothing more than physical, or else this would be a deal breaker.

"Sorry," he says. "I actually quit years ago, but after Thursday and finding..." He clears his throat. "After everything that happened on Thursday, I bought a pack. Stupid really. Your sister looks as angry as mine would if she could see me. Hopefully, I'll quit again once this pack is done."

"Oh, you have a sister, too?" I inquire, tilting my head, hoping to prise him open and find the pearl within.

He takes another drag and falls silent momentarily before saying, "That was heavy."

"Funerals often are," I reply, annoyed by his blatant evasiveness.

He shakes his head. "Not like that. Not unless it's a tragedy."

"Yeah," I sigh. "Yeah, you're right."

"It's just sick," he says, spitting on the ground. Another action that will go over well with my parents, I'm sure.

"Do you want to talk about it?" I offer. "We could, I don't know, grab a coffee or some food after the wake is over."

"No, you be with your family. I'll be fine."

"Are you sure? I don't mind. Honestly, you probably get how I'm feeling more than—"

"I said I'll be fine," he snaps, his shoulders raised.

"Okay."

"I'm surprised you'd even offer to be alone with me. Considering what the cops think of me."

"I'm not a cop," I counter.

He laughs coldly. "You might as well be. I bet they told you to keep an eye on me, and that's why you want to hang out."

"I was just being nice," I retort, wrapping my arms around myself. "I'll be sure to never do so again."

"Good. I don't need your pity."

"Wow."

"Oh, come on. I see through you. I can tell you have an agenda. And so I'll tell you this, and you can pass it on to your cop friends: I'm thirty-two, I don't know what the hell a tarot card is, and I never stepped foot in this town before last year. I didn't even know who Mia was, not really, until we found her body. I'm not your man, and I will not be labeled a murderer just because you're bad at your job."

"I'll be sure to tell Donna," I say dryly, as if she and I aren't already aware of these details. As if Noah isn't low on our list because of them.

"Donna," he says mockingly. "And you pretend like you're not in the police's pocket."

I scoff. "Whatever, Noah. If you're too dumb to see a helping hand when it's extended to you, then..."

"Then what?"

"Then don't expect to get another one."

"You're not trying to help me, *Birdie*. You're trying to convict me."

"Come on—"

"Buckaroo needs a walk," he snaps, throws his cigarette on the ground, and takes off. Then, sheepishly, he turns back, picks the butt up, and puts it in the local trashcan while I watch on reproachfully.

Shaking my head, I turn around and, with my eyes foolishly focused on the ground, run smack-bang into somebody. However, it's me, not them, who starts to fall, my ankle twisting in unfamiliar heels, and they reach out to grab me. As I steady myself, I look up at my victim and savior and see Stanley smiling at me.

"Oh my God, sorry!" I exclaim. "I'm all over the place today."

He keeps his hands on me, making sure I'm steady and then brushes off my arms as if he might have gotten dirt on me. "Are you okay?" he asks.

I melt and feel my face take on a sappy puppy dog-type expression. "Yeah. I'm okay. You?"

He shrugs. "That was pretty brutal."

"Yeah, it was," I laugh, and then my softened expression hardens as I cringe. "Sorry, I don't know why I'm laughing."

"I get it. My mom used to laugh at funerals. She couldn't help it. It's a nervous thing." He pauses thoughtfully. "They're always so awkward, aren't they? Funerals. It's like the Olympics of walking on eggshells. I never know what to say or how to say it. Or how to sit and walk and hold my face. It's all just..."

"Awful," I finish.

"Yeah."

"Are you coming to the wake?"

"Oh, I'm not invited. I just came out of respect. Ms. Ramsey was the librarian at school when I was a kid, and she was always so nice to me. I think she was the one that made me want to be a librarian."

"No one will mind if you tag along. In fact, the Ramseys told me I was welcome to bring a plus-one because my sister is bringing her husband."

"Are you sure? I don't want to intrude."

"No one will even notice you're there. Seriously. This is going to be the kind of wake with an open bar, if you catch my drift. And all of my parents' friends are coming, which means I'm going to be asked a lot of questions about my career and love life. I could do with someone being there to bail me out."

"I can do that," Stanley chuckles. "Or I can hype you up. I can tell people you're in the FBI and dating a billionaire."

"That works."

"Alright, I'm in. Wow, meeting the parents already," he jokes and then, realizing what he's said, looks mortified.

"And we haven't even been on a date yet," I tease, saving him from humiliation. "Come on. They'll love you."

I hold out my arm to take, and he links it, allowing me to drag him toward my parents, my sister, Patrick, and the latter two's waggling eyebrows. This is a terrible day, and in my eyes, Stanley is nothing short of a superhero, saving me from a burning building before I, too, turn to ash.

CHAPTER SIXTEEN

THE FOLLOWING MORNING, I FIND MYSELF SITTING CROSS-legged on the floor of Curio. The cops, as far as I'm aware, didn't find anything useful here beyond the bracelet and tarot cards, and unfortunately, I find myself in the same boat. Archie is not an organized man. Not even a little bit. His handwriting is also appalling, and it seems that any paperwork older than a year or two has been shredded or stuffed in a water-damaged cupboard to rot. I suppose he only keeps what his accountant needs and forgets about the rest. It's probably not the wisest decision, but it's worked for him for the past thirty years, so what do I know?

Stanley is here, too, and I hear him groan as he rips a stuck-together book open, and a flattened cockroach drops to the floor. I laugh, but I hate this. It's like getting to look behind the curtain at a magic show. The mundane inner workings are ruining the majesty of the shop itself. It's also making me sticky and filthy, and I think that if Archie is innocent, I'll hire him a cleaner as a welcome home present. Or maybe he'd hate that. He probably loves the chaos.

"I might hire a cleaner for Archie," I say, voicing my thoughts aloud. "He'll need a fresh start after everything."

"I wouldn't bother," Stanley replies. "I doubt he'll stick around. People accused of murder rarely do."

"But what if I find the real killer? Surely everything will be back to normal for Archie?"

"I don't know. I feel like people don't really come back from that kind of thing. Even if they're innocent. It's like a stain. His getting arrested is on his permanent record forever now."

"Sounds like you're speaking from experience."

He laughs. "No. Fortunately, I've managed to lead a very boring existence. I just watch a lot of true crime documentaries."

I smirk. "Me, too."

"Is that what inspired you to become a PI?"

"No, I think I just realized that I've always been good at solving puzzles and wanted to do something with my life that I'm good at."

"Makes sense," he says, failing to keep the disgust out of his voice as he pulls a particularly soggy folder out of the cupboard. "Seeing any puzzle pieces here?" he asks.

"Nope. No edges, no corners, no picture. Not even sky," I reply, getting to my feet and dusting off my rose-pink pants.

"So, what's next for PI Hartley?"

"Well, I'm talking to the Ramseys and Mia's ex-boyfriend tomorrow. But today, I'm looking at a different mystery. There's a jewelry thief at Sunny Side, and it's personal."

"Don't get too close to the case," Stanley warns jovially.

"I can make no promises. Somebody stole my grandmother's pearls and a diamond tennis bracelet. Her late husband, my grandfather, gave her both."

"Seriously?" he asks, looking even more disgusted at that than he does about the mold he wipes from his fingertips with a paper towel.

"I know. I mean, it's Sunny Side."

"What is going on in this town? It feels like it's gone to shit overnight."

"You're telling me."

"I don't know how you do it."

"Do what?" I ask.

"Everything. All of this. The cases. The kids. When do you sleep or relax?"

"Don't worry, I manage to get my eight hours in."

He narrows his eyes, skeptical. "Do you?"

"Okay, maybe six. Four if I count all the times I wake up. Which is why," I pause to sigh. "Which is why I'm going to turn in my notice at Sproutville today. I love those kids, but..."

"Your calling is elsewhere."

"More like my mind is elsewhere. They didn't used to be, but my jobs are too conflicting. Murder investigation versus shaping the minds of our youngest generation? I'm worried I might, I don't know, negatively impact them. Like, they'll be able to smell death on me." I laugh and shake my head. "Sorry. That probably sounds crazy."

"It doesn't at all. My grandfather was in the funeral business, ran a parlor in town decades ago, and it kind of followed him like a cloud."

I scrunch up my nose. "As in, he stunk?"

Stanley tilts his head from side to side. "Kind of. I mean, the business of death stinks. There's all the chemicals, you know. But it was more like you could tell he was thinking about it, or at least, you thought about it when you looked at him."

"That's reassuring."

"Sorry."

I swat his apology away. "Don't be. I chose this back when I started covering true crime cases in New York."

"But this is different?"

I nod. "Yeah. Maybe because I knew Mia or because it's happening in my town. It's one of those things like cancer or car accidents. You never think it will happen to you." I sigh. "There's another funeral tonight at the church for Gina Martin."

"Do you want me to come with you?"

"Yes," I say a little too quickly. He really was my saving grace at the wake, and my family liked him. I think he kept us all sane.

He smiles and moves closer to me as he trashes another ruined folder. "I can do that."

"Do you want to come to Sunny Side, too? Be my Watson?"

"As much as I'd love to come to Sunny Side and watch you pull a Sherlock on a bunch of rich old folks," Stanley says sadly, "I have work."

"Huh," I say mildly.

"What?" he snorts.

"I don't know. I think I forget you actually have a job. You kind of have old-money vibes. You know, like being rich is your job."

"I wish," he replies, pulling out his car keys that I know belong to a vintage Jaguar, which does little to alter my perception of him. "Are we done here?"

I look around at the mess we've created and stand slowly. "Yeah. For now."

We meander toward the front door, hug briefly, make plans for later, and part ways. He gets in his car, and I start walking toward Sproutville. This is going to be painful, and I could do with some moral support. At the same time, I don't want to be greedy and wring him dry so early on.

When I arrive at Sproutville, fortunately, the kids are outside with Luna, another part-time employee. Because of this, they don't notice my entrance, which sets me at ease. Especially when I see Maisy—the person I need to speak to in Dolly's absence—tidying up the fallout from a prior rampage. She shoots me a look I rarely receive from her. It's a little dirty and a lot frustrated.

"Finally," she hisses, sitting back on her haunches, hands full of wooden blocks.

"What do you mean?"

"You're on shift today," she answers.

"No, I'm not. I don't work on Mondays."

"Yeah, but you said you would *this* Monday, two weeks ago. Remember? Because Perry is out. I've texted you at least twice to remind you."

I open my phone to check and know I've made a mistake when Maisy's expression becomes indignant. I'm doubting her, to her face. This is a big no-no in general, but especially with Maisy and her history of dating gaslighters. I sheepishly tuck my phone into my purse and say, "I believe you. I'm sorry. I must've forgotten to add it to my calendar."

"Okay, if you forgot, then why are you here?"

I hesitate, then stammer, realizing what I'm about to say is going to blindside her. I almost decide not to say it. I almost shuck my coat and get on my knees to help clean. But I don't. Instead, I say, "I came to give my two weeks' notice."

"Seriously, Birdie?"

"It's just... the case. And my other case. Basically, it's my job. You know this was always going to be temporary while I got established, and now I have enough saved to risk going full-time as a PI."

"Alright, well, dive in. At least I have you for another two weeks."

I shift and put my hands in my pockets. "Maisy."

"What is it?"

"It's just that I didn't know I was working today, and I have an appointment. Down at Sunny Side. The residents are getting together so I can question them about this jewel thief."

"But we're understaffed. We need at least three people here."

"I—"

"You know what? Forget it," she snaps. "We'll manage. Or I'll get Mom to come help out."

"Maybe they can rearrange the meeting," I say, getting my phone out again and scrolling through my contacts, looking for Tanya.

"Seriously, Bridget. Forget it. You forgot. It happens."

If her tone was even a fraction more pleasant, I might be able to fool myself into thinking that she's telling the truth, but it's not, so I can't. She's mad. More than mad, she's angry. It's been a while since we had a falling out, but last time, at least—though protracted and involving a lot of forlorn music listening—wasn't either of our faults. Her ex-boyfriend got in her head. This time, it's all on me.

"Are you sure?" I ask, and in response, she lets loose an overly long sigh and looks away. Part of me thinks she's being childish, but most of me is guilt-riddled and apologetic. However, I know begging for forgiveness is only going to make things worse, so instead, I say, "Sorry again. Maybe I can come help tomorrow."

"The two weeks isn't mandatory. It's in your contract as a part-timer. So don't worry about it. Just solve that poor girl's case. I'll manage." This time, there's a softness there, as if she's remembered the gravity of my situation.

"Coffee then?"

"I'm having a caffeine break."

"Oh, okay," I murmur, my heart breaking as she refuses to look at me. "Good for you. Maybe I should do the same."

"Mm."

"I'll see you soon, then."

"You know where to find me."

I nod even though she doesn't see it and head back the way I came, up the high street toward my car. My fists are clenched in my pockets as I walk. I don't like having 'space' when it comes to Maisy. And it's not about my feelings, though that does play a part. She might be a few years older than me, but she's prone to bad decisions and worse men. If we're not talking, if she doesn't come to me for advice, if she's upset with me, I worry that she'll slip into old habits and dangerous beds.

I sit behind the wheel of my car and want to cry, but I think of Donna and save the tears for later. I have a thief and a killer to find. I'll pencil in emotions for later, 7:00pm sounds good; once I've eaten, but before it's time for a hot bath and a good book. I'll make time, but I must prioritize and privatize. The killer could be watching.

CHAPTER SEVENTEEN

At Sunny Side, I sit beside Tanya before a semi-circle of thirteen retirees. We both have clipboards, and she's recording the session for mysterious 'legal purposes.' I suppose it's so that if anyone complains about this non-police, and thus non-official, investigation, she can prove that I'm not being malicious, accusatory, slanderous, or libelous. I just want to get to the bottom of this without getting anyone in trouble with the law. I suppose it would be the same as a teacher trying to figure out who's been giving out exam answers. No one wants it to escalate to a federal level, and they certainly don't want anyone to sue.

"Good morning, everyone," Tanya says in her signature sunny fashion.

She's wearing black pants, a thin black sweater, and a neon pink blazer. Instead of turquoise on her neck and in her ears, she is wearing pearls. They're clearly fake, unlike Grandma June's, but she's pulling it off. I suspect her ability to pull off such a bold look has something to do with her black bob—not as cool as Donna's but just as striking—and her sharp cat eyeliner.

"Does everyone here know Birdie?" she continues, and everyone begins to talk over each other in the affirmative. Tanya clears her throat loudly and aggressively. "How about we raise our hands if we don't know Birdie. Hmm?"

In my opinion, Tanya is being a little condescending, but I suppose any group of people, from toddlers to the elderly, can get a little bit out of hand. There will always be the show-offs, the class clowns, the shy ones, the nerds, and the popular clique. Grandma June is both shy and popular—a little bit like me when I was at school.

Ten people keep their hands in their laps, but three raise their right, and I realize that I don't know them either. "Are you all newcomers?" I ask, and they all nod.

"Agnes Parker," says one lady, loud and clear. She looks quite a bit younger than the rest of the women, though maybe that's the dye job and tattooed eyebrows. "I've been here for three months."

"Leonard Simmons," the man next to her says. "Two weeks."

The third man lowers his hand and doesn't say anything until prompted by Tanya. "Charlie Wilkins," he grunts. "Four months."

"Hi, Agnes, Leonard, and Charlie," I say warmly. "I'm Bridget Hartley, but you can call me Birdie. I'm a local private investigator." Noting some people look left out by my lack of greeting, I laugh lightly and say, "And hello, Millie, Harvey, Evelyn, Walter, Bert, Enid, Ida, Penelope, Phillip, and Grandma June."

"What's all this about?" Walter, the resident grump, asks.

"This is about an issue that has been brought to my attention by your dear friend June. Now, I don't want to sound accusatory, and I want you to know I will also be speaking to staff, but I believe that there is a jewelry thief at Sunny Side." No one seems shocked, and half of them cast their neighbor knowing looks. "Okay," I continue. "I see that we're all aware of this. So, starting from left to right, I would like you to tell us what you think has been stolen and if you have any other information regarding this case."

Starting with Millie, one by one, they tell me, and though I keep my expression neutral, I'm taken aback by the sheer quantity of items stolen. At the halfway mark—when some of the residents begin to rise to grab tea, coffee, biscuits, and muffins from the back of the room—I've estimated the value to be nearing five figures. Then, we get to Charlie, one of the newcomers, who sits slightly apart from the others at the far end with his arms crossed.

"Rolex. Worth maybe twenty-five thousand dollars," he begins.

"Wow," I say, thinking that maybe I should involve the police if the stakes are this high. The others couldn't put an exact value on their items beyond the sentimental, but there's been a lot of gold, diamonds, and sapphires in the mix.

"Yeah," he grunts. "And three diamond tennis bracelets that used to belong to my wife. I suppose they still do," he adds, softening for the first time. "I bought those for fifteen thousand each."

"Baller," Agnes drawls. The joke goes over most heads except for mine and Tanya's, and I understand the implication. She thinks Charlie is lying.

"Are you with insurance?" Charlie asks, and Agnes's comment makes sense. He's here for a payout and thinks that he'll get one because there's no proof that he didn't own these things.

"No," I reply kindly. "And unless the belongings were insured—"

"No," he replies. "But the police give payouts, don't they?"

"I don't think they do," I reply slowly. "And I'm not police."

"Never mind then." He wilts a little, and what I see is a plan come undone. My question is, is he lying now in hopes of claiming money, or did he commit the crime in the first place because he thought this was how it worked? If so, he's a smarter criminal than most, making sure that twelve other people were also 'hit' so as not to draw suspicion. He might even think the others would also be compensated and that everything would turn out hunky dory.

"You don't have to worry about insurance," Tanya assures him, "Because we're going to make sure everything gets back to its owners."

"Exactly. Please continue, Charlie," I encourage. "This list is to make sure everyone gets their belongings back."

"And if you don't catch him?" Charlie inquires.

"Him?"

"Well, it's always a man, isn't it?"

I smile. "Sometimes. And I will catch them, I promise."

Charlie scoffs, and Tanya interjects. "In the case that Birdie doesn't succeed, Sunny Side will make financial amends."

"Why don't you just go ahead and do that?" he pushes. "And hire some damn security."

Some further tittering implies that some people agree with him, and some think he's being unforgivably rude. I think the gentlemen doth protest too much, and with any luck, the plan I have will go off without a hitch, and I won't even have to involve the staff, who run a greater risk than a slap on the wrist.

"Let's just give Birdie a chance," Tanya replies. "Then we can take further steps."

Charlie grumbles, and I can tell he's not going to give us anything further, so I move on to my next question. "Has anyone seen anything strange or suspicious? Better yet, has anyone actually seen or heard someone in their room?"

"It's probably one of their damn kids," Walter replies. "You know what young people are like," he adds, addressing me as if I'm regularly plagued by criminal youths. Maybe it's my outfit, but I always feel like one of the pack here, which is not as insulting as it perhaps should be. I must admit I am drawn to older people. They always have the best love stories and adventures. Yet, I simultaneously sympathize with my fellow millennials. It's hard to have an adventure when rent costs $2000 a month, and romance is tricky when Tinder has a monopoly on love.

"I don't think it's anyone's children," I say. "Unless one of your children is Danny Ocean." I worry the reference might go over their heads, but I get a couple of chuckles and uproarious laughter from Grandma June, who adores heist movies. "Whoever did the thievery knew where the security cameras were."

"They'd have to case the joint," Grandma June adds for me, using the appropriate lingo.

"Exactly," I say with a smile. "Which is why I think the guilty party is someone who's here full-time." One of the residents says something deeply offensive about the cleaners, but we ignore him, and I continue. "So, again, has anyone seen or heard anything?"

I'm met with shaking heads and then silence. I let the silence continue until it becomes unbearable before swiveling to Tanya, who presses stop on the recording device. "Well, please tell Tanya if you have any information you'd like to share privately."

"It's over?" Enid asks, disappointed. She's an Agatha Christie fanatic and is expecting something more exciting.

"Today's session is, but the case is not, I assure you," I reply, standing up, clipboard in hand. "Please help yourself to snacks and beverages, however, and I will stick around if anyone would prefer to speak to me directly."

Most of the residents rise, the rest turn to each other; and I take my chair over to the window, and Grandma June follows me. "You know, Charlie told me his Faberge egg was taken," she whispers conspiratorially. "But I notice he didn't bring that one up today."

I keep my expression neutral just in case somebody is watching, but I give a quick nod to let Grandma June know that the implication hasn't gone over my head. "What did he do before he retired, Gigi?"

"He was a plumber," she says bluntly, which furthers my theory. I know plumbers can be well paid, at least enough to own a nice home and car, but $45k worth of bracelets is pushing it. And a Faberge egg is downright impossible, not to mention irresponsible on that kind of wage.

"Was he a gambler? Or did he have rich parents?"

"No, no. The only reason he's here is because his son is an investment banker. Lives in Japan, apparently. Doesn't come around much."

"Well," I say, raising my voice a little as Charlie mooches around us, staring idly out at the hedge maze. "I got you a little something to make up for your things being stolen."

"Oh, Birdie, you don't have to get me things. You'll get my real things back in no time, I'm sure."

My plan hasn't landed with her yet, but it will soon. Even now, she's still sharper than I'll ever hope to be. I hand over the gift bag, and she rolls her eyes at me affectionately as she rummages inside and tosses balls of tissue paper to the ground. Several residents are watching her do so, including Charlie.

"Wonderful granddaughter you have," Ida coos.

"Don't I know it," Grandma June replies, smug, as she opens a velvet box and reveals a ring she bought me on a beach holiday. It's cheap, bought partly as a joke from a kiosk. It's the type of ring that will turn your finger green. She told me to wear it in rough areas when I get engaged. 'Most thieves won't be able to tell the difference,' she said. I can tell she recognizes it, and she meets my gaze for a second and admires it in the light before saying, "You really are a blessing."

"Keep going," I encourage her, knowing that she's now on board.

Next, she pulls out another velvet box and opens it, and I can see her resist a laugh. Grandma June knows her jewelry, and she knows costume when she sees it. I'm just hoping that our jewelry thief doesn't, and although I'm not looking directly at him, I can tell Charlie's gaze is fixed upon the faux sapphire set.

"Oh, darling," Grandma June says, reaching out and squeezing my cheek.

"One more thing," I say, akin to Columbo as she unearths a pink, fluffy teddy bear. She looks at me, a little perplexed, and I say, "I thought he could be a companion. A security guard of sorts."

"Oh, I love him. I'll call him Valentino. Thank you so much, Birdie, you've really cheered me up."

"I'm so glad," I reply, leaning in for a kiss on the cheek. I can smell her scented rouge and lipstick. "The bear has a camera in its eye," I whisper imperceptibly, my ears tilted into her ear canal. "Leave your door ajar and make sure the jewelry is in shot."

Grandma June parts from me and puts her hands on my shoulders. "What did I do to deserve such wonderful granddaughters?" she questions, acting as if I'd said nothing at all.

"By being a wonderful grandmother," I reply, and this time, I kiss her other cheek for real.

She tuts. "Tell me about Ada. How's the baby?"

"They're both great. She's actually coming by later. She's still at Mom and Dad's after the funeral."

"Good, good. And what about you?"

"I'm good."

She pulls me in again. "Oh, my darling girl," she says loudly before turning her voice into an imperceptible whisper. "I'm good with computers. I took a course. Send me the app for the bear. If I catch anything good, I'll send it to you."

We part again, and it's my turn to put my hands on her shoulders. "Well, I have to get going, but I'll talk to you soon."

"You better, my little bird," she says with a wink.

CHAPTER EIGHTEEN

"ARE YOU OKAY WITH ME RECORDING?" I ASK SAMUEL Henderson, the boy who was sobbing at the funeral. He's Mia Ramsey's ex-boyfriend and a person of interest because of this. Poor kid. I have doubts about the whole copycat angle, but I have to do my due diligence and turn over all the stones I come across.

"That's fine," he replies shakily, forcing a polite smile.

His hand trembles as he runs it through his floppy nineties-style bangs. His look, in general, is very derivative of a decade he wasn't even alive for: baggy jeans, vintage Nike sweatshirt, beat-up chucks. I suppose all trends come back around eventually, but it's

THE GIRL IN THE SPRINGS

strange being old enough to see it happen. Admittedly, I only saw six years of the nineties, but I still remember.

The age gap between Samuel and me suddenly feels very large, and I feel a little weird in noting that he's a good-looking kid. Obviously, he's too young for me, but I bet he's popular with the younger ladies. I bet he's popular in general, and I'd hazard a guess that there's a letterman jacket and football uniform somewhere in his wardrobe.

"Great," I say kindly to Samuel and press record. "And can you confirm that it is Tuesday the eleventh of March and that the time is 11:58am?"

Samuel checks his phone, which lies face-up on the kitchen island between us. "I would."

"And can you state your name for the record?" I ask, sounding like a character in a police procedural. I've never done this before. Not for a murder investigation, anyway.

"Samuel Jacob Henderson."

"Thank you. And thank you for agreeing to meet with me. In your email, you expressed that you would like to help the investigation as much as you can. I'd like to help you help us, Samuel. So I have some questions."

"Shoot," says Samuel, trying and failing to sound relaxed.

I smile. "And please remember. I am not a police officer. I'm not here to arrest you or accuse you. I just have a few questions."

He nods jerkily. "Yeah. Cool."

"Great. So when did you begin your relationship with Mia Ramsey?"

"Around the end of sophomore year. I asked her out by slipping a letter into her locker. Cheesy, I know. But she loved it."

"I bet she did. Most girls don't get letters nowadays."

"That's because guys my age don't have any rizz."

"Rizz?"

"Oh. Like charisma. Flirting skills."

"Right. Got it," I say, the interaction aging me by a decade. "And how did you hone your skills?"

"Watch a lot of chick flicks," Samuel answers coyly. "And it works most of the time. I dated a couple of girls before Mia and… a couple after. Thought it might help me get over her."

"But it didn't work?"

"It did not."

"Sorry."

He shrugs, and I move on to the next question.

"So, you're saying you could have anyone you wanted. Why did you choose Mia?"

He smiles. "I wouldn't say that. I had options, I guess. But I only *wanted* Mia. My friends were surprised when I told them. Mia and I ran in different circles. She was quiet, nerdy, never went to parties. And as a quarterback, I think everyone expected me to end up with a cheerleader."

"So, how did you two meet?"

"We were lab partners. And from day one, I was in love with her. Seriously. She was just *so* smart. Like so smart it blew me away. She was a babbler, too, when she was excited or passionate about something. She talked my ear off the entire lesson, and I literally just sat there, chin in my hands, listening like a lovestruck puppy. It took her months to feel the same way, but I was all in from the jump. I pined about her. My moms were probably sick to death of her name by the time they actually met her."

I'm smiling hard as Samuel speaks. I can't help it. I'm a hopeless romantic at heart. "What else did you like about her?"

"That she wasn't vain even though she was beautiful. She didn't care about fashion or fancy hairstyles or makeup. Not that there's anything wrong with that," he clarifies.

"I know what you mean. Please, continue."

"It's just that that isn't my thing. I wanted a partner. A best friend. So I wanted somebody who liked what I liked and vice versa. I wanted somebody I could go fishing, camping, and hiking with. I wanted someone who wasn't afraid of getting dirty and was happy to have my dogs jump all over them. And she was all of those things. A Girl Scout through and through. She knew more about most of my passions than I did. The first time we went camping, she made the most amazing fire just by rubbing sticks together. I thought that was a myth."

"Was there anything she wasn't good at?"

"Cooking and cleaning," Samuel laughs. "Luckily, I am good at those things, and I even took cooking lessons to get really good and impress her. Which worked," he adds smugly. "She also sucked at video games, but she practiced so that she could play with me and my friends. I don't know, man. She was just perfect. She was the first girl that I liked for more than her looks. It was like I was attracted to her soul." He blushes, and I don't know if he's embarrassed or about to cry. Possibly both. There are tissues at the ready for just such an occasion, and I slide the box toward him across the kitchen island.

"It sounds like you really loved her."

"I wanted to marry her."

"And you were together for how long?"

"Three years, eight months."

"So, I heard that she broke up with you?" I question, genuinely confused. It sounds like what they had was real. Certainly a lot realer than any of my relationships. "Why was that?"

"She didn't want to go long distance. We were going to different colleges, and I guess she didn't want to be tied down. Or she thought she'd meet somebody better, I don't know. I knew something was wrong on the flight back from Australia—we took a gap year to do some traveling—and then a week later, she dumped me." He sighs. "I might defer another year. I don't know. It all feels pointless without her."

I frown, and an empathetic knot forms in my throat. "What college are you going to?"

"Princeton."

"Wow. Congratulations."

"Thanks. But I don't know. Maybe if I hadn't gotten in, none of this would've happened. Maybe she'd still be alive. I should've gone to her school instead. I got accepted there, too, but Princeton is... Well, it's Princeton. Oregon is great for track and field but not so much for bioengineering. I mean, it's probably fine," he adds, studying my face for fear of offending.

"I get it. I went to NYU when I could've stayed local. Then I stayed for another ten years with my boyfriend, much to my parents' displeasure."

"What did you do?"

"Journalism. True crime mostly."

"So, is that why you're doing this?"

"Yeah," I reply.

I don't talk much about my time as a journalist, but it is why I do this. It's what gave me the bug. Sometimes, I miss it, but I needed a change after breaking up with Gavin, and I was burnt out by the never-ending crimes in New York. My parents were so upset when I quit, even though it meant moving back to Serenity Springs. I think they were embarrassed to tell people, mostly. When I was a journalist their friends would ask fascinated questions about my line of work and the cases I covered. When I became a PI, the best I got was passive-aggressive dismissals. 'Surely,' they would say, 'There's nothing around here to investigate.' How wrong they were. Unfortunately.

"Don't blame yourself," I say to Samuel, realizing I hadn't attempted to comfort him. "People break up all the time. It normally doesn't end in murder. The only person at fault is the monster that took her life."

"Unless I am the monster," Samuel says flatly, and I shoot him a confused look. "Sorry, it's just... The police questioned me. I'm a suspect, right?"

"Not exactly."

"But sort of?"

I sigh. "You're the 'jilted ex-lover.' And unfortunately, a lot of the time when a woman is murdered..."

"It's the boyfriend. I know. And I get it."

"Did they take you in for questioning?"

"No. They came here."

"And what did you tell them?"

"That she dumped me. That on the night she disappeared, I was here, and my moms could vouch for me. I know that's a weak alibi. They're my parents; of course, they'd protect me. But it's true. I was here, watching movies and eating popcorn."

"And is there anything you didn't tell the police?" I inquire.

"That she was cheating on me. Or at least I think she was. For the last couple of months that we were together."

"And why do you think that?" I ask, swallowing hard.

I'm taken aback, despite knowing what I do about the car picking her up and taking her to Lovebird's Nest. I think, before now, my brain hadn't fully connected the Mia I knew to the case at hand. Despite finding her body and going to her funeral, there's been some cognitive dissonance at play. It's as if I've been talking about a different Mia Ramsey this entire time. "Because she stopped wanting to hang out," Samuel answers. "And when we did, she didn't want to 'do it' anymore. She was also weird about her phone. If it was out, which was rare, it was always face down. And then sometimes she'd pick it up and start typing and smiling. If I asked, she'd say it was a friend, but I knew something else was going on. And then she sent me… a picture. A nude. Don't worry, we were both eighteen, but it was so weird. She'd never done that before, and when I replied, she ignored me."

"So you think it was meant for someone else?"

He nods. "Yeah. I do. I think maybe I was starting to bore her. I was the only boyfriend she'd ever had. First, everything, you know. Maybe she'd already gotten it in her head that she was going to leave me and decided to have some fun locally to, I don't know, prepare herself."

"And do you have any idea who this other person was?" I ask, thinking that, despite his shaky alibi, all of this sounds not only plausible but likely.

"No, but it was a guy. She sent a text, along with the photo, something about getting hard. But I never saw anything else. Never saw her with anyone, and I'm not the type to go through people's phones."

"Of course not," I agree. "But if anything occurs to you, please let me know. If you're right, I'd say the person she was seeing is the same person who picked her up, and I'd very much like to find out who that is."

"Yeah. Of course." He pauses. "What about Archie?"

"What do you mean? Do you think she could've been sleeping with Archie?" I ask, dismayed, remembering the bracelet.

Samuel scrunches his face. "I don't know. He's really old. I can't really see her being interested in him, you know? It's just… I heard about the other bodies, and he's old enough. And the cards. Maybe whoever Mia was seeing is another victim."

"Maybe," I agree. "There's a lot of possibilities here. And I'll keep you updated as much as legally possible."

"Yeah. Yeah. No worries," he says, pretending to be cool, even though I hear his voice crack.

"I think that's enough for today," I say, aware that he's reached his limit. "I'll get out of your hair."

"Have you spoken to her family?" he blurts out as I press stop on the recorder.

"No. Not yet. I'm heading over there next. Why?"

He picks at the tissue in his hands and scatters paper snow onto the counter. "I don't know. But there's clearly something weird going on with her dad's side of the family. I only ever brought them up once, and she got so mad at me. And sometimes her dad would get drunk and start talking about them, but her mom would take him to bed."

"Maybe I should get him drunk."

"Maybe you should," he says, deadly serious. "As you said, you're not a cop."

I smile as if he's told a joke. "See you around, Samuel."

CHAPTER NINETEEN

DESPITE EVERYTHING THAT'S HAPPENED, I'M SHOCKED TO see Lloyd and Kate smiling from their doorway as I finish parking. I return the gesture, but upon closer inspection, I can see their happy faces are forced and fading fast. Not that that means they're ungenuine. I can tell they are glad to see me and feel the warmth radiating from them. I can also tell that their happiness is being weighed down by something even stronger than gravity—grief.

From what I know of it, grief is a lot like being in purgatory; you don't know which way is up, and you don't know how to escape, and it's almost impossible to explain to someone still rooted to the earth where you are and what it feels like. Not if they've never paid it a visit. I've visited before when Grandpa Ken and my childhood pets passed away, but those forays were mere holidays that I think about sometimes. Kate and Lloyd aren't just visiting. They've set up camp. They might never leave.

Their house—a pink and white Victorian house not dissimilar to my parents' that everyone calls 'The Pink Palace'—is undeniably beautiful. Yet today, there's a misery about it. Much like the somehow still smiling couple, it wilts under scrutiny. The flowers are dying, the curtains are drawn, and the usually pastel pink looks dusty. I blame the weather, but maybe houses have feelings, too. Perhaps that's what ghosts are: houses grieving the loss of a previous inhabitant.

"Birdie!" Lloyd and Kate call out in sync, and I close the gap, hoping that once the hellos are done, they can let the facade crumble and stop straining their muscles.

"Hi," I say breathlessly as each pulls me in for a tight hug.

"It's so good to see you," Kate sniffles, hand on the back of my head, stroking my hair. Without looking, I can tell the smiles are gone. Thank God. They were starting to remind me of wax mannequins or clowns with painted grins. The falsehood unnerved me. I'm all for manners, but not at the cost of mental well-being.

"It's good to see you, too."

"Come in," Lloyd says, gently prising his wife off of me. "I've made a pot of coffee, and we still have sandwiches left over from the wake."

"So many sandwiches," Kate laughs, shutting the stained glass door behind her.

The laugh is genuine until it isn't, and she looks at me tearful and apologetic, her hands fretting. I put an arm around her, which turns into another hug. The mood swings are hardly surprising. Mia's body was found last Thursday, and her funeral was on Sunday. They've hardly had time to shake off the shock.

"It's nice to know that she's resting," Kate whispers and reluctantly pulls herself away from me. "I hated thinking of her being poked and prodded at. She's at peace with my parents. But I think we might do something in a couple of weeks. Just with our family and yours. Maybe at her grave and then back here.

Something less somber. Her nineteenth birthday is at the start of next month."

"That sounds lovely," I reply. "I'll make a cake."

"Oh, would you?" Kate asks, on the verge of tears. "Your cakes are the best. Especially that blueberry cheesecake. Mia never stopped talking about it. She always criticized my baking skills and said I should ask you for lessons."

"I'd be happy to teach you," I say, grabbing her hands, which float in the ether between us.

"Oh. Yes, please. She'd like that, wherever she is."

"I'm sure she would," I reply softly, spotting a photo of all of us on the wall next to the living room doorway. Mia and I have our arms wrapped around each other, and for the first time, it really hits me. I know I've been crying. I know I've been mourning. I know who I found in that trench. Yet it all seemed somehow distant. Now, it connects like a punch to the jaw. Mia, the actual Mia and not a clone or doppelganger, is gone forever. Mia, my only cousin, is dead.

I pencil in my tears for later, but Kate must sense my distress because she kisses my hands before releasing them. Then she chews at her nails—an old habit, much like Noah's smoking—and fiddles with the lank strands of hair near her temples. There are several centimeters of grey roots on her scalp, which starkly contrast the amber tresses. I always thought her hair was natural. As does my mom, who's always envied Kate's hair. It's funny how many unremarkable, ordinary secrets people keep. Not funny 'ha-ha' but funny like a Ha-ha. Funny, like a hidden trench that could break an ankle. Weird, disorientating, and sometimes dangerous.

I follow the pair into the living room. I take an armchair on the left side of the coffee table, and they take the couch to the right. Much like talking to Samuel, I feel a bit like I'm in an interrogation room with the flat surface between us. Not that I've actually been in an interrogation room, but I get the gist.

"Do you mind if I record this session for my notes?" I ask as Lloyd pours the delicious-smelling coffee into the mismatched mugs. Mine has sausage dogs on it, and before I can ask, Thumbelina, their newest Daschund, waddles into the room and, in an impressive demonstration of agility, jumps onto my lap.

"She misses Mia," Lloyd says, voice breaking but holding strong.

"I bet," I reply. "I think everyone misses her."

"Everyone except the killer."

Kate tenses beside him, and I notice there's an unusual gap between the usually cozy couple. I hope this doesn't break them. I can feel white-hot anger radiating from him, and from her, all I can sense is sadness. She doesn't want to rant or rage, but he does. It would be a shame to lose their marriage, too, but I am well aware from my time spent covering the worst of the worst that many couples don't survive losing a child.

"And, of course, you can record," Kate says, and Lloyd silently agrees. "Whatever helps you, Birdie."

"Do you need alibis for us?" Lloyd asks as I lay out the recorder on the table.

It's a strange question, and I raise my eyebrows slightly. "You were at home when she left, right?"

"We were. I just think it's weird that the police haven't questioned us beyond that. Parents can murder, too. I mean, you know that, don't you? You covered that Javier Ortiz case."

"Lloyd," Kate hisses.

"I did," I reply.

"I'm not saying that we murdered our daughter," Lloyd insists. "We didn't. I swear we didn't. We'd never—"

"You're worried they're not being thorough," I say.

Lloyd slumps in his seat and shoots his arms out toward me. "Yes, exactly."

"Well, that's why I'm working alongside them," I reply, "To be thorough." It's not true. I believe in Donna and her abilities. I'm just here to be the people person, to extract secrets from those who love and trust me. Which is precisely why I said what I said. I know Lloyd—and Kate, to a degree—don't trust the police. So, for now, I don't either.

I press record. "Can you confirm for my record that today is Tuesday, March eleventh, 2024, and that is it 1:15pm?"

"It is," Lloyd says firmly. "And I am Lloyd Isaac Ramsey."

"And I am Kate Rose Ramsey."

"Great. Thanks for that. So, the police already have a detailed timeline of what happened the night Mia vanished, and I've read that report. My interest lies more in the car itself. You heard it arrive and drive away. Was there anything that stood out? Maybe a weird horn or backfiring? Something to indicate it was big or small?"

"We've asked ourselves this a thousand times," Lloyd admits, "but the reason we didn't tell the police anything about the car is because there was nothing that we could identify about it. It just sounded like a normal car. And as you can tell from the beaters outside, we don't know anything about cars."

I can tell Kate resents her Porsche Cayenne being referred to as a beater, but she nods. "I've always gotten ripped off by mechanics because I don't know anything. I don't understand horsepower or what's under the hood. I might be able to tell you if it was a really noisy muscle car or one of those awful oversized gas guzzlers, but it just sounded normal. A sedan probably, or even something little like your car."

"See, you do know something," I say kindly. "We can rule out roaring V8 engines, things like souped-out Mustangs, Ferraris, and big old gas guzzlers like Dodge Rams."

"Oh, don't rule out anything on my account," Kate says frantically.

"I won't," I promise. "I just mean I'll prioritize something more ordinary. That is to say, if I find a suspect, I won't look at their Lamborgini and rule them out. But someone like Archie and his beat-up old Ford Dodge might be a better fit to the profile being established."

"And what is the profile being established?" Lloyd asks.

"Most likely male. Late forties at the youngest due to Carrie Olson and Gina Martin's murders. Local because of Lovebird's Nest, the graveyard, and where Mia was found."

"Older, male, and local. Aren't they all?" Lloyd asks. "Killers, I mean. Next, you'll be telling me he has brain trauma and mommy issues."

"Serial killers do tend to fit a certain mold, yes."

Lloyd tilts his head. "And that's what you think this is? A serial killer?"

"In Mia's case, it could have been a copycat. But then, how would he know about the tarot cards?"

"Ah yes, the cards," Lloyd says, scratching his stubble. I've never seen him with facial hair before. He's always been so clean-shaven I didn't know he could grow it. It doesn't suit him, and I feel bad for thinking this. Nobody in town looks their best right now, nor should they.

"Do you know anything about them?"

"I know that I shouldn't know anything about them. Somebody on the force has a big mouth, which makes your job more difficult."

"Do you think the killer is the person that picked Mia up?" Kate asks.

"I don't know. Whoever picked her up could be another victim. It would make sense considering the pattern of couples being taken from Lovebird's Nest, and I did find evidence that the location had been broken into."

"But then, where's the car?" Lloyd demands, not of me, but seemingly the universe. "No one around here owns a tow truck except for 'Tony's Tows,' and Sheriff Mercer says they're accounted for that night with CCTV footage."

"Stolen keys," I suggest.

Lloyd smacks his forehead a little too aggressively. "I didn't even think of that."

"Neither did I until now," I admit.

"Maybe he's still locked up. Whoever picked her up."

"It's possible. The police are combing the woods as we speak."

"Good. Glad they're doing something other than sitting around and eating doughnuts."

"Do you mind if I ask you some questions?" I ask brightly, trying to steer the subject away from the police. I can tell Lloyd is getting worked up, and I don't need a recorded rant; I need information.

"Go for it; we're open books," Kate says, to my surprise. I thought she was closing down, coiling in upon herself, but I see openness in her face. In contrast, I see Lloyd blanch before nodding, and I wonder what he thinks I'm going to ask.

"Samuel thinks that Mia was having an affair with another man. Do you know anything about this?" I inquire, and I can tell I have not prodded the sore spot as Lloyd had expected. Instead, he looks at me dumbfounded, and Kate seems equally shocked.

"Really?" Kate asks. "I... It's just Mia told us everything. We're a very open family. We gave her 'the talk.' She told us that she and Samuel were getting intimate, and we took her to the clinic to get birth control. We gave her condoms. I mean, she was eighteen. I got married at eighteen, for God's sake. Who was I to judge?"

"So you had no idea about this supposed affair she was having?"

"No," Lloyd answers very tersely. "We loved Samuel like a son."

"Maybe that's why she didn't tell us," Kate laughs meekly. "Because she knew we'd give her hell."

Lloyd slumps forward slightly, arms folded on his lap. "She was more secretive than usual toward the end. On her phone a lot. I thought she was just being a typical teenager."

"Maybe she was," I comfort. "But Samuel has reason to suspect that there was another man. I think this man is the one who picked her up from your house that night."

"And you haven't recovered her phone?" Kate asks.

"No. Her phone is actually the only one that was never recovered," I say. "But the other victims' phones didn't have anything of interest on them. At least not, according to the previous sheriff. I don't think they knew their killer. At least not well enough to text and call."

"It has to be a copycat," Lloyd states. "The lack of a car. Her not being buried. No phone. Someone is hiding something."

"And you've still had no success with social media?" I inquire.

"We have," Kate says. "Well, now that she's... They let us have her passwords, but there was nothing weird on Facebook or Instagram."

"Samuel said he received a weird text from her that he thinks was for someone else. They must've only been texting to cover their tracks."

They nod in agreement, and I worry I'm telling them too much, but none of this is confidential. I'm not a cop, and I'm sure Samuel would tell them the same story if they asked.

"Any strange calls?" Lloyd prompts.

"According to Mia's service provider, in the week before she went missing, she only called you two and a landline based in Idaho," I inform them, reiterating what I read in the reports Donna has shared with me. "We tried calling the number, but it just goes through its voicemail."

After I say Idaho, Lloyd stands and pours himself a large bourbon while leaning on the liquor cabinet. Kate seems unwilling to speak, so I wait patiently for him to sit back down. He ends up pouring drinks for all of us, but mine is small, barely a sip, which I appreciate. I take it, thankfully, and smile at him as he takes a seat.

"I was hoping it wouldn't come to this," he says at last, after draining half the glass. I can tell that this is his sore spot. Lloyd is not a drinker, not really, and my skin prickles into goosebumps, waiting for what comes next. "But as I'm sure you're aware, I'm not in touch with my family."

"I am."

"Well, the reason for that is because my younger brother Ben is a murderer. He killed his girlfriend, Shelley Pearson, back in 2017 when they were living just outside of Cascadia, one state over. He was acquitted, but I know he did it. My family—my parents in particular—don't agree, so I cut contact. He's who gave me this," he states, referring to his fading shiner. "And he's the one who tried to intrude on the funeral."

"And do you think that Mia—"

"She was trying to mend bridges, yeah. That's probably why she called Idaho. She was talking to him. Who knows? Maybe he was the one who picked her up."

"Do the police know about this?"

He nods. "They do. And they're looking into it, and I'd hoped he, not poor Archie, would be behind bars right now. But as expected, he's managed to disappear. Not that it would matter if they found him. He and his endless amounts of bullshit have gotten him out of trouble before. Streams out of him like a river. That's why I'm telling you. I want you to look into Ben."

"Do you have an address?"

"No. He's a drifter. Has been for the last seven years. That's probably why no one's picking up the phone. You probably called an empty rental."

"I'll find him," I reply with a confidence that surprises me. "And if I can ask you another question..."

"Go ahead."

"Why do you hate the police so much?"

"Because before Shelley disappeared, Ben was a homicide detective."

CHAPTER TWENTY

I spent my Tuesday evening in Donna's home office talking, theorizing, and playing her the recordings. She did a lot of pacing, and I did a lot of nervous chattering, and ultimately, we agreed that the person in the car was either the mystery man that Mia was sleeping with or Ben Ramsey. If it was the former, she was expecting to go on a date, and either he killed her, or he's also a victim. If it was the latter, it was because Mia wanted to repair the burnt bridge and was under the impression that Ben did, too, but really, he had much darker intentions. Ben Ramsey, at age forty-eight, could be our serial killer, and as to why he would murder his own niece, I'm not entirely sure. But he killed his long-term girlfriend,

THE GIRL IN THE SPRINGS

so why not his niece? Maybe she knew something about the missing teenagers and was confronting him.

Donna said she'd put out an APB on Ben in the morning and would also run his name through the databases looking for recent charges, parking tickets, that sort of thing. Hopefully, he has a car registered in his name. Then we tried the Idaho number again, and this time, somebody picked up—a cleaner for a long-stay holiday rental. Lloyd was right about Ben being a drifter. The cleaner then gave us the owner's numbers, and she confirmed that a Ben Ramsey had booked into this rental on the twentieth of December 2023 and had vacated upon the first of March 2024.

The owner, Aubrey, further elaborated by saying Ben had wanted to spend Christmas and New Year with his family and then had stayed for the fishing before moving on. She did not know what car he drove, as the property was remote, and he arrived via bus at her office in town to pick up and drop off the keys. This was also his mode of transport for paying his monthly rent, which he did so in cash. Beyond that, Aubrey couldn't tell us much. Ben seemed polite and left the rental behind in perfect condition, and there was nothing strange about him other than his insistence on paying cash. She blamed that on his line of work as a day laborer, but Donna and I were far more suspicious of this tidbit. It seemed to us that Ben didn't want to leave a paper trail.

After we wrapped up with Aubrey, we wrapped up in general, and I headed home and left Donna to enjoy her very late dinner with her husband. I then had dinner of my own—leftover pizza from Notte Stellata—and dug into the murder of Shelley Pearson.

In July 2016, just a few months after the murders of Sanya Gupta and Jayden Nelson, Shelley vanished from the small, rural home she shared with her boyfriend of seven years, Ben Ramsey. The house was located in the forests outside of Cascadia, a much larger town than Serenity Springs, where Ben worked as a detective. Shelley was a nurse at a private care facility and had made a lot of friends through her work. One day, one of these friends swung by to visit on their mutual day off—Wednesday the fourteenth—and when Shelley did not answer the door, she became concerned.

Upon rounding the house and looking through the bedroom window, this friend saw blood on the bedsheets. She then tried the front door and found it unlocked. She bravely looked for Shelley but couldn't find her and called the police.

Ben was then allowed to attend the scene along with several other officers, and when he failed to tell a convincing story about what he was doing on Tuesday night, he was brought back to his place of work for questioning. Whatever he said to them got him off the hook, but it seems that most of the town and his brother were not convinced, and he was ultimately let go from his job. He then moved to Idaho to live with his parents and start again.

That's about all I could find about Shelley's case, but two things stood out to me. One was the fact that Cascadia is a mere thirty-minute drive from here, and the other was that Shelley Pearson's body was never found. Something clicked, and I rushed to text Donna.

"Could the Jane Doe be Shelley Pearson?"

I wake up to my phone buzzing on my pillow again. I keep falling asleep reading articles about the murders, and if my nightmares are anything to go by, I need to swap back to books. It's hard to not let this consume you, and I wonder how Donna does it, balancing this type of work and life. Maybe she doesn't. Maybe she fell asleep reading about corpses, too.

One of the texts is from her. "Will contact Shelley Pearson's family. No car is registered in Ben Ramseys's name. The APB is out." Simple and efficient. I like it.

The second text is a lot longer, and, to my surprise, it's from Noah. I don't have his name saved to my phone, but he's texted me previously about the house, so I know it's him. He says, "Hi, Bridget." Very formal. "The building site isn't a crime scene anymore, so we're all back to work. Would you like to come over and go through some options with me? I have the exterior wood and paint samples."

"Sure," I reply. "I will be over soon," I add.

THE GIRL IN THE SPRINGS

Work and life balance. It's hard, but it must be done, and while I'm waiting for Donna, I might as well fill my time with something productive. And it's not like Ada's pregnancy can be put on pause. That baby is still coming, and it needs a house to live in.

I pull on a dress decorated with daisies, a similarly yellow sweater, thick socks, and Wellington boots and make coffee to go. I'll get breakfast afterward; I'm never hungry until after 9:00am at the earliest. Honestly, I'm barely a breakfast person at all. I'm all about lunch. Sandwiches, wraps, and salad? Count me in. I'm a hot drinks and cold foods type of girl.

However, as I drive out of town and into the woods, I think that maybe waking up so early all week has thrown off my body clock. My stomach is roiling. Yet, when I picture myself chowing down on a poached egg, I feel nauseous. I'm not hungry. I'm nervous.

Donna told me to stay away from Noah, and for good reason. And never mind the fact that Keith still hasn't turned up.

I also think about what Donna said about killers turning up at funerals, and I think about Noah in the back of the room, lighting a cigarette afterward, flouting my questions, and disappearing. What if it's him? He's too young to be our serial killer, but he could be a copycat. He does live extremely close to the makeshift cemetery. Maybe seeing it gave him an idea and made it easier to blame Mia's death on someone already well-established. He's handsome, too, which means he could've been Mia's secret boyfriend, and he was a secret because of the inappropriate age gap.

When I reach the clearing, I notice the tape and tent are gone, and nobody is here. Nobody except Noah, who comes bounding over as I park. I tell myself that I can leave, that I have a choice. I reach for my crochet daisy purse, feel the mace inside, remember my self-defense training, and exit the car. I do have a choice, and I choose to stay.

"Bridget," Noah says, holding out his hand to shake.

I don't accept. "You tricked me," I hiss, pointing accusingly. "There's no one else here. You're not 'all back at work.'"

He holds up his hands in surrender. "I know how it looks, and I know what the cops think of me."

"Well, I'm starting to agree with them," I say, gesturing around at the empty clearing. "How do I know you didn't lure me out here to kill me?"

"Okay, I get it. It's weird. Maybe I should've just called you, but I wanted to see you face-to-face. I didn't think you'd come out willingly if I told you the truth, so, yeah, I lied. But I need to talk to you, and only you."

"Why only me?" I ask hesitantly, scanning his threadbare jeans and flannel shirt for weapon-like shapes.

"Because I like you. Because I think I owe you an explanation." He sighs and bends forward as if bowing. "Because I feel, I don't know, attached to you after finding Mia, and I've been rude and... Come on, Birdie, please."

I hear my name in his mouth, on his lips, and feel a peculiar fluttering inside. That, paired with his hangdog expression and reaching hands, makes me relent. "Okay. Then talk."

"Can we walk and talk? I totally forgot to feed Buckaroo."

"I don't believe you," I say without thinking, toying with my purse.

"I'm telling you the truth. I was so nervous about talking to you that I left the house without thinking."

"You are literally trying to lure me into the woods," I scold.

"I'm not, I... God, being a man sucks sometimes."

I laugh incredulously. "Try being a woman."

"Sorry, that was a stupid thing to say. It's just... I'm not trying to kill you."

"Sounds like something a serial killer would say."

He groans. "Come on."

"Fine. But keep your distance. I don't want to have to kick your ass."

"No problem. I'd hate to get my blood on your pretty dress."

"Oh, this isn't too granny-like for you?" I ask bitterly.

He smirks, and I hate that that expression of his makes me instantly hot under the collar. "I think it's just the right amount. Your bag is adorable."

"It has mace in it."

To my annoyance, his grin only widens. "You know what you remind me of?"

"What?"
"Lily of the Valley."
"And why is that?"
"Because you're pretty but deadly."

The heat rises from my chest and throat and into my face. I can tell that I'm blushing from his self-satisfied expression, and I compose myself. "Touch upon pain of death."

"Oh, I wouldn't dream of touching you."

I roll my eyes. "Come on. Let's go feed Buckaroo." I walk toward him, and he jumps out of my path as if I'm plagued with an infectious disease. I don't give him the satisfaction of laughing. Though, I'll admit that I like the descriptor. Pretty but deadly. Gavin just thought I was a wet blanket.

He jogs ahead of me, forcing me to pick up the pace. "Hurry!" he calls back at me. "You won't like Buckaroo when he's hungry."

"Categorically untrue," I call back. "Buckaroo could eat my hand, and I'd still like him."

"Don't tempt him. I could see how he was looking at you."

I catch up to him as we reach the edge of the clearing, and Noah holds a tree branch high in the air, allowing me to duck beneath it. "So what's all this about?" I ask.

"It's about me being sorry," he admits, the words exploding out of him in a rush. I watch his hands clench and unclench before one moves to his pocket and the other to his throat.

I stop dead, not wanting to get any closer. "For what?"

Noah turns toward me and softens his tense posture. "You don't have to be scared of me. I'm not going to hurt you, and I didn't hurt Mia."

"So why are you sorry?"

"For the way I've been acting. For running off after the funeral. For avoiding you."

"That's fine." My voice is even slower this time, and I feel as if I'm trying to calm a spooked horse or a snarling dog. Noah's energy is frenetic. "I mean, you've been behaving a little weirdly, but I've only met you like three times, and the first time you cut in line. I just assumed you were like that."

He chuckles sadly. "I'm not. Not really. This whole thing has…" He exhales, clearly frustrated and struggling to get the words out.

"My sister died," he says at last, loudly and bluntly. The words hang heavy in the air, echoing through the forest like a gunshot.

"Oh, Noah. I'm so sorry." My voice is a whisper, my throat suddenly tight, all of the fight in me draining away. I can't imagine losing my sister.

"It was years ago. In 2018."

"That's not that long ago."

He laughs bitterly. "That's not what everyone else says. They think I need to move on, but it's..." His voice breaks, and he pulls off his beanie and rubs at his head. I can tell that he's only a few steps away from a panic attack, and I move toward him, listening intently. "She was, uh, she was living in Canada with a friend and doing a bit of everything: acting, modeling, fashion design. She was an 'It girl' with money to match, which is why she always came to me for the holidays. That was the deal. She pays for the pricey ticket, and I spoil her when she lands. Except, that year, she didn't land. Well, she did. In a sense. But not at the airport."

"The plane crashed?"

Noah's jaw is twitching, and he hangs his head. "Right into the goddamn mountains. It took days to recover the bodies, but I never stopped holding out hope until I got the call to identify her. Seeing her like that, on the slab, I..."

He sounds like he's going to be sick, and I take another step forward. "And finding Mia dredged everything back up?"

A tight nod answers my question. "Even you talking about your sister makes me... And I know that isn't fair. The world doesn't stop for everyone else just because my world ended. And this is why I don't..."

He can't say what he feels, but I can read between the lines. This is why he lives off-grid in the woods. This is why his only companion is a dog. This is why he doesn't get close to people.

He's getting worked up, looking at me, embarrassed for having shared all of this, annoyed that I can see the chink in his armor, mad at me for not having anything to say. He's going to tell me to forget it or to leave him alone. I can sense it. It's forming on his lips. He's already saying it in his head. Yet, I can also tell that he doesn't actually want that to happen. He just hates this feeling, this vulnerability, my eyes on him.

So I tell him, firmly, to, "Come here."

And he does. He walks over to me and towers above at least a head taller, and I stand on my tiptoes, wrap my arms around him, and hug him tightly. I can feel his hesitation and the pain in his tense muscles, but slowly but surely, it all disappears, and he's soft despite his rock-hard physique. He sighs, wrapping his arms around my waist and burying his face into my cardigan.

I swallow hard, chin on his shoulder. I don't want him to let go. My body is tingling, warmth is spreading and pooling, and butterflies hatch from cocoons I thought were dead, considering how long they've been dormant. I don't think I've ever experienced a hug this powerful.

His arms around my waist tighten, a hand drifts up and down my lower back, and for a second, I think he might pin me against a tree and take me. I don't know if I'd let him, but I think I want him to try. I've never done anything like that before.

My phone begins to buzz, and I ignore it at first, but when the fourth text arrives, I pull away and look at him dazed as if breaking free of a trance. His face bears the same expression. I want to throw my phone into the leaf litter and throw myself at him. I want to take his pain away. I want an escape from the world. But the moment is gone, so instead, I check my phone and see four grammar-perfect texts from Grandma June.

"Sorry," I murmur sheepishly.

"No problem," Noah replies, red in the face.

I skim the texts as quickly as possible and look up at Noah. "Want to help me catch a jewel thief over at Sunny Side tomorrow? My grandma caught somebody stealing from her on tape, but it's a bad angle. She's going to lend her friend the nanny cam I gave her and try again tonight."

"Jesus, this place has more criminals than eighteenth-century Australia."

"That's not an answer."

He smirks. "I'd love nothing more."

CHAPTER TWENTY-ONE

AS THE SUN DESCENDS ON A PARTICULARLY GRUELLING Wednesday, I head to Notte Stellata. It's the closest I'll come to experiencing Italy for a while, and considering recent events, I need to maintain some semblance of normalcy so that I don't lose my mind. This week has been exceptionally difficult; even though we have a new suspect in Ben Ramsey, the body count has risen to at least eight, and a dangerous killer remains at large.

Archie has also been released from custody, which was a fleeting bright spot as his shop was vandalized shortly after by Carrie Olson's younger brother and Gina Martin's nephew. And who could blame them? The media circus has riled everyone up, and now poor Archie is hiding out at my parents' cabin two states away. I pray nobody finds him while we hunt for the real killer—however long that takes—and I hope Stanley is wrong about Archie's reputation being permanently ruined. Surely, the residents of our once-perfect town know when to apologize. Right?

Stepping into Notte Stellata feels like being wrapped in a warm hug to rival Noah's. The air is thick with the aroma of garlic sizzling in olive oil, fragrant basil leaves freshly plucked from the garden, crusty loaves of bread cooling on wooden racks, and ripe tomatoes bubbling away in pots. My stomach rumbles in time to this sensory symphony, reminding me that I have barely eaten anything all day. In fact, I feel like I've barely eaten anything all week. I am fueled by nerves, adrenaline, and caffeine.

Isabella Rossi greets me with her usual warmth, but there's a hint of sadness in her expression as she wraps me in an uncharacteristic hug. "Darling, how are you doing? Are you alright?"

"I'm managing," I reply as she releases me before offering a weak, unconvincing smile. After walking for miles with Buckaroo, every inch of my body is sore, and the enormous weight on my shoulders doesn't help either.

"Your usual table, bruschetta and a glass of wine await you. On the house."

"Thank you," I say gratefully, patting her arm which is sheathed in the usual polka-dot chiffon.

She hurries off abruptly after a quick air kiss, and I suddenly realize how chaotically busy it is tonight. My shoulders tense at the sound of a plate shattering in the kitchen, and I can feel eyes on me as people turn to look. It feels like I'm the one who caused the sound, and I flush. I don't recognize any of the faces staring at me, and I start to feel uneasy. They could be media or, even worse, dark tourists. I accidentally make eye contact with a sketchy-looking guy with a neckbeard and quickly make my way up the stairs. While I haven't checked, I'm now certain that my face, or at least my name, is plastered all over the internet.

I cautiously navigate my way through the tightly packed upper dining room, careful not to disturb any of the coats slung haphazardly on the backs of chairs. Eventually, I re-adjust my vibrant cherry red dress and relax to the sound of the music filling the air. I reach for my glass of wine and take a small sip before indulging in some bruschetta, and already I'm feeling better.

The door behind me opens, and, expecting a staff member coming to take my order, I turn eagerly to face them. I am surprised, and disappointed, to see the unsavory man from downstairs accompanied by a very scrawny woman whose bleached hair reminds me of burnt plastic. Normally, I don't judge people based on their appearances, but in this case, I can't help it. There is something so off-putting about both of them. Their expressions are leering, making me feel like a rabbit being cornered by rabid coyotes.

"Hello," I say cooly, my smile tight.

"You're Bridget Hartley, right?" the woman squawks.

"I am. And you are?"

"Trina and Melvin."

"Uh-huh. And how may I help you, Trina and Melvin?"

I already know the answer. They want to eat me up and spit out the pieces onto their insipid true crime blog. I know this because, once upon a time, back in New York, when I covered crime, I was them. To my credit, I was a lot subtler with my slathering, but still, I know a hankering for the macabre when I see it.

They begin to speak when the door opens again and interrupts them. This new intruder—a woman with an ombre blowout and a dark purple power suit—looks at the first two scathingly. Unlike them, she is a journalist and a professional, and she clearly wanted me all to herself.

She laughs, "Looks like you both have beaten me to the punch." She introduces herself as Miranda Rogers, but I can't hear the rest over Trina and Melvin's indignant protests about first come, first served. They act as if I'm the last blueberry muffin at Cobblestone Cafe. The urge to yell at them and tell them to leave washes over me, but I know it won't end well when dealing with people like them. People who have no qualms about harassing someone just trying to enjoy some bruschetta. I may have been a journalist in the past, but I never behaved like that. I always made appointments and got consent before intruding on someone's space.

The door opens again, and I groan, look away, and snatch my glass of wine from the table. "Can I help you?" the fourth intruder asks, addressing the rabble. I swivel back. I know that voice, and sure enough, Stanley is standing beside Miranda, looking very displeased.

The group begins to answer, talking over each other, and Stanley holds up a hand. "I'm sorry, you three seem to have mistaken me for someone that cares." He looks at me and extends a hand. "Would you like to get out of here?" he asks.

"Yes, please," I reply breathlessly, snatching up my purse and jacket.

I pause momentarily, my hand in his, looking back longingly at my half-eaten bruschetta and a mostly undrunk glass of wine. I'd really been looking forward to this. Then I look back at him, pouting like a child, and he holds up a plastic bag filled with boxed-up food and a bottle of my favorite wine. He smiles, pleased with himself, and for the first time all day, I forget all about that moment with Noah in the woods and what it meant. Our attraction to each other might be potent, but this is what I want, this is what I need, this is what I deserve.

The rich aroma of savory dishes fills the interior of Stanley's vintage Jaguar as we make our way to his home. My stomach grumbles incessantly, but if Stanley notices, he is too polite to mention it.

"Now, try not to be shocked," Stanley says as he slows down on a narrow country road. A grand wrought iron gate comes into view, and he points towards it.

"Okay," I reply slowly, curiosity piqued. "Shocked about what?"

"My house," he replies simply, veering right.

My jaw drops despite his warning. The mansion before us is colossal, at least twice the size of my parents' home, but it lacks any of the warmth that theirs possesses. Its grey brick facade looks cold to the touch, and it is surprisingly stark in style. Squinting, I recognize the architecture as "English Manor," a style I have always associated with haunted houses in old British movies. The small, sunken windows seem to stare back at me like vacant eyes, and the excess of ivy reminds me of moss on a tombstone.

Suddenly, I realize why Stanley's last name, Crawford, has been bugging me. My classmates used to tell tall tales about this place back at school. Crawford Manor. They all said it was haunted, and according to rumors, if you dared approach it at night, awful faces would appear in the windows. I was, of course, too chicken to join those late-night adventures, but the stories still kept me up at night.

"I told you not to be shocked," Stanley laughs.

"That is a tall order."

"Yeah, I know. It blows my mind, too, sometimes."

"How... How do you maintain it? The bills must be..." I gesture wildly, momentarily struck dumb.

"Astronomical? They would be if there wasn't a fireplace in every room. As for repairs, well, I've got to spend my money on something."

"And the land," I exhale, gesturing around.

"Ten acres," he concludes.

"Wow."

"And a cemetery," he says lightly.

"Wait, really?"

"Yep, every Crawford family member and a few others are buried here, spanning generations. Even my dad, who passed away in Northern California, insisted on his final resting place being here." Stanley parks the car at the front of the house in the circular driveway and turns to me with a mischievous glimmer in his eyes. "Want to take a look?"

"Sure!" I agree, overenthusiastic even though I'd much rather retreat into the warmth and tear into my doggy bag. My stomach growls loudly, emphasizing this.

Snickering, Stanley adds, "We'll check it out and then head inside for some grub."

I blush, but it goes unseen in the darkness, and I traipse after Stanley through long, boggy grass, around the side of the house.

THE GIRL IN THE SPRINGS

I almost stop before rounding the corner. I've seen too many cemeteries as of late and have no desire to see more. I suddenly feel unwell and panicky, but I pull myself together and catch up to the oblivious Stanley.

The cemetery is larger than I expected, and though it's overgrown, it was clearly very expensive. There's an old fountain, sculpted angels, tall iron fencing, and large intricate headstones. There are also some smaller gravestones and a chill runs down my spine despite Stanley's casual demeanor.

"What are those little ones?" I ask, terrified of the possible answer.

"Pets," Stanley replies, which is admittedly a relief. "All the dogs and cats I've ever had."

"Wow," I say softly, not sure if this is sweet or eerie. "What's it like living next to a cemetery?"

"Well, let's just say it certainly adds credence to the haunted rumors," he chuckles. "As if this place wasn't already creepy enough."

"No wonder you're a fan of Edgar Allen Poe."

"Yes, I suppose my interest was predestined."

As I take in my surroundings, I feel the tension leave my body. However, something catches my eye, and it seems out of place—Earl Crawford's grave is not next to his wife Joanna's. I remember her name from a conversation we'd had at the wake.

"Your parents aren't buried next to each other," I observe, and then I cringe at how nosy the statement sounds.

Stanley's demeanor changes slightly, his smile falters, and I resist the urge to smack my forehead. "No, they certainly are not. He requested it, but I denied it. It didn't feel right. She put up with enough crap from him in life without making them eternal neighbors."

"So, I'm guessing there wasn't much love lost when he died?"

"Not really." And with that, I can tell that the conversation is over. Stanley softens and returns to his usual smiley self. "Let's eat."

Fully satiated and sprawled out on a loveseat by the fire, I take a more focused look around the largest of the living rooms. The floors, walls, and ceiling are all crafted from a glossy dark wood that exudes opulence. Yet, despite the darkness, it doesn't feel cramped or claustrophobic; quite the opposite, actually, due to its immense size. I actually wish it was smaller. There are a lot of dark spots where the light of the candles and fire don't reach. Sometimes, I think I see someone lurking in those shadowy spots, their backs pressed against the wall, only to realize it's only a pale face in an old oil portrait.

"How do you stay here alone?" I ask, the ceiling overhead creaking as if there's someone in the room above.

Stanley stands from his armchair, bottle in hand, and moves toward me. "I've spent twenty-six of my twenty-nine years in this house. After a while, you just get used to things, no matter how creepy they are."

"And what about those other three years? Where were you then?"

"Northern California, with Dad and my grandparents after Mom died. Then he died, I inherited the house, and came back. And no, I've never seen a ghost. I haven't heard one or sensed a presence either." He pauses, and gives me a sly smile. "I know you were dying to ask."

"I was," I admit. "Even though I don't believe in them."

"Oh, I believe in them," Stanley clarifies, "but I don't think there's any here."

"You do?" I ask, surprised.

"Oh yes."

"Well, why wouldn't there be any here? Considering its age and the cemetery you'd think it would be prime real estate for specters."

"Honestly, I have no idea."

"Nobody died a horrifying death?" I joke.

"Nope. Health issues and natural causes." He tops up my glass of wine. "It's disappointing, I know."

I realize this is the third time he's topped us up, which means he's had too much drink to drive, and so have I. My car isn't even here. At some point, he must have made the assumption that I intended to stay the night. I can't blame him for his wishful thinking. This place might not creep him out, but it must be lonely. I just hope he's not hoping for anything sexual to happen, as I don't do that on first dates, which is what I presume this is.

I consider whether *I* want to stay as he sits back down, his lips slightly purple-tinted. He is beautiful. This is fun. I'd even push my limits and have another glass if he turned on a movie or some music. Yet, I feel more like a kid at a sleepover than a grown woman on a date.

I stand, put my glass down on the coffee table, sidle over, and kneel down by his legs as if I want to rest my head on them. He seems to realize what I'm doing, and we meet in the middle, me on my knees, him bending forward, his hand on my jaw. We kiss, and his lips are soft and gentle until I push deeper. He tastes of wine, and all the sensations are pleasant and right, but still, I pull away. He looks down at me lustfully and moves in for more but stops when he feels me hesitate.

"What is it?" he asks.

"Sorry," I say, scooching backward out of his grasp, arms wrapped around my knees.

"Ah. No fireworks?"

"No," I reply, and in truth, it felt like I was kissing Maisy. Which wouldn't be unpleasant, I'm sure, but it's not my cup of tea. "I'm so sorry."

"Please, don't be. I didn't bring you here in the hopes of anything happening. I enjoy our friendship and am more than happy to remain friends."

"Did you feel..."

"No," he says, a little hastily, and I have an inkling he felt something, even if it wasn't fireworks. "But at least we tried!"

"Yeah," I respond heartily before returning to the loveseat. "Now we know for sure."

"Exactly."

I don't settle into my 'spot' quite right this time. I feel the wooden bones beyond the upholstery and shift frequently with discomfort. We attempt to pick up where we left off in our conversation but end up starting a new one instead. Even though we eventually manage to get back into it, and I take a few more sips of wine, it becomes evident that neither of us has much more to say. So, I text my dad to come pick me up and Stanley looks relieved that I do so.

CHAPTER TWENTY-TWO

"Poor Stanley," Dad murmurs as soon as I watch Crawford Manor shrink in the sideview mirror.

"Why do you say that?" I ask, nervous that my own father might be about to scold me for ditching a date.

Dad fixes me with a strange look. "He didn't tell you? About his dad?"

"Only that he's dead, and he doesn't seem to care that he is."

"If you knew Earl, you would not find that surprising in the slightest. I just still can't believe that the old bastard is really gone. I thought he'd outlive us all out of sheer spite."

"You knew him then?"

"Oh yeah, everyone knew Earl. They hated him, too. He was a real bloodsucker. Every room that he walked into would turn quiet. People would leave. Your mother would get nauseous. There was just something wrong about him. And then, eventually, we figured out exactly what that was."

"And? What was it?" I prompt after Dad's silence goes on for too long.

"Oh. Sorry, darling. Past my bedtime."

"Uh-huh."

"Earl was a murderer," Dad says, cavalier as anything.

"I'm sorry, what?"

"Well, a suspected murderer." Dad pauses. "Stanley didn't tell you any of this?"

"It didn't come up."

"Well, I suppose that makes sense. He probably avoids thinking about it. Poor kid."

"Who did Earl kill?"

"His wife, Joanna. In—oh, let me think—February 2017. Well, everyone thinks he did, anyway. They'd been having serious problems, and we'd seen her around town covered in bruises and the like. Stanley, too. I don't know all of the ins and outs regarding, you know, the crime scene. But I know it was ruled a suicide. He may have been unpopular, but he still had friends in high places thanks to his deep pockets. All dead now, too, of course, as they were much older than he was."

"So he got away with murder?"

"In a way. Despite these friends—doctors, coroners, police— Earl was chased out of town toward the end of the year, and for whatever reason, Stanley went with him. I suspect by that point he was brainwashed." Dad shakes his head. "I'm so glad that he's finally free, but I have no idea how he lives in that house."

"Me neither. It's seriously creepy."

"I imagine it is. It's foreboding enough on the outside."

"Amazing antiques, though. Most of it is original."

"Oh, wonderful!"

"There's also a cemetery out back."

Dad's expression hardens. "Good lord." He shakes his head again before clearing his throat. "Are you two…"

"No," I laugh. "We're just friends."

Dad hums, and I sense a note of disapproval. "Well, he's a very nice boy. I think you two would be a good match."

"I agree." I really do. And I think that maybe if I try really hard, I can make it work with Stanley. Maybe our romance is something that will grow on me. I didn't like olives or anchovies straight away, but now I can't have a pizza without them. Maybe he's just an acquired taste, and the reason Noah was immediately delicious is because he's bland, like a cheese pizza. Now I'm thinking of Noah again. Great. And even worse, I'm craving him.

In the end, my thoughts of Noah led to pleasant dreams filled with romantic escapades in the forest instead of dreary haunted mansions and murders. Better still, Mia did not make an appearance, nor did any other dead people. It was just Noah and me and all the pleasure I could handle. Which turned out to be a lot. It's been a while.

When I wake up, I remember that I have plans with Noah today, and a rush of nerves floods my system. I don't know how I'm going to face him after such a steamy dream session. More frustrating still is I know that it will never happen in real life because he doesn't find me attractive and has been very open about this. Sharleen may be a joke, but he seems to be drawn to girls like Maisy, who are fun and glamorous. He probably sees me as an uptight nag compared to them. For him, hugging me was probably how it felt for me kissing Stanley—close but no cigar. Why can't I want the ones who want me? Now, all I need is for Noah to form a crush on Stanley, and it'll be a perfect circle of unrequited love.

The thought makes me chuckle, and the rush of embarrassment fades away. I quickly get ready to head over to Sunny Side before I can lose my motivation. Even though I still haven't solved Mia's murder, at least I can do something productive by catching this thief.

As I'm about to leave, I decide to do a quick Google search on Joanna Crawford. The details my dad shared with me were few and far between, and I don't want to accidentally say something insensitive again like I did last night when I joked about tragic deaths. Fortunately, Stanley didn't seem upset. Maybe he's had time to process it over the past seven years. But still, I should be more careful.

Surprisingly, not much comes up. Maybe the Crawford family is wealthy enough to keep their dirty laundry stashed away and their skeleton-containing closets locked. Or perhaps this was simply another case of a sheriff not fit for his line of work. In the end, all I can find is a vague article with no cause of death and an obituary that mentions a loving husband and son. It all seems so impersonal. As if Joanna never really existed. As if she wasn't a person with hopes, dreams, and hobbies. I can only find one picture of her. It's on the obituary website and is abysmally low quality. Even still, I can tell that Stanley got his looks from her.

I shoot Donna a text, asking, "Hey, do you have any information on what happened to Joanna Crawford? Her cause of death, for example."

She texts back instantly. "Is this a lead?"

I pause and think. It wasn't before she asked, but Joanna getting murdered in 2017 is suspiciously close to all the other killings. Mind you, Earl was in Northern California when the last pair went missing and was dead when Mia's body showed up, but I reply to Donna with a "Maybe."

"Okay," she replies, and I know she'll find out for me soon enough.

I approach Sunny Side and spot Noah, his back to me, standing in the misty morning air, completely still. The oncoming lousy weather must be keeping everyone else inside, but for whatever reason, he hasn't joined them. I wonder if he's nervous; most people are in places like this, though there's no reason to be.

THE GIRL IN THE SPRINGS

I suppose it brings up a lot of feelings of mortality, and everyone would rather bury their heads in the sand.

When Noah hears the gravel beneath my feet and turns to me, I see that he's not nervous at all. In fact, he's beaming with joy. I approach him, rubbing my arms to stay warm.

"Hey," he greets me.

"Hi," I reply hesitantly. "Why do you look like that?"

"Like what?"

"Like you've hit the jackpot."

He shrugs. "I have a soft spot for old people."

So he's not happy to see me. Damn. "Really?" I ask skeptically. From what I know about Noah, I didn't think he liked anyone.

"Yup. Our personalities just click. I'm probably the emotional equivalent of a sixty-five-year-old."

I study him for a moment, then shrug. "Yeah, I can see that."

"Because I'm so wise?"

"No, because you're one of those guys who probably really loves mowing the lawn and has a garage filled with random tools and junk."

"Don't forget the piles of old newspapers."

"You don't," I say, aghast.

"I do. They make good kindling."

I narrow my eyes. "I'll let you off for that."

"I also like to go to bed early."

I shake my head. "And you had the nerve to call me granny."

"You *are* a granny," he says. "And that's not an insult."

I roll my eyes. I get what he's saying, but I don't want to be a granny. I want to be the girl he wants to pin against a wall. I want him to have sexy dreams about me. Ugh. Said dreams are getting to me. "Come on," I murmur. "Let's go watch this tape."

As we enter the lobby, I notice that most of the crew—those who are close to my grandmother and me—are gathered around and whispering. They stop and their eyes widen as they spot us. Then they move toward us eagerly in a pack, and for a moment, I think they're going to embrace me and shower me with thanks for saving the day. I've even prepared a short and humble speech in my mind. However, I am completely and utterly ignored, and instead, Noah is swarmed. They place their hands on his arms and gaze up at him adoringly as if he's some sort of celebrity.

I shoot him a glance, silently asking, "What the hell?"

"Sorry, Birdie," Grandma June coos, turning to me and giving me a big hug. "Noah is a bit of an A-lister around here."

"What? Why?"

"Because he runs the woodworking shop," Ida answers.

"And the whittling class," Walter follows up.

"And he brings us DVDs," Grandma June says. "Funny, raunchy ones that Tanya won't buy."

"Unbelievable," I say, shaking my head at Noah, unable to tamp down my grin.

He nonchalantly shrugs and revels in the limelight until I reach my limit and grab him by his jacket, swiftly leading him and Grandma June toward Tanya's office. It's time to crack this case, and to be honest, I'm feeling a twinge of jealousy. Maybe it's time for me to start my own class. I think Noah would be open to a bit of friendly competition.

Just as I am about to knock on Tanya's door, she opens it for me. The walls in this building are paper thin, so she always knows when someone is approaching. She likes to pretend she has psychic abilities, but I know the truth. As we enter her office and close the door, the sound of the bustling lobby still rings loud and clear.

Grandma June approaches Tanya with a USB stick, and Tanya puts it into her desktop computer. As we all crowd around, she looks at me and asks, "Is this legal?"

"To record in your own domicile? Yeah. Plus, I think the police would be more concerned with the thievery in any case."

Tanya nods and clicks the newest file, and just as she's about to press play, Grandma June stops her. "Who do you think it is?" she asks me.

She's wearing an impish expression, and I ask, "Have you watched it?"

"I wouldn't have called you in if I hadn't. Go on, Detective."

"Charlie Wilkins," I say without hesitation, and she smirks as she turns her gaze back to the screen.

THE GIRL IN THE SPRINGS

Tanya presses the play button, and my suspicions are confirmed as Charlie Wilkins slinks into Ida's room with ease, snatching another decoy trinket before leaving undetected. He must have taken off his shoes to move so quietly, and it wouldn't have been difficult for someone as cunning as him to steal a spare key and return it without being noticed. Only after Tanya confiscated all the keys did he change tactics and start using the trap we set up with the slightly ajar doors. The mystery is solved; the suspect I had my eye on is guilty, but now I'm left with one question: why? Was this some sort of insurance fraud scheme? But then again, why continue after I explicitly told him there would be no payout?

"Can I talk to Charlie?" I inquire.

Tanya nods slowly, blinking over glassy eyes. Then she sharpens up and clears her throat. "You'll have to wait until he gets back, though. He's on a fishing trip with his son."

"Does he go fishing a lot?"

Tanya looks grim. "No. He does not. This is the first time I've ever seen his son."

And maybe that's the answer to my question. Charlie is lonely.

CHAPTER TWENTY-THREE

NOAH AND I ENDED UP SPENDING MOST OF THE DAY AT Sunny Side yesterday. After some seriously shameless pestering from the residents, he not-so-reluctantly volunteered to do an impromptu whittling workshop for them in the assembly hall. He'd 'conveniently' left his supplies behind, and I suspect someone may have hidden his bag to ensure he'd definitely come back. Or maybe Noah was feeling soft-hearted and left it behind purposefully like an overzealous one-night stand might leave a trinket behind. Secretly, I think it's the second option.

I obviously joined the session, excited to watch Noah in his element. And I have to admit, he was incredible. We were tasked with creating basic wooden figures with round heads and flat, curved bodies. No need for intricate details or faces, just a simple design. Thanks to Noah's expert guidance, ours all turned out beautifully. Well, mostly. Mine ended up a bit lopsided because I couldn't take my eyes off Noah as he whittled, sanded, and polished. But that's okay. Not everything needs to be perfect.

Noah, of course, then challenged me to come up with my own workshop on the fly. As suspected he was not afraid of some friendly competition. Fortunately, I didn't blank and came up with the idea of painting our figures and clothing them in thread and felt. And for those who were lacking in inspiration, I suggested they model their figure after a loved one. Sadly, in a place like this, many loved ones have already passed on, and it hurt my heart when half the class opted to recreate their deceased spouses. However, it wasn't all doom and gloom. In fact, it was quite poignant and led to a lot of residents opening up about their feelings. Grandma June then—stirrer that she is—began to beguile everyone with hilarious stories of Grandpa Ken, and before I knew it, the conversation went from PG to R-rated. I couldn't stop laughing, and Noah looked as if he wanted to melt into the ground, which brought me to tears.

I created Noah, and in turn, he created me. However, I quickly realized he was not in on the joke, as when it came time to reveal our creations, mine was a caricature, while his was utterly sincere and really rather beautiful. I have no idea how he managed to make the hair look just like mine, but it's obvious that his artistic skills far surpass my own. Luckily, he found my buzzcut, grumpy lumberjack hilarious and complimented me on the ripped jeans made of felt. We ended up exchanging them as gifts, and I went home with my mini-me in my pocket, excited to display her in my apartment.

As I wake up and reach for my phone, the Birdie doll on my bedside table stares at me with a serene expression. I feel almost as good as she looks after a sound night of sleep. I haven't slept that deeply in weeks, and I imagine it had something to do with the third class of the evening—Grandma June's 'Zesty Zumba.' That woman is unbelievable. I knew she was in good shape, but to see her in her leggings and tank top was mind-blowing. The way she's going, she'll end up being 120 and fitter than I am at thirty. Almost all of us were near collapse at the end, except for Noah. Though, I have the feeling that he was just putting on a brave face to outdo me.

I unlock my phone and see that Noah called me ten minutes earlier. That must've woken me up, that infernal buzzing of the phone against wood. Yet, I'm glad he did call. Smiling, staring at my mini-me, I call him back, and when he picks up, I say, "Let me guess. You're dying for another round of Zumba. Well, you're in luck. There's one at 9:00a.m. today."

"Birdie," he whispers, audibly swallowing saliva as if he's trying not to be sick.

I prop myself up on my elbows. "What's going on?"

"It's, uh, it's Keith."

"Keith?" I prompt, my heart thrumming like a hummingbird's wings. "Is he okay?" I already know that the answer is no, and Noah's choked-out confirmation, his body heaving with grief, leaves no room for doubt. I give him a moment to breathe before asking, "What happened?"

"I don't know. I found him on my doorstep this morning. Bullet to the head."

My hand instinctively flies to my mouth, trembling with shock. I am at a loss for words, unable to form a coherent thought. The only thing escaping from my lips are hushed repetitions of "Oh my God," as if it's the only phrase in my lexicon.

"I know, I..." He trails off, still unable to get the words out.

"I'm so sorry, Noah. I..." I trail off, my voice rattling from shock and my head spinning. "Did you hear anything? Did you see anyone?"

"No," he replies, small and quiet. "No gunshot. No nothing." He lowers his voice. "The cops are here. I think they think I did it. They keep asking about an altercation, but I haven't seen Keith since the day before we found Mia."

I try to sound composed as I speak into the phone. "Is Donna there?" I ask, hoping that she'll see reason. I refuse to let Noah take the fall for this, and as someone who has covered a plethora of crime cases, I know what the cops are thinking. They think Keith killed Mia and then showed up at Noah's house in the middle of the night, confessing and begging for help. And in a state of shock, horror, and trauma, Noah shot him. It's a common narrative, but I know Noah well enough to know it's not his story.

"Not yet," he whispers. "Actually, I have no idea. I'm hiding out in the truck with Buckaroo. There's a group erecting a crime scene out the front now, but I can't see from here."

"Have they found a weapon on Keith?"

"No."

"Okay, so that rules out suicide. Will they find a weapon in your home?"

"No. Not unless somebody planted one, but they'd be hard-pressed. I built this place like a bank vault."

"Okay, that's good."

"Hang on, somebody is coming over." Noah becomes muffled as he puts his phone in his pocket, and I distantly hear another male voice, but I can't make out the words. "Sorry," he says after a few minutes, his voice crisp and clear again.

"What was that about?"

"They want to search my house, and they want to take me down to the station for questioning, fingerprinting, and I think he said ballistics?"

I give a slight nod, even though he can't see me over the phone. "That sounds like typical protocol for a homicide case. As long as they're not accusing you of anything, just cooperate. You have nothing to hide. But if, for some reason, they do arrest you, use me as your one phone call and I'll speak with Donna and my family's lawyers if necessary."

"Okay," he exhales. "Okay. You're right. I have nothing to hide. I've never owned a gun. I've never fired a gun. I didn't kill Keith, and he didn't kill himself. Or, if he did, he did it elsewhere, and somebody dumped him here."

"I think this is a warning," I say. "Like Mia and the building site. I think the killer is playing with me, and you've been caught in the crossfire."

"Don't you dare apologize," he warns me just as I'm about to do so. "This isn't your fault."

I remain silent. My mind is consumed with worry for all the other people I care about, and I can't help but wonder if they are in danger of discovering a corpse or, worse, becoming one themselves.

"Birdie," Noah says firmly.

"Yeah. I'm here. Sorry."

"Are you okay?" he asks.

My heart pangs. "Yeah," I answer. "Are you?"

"No. But I've got to go."

"Okay, call me when they release you. I'll come and pick you up."

"Thank you," he murmurs faintly.

"Bye," I say, but he's already gone.

Impatience gnaws at me, driving me to pace restlessly around my apartment. Every tick of the clock feels like an eternity as I anxiously await an update. My mind is consumed with thoughts of Keith's death. Was he murdered because he stumbled upon something he shouldn't have? Or did he try to save Mia? Another pressing question is: was his body still fresh when it was discovered? Of course, I couldn't bring myself to ask about the state of his body, and I can only imagine that Noah didn't look for long. And if he did, I doubt he would ever want to talk about it.

In a state of desperate impatience, I reach for my phone and text Donna, "Did Keith die recently?"

The reply is a simple "Yes," and it sinks in that wherever Mia had been held captive in the forest, Keith must have been imprisoned there, too. And, like her, he was there for an entire week. What I don't understand is how this location has gone undetected for so long. Despite the vastness of the woods and our limited group of volunteers and police force, it feels insane that this murder shack—located somewhere between my parents' plot of land and Lovebird's Nest—has evaded discovery. Surely, the victims must've been screaming.

Maybe I'm being unfair to the police force and the wonderful volunteers because I'm frustrated. But I also think I am understandably so. Two people are dead now that could have been saved if only we'd found this mystery location. This murderer isn't killing onsite. He's drawing it out, playing with his food. Just like he's playing with me. Does that make me food, too?

Before I can put more stake into this question, I get a text from Mom. "Did you bring Noah Fletcher to Sunny Side yesterday?"

"Yes," I reply.

"Why?"

There's no emoji following the question, which means I'm in trouble. "The residents love him," I say at first. "He teaches whittling and carpentry there. He thought an impromptu class might mellow everyone out," I add.

"I think you should stay away from him, honey."

"He's a good guy."

"I know you think that," she replies, and I can practically hear her exasperated sigh.

She thinks I'm being naive, and frankly, I think the whole town has gone crazy. We've never cast stones like this before. I mean, sure, I was a little suspicious of Noah at first, but now I realize that never made any sense at all. I suppose we just can't bear the thought that it's a beloved local that's committed these atrocities. It's so much easier to blame crime on a drifter. Then it's not our fault. It's another town's fault for infecting ours. It's never us; it's always them.

Ignoring my mother's persistent texts, I set my phone aside and pour myself a steaming cup of green tea. It warms my hands and calms my mind as I wait for Noah to call. Outside, birds chirp, and cars pass by, but at this moment, all I can focus on is the anticipation for Noah's voice on the other end of the line.

The purple-orange hues of the sunset cast a somber glow over the precinct as I wait in my car for Noah's release. When he finally appears, he looks haggard and worn, his normally rigid posture now stooped and tired. The bags under his eyes are pronounced, evidence of the turmoil he's been through. He moves slowly towards the car, almost as if he's been confined for days. His exhaustion is palpable, but there is also a sense of restlessness in the way he fidgets and shifts in his seat as he climbs into the car beside me. It's clear that he desperately needs some rest, but it seems like his anxiety won't let him settle down just yet.

"Want me to grab us some food?" I ask.

"Yeah. Sure," he murmurs, rubbing at his stubble.

"Thai?"

A flicker of a smile. "Sounds good."

"Then we'll go walk Buckaroo?"

"Yeah," he exhales, closing his eyes, some of the buzz about him diminishing.

"Do you want to crash at my place? Buck is welcome, too," I ask, my voice filled with hope and a touch of desperation.

"No," he replies firmly, his voice leaving no room for argument.

"Come on, Noah," I groan. "Give it a rest with the stoic thing. Don't make me not want to help you."

He sighs and looks sideways at me, his eyes filled with sadness. He leans his head back against the car seat's headrest. "Fine. I'll think about it."

"Good. You better."

"But I'm paying for the food," he adds with a sleepy smirk.

"You're impossible," I mutter under my breath, though I can't help but match his upward expression.

"I know," he says softly, his eyes meeting mine for a brief moment before closing his eyes.

I'm about to apologize—it's not the right time for our usual banter—but before I can even open my mouth, he interrupts me.

"Can we make a quick stop and get a two-liter bottle of Diet Coke?"

"Sure. Got a craving? Personally, I'm more of a full sugar girl."

Noah lets out a sad chuckle and says, "It was Keith's go-to drink after he got sober. I thought we could raise a glass in his honor."

Touched by the sentiment, I reply softly, "Yeah, that sounds nice."

"And Thai food, of course," he continues, mostly talking to himself and reassuring himself that everything will be okay.

"And we can take Buckaroo for a walk" I repeat.

"And sit by the fire."

"And have a drink."

"And then we'll go to sleep," Noah murmurs.

"Yeah. And then we'll do that."

CHAPTER TWENTY-FOUR

THE MOON IS HIDDEN BEHIND A BLANKET OF CLOUDS, shrouding the densely-packed pine forest in almost total darkness. We rely on our flashlights, but despite the lack of visibility, Noah decides to let Buckaroo off his leash after only five minutes of walking. I watch nervously as the big, goofy dog bounds into the black, concerned that this decision was influenced by the several shots of whiskey Noah downed back at his house. Three shots might not be that much, but he said it was his first sip in at least two months. Like me, he doesn't really drink, and his reason for this was to support his friend. It's commendable, and I love that he's not a heavy drinker, but I imagine his tolerance must be low.

THE GIRL IN THE SPRINGS

Noah must sense my unease because he quickly reassures me. "Don't worry. He may be a failed K9, but he's still better trained than most dogs. He always comes back."

"What about wild animals?" I ask, looking around.

"Still have that mace?" he inquires.

"Always," I say, patting my daisy-shaped handbag.

"Then I'm sure you can come to his rescue if needed."

I hum, still anxious, an event unfolding in my mind. Buckaroo barking. Noah and I running. A bear snarling. Me spraying the bear. Noah grabbing the dog. Us running like hell through the woods. I also envision a version in which I use my physical prowess to take the bear down, but unfortunately, I know my self-defense skills aren't up to the task. Yet, through this daydream, I can understand Noah's desire to wrestle with nature. It's a powerful feeling to take down something bigger than you are.

"That Thai food was amazing," Noah says mildly, his tone not as enthusiastic as his words.

"Yeah, that place is the best. It's been here forever. Two generations of owners," I reply, helping him to fill the silence.

"They didn't find anything," he adds abruptly. "In my house, or on my hands."

"I know. Donna texted me."

"But the media was there when they took me in. They took photos."

I sigh. "I'm not surprised. They harassed me at my favorite restaurant on Wednesday night."

Noah shakes his head and reaches into his deep jeans pockets. For a moment, I think he's going to pull out a pack of cigarettes, but instead, he reveals an AA chip. "Day one," he announces, displaying it proudly to me. "It belonged to Keith. He said it was lucky because it symbolized the time that sobriety finally stuck." A hint of bitterness taints his following scoff. "Maybe he should've held onto it. He could've used some luck."

I move closer to him, closing the small gap between our bodies. I wrap an arm around his waist and feel the warmth of his body seep into mine. He responds by slinging one arm over my shoulders, and we bump heads affectionately, letting out a soft laugh. "I bet he gave him hell," I say gently.

"Oh yeah. He probably sang 'Camptown Races' at the top of his lungs on repeat all week. That's what he used to do when I was in a bad mood or ignoring him." His cheerful nostalgia is tinged with grief, and I feel muscles go taut under my fingertips as he reminisces. "Shit."

"I know."

"No, it's just… This guy must be huge. I mean, Keith was a goliath."

"He was," I agree, shivering not just from the cold but from the idea that an enormous apex predator roams these woods, and it's not a bear but a man. "And I'm so sorry."

"Birdie, I…" He exhales sadly, and we slow, turning toward each other. I am primed to hug him, my arms at the ready, when Buckaroo unleashes a primal howl and takes off running ahead. We turn sharply and quickly peel apart, following after him, guided by Noah's high-powered flashlight. Without it, we would probably break an ankle on the uneven terrain—full of slick mud and unexpected drop-offs—but with it, we're quick and capable. Yet Buckaroo outruns us and the light all the same and disappears into the dark.

Noah's desperate cries fall on deaf ears as we struggle to keep up with Buckaroo. The only sounds guiding us are the muffled crunch of leaves under his feet and the occasional snap of a twig breaking. Suddenly, everything goes eerily quiet, and we, too, draw to a standstill, listening out for the gone rogue dog.

Noah's flashlight beam cuts through the darkness ahead like a beacon, and he signals for me to keep quiet by placing a finger over his lips. I spot something brown in the distance, and with relief, I gesture urgently toward Buckaroo, whose tail is wagging excitedly against a sapling. Yet, as we inch closer, his happiness dissipates, and I can see his fur standing up on end and hear a low growl emanating from deep within his chest.

My hand instinctively reaches for my mace as I prepare to fight a bear after all. But as Noah directs his flashlight towards Buckaroo's new nemesis, I sigh with relief. It's only a hunting cabin, small and unassuming. Still, despite my relief, I can't help but feel perturbed by its sudden appearance in the middle of nowhere.

THE GIRL IN THE SPRINGS

"Have you ever seen this before?" I ask, looking around, unsure of where we are and even less sure of how to get back. I check my phone, and luckily, I have enough bars to get us out of a potentially sticky situation.

"No. We don't normally come this way because of the terrain."

I nod, remembering what he'd said during the hunt with the cadaver dogs. "Do you think we're close to the cemetery?" I ask.

Noah nods slowly, his gaze focused on the cabin.

"Then surely the search must have covered this area already," I point out.

Noah nods again, not really listening.

"Has Buckaroo ever acted like this before?" I question, trying to coax a response out of him.

This time, Noah shakes his head, seemingly unable to verbalize his thoughts. But I can see the gears turning in his head as he tries to make sense of why Buckaroo has brought us here. With caution, and without consulting me, Noah moves toward the cabin and grabs Buckaroo by the collar before reattaching him to his lead. He holds out the rope to me and says firmly, "Wait here."

"No way, I'm coming with you."

"Birdie."

"This is my case," I reply indignantly, not like an impudent child but with a growl to match Buckaroo's.

"Fine. We'll all go," Noah says, folding like a bad hand. "If this asshole is here, we'll need Buckaroo's teeth and your mace."

My gaze lingers on the dilapidated shack, its windows boarded up and dark. Despite my determination to catch the killer, a wave of terror washes over me at the thought of facing such a dangerous and clearly enormous man. Especially in the middle of nowhere without a weapon.

We approach regardless, Noah just as cautious as I, and Buckaroo more careful still. Our senses are on high alert for any sign of movement, and as we inch closer, I can't help but picture a gigantic figure kicking down the door, brandishing a shotgun. It's just that type of cabin. The one you see in horror movies about terrifying hillbillies who spend all day on creaky porch swings sipping moonshine.

I hand my mace to Noah, who is determined to take the lead as we approach the door. As he does so, I struggle to hold back Buckaroo, who coughs as he strains against his collar, desperate to protect his master. I hold on as best I can, the skin of my palms burning. I can't risk him, an innocent, getting hurt.

Surprisingly, the door is unlocked, and Noah quickly steps inside, turning sharply as if entering a drug den, his flashlight and the mace stacked on top of each other like a gun. After doing a 360, he gives me a thumbs up to follow, and I do so eagerly, with Buckaroo pulling me along. At first, the interior appears to be completely normal and downright cozy, but when Noah shines a light on the left corner, I gasp in shock. There sits a cage, or more accurately, a large dog crate. Inside is a tattered blanket and what looks like a rotting bone.

"*That* is police issue," Noah states. "High quality. Used for guard dogs and K9s. Buckaroo came with one."

I can agree that this is no ordinary pet store crate; the bars are thick, likely made of stainless steel. It's also massive in size, capable of holding two or three dogs or even a bear. And considering its sturdy construction, I wouldn't be surprised if it could contain someone as strong as Keith.

"You don't think..." I say, trailing off.

"I do," Noah confirms with a grim tone. "I think this is where that freak keeps them."

My fingers fumble with my phone, suddenly slick and sweaty despite the cold, as I hastily call Donna. Noah can tell what I'm trying to do, but he doesn't protest. He doesn't say anything. Instead, he moves toward the small fireplace on the right side of the room and grabs something from the adjacent shelf. My curiosity piqued, I look up from my phone to see a delicate golden, heart-shaped locket dangling from his fingers.

I step forward, hands outstretched, even though I'm unsure if we should be touching anything in this place. Noah hands it to me, and I press the catch, popping the heart open. There are two photos inside, water-stained and worn, but I can still make out the faces of a young man on one half and a young woman on the other.

THE GIRL IN THE SPRINGS

I'm able to drop Donna a pin, and she and the rest of the force arrive, along with CSU, within half an hour. They'd have been able to get here quicker if they didn't have to go on foot for part of the way. They get to work quickly to make up for it, and Noah and I wait outside while a forensics team dips in and out of the building with plastic bags, yellow markers, and cameras in hand.

A young police officer approaches Donna and presents her with a small trashcan, interrupting Donna's intense inspection of the locket. "Does this look fresh to you?" she asks, nervous in her boss's presence.

Donna peers inside, and the pungent smell of stale KFC wafts towards me. "Yeah," she answers, her nose wrinkling in disgust. "Test it for saliva."

The officer wanders away, and Donna shakes her head, disappointment etched on her features. "I can't believe we missed this place."

"What do you think about the cage?" I inquire, struggling to keep my voice steady. The adrenaline is making my teeth chatter.

Donna turns to me, her eyes surveying me thoughtfully. "What do *you* think?"

"I think it could hold a person."

"I would agree with that assessment."

"So you think this is something?"

Donna remains silent, deep in thought. "Do you recognize these people?" she asks at last, turning the locket to me.

I squint but ultimately shake my head. If I do know them, it still hasn't clicked. Donna huffs in frustration, not at us, but at the situation, and calls out, "Miller! Get over here."

Miller jogs over, his thin hair damp with sweat. Donna uses a combination of her flashlight and Noah's to illuminate the faces in the locket. "Do you know these people?"

Miller leans in, studying the photo closely before nodding intensely. "Oh yeah. That's goddamn Ben Ramsey and his girlfriend, whatshername..."

"Shelley Pearson," I interject.

"Yeah, that's the one. I was working in Cascadia when all of that went down. That guy was a real freak. I hated him from day one."

"Thank you, Miller," Donna says curtly, clearly wanting him to leave as soon as possible, and with a quick nod, he does just that.

Donna turns directly to me for the first time in twenty minutes, her expression serious and troubled. "The seventh body wasn't Shelley's," she whispers, not seeming to care that Noah is well within earshot. "Her parents confirmed that none of the items found belonged to her."

"Then who is it?"

"No idea. It could be anyone. This freak was on a rampage."

"What about Joanna Crawford?" I ask, hoping that family might be *something*.

"I looked into that," Donna answers, jaw set. "Not much to be found, unfortunately, thanks to my predecessor, but she was definitely buried at Crawford Manor." She pauses and tilts her head just so. "What's the deal with her?"

"I don't know. My dad told me that her husband Earl murdered her in 2017. Or at least everyone thinks he did. I thought it could be relevant."

"Interesting."

"I'd agree if he was still alive and hadn't been living in Northern California when Sanya and Jayden were killed," I add.

"Still interesting," Donna states firmly. "As I've said before, I clearly don't know enough about this town, and the file-keeping is abysmal. So, I want to know about every murder, not just the ones that pertain to this case. I'll have someone look into Earl, but for now, me and you? Let's stick to Ben."

"Agreed."

"He was in town recently, if the food is anything to go by," Donna says, wrinkling her nose again.

"Yes."

"And he has a cage strong enough to hold a person."

"Also, yes."

"And Mia called him in Idaho."

"Yes," I say, feeling stupid for repeating myself, but I'm numb from the cold, and the horrors of the day are seeping into my skin.

THE GIRL IN THE SPRINGS

Donna seems to understand this. "Go get some rest, Birdie. And good job today. I'll take it from here. I'll enforce a curfew and 24/7 patrol. I'll be damned if anyone else dies on my watch."

I nod numbly, my eyes glazing over, and Noah moves closer to me, protective, his arm wrapping around my waist. I watch Donna's eyes flit between us. I've flouted her advice, or rather instructions, to stay away from him, but at the moment, I don't care about the judgment being hurtled my way from her or my parents, no matter how much I respect them. They're wrong about Noah, so wrong, and when Donna moves back toward her team, I bridge the gap and hug Noah as hard as I can. If I hurt him, he says nothing, and eventually, my strength gives out, and he continues to hold me, weak as a kitten. Then, when I regain the strength in my knees, the two of us and Buckaroo traipse back through the dark forest, hoping our instincts will carry us home.

CHAPTER TWENTY-FIVE

SILENCE FILLS THE FOREST AS WE MAKE OUR WAY BACK TO Noah's house. Shock courses through our veins, leaving us dumbfounded and unable to form coherent speech. I just don't understand. How could this have been happening right under everyone's nose and practically on Noah's doorstep? And how could Ben, a former homicide detective, do such a thing? The fact that his own niece, Mia, is one of the victims makes it all the more unnerving.

I just can't understand why he chose her. If he is indeed the one responsible for the deaths of all those couples, it's likely that he targeted strangers to avoid his crimes being traced back to him. So why deviate now? Or maybe Ben isn't responsible for all the murders. Maybe I'm chasing two killers. What if there are two maniacs on the loose, primed to strike again?

I shudder as if someone has just walked over my grave, and my eyes dart around the forest, nervously surveying. Noah moves close to me. "Are you okay?" he asks, his voice sounding far too loud after so much quiet.

"I'm fine. How are you?"

"I've been better. But this feels like progress, at least."

I nod. "I guess Buckaroo is a police dog, after all. He led us right to the evil lair."

Noah chuckles weakly. "Yeah, he showed those other dogs up, didn't he?"

"He really did. You're a good boy, Buckaroo," I call ahead to him.

Buckaroo looks back at us, panting and smiling as if acknowledging that he is indeed a good boy, before running ahead, guided by the lamp light emanating from the windows of Noah's house. We made it in one piece, thank God. No bears or maniacs for us—not tonight.

"Are you coming in?" Noah asks, gesturing toward my car, which is small enough to easily traverse the path he's trodden from here to the road.

"Do you want me to come in?"

"Yes."

I bite my bottom lip, torn between wanting to stay and knowing I should probably leave. I'm more than capable of driving home, but I don't want to go home alone. The problem is that if I do stay, and we drink and talk, something will happen between us. I know it will. Not because he has romantic feelings for me, but because he's trying to fill a void. Then tomorrow, things will be weird and I'll have broken a cardinal rule for no reason. Then everything will be ruined, and I'll have to force myself to love Stanley because when are more eligible, handsome men going to come into my life in a small town? I don't want to wait another decade for happiness.

"Come on," he says gently. "Let's heat up some more food. We've earned it."

I hardly ate half of my portion earlier, and I could definitely go for more shrimp pad Thai. I think about my empty fridge back at home and give in, following Noah toward the light. It might not be the wisest idea, but I'm not sure if Noah should be alone right now, and I'm not sure I should be either. It's been a harrowing day, to say the least. I'll just have to be on my best behavior and keep him at arm's length.

Once inside, I can see how muddy Buckaroo is, but Noah seems past the point of caring. He merely watches blankly as the dog runs at the cream couch, throws himself upon it, and enthusiastically rubs all filth onto the upholstery.

"Well, it seems the couch is off limits," he says, his words tinted with amusement. "So how about some star gazing? I have two deck chairs out back. Keith and I used to sit out there for hours. He'd listen to an audiobook, but I'd just watch the world spin."

"That sounds great," I reply, not mentioning the fact that the sky is still covered in a thick layer of clouds. "You bring the Thai food, and I'll bring the Diet Coke."

The heavy cloud cover obscures the sky, as I predicted. Noah, beside me on a deck chair, takes it all in stride, laughter ringing out. "That's just typical," he says with a shake of the head.

I join in with his amusement. "It really is."

"Can't even stargaze in this goddamn town."

"It's not the town's fault."

"If I hadn't come here, then Keith would still be alive," he retorts bitterly, making a strong argument against my defense.

It's an uncomfortable truth that I haven't considered before. For Mia, me, and all the others, this town is our home, so I don't think about it that way.

"You haven't fantasized about being born somewhere else?" he asks.

"No," I reply honestly.

"Please don't tell me you believe all that 'things happen for a reason' crap."

"No," I answer. "But I do believe that bad things happen everywhere. And so do good things. Maybe I could've been born in Kansas and lost my entire family to a tornado. Or maybe I could've been born in Wisconsin and lived a life where nothing bad ever happened."

"What's your point?"

"That I don't like to linger on the 'what ifs,' because I wasn't born in Kansas or Wisconsin. I was born here, and everything that's happened has happened. I'm not a time traveler. I can't change it. I couldn't predict it. And I don't blame the town. It's just a place. It's not capable of being evil."

"But humans are."

"Yeah, sometimes. But most aren't. Well, I guess everyone's capable, but most people choose to be good."

Noah shakes his head and looks up at stars that aren't there. "I wish I could see the world through your eyes."

I titter. "It's not all sunshine and rainbows. I'll tell you that much."

"But despite everything, you're not bitter."

I hold up my thumb and pointer finger and bring them almost to the point of touching. "I'm a little bitter. Not finding that cabin in time... Ugh." I suck my teeth. "I know hindsight is 20/20, and that's the point I'm making here, but it was right there!"

"I know," Noah says gravely. "And I don't think I've been hearing animals at all. I think I've been hearing them—Keith and Mia—locked up and screaming."

A chill runs down my spine like a trickle of cold water, and I shudder visibly and audibly despite the thick blanket that covers most of my body. I can't think of what to say. Noah's words ring in my ears, the horror of them weighing down on my chest like a dumbbell, as I envision Mia and Keith locked in that cage, calling out for help. I turn to Noah, our deck chairs pressed up against each other side by side, and reach out to grasp his hand.

He doesn't reach back. "I could've done something. I could've saved them."

"You could've gotten yourself killed. He has a gun. And he's clearly big and strong enough to take down Keith. Far be it from me to emasculate you, but—"

He sighs. "No, you're right. Keith nearly broke my arm once arm wrestling. If somebody could wrangle him into a dog cage, there's no way I'd have made it out alive. But maybe Ben wasn't there all the time. Maybe that's why they were yelling."

"You're going to drive yourself crazy wondering," I say softly.

"I know. But I can't make it stop."

I want to make it stop. I want to kiss it better as if my mouth is powerful enough to cure something like this. How narcissistic. I want to try anyway. "Can I help?" I ask, keeping very still and brushing those impulses aside.

"You can stay," he answers. "I'll worry about you if you're home alone. I know you've got a cop watching your place, but I'll be up all night anyway, wondering, texting, imagining."

"Okay," I reply.

"I've got a couch bed," he adds as if he still needs to sweeten the deal, not realizing that I'm already sold.

"Sure," I say, smiling at his strong, perfect profile. "Anything is fine with me. I'm so tired."

He twists to face me, but he doesn't smile back. Instead, he's earnest, and normally, I'd balk at such intimate seriousness, but right now, I don't. I let it wash over me, the intensity of his gaze.

"Thank you," he says.

"Don't mention it," I whisper.

"I hate that I met you like this."

"How would you have liked to meet me?"

"In a cafe in Chicago," he answers quickly as if he's already thought about it a million times. "You'd be reading a book, and I'd be in a good mood, so I'd strike up a conversation while I wait for my coffee. We'd click, talk for a while, exchange numbers, and I'd take you out to my favorite restaurant."

"What's your favorite restaurant?"

"I don't actually have one. But the point is that we'd be normal, you know? Instead of bonding over a murder investigation."

"This doesn't need to be a tragedy for us," I say softly. "Maybe we can be a silver lining."

Before I've even finished the sentence, I scrunch up my eyes and feel burning embarrassment consume my body. What I have said is ridiculous. Noah is only here because of my parents. He only found Mia because of me. Keith only died because of Mia. I am intrinsically linked to the worst happenings in Noah's life.

He doesn't reply, and I feel stupider and stupider with each sorry, silent second. I'm about to roll onto my back, apologize, and leave when I feel a rough hand on my jaw and a thumb on my lower lip. I open my eyes and move in, opening my mouth with a small moan. Our tongues eagerly press together, and the movement feels like a well-oiled machine. I can't stop, nor do I want to, and when his hand is in my hair, massaging my scalp, I moan again into his mouth. I shift, moving onto his lap, surrendering entirely to the desires of my body.

We part, and I sit, looking down at him, awash in dimmed moonlight, and he stares up at me like a goddess. "You're right," he says, breathlessly, awestruck. "You are a silver lining."

Then we're intertwined again: legs, arms, and lips. He burns hot and I overheat quickly and shuck the blankets, letting in the cool night breeze, feeling it whisper across my skin. It feels amazing but doesn't compare to his touch. Eagerly, I unbutton my cardigan, revealing the thin straps of my dress and the shoulders I so often keep secret. Noah caresses my upper arms, my shoulders, my collarbones.

"You're so soft," he says. "And smooth like porcelain."

He pulls me closer, kissing my neck, and I could just about scream. I'm ready to rip off my dress, too, but before I do, I pause to ask, "Are you okay?" I try to say it as seductively as possible, but I still feel him tense beneath me.

He looks at me, green eyes a deep emerald in the low light, and nods affirmatively. "I've wanted this ever since I laid eyes on you at the cafe," he replies. "Are you okay?"

"Yes," I smile, my hand on his jaw. "I'm more than okay."

I slowly wake in the morning, bleary-eyed and cozied up in the soft sheets of Noah's bed. Despite the modest square footage of his room, the bed is surprisingly large and much more comfortable than my own antique bed frame and hand-me-down mattress. Every muscle aches and my body begs me to stay in this warm cocoon all day. I reach out, tempted to do just that, but when I feel Noah's absence, I sit bolt upright.

Panic instantly sets in. Nervously, I quickly dress myself and try to distract myself by skimming through my texts from Grandma June, but I can barely absorb any of the information. My thoughts are consumed by what to do next. Should I make a quick escape and pretend like nothing happened? Or should I wait for him to come back and face the awkwardness head-on?

I opt to carry my shoes in hand, in the event that he does want me to stay, and creep downstairs. Halfway down, the mouth-watering smell of bacon and eggs wafts toward me, and tentatively, at the bottom of the stairs, I peer toward the kitchen. The table is set for two with matching beautiful handmade plates and quirky-looking silverware. There's a beautiful arrangement of wildflowers sitting in a vase in the center. It's clear that Noah went out of his way to make this breakfast special and the butterflies in my stomach begin to flap their wings.

A smile tugs at my lips, staring at Noah's broad back as he cooks up a storm, and I clear my throat, causing him to start and turn to me. He looks at me in the same way he had last night—lovingly. My smile widens, and I drop my shoes and run at him.

"You're up!" he says as I throw my arms around him.

"I am."

"I was just about to come wake you." He pulls back, eyeing my slightly muddy clothes from the night before. "I left you a dressing gown out."

"Oh," I say. "I must've missed that."

"Did you think I was going to kick you out?"

"Little bit," I admit, utilizing the same hand gesture as I had the night before.

He frowns. "I might be a jerk, but I'm not that type of jerk."

"Well, that is very good to know."

He tilts my chin up and kisses me gently before turning back to the eggs. "What are your plans for the day?"

"Sunny Side. Gigi says Charlie Wilkins is back. So I guess it's time to get a confession."

"That's great. At least that's one case you can solve," he enthuses, then stops himself. "I didn't mean. God. I just meant—"

I laugh. The energy is awkward but sweet. We're both walking on eggshells like shy, lovestruck teenagers. "It's fine," I assure him. "I know what you meant."

"Do you want me to drop you off? We could take the bike. Could be fun."

The idea of having my arms wrapped around Noah, rocketing around on a motorbike, thrills me, and I nod enthusiastically, wanting to get as much time with him as possible. "Yeah. Please. What are you doing today?"

Noah's jaw muscles twitch. "I'm talking to Keith's mom. Helping with the funeral. And then it's back to business."

"Jesus. Have you asked my parents for time off?"

"I think it's better to keep busy."

I can't disagree with that. I take a seat at the table as he serves up toast topped with avocado, bacon, and a fried egg. I look up at him as he leans over and he moves in for another gentle kiss, and it feels as natural as breathing. It feels like our mouths were made for each other, and if I wasn't so hungry, I'd move in for more. Honestly I'd do almost anything to get back into bed.

It's crazy, but I was with Gavin for almost a decade, and it never, ever felt like this. Not even during the honeymoon phase at the start. In retrospect, I have no idea why I stayed. None at all. We borderline hated each other and did everything to avoid each other. The sex sucked, the kissing was worse, and he never cooked for me. Not once.

"Sorry," I murmur. "I haven't brushed my teeth."

Noah looks at me curiously, puts the pan down, and strides back over before moving in for another, deeper kiss. He pulls away and kisses his fingers like a chef. "Delicious," he murmurs, faux-seductively. "Diet Coke and Pad Thai."

I slap his upper arm gently, flushing as I laugh. "You're nasty."

"I could say the same to you."

I look away, then flip him off before chowing down. He watches on in amusement before sitting opposite to me, almost too focused to eat. "The sky is going to be clear tonight," he says, deep and gentle.

My body tingles. "Well, I guess I'll have to stay over again."

"Hmm. I don't recall inviting you."

"Too bad," I mutter, mouth half full. "This is like feeding the local wildlife. I'm never going to leave."

"Please don't," he laughs.

CHAPTER TWENTY-SIX

I TAKE A DEEP BREATH AND TRY TO CATCH THE ATTENTION OF the old man who sits before me. Charlie, with his gaze fixed on anything and everything but on me, is clearly trying to avoid confrontation. I decide to play along, taking a moment to fully absorb my surroundings. As I do so, I can't help but notice the plethora of birds that adorn Charlie's room. From hand-carved wooden sculptures to framed photos and even a collection of feathers, every inch of the room is dedicated to these creatures. There are also even a few photos of a younger man who bears a striking resemblance to Charlie, perhaps his son. Yet it's clear that it's birds that dominate Charlie's heart.

I wonder if he's also a birdwatcher. He must be considering his passion for the species, and I tuck this piece of information away for later, certain that it will come in handy if only to expand upon my knowledge of the hobby.

Trying to maintain an air of authority, I clear my throat and address Charlie for the third time. "So, Mr. Wilkins. We have you on videotape stealing jewelry from your fellow residents."

"Then, call the cops," he spits out, putting on a tough front. He is intimidating, I can't deny that, but I have to say, the carved ducklings that sit between us on the coffee table soften things somewhat.

With a weary sigh, I say, "I don't want to call the cops, Charlie."

He's still looking away, but my gaze is fixed on his face. Despite the lines etched into his skin, he's still very handsome, and imagine, back in the day, he was a real hit with the ladies. There's something of Elvis Presley about him with the slicked-back hair and a hint of sideburns. Most of his hair is gone now, but what remains is fluffed within an inch of its life and slicked with pomade. He clearly still takes a lot of pride in his appearance.

"Why not? I'm a criminal, ain't I?"

"Because I'd rather not take things to that level if I can help it, and Tanya and the residents agree. They just want their belongings back."

"Better to be in a jail cell than evicted," he mutters. "If they kick me out, I'll have to go to a state home or move in with my son. I don't want to live in one of those places, and he doesn't want to live with me. Who could blame him? You can barely stand being in the same room as me."

"That's not true," I say sternly because it isn't. "I don't dislike you, Charlie. I just want you to give everything back."

"Pshh."

"Was the fishing trip no good?"

"It was good when we were fishing. Everything else was... I just don't know how to talk to him anymore. I never was good at talking."

"I'm sorry, Charlie."

"Yeah, yeah," he grumbles, waving me off.

"I think if you come clean and apologize, Tanya will let you stay."

"Too late. Damage is done. Everyone's going to hate me. They did already, mind you. But now..." He shakes his head, waggling his jowls, and he makes a retching noise like he might phlegm into his teacup. I'm glad that he ultimately decides against it.

"Is that why you took their things? Because they don't like you?"

He shrugs. "I don't know why I did it. I just know once I started, I couldn't stop."

"Have you done it before? Stealing, that is."

"Yeah. From my family and friends. Normally, it's when I feel like they don't like me. I guess it's my way of revenge." He tuts at himself. "It's disgusting, I know. My mom was like that, too. Couldn't keep a job because of it."

"Charlie, I think you might be a kleptomaniac."

"A what maniac?" he demands defensively.

"It's an uncontrollable impulse to steal items. But don't worry, it's curable. I could find you a counselor—"

"No," he interrupts firmly. "No need for that. I'll just stop."

"Are you sure?" I ask hesitantly, sensing that this is a deep-rooted problem that might take some work beyond quitting cold turkey. Especially because he's been doing it for eighty years.

"Yeah. And I'll give everyone's stuff back. It's in a lock box in the wardrobe," he says, jerking his head to the wooden door.

I move quickly to the wardrobe, slide the slatted wooden door across, and inside, nestled amongst some sweaters, is a small safe. I look over my shoulder. "What's the code?"

"12, 03, 38. My wife's birthday."

A triumphant smile spreads across my face as I turn the dial and hear the satisfying click. I pull the door ajar, and my jaw drops at the treasure trove before me. It's a veritable dragon's hoard, overflowing with glimmering gold and sparkling diamonds. It's a lot more than I had anticipated, and I have a feeling that many residents don't realize that their belongings are missing. That or this collection has been years in the making.

"Was all of this taken from Sunny Side?"

Charlie sighs. "Yes."

"Jesus," I whisper.

"I know," Charlie murmurs, voice laden with regret, his sagging ears apparently still as sharp as a bat's. He looks down at his gnarled hands in anger, as if they're to blame. "As I said, I couldn't stop. I don't know what I planned to do with any of it. Nothing, I guess. It just made me feel like I had power over all of those rich assholes who never gave me the time of day."

"That makes sense," I say.

"Does it?"

"Well, I can see where you're coming from."

He frowns, and rubs at his wrinkled forehead. "It was funny at first. My little secret. But it stopped being funny a while back."

I can see the genuine remorse in his eyes as I approach him with the heavy safe cradled carefully in my arms. "Come on," I say softly, "let's give this back." The weight of the safe is a burden on my arms, but it pales in comparison to the weight on Charlie's conscience. He stands slowly and follows me out of the room without complaint. We both know it's time to make things right.

In the end, Charlie Wilkins was neither evicted nor hated by all. Honestly, everyone just seemed grateful to get their things back and were more polite than I expected about the whole affair. Tanya also agreed that he could stay on the condition that he be tailed by security for the next few weeks. Then, after that, if anything else goes missing, at least they know where to look. Charlie accepted the deal, and after the dust settled and everyone went back to their rooms and activities, I approached him and asked if he'd like to join me on a birdwatching walk. And wouldn't you know it, but the old grump lit up like the sun.

Now we're walking through Salish Pines Forest. He—a seasoned professional—is dressed in full hiking gear, complete with a walking stick, backpack, water bottle, and binoculars. Meanwhile, I'm still wearing yesterday's clothes, which keep me warm but aren't designed for where Charlie prefers to walk.

Neither are my shoes, but I follow along diligently, hanging on his every word.

"Red-winged blackbird, *Agelaius phoeniceus*," he informs me, pointing dead ahead and pressing his binoculars hard against his sockets like swimming goggles. "A male. A big one, too."

"He's beautiful," I say, squinting at the distance.

"American Goldfinch. *Spinus tristis*. A female with a nest. No eggs yet, though."

I *ooh* and *aah* appropriately, but wish I had my own pair of binoculars so that I could properly appreciate these discoveries. Still, there are much worse ways to spend an afternoon, and as a bonus, Charlie is in high spirits. In fact, he can't stop smiling, and neither can I. He probably doesn't get to do this that often. Not without having a care home worker come with him and having his doctor and Tanya sign off on it.

"Is this your first time in a care home?" I ask, wanting more from this venture than distant specks of feathers and colors. I have a feeling Charlie is a treasure trove of information if you can make it past the tough barrier.

Charlie laughs loudly for the first time, and it's a nice, warm sound, not unlike my own grandfather's. "You make it sound like a prison," he says.

"Well," I start, having already detected Charlie's feelings about his current situation, "It's like a very nice prison."

"You're not wrong. Locked in your rooms at night. Group sessions. Communal areas. Bah."

"So you hate it?"

"No. Not at all. But I hate living without my wife."

"When did she pass away?"

The binoculars slip from his grasp as he lets out a heavy sigh. He gazes up at the lush canopy above, lost in thought for a moment before speaking. "It's been four years." He looks at me, baleful eyes red-rimmed. "I stayed in the house for a couple of years after that, but then I fell and..." He trails off, gesturing vaguely with his hand. "You know how it goes. My son wants me to sell, but I won't. He'll have to wait until I'm dead."

"Tell me about your house."

"Oh gosh," Charlie starts, surprised by the question. "It's just the prettiest little place. A three-bedroom cottage on the other side of Willow Walkway. Surrounded by flowers. Emerald shutters."

"Why doesn't your son move into it?"

"He's got a big flashy place in the city. It has a pool, you know? Not that I've ever been there."

"Would you consider selling to a friend? Someone who'd preserve it?"

Charlie sighs wearily. "I suppose that would beat my son tearing it down and turning it into apartments. But I don't have any friends. Not anymore."

"Charlie, you wound me."

He looks at me and chuckles. "You're too young to be friends with me." He pauses and furrows his eyebrows. "Why? You looking to buy?"

I shrug. "I could definitely swing by and take a look. Sounds like it's my cup of tea."

His expression is torn between suspicion and happiness, and I suppose I'll just have to prove to the guarded side that he can trust me. I genuinely would like to be his friend. I'm not just saying it. Everyone needs at least one, and no one else wants to go birdwatching with me.

"I'm sorry about your wife," I say as we keep walking. "What was her name?"

"Pearl. And I'll tell you, she was every bit as beautiful as her namesake."

"I bet," I reply, picturing a woman not too dissimilar to Grandma June when she was younger. "How did you meet? Are you both from around here?"

"I feel like I'm on the damn Letterman show," Charlie says, amused rather than angry, shooting me another one of those mixed glances. "But yeah, we're local. High school sweethearts."

"What did you do for a living?"

"She was an artist, and I was an electrician when I wasn't a soldier. During my army days, we moved around a lot, but we always seemed to end up back here."

"I know the feeling. I spent ten years in New York, but this place has a certain pull."

"It's magnetic," Charlie agrees. "Though I'm not sure that's always a good thing."

"What do you mean?"

"Well, there's that goddamn place for starters," he says, passing the binoculars to me.

I press them to my eyes and gasp slightly as Crawford Manor comes into view. I have to say, it's not less intimidating during the day. As I continue to stare at it, I hear Charlie spit on the ground beside me. "Not a big fan of the Crawfords, I take it?" I ask.

"Actually I was good friends with Harold and Wilma, Earl's parents. I liked Joanna, too, and the kid. It was just Earl I didn't like."

"So what's the deal with Earl?" I ask, my intuition about Charlie's knowledge paying off.

"I'm surprised that someone as nosy as you doesn't already know."

"Humor me."

"Well, the guy was a creep, and everybody hated him. I suppose a young person such as yourself might say he had bad... what do you call 'em? Vibrations?"

"Bad vibes?" I offer.

"He had bad vibes. And I think that's a pretty accurate assessment. Anyways, cut to him turning eighteen, and a hitchhiker known as Bunny Sullivan goes missing, last seen on the side of the road by a long haul trucker just outside of town. Nobody really thought much of it. This was the eighties, and unfortunately, hitchhikers went missing all the time. There was a titter here and there from the local gossips, and then nothing. Now as I said, I was friends with Earl's parents, and one day they were over at our place for dinner, and they got a little tipsy, which wasn't unusual. But they were also acting strange. They ended up confiding in Pearl and me that they thought their son killed that poor girl."

"Why did they think that?"

"I have no idea. But they must've had a good reason because they moved to Northern California shortly after and left him behind."

"*Wow*."

"Yeah, that about sums up my feelings on the matter. I think they should've handed his ass over to the cops instead of running away, tails between their legs."

"Why didn't you go to the police?" I question.

"Because they didn't give me anything to go on. Just some slurred ramblings."

"But do you think he did it?"

Charlie laughs dryly. "Oh yeah. And I'd bet my house that he killed all of those kids and his wife, too. And if he was still alive, I'd say he killed Mia Ramsey as well."

"He was that bad, huh?"

"And worse. He killed animals. At first for sport, but then local pets started going missing and would turn up on the side of the road in trash bags. He hurt girls, too, strangling them on dates and beating 'em black and blue. He even got thrown in a cell a few times for that. I always hoped he'd give the wrong guy a reason to knock his lights out permanently." Charlie tenses as I lower my binoculars, his hands balled into fists. "I hope he's enjoying hell."

"He sounds like a monster," I say, and not just because it's what Charlie wants to hear. This testimony, combined with my father's account and Stanley's disdain, paints Earl Crawford as a despicable human being, and I am honestly surprised that nobody ever took matters into their own hands. It seems the sheriff wasn't interested in doing much about this bogeyman roaming the streets.

"He was. He..." Charlie swallows, his Adam's apple bobbing. "He murdered our granddaughter Carrie. Our daughter's kid. She and Pearl never really got over it. Lucy has been in and out of facilities ever since, so I don't get to see her much either. And with my son, Shane, I start drinking, and I start ranting, and he doesn't want to hear it."

"Charlie, I am so sorry," I say, choking up halfway through my sentence from shock and empathy.

"Was it you? That found her body? Lucy mentioned something about the case being reopened, but the names... I'm getting old. And Bridget used to be a much more common name."

"It was. Sort of. I set the sheriff on the right track."

"Don't be so modest," Charlie scolds me. "You're the first person who's ever…" He trails off, his voice brimming with emotion. "You should go and visit Wilma and Harold. I used to get Christmas cards from them up until a few years back, and I doubt they would've moved. Got a place in San Jose for a song. I can give you the address. Maybe they can shed some light on the whole thing."

"That would be great; thank you, Charlie."

"Please don't. Call it a favor for saving my ass and being the first person in twenty years to give a crap about my granddaughter." He hums. "You must be worth your salt for the cops to give you the time of day. They certainly didn't for the rest of us."

"I hope so."

"Yeah… me, too, kid. Me, too."

We both stare out at Crawford Manor, and I press the binoculars back to my eyes and gasp again before loosening my grasp. They swing down and whack me in the chest, and Charlie looks at me concerned.

"What is it?"

"I thought I saw…" I trail off and look again, but this time, the window is dark and empty. "I thought I saw a woman," I say because I really thought I had. She was pale and gaunt, with dark, sad eyes, and her hand was pressed against the window. She was so vivid.

Charlie nods sagely as I lower the binoculars again. "*That* would be the ghost of poor Joanna Crawford."

CHAPTER TWENTY-SEVEN

As we arrive at the modest Spanish-style home of Wilma and Harold Crawford in San Jose, California, my hand trembles in Noah's grip. He assumes it's the nerves, and he isn't wrong—with my bobbing legs and incessant fidgeting I am definitely feeling anxious. Yet, beyond that, I am elated and downright manic with excitement. This couple may hold the key to everything I have been tirelessly investigating.

And while Noah couldn't quite understand the purpose of meeting a dead man's elderly parents, he could see how important it was to me. I've tried to explain it to him during the drive, but he still hasn't grasped it. After all, why would Wilma and Harold reveal any incriminating information about their son if they haven't told anyone else? Especially after all of this time. Except that they abandoned their own eighteen-year-old son and moved all the way to San Jose to escape him.

I open the passenger door, and my feet touch down on the tan stepping stones that lead me toward the white stucco and terracotta home. The exterior almost blinding in the sunlight, an effect that is emphasized by how immaculately clean it is. There is no dirt, no junk, no imperfections. Even the lawn is perfect despite the frequent droughts, and its manicured evenness and density remind me of a carpet. I inhale, and the smell is delicious, and suddenly, I am willing for summer to come sooner and the rain to stop. I need a picnic. I need to bask. My body compels me to lie down, but I continue on, focusing on the house. It might be a major downsize from the imposing Crawford Manor, but it is far more charming and cozier. And considering our proximity to San Francisco, it's probably worth even more.

I gently rap my knuckles against the curved, white door, and it swings open enthusiastically to reveal an elderly woman with a stunningly coiffed 'Gibson Girl' hairstyle. Her delicate features are slightly pinched, giving her a mousy, suspicious expression, and though she does not smile, I do. I try to maintain eye contact, but I'm curious and find my eyes flicking downward before returning. Though she looks straight out of the nineteenth century from the neck up, her ensemble is more modern than my own, comprised of crisp linen pants and a tailored blouse accented by an array of elegant and timeless gold jewelry.

"Hello?" she asks, her voice small and croaky. Undoubtedly a smoker in her past.

"Hi, my name is Bridget Hartley, I'm a private investigator," I inform her, my sunny disposition likely the only thing preventing the door from being slammed in my face.

"Oh?" the woman inquires, eyes widening. "How may I help you, Ms. Hartley?"

"Please, call me Bridget or Birdie."

"Birdie," she hums, looking distant. "That was my older sister's name. Long gone now, I'm afraid."

"Oh. I'm sorry for your loss."

She nods sadly, her lips paling as she pulls them into a taught frown. "Me, too. But she lived a long, successful life. A prima ballerina when she was young. A breeder of Persian cats when she was old. Four husbands. Six children. Twelve grandchildren. Lucky duck."

"It sounds like she was amazing."

"Oh, she was certainly something," the woman titters fondly.

"And are you Wilma Crawford?" I ask, double-checking.

"I am."

"Great. And is Mr. Crawford home?"

Her expression crumples, and her sapphire eyes become distant. "No," she answers at last. "Well, not unless you count the urn on the mantle. I do."

"I do, too," I say softly.

"Well, do come in," she says, surprisingly friendly despite appearances. "Is that your friend in the truck?"

"My co-worker," I say. "But as your husband isn't home, maybe you'd be comfier just us girls."

She tuts affectionately and smacks my arm gently. "Girls. I haven't been called a girl since the fifties. But yes, just us girls. Do come in, Bridget."

As I step inside, I am struck by the impeccable taste of the homeowner. The interior is a perfect blend of clean lines, chic decor, and minimalist design. It's evident that every piece of furniture and decoration has been carefully chosen and placed with intention. A sense of balance and harmony fills the space, and I would hazard a guess that Wilma, or her decorator, is well-versed in Feng Shui. From the multiple Zen gardens to the ergonomic layout of the rooms, this home is not just aesthetically pleasing but thoughtfully arranged for maximum relaxation, like stepping into a waiting room for a luxurious spa.

"So, what is this about?" Wilma asks, lowering herself onto a cream couch and sheepskin throw and gesturing toward a nearby bone-white armchair, which I hastily occupy.

I clear my throat, the nerves finally beating out excitement for dominance. "Do you mind if I record?" I ask.

"Knock yourself out."

"Thank you. Can you state your name and the date for the record?"

"Sunday the seventeenth of March 2024. It is 2:33pm. And my name is Wilma Crawford."

"Perfect."

"So what is this about, Bridget?"

"I want to ask about your son, Earl Crawford."

"Oh," Wilma replies bitterly, her jaw clenching. She plucks a full glass of chilled white wine from the coffee table. Her eyes avoid mine, offering no explanation for the midday drinking, but as I follow her gaze to Harold's urn on the mantle, I understand. The curved plaque tells me that it has been four years to the day since his passing, and I have intruded on an anniversary of sorts. Wilma takes a long sip of her drink, and I wait for the effects to take hold before I proceed.

"Sorry," I say, "I don't want to blindside you."

She shakes her head fervently. "No, no. I should've known you were here for Earl. It's never my charity work or Harold's role as a councilman that garners attention; it's always Earl."

"So, people have come asking before?"

"Mm," she replies affirmatively. "Not for a long time now, though. But back when Joanna died, there were police officers and the occasional reporter. None of it ever made it to the papers, mind you. It was ruled a suicide, officially." She looks at me over the top of the glass, an over-plucked eyebrow cocked.

"I'm taking it that you don't believe that she killed herself."

She scoffs. "Don't play coy, *girl*. Would you be here if she had?"

"I guess not."

"Exactly." She takes another swig. "No, he killed her. Joanna. My beautiful angel Joanna. I loved her as if she was blood."

"So you two were close?"

"Apparently not enough. I never knew about the abuse. And this will sound awful because I am so grateful for my darling Stanley, but she should have never married him."

"Did you ever tell her that? Before they got married?"

"I would have if we'd known he was getting married. He only told us after the fact and once she was pregnant. And by then, it was too late."

"I know your grandson," I say. "Quite well, actually. I'm from Serenity, too."

"Ahh," Wilma says, taking another sip. "So this is personal."

"A little bit."

"You knew one of the missing teenagers?"

"Yes," I reply, a little taken aback by how much she knows and how forthcoming she is. "Lucia Nunez. Do you think Earl had something to do with that?"

"I really don't know. Not for sure. But I do know that I didn't want him living here. I didn't want the plague to spread, so to speak."

"And do you think it did? Spread, I mean."

Wilma turns her gaze to the window. "There were missing girls. Plenty of them. But this is a city, not a small town, so it's hard to say for sure."

"Why did you let him stay here? Three years is a long time to live with somebody that... Well, you know."

"It is, and it was. But Harold and I didn't exactly see eye to eye on the whole situation. Certainly, at first, he thought that our son did kill that poor hitchhiker, Bunny. But then he turned soft in his senility, and when Joanna 'killed herself,' he got all these silly ideas about how wrong we were and how much our 'baby' was suffering." Wilma tenses, every muscle in her sharp jaw twitching. "I was outvoted. Or overpowered. And I suppose I was weaker than usual because Stanley was coming with him."

"What was it like? Living with him again after all those years?"

"I made myself very busy," Wilma replies curtly. "A silver lining, really. At least for the community."

"And then Stanley left when his dad died?"

Wilma looks at me quizzically, head cocked. "No. I kicked Earl out when Harold died, and unfortunately, Stanley went with him back to Serenity Springs."

"Wait, what?"

"What do you mean 'what'?"

"It just... Stanley told me that his dad died here."

"Oh no. Harold died in March, and then they went home, and Earl died that same August of a heart attack at the manor. Stanley was the one who found the body. And before you ask, yes, this is all confirmed, and I did attend the funeral."

"Why would Stanley lie to me?"

"Well, Bridget, you're the investigator," Wilma says condescendingly.

A penny drops with a loud, metallic ding inside my skull. "Do you think he could've killed Earl?"

"If he did, then he's the bravest man this family has ever seen," Wilma retorts, indifferent at the idea of her grandson murdering her son. "He used to beat Stanley, you know. It never happened under my roof, but who knows what happened when it was just the two of them. Maybe Stanley had enough and slipped him some potassium cyanide or strychnine. Again, I couldn't really say for sure."

Those are some very specific examples. "Do you have a medical background?" I ask.

"I was a nurse, and I also watch a lot of true crime," Wilma retorts. "Not to mention everything is on the Google nowadays."

"If I had a dollar," I murmur.

"Speak up, dear," Wilma instructs sharply, though I'm certain she heard me.

"It's just… I used to be a crime reporter, and you'd be surprised how many people try to get away with things by claiming to be true crime fanatics."

Wilma leers at me. "What are you implying?"

"Absolutely nothing at all," I state emotionlessly, holding her gaze. "But I'm surprised you'd be interested in such a grim genre, considering."

"I'm not an ostrich. I refuse to bury my head in the sand. I did once, and look where it got me and all of those poor women. Ignorance is not bliss, Bridget. It's just ignorance."

I nod curtly, though I fully agree. "Are you still in touch with Stanley?"

"Oh yes!" she exclaims, lighting up. "We do a Facetime every Saturday night if he's free. He seems happy now. Working at the library. And I'm so glad to hear you're friends."

I smile at her as her expression turns dreamy, and she drains the rest of her drink. "I'm glad we're friends, too."

"He's a lovely, lovely boy," Wilma coos before snapping out of her daydream. Her sharp gaze pierces me like a hawk's talons. "You won't say anything, will you? About Earl's death?"

"No," I say. "No, I will not."

It was a challenging question but one that was easily answered. I am here for the victims, and Earl, murdered or not, is not a victim.

"Good girl. Now, stay a while, won't you? Have a drink? I'd love to talk about Harold."

Much like her grandson, Wilma is very persuasive, and I wait patiently for her to bring me a glass, information rushing around my head as if I've stood up too suddenly. Earl was a killer. Stanley might be, too. And this journey to San Jose has been more than worth it.

CHAPTER TWENTY-EIGHT

M Y EYELIDS OPEN SLOWLY AS MY PHONE BUZZES incessantly on the bedside table. Once again, a phone call has trumped my alarm, and at this point, I'm not even sure why I bother to set one. This is my new normal. I sit up abruptly, forcing myself awake and causing Noah to grumble and pull the covers up high. Despite this and the fact that my bed is a significant downgrade from his own, he remains asleep.

I press the off button on my phone, hanging up on the caller, and swing my legs out of bed. I groan as I feel sand scrape against my skin. We showered when we got back yesterday, but it still feels like it's everywhere, under my nails, in my hair, between my toes. And this is precisely why I am only an occasional beachgoer.

I grab my phone and tiptoe into the bathroom, clad only in my underwear—a decision that I soon regret. The cool tiles beneath my feet send shivers up my spine and I can see my breath as I sit down on the closed toilet seat. I turn my phone on, go to missed calls, and seeing Donna's husband's number, press the call button.

"Birdie," Donna answers. Her voice is hushed and conspiratorial, and I wonder if she's also hiding away while her partner sleeps.

"Hi," I reply just as quietly. "What's going on?"

"I just wanted to give you an update about the hunting cabin."

"Okay," I say, trying to contain my excitement, my fingers drumming on my lap.

"Unfortunately, it's not good news," she replies with a heavy sigh. "The only DNA we found in the crate is canine. No trace of Mia or Keith or anything human. Ben's saliva was on the KFC, but that's it."

I search for a silver lining. "So that means he was definitely here, and recently."

"Yes, he was, but merely existing is not a crime. Neither is talking to Mia on the phone. We need a lot more than that to arrest him."

"But we're so close," I protest.

"I know. And when we find him we'll bring him in for questioning and, hopefully, he'll slip up or confess. But we can't hold him or press charges without hard evidence. Aside from the possible murder of Shelley Pearson, what we have is circumstantial at best."

I grit my teeth and grip my phone so tightly it feels liable to break. I feel like this case is slipping through my furled fingers like smoke.

"I know," Donna sighs. "Which is why I need you. My hands are tied, but yours aren't. You can continue to snoop and find out everything you can about Ben."

"Yeah, okay." I like the sound of that, but I have no idea where to start. I thought the hunting cabin was a wrap. I thought that was the final piece of the puzzle.

"Also, I'm curious. Where did you go yesterday? Your 'bodyguard' told me that you left town."

"To visit Earl Crawford's mother," I reply truthfully. After all, Donna and I are partners in this. I'm just glad that she doesn't mention Noah. My security detail would have undoubtedly seen him enter my apartment.

"And what did you find?"

"A lot more than I expected. To sum it up, Earl's parents believed that he murdered a hitchhiker named Bunny Sullivan in 1982, right here in Serenity Springs. But instead of turning him in, they left. After that, according to Wilma, Earl's mother, her husband Harold began to doubt their convictions, and 'went soft,' allowing Earl to stay with them after Joanna died. Earl then stayed for three more years until Harold passed away in early 2020 and Wilma kicked him out. Earl then died shortly after at Crawford Manor of a heart attack." I pause to breathe. "Wilma also thinks that Earl is responsible for a bunch of other murders, including the Lovebird's Nest couples."

"And what do *you* think?"

"I think she could be on to something."

"Then where does Ben fit into all of this?"

"With Shelley, Mia, and Keith. I think he killed them, but now I don't know why. If he didn't kill the Lovebird's Nest victims then he had nothing to hide."

"Maybe Mia found out the truth about Shelley. And it's not as if domestic homicide is unusual."

"Yeah," I say, gaining confidence.

"But two murderers in a town like this…" Donna trails off. "If I wasn't so confident in your abilities I'd think you were crazy."

"And I wouldn't blame you."

"But you're certain about everything else?"

"At this stage, yes."

"Well, then let's assume your theory is correct, and investigate accordingly until we know more."

"What do you think?" I inquire. "What's your theory?"

"I believe that Ben is the killer, but after hearing what Earl's mother had to say, I'm willing to consider other possibilities. I'll definitely be looking into Earl further. Especially considering the murder in 1982. Ben is only forty-seven. He would've been much too young."

"Could the seventh body be—" I stop myself realizing how absurd my question sounds.

"Yes?"

"Sorry, I was going to say Bunny, but that's not possible. Not if she died in 1982. She'd be a skeleton."

"Yes, she would be. Our Jane Doe has only been dead for a decade at the most."

"He probably disposed of her," I say, and then flush, hoping that I don't sound overconfident. Donna is the serial killer expert, not me.

"If she was his first, I would say that is likely. Most tend to panic and dismember or dump."

"She couldn't be Joanna, could she? She was definitely buried, right?"

"That's what the records claim. Although, we could always exhume her body to make sure."

I cringe at the thought. Stanley has already endured so much pain when it comes to his family. Digging up his mother's seven-year-old remains is the last thing he needs right now. "If it's okay with you, I'd rather investigate further before making that decision."

"Not a problem. It's a godawful process anyway and requires the family's permission, which we might not get. Now before I head off, is there anything else?"

"No, I don't think so," I say, rubbing a tired eye with the back of my hand.

"Well, this is good stuff, Birdie. You're doing an excellent job. Call me if you find out anything further, and I'll return the favor."

"Will do," I yawn.

"Be careful," she cautions as Noah grabs the handle and strolls into the bathroom, dressed in only red gingham boxer shorts, his impressive physique on full display. I know she's talking about him, but I pretend she isn't as I wrap up the call.

"Good morning," I say, smiling up at Noah.

"Good morning to you," he replies, stooping for a kiss. "Was that Donna?"

"Sure was. Apparently, there was only dog DNA in that crate."

"Seriously?"

"Yup. So now we have no evidence, and because of that, we can't arrest him."

"Bummer."

"No kidding."

"Well, this is for you," he says, handing over a blank envelope. "I went to make coffee, and it was just lying there, shoved under the door."

"Weird," I say, grabbing it and turning it over. It doesn't even have my name on it, which means that whoever delivered it, did so in person. Which also means they also know where I live, and somehow got past the lobby door downstairs.

"No address," Noah notes, on the same page as me, his expression perturbed.

I tear the envelope open and reveal a folded piece of paper inside. I unfold it and see that it's a letter, written in a scrawling, masculine font. "Dear Bridget," I read aloud, "I know that you have been looking into my niece's case. I would like to help you do so, if you'll let me. Which means I'd like to meet in person and talk. Below is an address where we can meet. Bring a friend if you need to, but I beg you, do not call the police. Not yet, anyway. Hear me out first. I think you'll find my story convincing. Regards, Ben Ramsey."

"Holy crap," Noah replies.

"That about sums it up, yeah."

"What are you going to do?"

I look up at Noah. "We're going to go meet him."

Following the address leads us to the state border, closer to Cascadia than Serenity Springs. More specifically, it leads us down a winding path, surrounded by towering trees and dense foliage, and after fifteen minutes we come across a cabin, this one much larger and more liveable than Ben's hunting hideaway. Yet that doesn't make it any cozier, and I am still very much aware of how far we are from anywhere. My guts roil as we park, and Noah's features are tight and tense. I get it. We're a pair of deer wandering toward a trap waiting to be sprung.

"Are you sure about this?" Noah asks.

"Yeah," I say, more confidently than I feel.

"Okay then," Noah says, reaching across me, opening the glove compartment and shoving a sheathed hunting knife into his boot.

I open the passenger door and begin to walk toward the log cabin. Before I can reach it, a man opens it and stands before us, exhausted and wilted. He's short, with receding brown hair, a lower-gut paunch, dark eye bags, and ill-fitting stained clothing. Yet he is not repulsive. His face is handsome, and despite the extra weight, his build is thick and muscular. He reminds me of actors in the seventies before everyone was forced to get plastic surgery and work out three times a day. That is to say, there's something very charismatic about his schlubby appearance.

He lifts a hand as a greeting. "Bridget, right?"

I nod. "And you're Ben Ramsey?"

"I am. Who's your friend?"

"This is Noah."

"Hi, Noah," Ben says, holding up his hand again. His expression is friendly, as is Noah's, but as I look back and forth between them, I can tell they're sizing each other up. Honestly, Ben doesn't stand a chance without weapons, which is quite reassuring.

"Would you mind emptying your pockets?" Noah asks.

"Not at all," Ben replies, turning his sweatpant pockets inside out and littering the ground with coins and lint. "I'm not going to hurt you. And I know that's hard to believe, but I'm like a spider, pal. I'm more scared of you than you are of me."

"I'm not scared of you at all," Noah says.

"Really? Well, color me terrified."

"Let's talk outside," I say, not as brave as Noah, but not terrified either.

"Yeah. No problem," Ben says, his voice raspy and laden with time spent in New York. "Pull up a chair," he adds, gesturing to some dirty plastic chairs next to the tree line.

THE GIRL IN THE SPRINGS

We do so and sit ten feet away from him as he makes himself comfortable on a worn-out deck chair. He puts his feet up, puts a cigarillo between his lips, and reaches for a silver flask that was lying atop particle board balanced on a stack of tires. He lights up and takes a swig.

"Thank you for coming," he croaks. "Seriously."

"What's this about?" I ask, trying to sound 'hard' but failing. I've never played a bad cop before; it's just not in my nature.

"You went to go see Wilma Crawford, yes?"

"Yes," I reply slowly. "How did you know about that?"

"Because I know everything that happens regarding the Crawfords. I know you've been to the manor. I know that you've been befriending the son, Stanley. And I know you paid Wilma a visit."

I don't ask how he knows because, honestly, I don't want to know. The thought of someone having such intimate knowledge of my actions makes me uneasy. "Okay. And what about it?"

"Well, Bridget, I want to know what you think."

"As in?" I ask, playing dumb.

"What's your theory? Do you find them suspicious?" Ben questions, face obscured by a veil of smoke.

"I think that Earl killed his wife and the missing teenagers. I think that Stanley killed Earl. Then, I think that you, separately, killed your girlfriend, Mia, and Keith."

To his credit, Ben doesn't look outraged at the accusation. He must've known it was coming. "Smart girl," he says, taking another swig. "And you're close. I'll give you that. Except there is no blood on my hands."

"Enlighten me," I retort.

He bobs his head, swilling the liquor around in his mouth before taking a puff. "I intend to. So, I was a homicide detective, right?"

"Right."

"Rhetorical," he chides impishly. "But anyway, that was my job. And I catch wind of these missing kids over in Serenity Springs and the botched job the sheriff is doing. So, when the second pair went missing in 2010, I decided to look into it. I ask around, blah, blah, and catch the drift that this Earl guy is a real asshole. Nearly got pinned for a missing hitchhiker case back in '82. So, no, she's not the seventh body. And yes, I know about that."

Ben is rambling, eccentric, and already drunk, but I have to admit that I'm hanging on his every word. I don't think I've even blinked since he started talking and every muscle is rigid, and my body is angled toward him.

"Do you know who the seventh body is?"

Ben nods curtly. "Joanna Crawford. The famous ghost. You've seen her, I'll bet."

"I..." I can't lie. I never believed in ghosts before, but I saw a face in the window that day, clear as crystal.

"Yeah, I thought so," Ben says gravely. "I've seen her, too. And let me guess, you don't believe in ghosts."

"I don't."

"Hmm. It's funny how things can change, isn't it?"

I feel Noah's eyes on the side of my face, but I keep my eyes fixed on Ben. "The police told me that Joanna—"

Ben interrupted. "That she's buried in the Crawford cemetery? Yeah, that's all Earl's doing. Paid off the old boys. Convinced them that she ran away and drowned in the river. There was no body. They buried an empty casket."

"What? Does Stanley know?"

Ben shrugs. "No clue. Probably, if he decided to murder his dad. Must've found out that Pops lied to him, too."

"So you think Stanley killed Earl, too?"

"It's crossed my mind, but I'm not as convinced as you seem to be." Ben coughs loudly; the sound is wet and deep. It seems painful, as he quickly washes it down with another swig. "Anyway. Timeline. I'm sure you know most of it, but hey, let's make sure we're on the same page. So, Earl was born in 1964. He starts off with animals like most of these freaks do, and then in 1982, at only eighteen, he strikes for the first time. He goes on to kill more in the eighties and nineties. Hitchhikers, out-of-towners, and prostitutes. Then he gets overconfident and changes his MO. He kills Gina and Carrie and has to lay low for a while. Then, along come Lucia and Chad. That's where I come in, and it takes me a matter of weeks to make him a suspect. Then *boom*. My life blows up. I'm getting anonymous threats. My tires are slashed.

Somebody kills my goddamn cat. Then, Shelley goes missing—leaving a bunch of blood behind in our bed—never to be seen again. Of course, people suspect me, and though they can't prove anything, I'm cut from the force, and I lose all my power. Earl goes on to kill more—including his wife—and runs away to San Jose. He presumably kills more there, and then his dad dies, and he's forced to come back here. He dies, and then nothing. The reign of terror is over. Until now. Double homicide. Mia Ramsey and Keith Hicks." Ben's voice cracks when he mentions his niece's name, and he quickly takes another drink.

"So you're saying you didn't kill anybody?" I ask.

"No. I swear to God. I've never hurt a fly. Not even a convict. Sure, the other guys would rough them up, but not me. Though I'll tell you, I wish to God that I was the one to kill Earl."

"What were you doing in that hunting cabin?"

"Me and my pal, Eric," he says, pointing at a basset hound in the window, "Were scoping the cemetery out."

I frown. I'm still not entirely convinced.

Ben holds his hands up, liquor sloshing, cigarillo in the corner of his mouth. "I get it. So, I'm going to show you something. And maybe you'll think it's all been me because of it, but I wanna show you it anyway."

He gets to his feet and stumbles into the cabin, using the door frame and walls as support. I wait holding my breath, keeping my eyes fixed on the dark doorframe. When Ben emerges, I hone in on what he's holding and put my fingers to my lips. It's a battered, yellowing tarot card.

"The ten of swords," Ben says. "A bad one, apparently. This was left on the bedside table when Shelley was taken."

Ben approaches me cautiously like I'm a wild animal and prone to biting. He hands the card over, and I examine it. It matches the Sola Busca style of the rest of them. "But how do I know—"

"You don't. But I'm telling you, I haven't killed anyone."

"Then why did Mia call you?"

"Because she believed me. She wanted to make things right with me and her dad."

"Were you the one in the car with her that night?"

"I was not," Ben says, meeting my gaze.

"Then who was?"

"Come on, Bridget," Ben says encouragingly, his voice not much louder than a whisper.

"Seriously, I have no idea."

"I think your boy Stanley might've taken over the family business."

CHAPTER TWENTY-NINE

A STORM IS ROLLING IN AS WE MAKE OUR WAY BACK TO Serenity Springs, tinging the sky with green. The clouds are laced with ash and black smoke and though I feel Noah's eyes on me, I can't peel my gaze away. I can barely even blink. Even though it's frightening, it's so beautiful—the sky and the town. I'd almost forgotten. I haven't been looking lately.

"What are you thinking about?" he asks, his voice cutting through the quiet of the car.

I finally blink. "Hmm?" I reply blankly.

"You haven't said a word since we left the cabin. So I was just wondering what you think about… all of that. Do you think Ben is telling the truth?"

"Maybe," I say slowly. "I mean, it all adds up."

"Even the part about Stanley being a murderer?"

"No. He's definitely wrong about that. But everything else is within the realm of possibility."

"Should we call the cops? We could tell them what he told us. I'll back you up."

I rub my exhausted eyes and feel wetness on my fingertips. "I have no idea," I admit. "We probably should. I don't want to get in trouble for withholding information."

"But you don't want to?" Noah prompts, sensing my hesitation and uncertainty.

"Ugh. I don't know. I trust Donna, but this is complicated. She's sure that Ben did it, and she has an officer in her ear who knows Ben and thinks he's guilty of killing Shelley."

"So the force might be biased."

"Maybe. I'd like to think otherwise, but it's hard to say. I think… I think I want to look into Earl some more before I cause another Archie situation. And when I have some more information, I'll tell Donna about Ben."

"Alright, whatever you want to do."

I bury my face in my hands. "God. I don't know."

"Sleep on it," Noah advises. "You can tell her in the morning if you see fit."

"Yeah. You're right. I'm too tired to think right now. All I know is that I need to talk to Stanley. Hopefully, he knows more about Earl and his mom's suicide than he lets on." Noah becomes strangely quiet, and I turn to him. "What is it?"

"I know Stanley is your friend, but could Ben be right about him? I mean, he wouldn't be the first 'nice' serial killer. A lot of these guys have been well-liked."

"I get what you're saying, but why would Stanley 'take over the family business'? He clearly hates his dad."

"I don't know. Trauma, grooming, head trauma. All of the above." He shrinks, slightly. "Sorry, you're the investigator."

"Don't apologize. You're making many a valid point, and I don't want to overlook anything. There's been enough of that in this town. So consider Stanley to be officially on my list. Mind you, I think I'd notice if he had head—" My mouth falls open, but no words come out.

"What?" Noah asks, wide-eyed.

"Speak of the damn Devil," I say in disbelief, gesturing at the dark-haired figure walking along the Knobbles, his hands shoved into his coat pockets.

"Oh, wow. That's Stanley, isn't it?"

"Sure is. Pull over so I can say hi." Noah doesn't need to be told twice, and we pull alongside Stanley with smiles on our faces. I roll down the manual window as quickly as I can, and call out, "Stanley!"

Stanley turns on his heel, beaming back. Then, he looks past me, and his expression darkens as he lays on Noah. "Birdie," he says neutrally. "What's up?"

"Just wanted to say hi," I chirp merrily as if I can't sense the building tension between the two men.

"You didn't reply to my last email," Stanley replies, pulling his eyes away from Noah with seemingly great effort. "It was about the other night."

"Crap, sorry. I've been so busy, and my inbox is overflowing. Sooo many journalists."

"Well, do me a favor and delete it. I'd had a lot to drink when I wrote it." He flushes furiously and drops his gaze. I can't tell if he's embarrassed or incensed, but it's unpleasant to watch all the same as he begins to kick his feet. "I kind of poured my heart out. Ridiculous, really. You told me how you felt, and I should've left well enough alone."

"Oh," I reply, completely mortified.

"I suppose this is why you weren't interested?" he asks, gesturing vaguely in Noah's direction.

"No, Stanley, it's not like that. We just weren't a match romantically. I didn't get with Noah until after our date."

"It's fine. You were playing the field, and he won." He eyes Noah scornfully. "Nice truck," he adds sarcastically.

"Thanks, man," Noah says enthusiastically, as if Stanley's tone went over his head. I know that he's just playing nice. After all, Stanley isn't wrong. Noah did win my heart.

"Well, I have to get going," Stanley replies. "Nice seeing you, Bridget."

"Yeah," I say slowly, watching him in shock as he stalks away.

Noah pulls back onto the road, and as I wind up my window, he says, "I don't think that guy is your friend."

"No," I say distantly, my mind reeling. "Not anymore, anyway. Or, I guess, not ever. I guess he just wanted to get in my pants all along."

"I'm sorry, Birdie. That really sucks. Are you okay?"

I smile weakly. "Yeah, I'm fine. But maybe there's more to Stanley than meets the eye."

Noah and Buckaroo stay over again, and mercifully, Buckaroo did not destroy the apartment in our absence. I know he's a good boy, but he's also a big hyper boy. Yet, there he is, lying on the couch, a perfect angel. Both he and his dad are easy-going house guests, happy to entertain themselves and let me get on with what needs doing. This works for me; I don't like hosting. At least, not all of the time.

I'm stressed, so I take a long bath and wash away a weird morning, and then I turn to deep cleaning, reorganizing, and shifting furniture. Sometimes, a clean space, a good rearrange, and a lit candle can do wonders. After that, I cook, even though Noah tries to force me to sit down and take a nap. I make ravioli from scratch, and it's not very good, but it keeps my hands, and later my mouth, busy. When it's all over, and there's literally nothing left to do, I begin to pace, making notes about the case on my phone and to his immense credit, Noah doesn't complain once about this. He simply watches TV on my laptop while sipping on a cup of decaf.

"I'll call her in the morning," I say, my mind finally made up, as I jump into bed with Noah. "It'll weigh too heavily on my conscience otherwise, and I won't be able to sleep."

"Good idea. And she can only bring Ben in for questioning, right? Like he's not going straight to the gallows."

"Yeah, exactly," I say, gaining confidence. "And Donna will listen to me. I'm sure of it. Plus, who knows? Maybe Ben is guilty, and he's playing mind games to throw me off the scent. He's smart enough for a little subterfuge." I pause and narrow my eyes as I look at the laptop screen. "What are you watching?"

"Deep sea fishing."

"Jesus," I say, tilting my head at the grim and stressful-looking scene. The rocking of the boat is making me feel unwell.

"It helps take my mind off things," Noah explains. "Because nothing could be worse than that."

I continue to stare, and though my cortisol levels don't lower, I am wholly distracted from my own life. All I can think about is those fishermen. "You might be on to something."

I flop my head onto his lap, and he begins to toy with my hair as the episode comes to an end. "Do you want to watch another one?"

"Yes, please," I moan as if the idea is somehow erotic. I'll take all the escapism I can get, even if it's terrifying.

"Popcorn?"

"Please."

"Your wish is my command," Noah replies dutifully, moving from the bed toward the living room.

"It's in the cupboard above the oven," I say, missing his fingers on my scalp. "Triple butter."

"I like your style."

As Noah takes care of snacks, I change into more comfortable clothes—just my underwear and a tank top—and slip into bed. I changed the sheets earlier and shaved my legs, and the feeling is heavenly. I love cleanliness. Perhaps to an obsessive degree. Luckily, Noah has seen this aspect of my personality in action and doesn't seem to mind.

Then my phone buzzes, and my relaxation is shattered. I resist the urge to scream into my pillow as I reach for it. It could be anyone calling, but I fear that it's Donna. That she's somehow found me out. That I'm in for a timeout and a scolding.

I flip it over, see 'Dolly' on the screen, and hastily answer my ex-boss's call. Her voice crackles, and I can't understand a word. The connection must be poor, wherever she is, but I wait it out. Dolly wouldn't call me late if it wasn't for a good reason, though I fear I might still be in for an earful. I did quit unexpectedly after all and did not fulfill my two weeks. I haven't heard from Maisy either, and I expect that she hasn't been saying the most flattering things about me since my abrupt departure.

"Birdie," Dolly eventually says. "Sorry, horrible signal at Sproutville."

"You're still there?" I ask, checking the time and seeing that it's ten past nine. Far later than I thought it was.

"I had a bit of paperwork to catch up on after my holiday. But if I'm honest, I've hardly looked at it."

"What have you been doing instead?"

"Calling everyone I know."

"Wait, why? What's going on?" I ask, eyeing Noah, who stands in the doorway looking concerned.

"Maisy didn't show up for work today. She had an afternoon shift, the one to seven. And at first I didn't think much of it. I mean, it's not like it's the first time. No offense, but none of you are particularly reliable, Maisy least of all. But she always texts me with some sort of cockamamie excuse, which I know is code for 'shacked up.'"

"But not today?"

"No. And she wouldn't answer her phone, not for me or anyone. Tracy thinks she's run away with a man. Some sort of Twitter post alluded to it. Something about a 'divine reconnection.'"

"That doesn't sound good, considering her exes."

"Exactly my thoughts."

"When did she post that?" I question, reaching for a scrap piece of paper and pen.

"Ten to two. Today."

In a way, this is a relief. That means that as of only eight hours ago, Maisy was alive and well. And while she usually contacts Dolly when she's going to miss a shift, that's not always the case.

Dolly is over seventy, and her memory is not as sharp as mine. There have definitely been a few instances of radio silence, especially when Maisy was hooking up with an ex. This concept of 'divine reconnection' and fate intervening is not a new one.

"I'll message some of the exes on Facebook," I say, putting my pen down after scribbling some notes.

"Have fun with that," Dolly replies snarkily, and I prickle slightly. Yes, there are a lot of them to remember, and yes, it will be challenging to recall each one, but there's no need for criticism. No one is perfect. We all have our flaws. Maisy's weakness may be shady men, but I understand her struggle the same way I would sympathize with someone addicted to alcohol or drugs. It stems from pain and trying to fill a void. Breaking a habit takes tremendous effort, as poor Keith could attest to.

"Thanks," I reply, trying my best not to sound moody. "And, please, go home. I've got it from here."

"Will you call the police if you can't find her?"

"Of course," I reassure her, and it's the truth. It may be embarrassing for her when she resurfaces, but perhaps hitting rock bottom will encourage her to finally climb out of the hole she's dug.

CHAPTER THIRTY

SLEEP EVADED ME ONCE AGAIN, AS MY PHONE BLEW UP repeatedly with messages from Maisy's nocturnal ex-boyfriends. When their replies—and attempts at hitting on me—yielded no results, I called the police as promised. Annoyingly, despite there being a serial killer on the loose, the discovery of nine bodies within the past fortnight, and my relationship with Donna, they were very blase. Which is probably because this is not the first time Maisy has been reported missing since moving to Serenity Springs, a fact unbeknownst to me until now. In fact, this marks the fifth time. Her concerned out-of-town parents were the ones who contacted the police the previous four times. And just as Dolly said, every time they located her, they found her safe, sound, and 'shacked up.' I'm still not reassured when the call ends, and I call Maisy ten times before falling asleep with my phone in my hand.

I am jolted awake by the sound of Buckaroo's frenzied barking and howling. His paws are pounding against my front door as if he's trying to break it down. In a panic, I throw off the covers and rush out of bed with Noah at my heels. As we struggle to calm Buckaroo for the sake of my poor neighbors, I assume it's just a false alarm caused by Buckaroo's first time in a complex. However, when I finally manage to pry open the door, with Noah holding Buckaroo back, I'm met with an unusual sight. A crudely made cardboard box sits on the tiled floor, and much like Ben's letter, it has no address or name on it.

"What is it?" Noah asks from afar, carrying Buckaroo into the bathroom and shutting the door. The dog quickly falls quiet. For whatever reason, he's obsessed with the bathtub and views it as some sort of luxury dog bed.

I hold the package in my hands, unsure of what to make of it. I don't remember ordering anything, but here it is on my doorstep. I cautiously bring it inside and shut the door behind me. Placing it on the kitchen table, a sense of unease washes over me as I'm reminded of the ending to *Se7en*.

Noah and I must be on the same page because as he returns to the kitchen, he asks, "What's in the box?" in his best Brad Pitt impression.

It almost makes me smile. Almost. But I'm too anxious about the unknown contents to do anything other than grimace. I wonder if I should call the bomb squad and press my ear to the cardboard before dismissing the idea as ridiculous.

"What's up?" Noah asks, sensing my unease.
"I didn't order this, and it's not addressed to me."
"Who is it addressed to?"
"Nobody."
Noah's grimace matches my own. "Want me to open it?"
"No. I'll do it. Hand me a knife."
"Are you sure?"

"Yeah," I say, only semi-confidently. "Are we the people who die in horror movies?"

"I guess we'll find out."

"Great," I say sarcastically before slicing through the packing tape with the dull blade. It cuts like butter, and with a deep breath, I peel back the cardboard folds. As I reveal the innards, I realize why it was so lightweight. There are only three items inside the cavernous space. A phone sits in one corner, while an empty Sola Busca tarot box taunts me from another. Then I see it—a lock of hair, carefully braided. My stomach churns as I recognize the curly, navy blue lock. It's Maisy's, and I retch with revulsion as Noah hurries to my side.

He looks down into the box and then backs away, holding his chin parallel to the ground, not wanting to look. "Is that—" he begins.

"Yeah," I say, confirming the worst. "I think he has Maisy." At least that's what I try to say; the last sentence is distorted, interrupted by abnormal breathing and a lump in my throat.

Noah suggests calling the police, but I'm already focused on unlocking Maisy's phone. I type in the passcode 811994. It's a simple code that we've joked about before: 81 for the first two letters of "Birdie"—if you squint you can see that the 8 kind of looks like a B—and 1994 for my birth year. It was our little secret.

Unlocking the phone, I see texts—lots of them—but one name stands out in particular as I begin to scroll. Ben Ramsey. I turn the phone to Noah, tap the contact name, watch as his jaw drops, and swivel it back to read.

'I'm in town and want to catch up,' said Ben.

'I don't know,' Maisy replied.

'Please. We were good together.'

'No, we weren't.'

'Well, maybe we could be. I have some whiskey with your name on it.' Ben's message is followed by a childish, winky face.

'Ugh. Pull my leg.'

'Let me pick you up.'

'Fine.'

Maisy's responses may seem nonchalant, but I know there's more to them than that. She has a tendency to act distant and play hard to get when she's interested in someone, and it's clear that she is attracted to Ben despite their age difference and his reputation. Personally, I don't see what she sees in him; he doesn't fit her usual type. At least not physically. But clearly, there's something there that I'm not seeing.

"Get dressed," I command. "We're paying Ben another visit."

As Noah drives, I call Donna's number with trembling fingers. I don't even bother with a greeting as she answers. "Has anyone attempted to access Lovebird's Nest?" I ask urgently.

"No. I have security measures in place—cameras and armed officers. Why do you ask?"

"My best friend, Maisy, didn't show up for work yesterday. And this morning, I found a box on my doorstep containing her hair, phone, and an empty tarot box."

Donna's response is filled with expletives and possibly the sound of something being punched. I can relate to her fury.

"Was there anything else in the box? Some sort of clue?" she asks, panting.

"Yep," I reply bitterly, clutching my phone tightly. "Ben Ramsey sent her a text. Apparently, they're 'exes' of some sort."

"Jesus. Okay. Wait, what are you doing? Is that a car I hear?"

"I'm going to talk to him," I say firmly, grateful that Noah is willing to go along with my plan as he puts the pedal to the metal.

"Birdie," Donna says warily.

"I'll drop you a pin," I say before doing just that. "Just give me a head start. I need to talk to him myself."

"How did you find out where he is? Actually, never mind. I don't want to know. And fine, but please stay safe. Does he know you're coming?"

"No. I don't think he knew that I had Maisy's passcode. He was taunting me, but now the tables have turned."

"Birdie, honey, you sound unhinged. Pull over and let me handle this."

"I'm not behind the wheel," I retort, feeling just as unhinged as Donna thinks I sound. "Please, just let me do this. This is my best friend we're talking about."

Donna sighs. "I'll give you five before I send officers over. The location you've dropped is ten minutes away. If you're nearly there, that gives you fifteen."

"Thank you. Seriously."

I hang up before she can further attempt to dissuade me, and I nod at Noah, my adrenaline pumping. He doesn't slow down, doesn't doubt me, and we are at Ben's house within three minutes. It doesn't give us long, but it's just enough.

I exit the car and slam the door so loudly behind me it sounds like a gunshot, and before long, Ben is in the front doorway, wearing a shirt and jeans and looking like he's seen a ghost.

I bellow Ben's name, my voice ringing out with a deep, almost growling timbre. "Where is she?" I demand, my anger ringing clear via every syllable.

"Where is who?" he stammers, his tough-guy, noir-detective facade crumbling under my intensity.

"Maisy. Maisy Jenkins, my best friend," I snap back at him.

"Maisy?" He looks genuinely startled for a moment before regaining his composure. "God, I haven't seen her in..."

"So, you do know her?" I interrupt impatiently.

"Yeah...we dated briefly a few years ago. If you can even call it that."

My hands shake with rage as I unlock my phone and shove it in his face, revealing the incriminating messages between him and Maisy. His already crumbling demeanor weakens, and he stumbles over his words, trying to come up with an excuse.

Then I see it—the button on his plaid shirt. It matches the missing one I found at Lovebird's Nest. Without a word, I reach into my pocket and pull out the button, holding it up to the gap in his shirt. His eyes widen in fear as he shakes his head frantically. "No, no. It's not what you think."

"I think it's exactly what I think. So, where is she?"

"No, seriously, that button... Where did you find it?"

"Lovebird's Nest. The same place you've taken all your victims. I found it after Mia went missing. It was in the mud by some tire tracks. I figured it belonged to the killer."

"No, Bridget, that button—"

"Save it," I snap, my heart pounding in my chest. "The police are on their way. But if you tell me where Maisy is, maybe they'll let you off easy." My composure cracks and breaks as we make eye contact. I want to get down on my knees and beg the question, 'Is she still alive?'

"Bridget," Ben says softly, holding out his hands, palms up.

"Fuck you," I hiss, striding back to the car, before calling out over my shoulder, "I hope Sheriff Mercer tears you apart."

"It's Stanley!" Ben calls after me. "It's always been the goddamned Crawfords!"

I scramble back into the car, slamming the door shut with a resounding thud. Ben's cries are muffled by the metal and glass, but I can still see the desperation etched on his face as Noah puts the car in reverse. In an act of sheer desperation, Ben throws himself at the hood of the car and ends up sprawled face down in a pile of wet mud. I grip even more tightly on the wooden button of his shirt.

"Hi, Birdie." Donna's voice comes through the phone speaker, soothing and soft.

"Hi," I reply shortly, unable to hold back my frustration as I lay in bed, my eyes puffy from crying. Noah sits beside me, rubbing my arm, primarily fixated on a *Pawn Wars* rip-off playing quietly on my laptop. I'm grateful for his distraction; I was getting sick of him treating me like a hospice patient.

"We went to the pin you dropped," Donna says.

"And Ben is in custody?"

"No. Unfortunately, by the time we arrived, Ben was gone."

I cover my mouth with my hand, stifling a sob. Why didn't I just call the police in the first place? All I've done is let Ben into my life, and they would've been able to get much more out of him than I did. All I have is this stupid button and a bunch of lies.

"God," I whimper.

"It's not all bad news," she continues. "He left a note confessing to all of his crimes, even going back to Gina and Carrie."

"Does he mention Earl Crawford at all?"

"Yes. He says he used him to cover up his crimes," Donna says, maintaining her soothing tone.

"Did he kill Joanna?"

"It doesn't say, I'm afraid. Perhaps Earl did kill his wife, which would've given credence to Ben's pick of scapegoat." Donna sighs, listening to my insuppressible sobs. "We'll find him. I promise."

"What about Maisy?"

"He didn't mention her in the note, but I'm sure that we'll know more soon. I'll be in touch, but I have to go for now. Please, look after yourself."

The call ends, and I slap my palms over my eyes. "God," I cry, wanting to scream.

"Is there anything I can do?" Noah questions, pausing his show and lying down beside me.

"Yeah. You can take me to see Stanley."

"Are you sure that's a good idea?"

I nod. "I can't just sit around and do nothing. I need to know everything."

"But the texts… Birdie, I think the case is done."

"I know," I sob, frustrated, rolling onto my front. "But I'm not."

"Okay," he whispers, rubbing my shoulders. "We'll go pay Stanley a visit."

CHAPTER THIRTY-ONE

I don't tell Stanley that I'm coming. For one thing, the only contact information I have for him is his email address, and I highly doubt he would even bother responding. But as they say, it's easier to ask for forgiveness than permission. And in this moment, I care little about either. All I want is the truth and for my best friend to be found, safe and sound.

As we turn into the unlocked wrought iron gates, Noah gasps audibly. "I know," I say with a hint of unease in my voice. The imposing house looms before us, its size amplified by the long shadows stretching across the lawn in the bright moonlight.

"Now I see why people think this place is haunted," he says, eyeing the windows suspiciously.

"Funny you should mention that."

Noah looks at me, appalled. "Please don't tell me you've seen a ghost here."

I fall silent, a smirk playing across my lips despite everything.

"Birdie?" he prompts impatiently.

"You told me not to tell you!" I protest.

"You're right. I don't want to know."

"It was probably just a trick of the light," I say. "I was also looking through binoculars." Thinking about it, I don't know what I believe. I've been so busy I haven't had much time to contemplate the afterlife or the spiritual realm. I suppose before now I vaguely believed that there was *something* after death, but I didn't know what. Suddenly what we're doing seems a lot less funny. We're about to enter—if Stanley permits it—a possibly, actually haunted house. "I saw a pale woman in one of the top-floor windows," I say, pointing upward.

In the glow of the headlights, a pale figure materializes before us in the dark, and I scream as I slam on the brakes. Noah and I lunge forward from the sudden halt, and I clasp a hand to my mouth in embarrassment as Stanley turns to look at us. and my heart leaps into my throat, causing me to let out a blood-curdling scream. He cocks his head curiously, like a dog, as I offer a sheepish wave.

Hesitantly, he waves back. He's dressed for the weather in a long wool coat, buttoned up to his neck, pleated slacks, and rubber boots. He's clearly been outside for a while—his shoes are coated in mud, as are the ankles of his pants.

"Stay here," I tell Noah, and I exit the vehicle before he can protest. I can feel his eyes on me like a hawk as I approach Stanley. Stanley is also staring, unblinking. I feel like I'm trying to mediate a hostage situation. That Noah is the FBI—waiting to strike, the red dot of his sniper rifle aimed squarely at Stanley's forehead—and I am the loved one, hoping to talk Stanley out of what he's doing. It's tense, to say the least, and I stop within a safe distance.

"Hi," I say.

"Hi. What are you doing here?"

"I came here to tell you that I'm sorry."

"What for?" he asks, as if our interaction yesterday hadn't been beyond bizarre.

"I wasn't honest with you, and I didn't mean to hurt your feelings. I really wasn't with Noah yet, when I came here and we kissed, but he was in my life, and I did have feelings for him."

"No, Birdie, it's fine, really. I overreacted," Stanley says, holding up his hands, metaphorically waving a white flag. "I'm jealous, sure, but I shouldn't have behaved like a child. And I hope you didn't feel that I was 'slut shaming' you or anything like that. Of course, a girl like you would be in high demand."

"Honestly, this is the first time in my life that two guys have liked me at once."

"Well, I could say my timing was off in that case, and that I wish I met you sooner. But if there's no spark now…" He trails off and shrugs, before offering me a small smile. "He can come out, you know. Your boyfriend."

"He's not—" I stop myself. If Noah isn't my boyfriend, then what is he? I smile back, and turn toward the car, beckoning Noah toward us.

He almost crawls out from my tiny Fiat 500, and approaches, polite as ever, hand outstretched for Stanley to shake. "Noah Fletcher," he says, voice low and measured.

"Stanley Crawford," the other man replies, his smile faltering ever so slightly. "So, did you two really come all the way out here just to apologize? Because while I appreciate the gesture, it wasn't necessary. And you know I'd never hurt you, right?" Stanley asks, concerned, looking between Noah and me, realizing that he is here as my bodyguard.

"I'm finding it a little hard to trust people right now," I say. "No offense."

"None taken. Just wanted you to know."

I clear my throat. "But no, I didn't just come to apologize. Can we walk and talk?"

"Sure," he says lightly, shrugging nonchalantly. "That's what I was doing anyway. The walking part, I mean."

Stanley moves closer to me, cautiously, clearly not wanting to spook either me or Noah. Noah, too, moves to my side, and in a line, we wander aimlessly into the dark. The only light guiding us is from the soft glow emanating from the house and the now-distant beams of my car's headlights. As we venture further, the ground beneath my feet becomes soft and squelchy, and soon my boots are also caked with mud. I feel guilty for judging Stanley for being out at night; before recent events, I used to take nightly walks without a second thought.

As we continue on, we form a triangle with Stanley in the lead, and I realize that I am not speaking at all. Instead, I am simply following in his steps. It becomes clear that he has a destination in mind, and soon enough, we come upon the cemetery with its solar lights and stone benches. It's a good place to talk, no doubt, but I hear Noah's breath catch as he lays eyes on it. I hadn't warned him about this, and like me, cemeteries are not his favorite locale. I make a similar noise when I see a fresh patch of earth, recently dug. A chill runs down my spine at the thought that Ben may have been right—what if Maisy's body is buried here? It would certainly be one hell of a hiding spot.

"New arrival?" I ask before cringing at my insensitivity. "Sorry. It's not your grandmother, is it?"

"It's fine. And fortunately not. Grandma, I imagine, will live to see triple digits. No, that is the last of my cats. Boudica," Stanley replies, his voice thick with emotion.

"Was it old age?" Noah asks sympathetically.

"Yes, in a sense. I made the call, but she was twenty-one, believe it or not. I got back from the vet's around lunchtime." He sighs. "I went for a consultation with her yesterday and me and the vet agreed it was time. I was in town buying her some treats when I saw you. And, again, I'm sorry for taking it out on you."

"No, it's fine, seriously," I say softly. "I'm so sorry about Boudica."

"She was an asshole and ruled over the others with an iron fist, but I'll miss her all the same."

"I had a cat just like that," Noah chimes in. "Sultan. I rescued him. He only had three legs and one eye, and he was a real shit. Spiteful. Bullied me and my roommate. But I still miss him like crazy. Every time I put a glass of water on the counter I'm waiting for him to come knock it over."

Stanley looks at Noah, his features soft, and he nods. "Even the most difficult loved ones are still loved. And it's not always in spite."

"Do you feel that way about your dad?" I ask boldly.

Stanley looks at me, and his smile is lopsided as if he's only half-amused. "Is that why you're here? To talk about dear Dad?"

"In a way."

Stanley stares at me expectantly and sits on one of the stone benches. He's giving me the stage.

I shift uncomfortably. "You told me this place wasn't haunted."

"Because it isn't."

"Well, I swear I saw a face in the window."

Stanley leans forward, eyes wide, before glancing upwards at a row of windows. "Really?"

"I think it was your mom. At least that's what Charlie Wilkins said."

"Charlie...?"

"He's Carrie Olson's grandfather. One of the murdered teenagers."

"Ah. And he suspects my dad had something to do with all of that."

"He definitely thinks he murdered your mother. So does your grandmother."

"Do they now?" Stanley asks, his expression darkening ever so slightly.

"What do you think? I know they buried an empty coffin."

Stanley stiffins, frowning. "What? Who told you that?"

"Wilma. She says your dad paid off the coroner and the sheriff. Convinced them it was a suicide even though the body was never found."

As Stanley stares at me, his eyes become wet, and though he hastily reabsorbs the fluid, I can tell that this is brand-new information for him. "Why were you speaking with my grandmother?" he asks.

"Because Charlie Wilkins recommended I do so. I'm so sorry. You didn't know."

"I did not. He told me he found her hanging in the attic and locked me in my room until everything was 'done.' I assumed he was being kind. Not wanting me to be traumatized by the sight. In retrospect, that was wishful thinking. My father never did a kind thing for me, not ever." He pauses. "And you really think you saw her in the house?"

"I don't know for sure, but that's what it looked like."

"Hm," he says mildly, though I can feel his pain from a distance. "Well, I suppose if anyone has unfinished business, it's a murder victim."

"Yeah, I guess so," I reply quietly, worried this information might send him down an unhealthy grief spiral.

"So, Ben Ramsey confessed to everything," I say, getting to the real point.

"Ben Ramsey?" Stanley questions, well-groomed brows knitted together.

"He was a homicide detective over in Cascadia from 1999 to 2017. He was looking into your dad for a while. Apparently, he thought he was a serial killer."

"Really? I've never heard of him."

"I guess your dad kept a lot from you," I say lightly, trying to keep the frustration out of my voice.

"Apparently," Stanley says coldly, vitriol aimed at the dead, not me. He reaches inside a coat pocket and produces a flask before sipping. He doesn't glug it like Ben did from his own flask. His sip is cautious and mindful, a small layer of padding against the blows I'm dealing with. "So what did he confess to?"

"That he was using your dad as a scapegoat and that he killed Gina, Carrie, Lucia, Brad, Sanya, Jayden, Mia, and his own girlfriend, Shelley."

"Jesus," Stanley says, taking another swig, this one borne by shock. "But not my mother?"

"Not your mother. And not my best friend either."

Stanley looks at me sharply. "Your friend is missing?"

"Yes. Maisy Jenkins."

"Sorry, another name that doesn't ring a bell," Stanley says sheepishly. "I hope you get the answers you're looking for. Really, Birdie. And I'm sorry that I don't have the information that you're looking for."

"It's fine," I exhale, exhausted. "I just thought…"

"That I was the last piece of the puzzle?"

"Yeah."

Stanley nods and looks at me sympathetically. "I'm afraid I've been living in the dark. My grandmother would know far more than I do."

"Was there a note?" I ask.

"A note?"

"Yeah, a suicide note from your mother."

Stanley blinks rapidly as if trying to remember. "Yes. There was. And I believed it to be authentic. I knew her handwriting well because we wrote notes to each other all the time. I'd slip them under her bedroom door when she'd lock herself away for days on end. Then I'd sit and wait in the hallway for her to send one back. In the last year of her life, I saw her more on paper than in the flesh."

"What did the note say?"

Stanley sips again. "I can't remember exactly. It's been seven years, after all. But she mostly just apologized to me."

"Do you think it could have been coerced?"

Stanley sighs. "Does it even matter anymore? He's dead. She's dead. There's no one to arrest. I advise you to leave me to my family drama and focus on this Ben guy."

"You're right," I say, holding up a hand apologetically. "Forgive me. It's just my investigative nature."

"I get it," he says genuinely, surprisingly unfazed. "But I'm afraid I have little for you, and I don't think any of it will lead you to your friend."

"Do you mind if I—"

Resisting an eye roll, Stanley holds out a hand to me to continue before taking another swig.

"Was he abusive, your father?"

"Of course he was. The man was a monster."

"And do you think that maybe he could have killed other people?"

Stanley sits with the question for a moment while Noah takes a seat on the back doorstep. "Yes. But if he killed those teenagers, then who killed Mia?"

"Exactly my question. This is why, at this point, I'm willing to believe Ben's confession. But does the name Bunny Sullivan ring any bells?"

"Nope. Not even a little bit. Who's she?"

"A hitchhiker that went missing in 1982. She went missing, and your grandparents believed your dad was responsible, which is why they moved to Northern California."

Stanley's expression turns from ambivalent to angry. There is so much he doesn't know about his own life. "Seriously?"

"Deadly."

He curses under his breath. "Any more big reveals, Birdie? I'm thinking I should've been taking notes."

I balk. "Sorry. I kind of… I thought you knew everything."

"Well you thought wrong," he snaps before softening. "Sorry. Sorry. This is just a lot, you know?"

"I know. Just two more questions, and I'll leave you alone."

"Okay. Fine," he retorts, clearly at the end of his rope.

"Why did you tell me that your dad died in Northern California?"

Stanley pales as if that were even possible, considering his already alabaster skin. "I… I didn't want to tell you the truth. That I found him on the kitchen floor. It messed me up. And it's hardly first-date conversational material."

He's not wrong. I hesitate before asking my next question, but I do so anyway. "Did you kill him? Your father? Your grandmother believes that you did. She even gave specific examples of how you could have induced a heart attack."

Stanley laughs loudly and abruptly, looking at me as if I'm telling a joke. "You're not serious."

"I'm curious as to why she thinks that. I mean, who could blame you?"

"No. I didn't kill my dad. Was I glad when he died? Sure. But I had nothing to do with it, I swear. And it's not as if I could've paid off the coroner. They were best friends. If I'd killed my father, I'd already be in prison."

"Okay," I say, trying to defuse the increment of anger. "I believe you."

"Who knows? Maybe this Ben guy killed my parents, too," Stanley spits, grief making itself visible in his delicate features, aging him by a decade. "Maybe he owed my dad money. Maybe my dad knew what he was up to. Maybe he was in love with my mom—plenty of guys were."

"Well, hopefully, Ben will come clean about everything. Including your parents."

"Well," Stanley says, getting to his feet. "If you're going to find this prick, you better get a good night's sleep." He walks toward Noah, who hastily stands and clears a path. "Goodnight, Birdie. Noah. Don't show up here without permission again."

"Understood," Noah says, and I half expect him to salute Stanley.

"Goodnight, Stanley," I say softly. "And please, email me."

"You first," Stanley says before opening the door and disappearing into the terrifying haunted house.

CHAPTER THIRTY-TWO

RELIEF WASHED OVER ME WHEN WE RETURNED FROM Crawford Manor. The tension between my friend and I had been mended, and no more secrets lingered. At least not answerable ones. I was so relaxed that I was able to eat, wash, and do some ironing, and was generally in a good mood.

Then, 10:00pm rolled around, and Noah and Buckaroo fell asleep, leaving me all alone in my drafty apartment. The breeze seeping through the cracks seemed to whisper to me, and no matter how comfy I made myself or how much I focused on reading, I could still hear it. Eventually, I opted for earplugs, and after a lot of tossing and turning, I managed to fall asleep. Boudica—the warrior, not the cat—filled my dreams. She, red-haired, wild, and beautiful, led me back to that grave at the Crawford cemetery and shook her head at the overturned earth.

"The grave," I gasp, jolting upright in bed as my grandfather clock announces that it's midnight.

"What?" Noah mumbles.

"Boudica's grave."

"Yeah?"

"It was fresh."

"Uh-huh," he says, rousing himself from his slumber and rubbing his bleary eyes in confusion.

"Well, what if Ben was right about Stanley taking over the family business? What if it was Maisy down there?" I ask, my voice trembling.

"Birdie," Noah says softly. "You've spent all evening talking about how much you believe Stanley. Plus, that patch of dirt was way too small for a person."

I chew my lower lip. "I know what I said, and I know that it's small, but maybe he…" I stop myself. My unspoken words sicken me.

"Maybe he what?" Noah asks, propping himself up in bed, staring at me in awe.

"Maybe he dismembered her," I whisper, my stomach continuing to churn. I suddenly regret eating so much cheese.

"Jesus, Birdie," Noah exclaims, his face contorted by disgust.

"Well, it's possible."

"Are you serious? You think he could've done something like that?"

"I don't know," I say, throwing myself back and missing the headboard by an inch. "He seemed like he was telling the truth, but did you see how muddy he was?"

"Yeah. I did. Did you see how muddy we were when we got home?"

I groan. "I know. It's just bugging me. I mean, I've been to the manor before, but I never saw a cat."

"He did say Boudica was an asshole. Normally asshole cats keep to themselves around strangers. Maybe he locked her away in the bedroom so she wouldn't attack you."

"That's true," I say, a little bitterly.

"Birdie," Noah soothes, "I trust you implicitly, but I think you're overthinking things."

"Yeah," I sigh, rolling onto my front before burying my face in my pillow.

"Hey."

"What?"

"You're amazing."

I smile into the fabric, and I very nearly tell him that I love him, but it's way too soon for that. "You're not so bad yourself," I say, muffled.

"You're not going to do anything crazy, are you?"

I slowly roll onto my side and turn to face him, shifting closer so that our bodies are pressed together. I lean in and kiss him deeply, feeling the warmth of his lips against mine. He moves a hand towards my waist, but I gently retract.

"Sorry," I say apologetically. "I'm just so exhausted."

"Don't worry about it," he replies, kissing my cheek.

"I promise I won't do anything crazy. Go back to sleep."

His eyes are heavy with sleep as he nods, and within seconds, he is snoring softly. Taking advantage of his deep slumber, I quietly slip out of bed and make my way over to the built-in wardrobe. I carefully select a comfortable white tank top, a brown boiler suit, a navy puffer jacket, and a pair of thick socks. The boiler suit and jacket I have been meaning to sell for months because they don't suit me. But tonight, they are perfect.

Pulling my hair into a bun and covering it with Noah's beanie to hide its luminous color, I slip on my trusty Wellington boots before grabbing my flashlight, car keys, and phone. With one last glance at Buckaroo, who is happily munching on a treat, I move towards and then through the front door, close it behind me, tiptoe down the stairs, and slip outside into the cool night air.

With each step closer to the cemetery, the same sentence loops through my mind like a broken record. *This is crazy. This is crazy. This is crazy.* And it truly is, I know that. Common sense and fear scream at me to turn back before I get myself into trouble, but I can't leave, won't leave without knowing for sure. If it's Maisy down there, in that dark, dirty pit, I need to see her one last time and say goodbye before she becomes evidence, inaccessible, a body, not a person. It may be reckless and foolish, but she's my best friend, and I refuse to wait for bureaucracy, legalities, and red tape to catch up with my investigation. So, I'll just dig it up unnoticed, check inside the hole, and if it's Maisy—or whatever is left of her—I'll call Donna. If it's not, I'll cover it up regardless. Either way, at least I'll know for sure, and worst case scenario, at least I can start grieving. At least she'll be found.

She's not dead; she can't be dead is my next mantra as I stalk toward my destination without the assistance of light. I almost believe it. Or, at least, I hope that I'm wrong.

You're being ridiculous, I tell myself as the cemetery comes into sight.

Shovel in one hand and flashlight on its dim setting in the other, I creep inside. The house is completely dark, which is good news. Stanley must also be asleep. In fact, the whole town seemed to be on my drive out here, which doesn't make me feel any less deranged. I guess it's the person I've become.

As I see the fresh grave, which is lacking a headstone, I push the shovel into the soil, gently. I question myself yet again, and then I think of Maisy, and the adrenaline kicks in, fuelling my temporary insanity. I scoop a pile of dirt from the surface and pile it next to my right foot. Then, I pause, not sure if I want to keep going.

"What the hell are you doing?" I ask myself aloud.

"I was about to ask you the same question," Stanley says from behind, holding a candle in an antique brass holder like a Dickens character. He is, unfortunately, not wearing a nightgown or cap, which would've brought some much-needed levity to the situation. "Electricity is expensive," he explains, tilting his head toward the flame.

"I bet," I say.

"So, would you like to explain yourself, or should I go ahead and call the police?"

"I would like to explain myself."

"Alright," he says, sitting on the stoop that Noah had occupied earlier.

I pluck the shovel out of the soil. "My best friend Maisy is missing."

"I'm aware. You told me earlier today."

"Yeah. But..."

Stanley laughs mirthfully, his upper lip coiled. "Oh, so you think that because I killed my father, that I killed her, too? That maybe I got a taste for blood and killed Mia and that other man as well?"

"Did you?" I ask, taking a step backward and finding myself pressed up against a fence that is too high and too sharp to jump.

"No. And I didn't kill my father either. He was an overweight alcoholic with a congenital heart defect. I can bring you the pathology report if you'd like?"

"No, that's okay," I whisper, scooting along the barrier.

"I'll email it then," he says faux-chipper. "I must have it here somewhere." He opens his phone, begins to scroll, and then tuts. "I had to scan it in ages ago, but it *should* be in my files. I can give you the death certificates, too."

"Stanley, no, it's fine," I stammer, hands up protectively.

He looks up at me. "Oh, don't let me stop you. Keep going."

"What?"

"The grave. You need to know... So, *know*."

"No, it's fine. I was just being stupid."

"Keep going," he growls, pointing at the shovel.

I do as I'm told, almost without resistance, feeling embarrassed.

"Come on, you can do better than that," he coaxes. "I buried her deep."

I keep going, and when the shovel makes contact with a hard, wooden surface, I drop to my knees, humiliated, and proceed with my hands. My nails are soon unpleasantly caked in thick, wet mud, and I want to cry.

"Keep going," he encourages, a sick smile playing across his lips. He is not the man I thought he was, and in a way, I think I might have been right to come out here. I never would've seen this side of him if I hadn't.

I continue to scrape away the earth with my hands to reveal a small wooden coffin with the name Boudica on a bronze placard. I cringe. I wince. I know what he's going to ask me to do next.

"Finish up," he says. "I'd like to go back to sleep. I have work in the morning."

Tentatively, I open the lid, and sure enough, a ginger cat is curled up inside. She looks as if she's merely sleeping, which is a small mercy, but when I look back up at Stanley, I can see tears brimming in his eyes once again. Carefully, I close the lid, place the coffin back into the ground, and stand to rebury her.

"No, let me," he says, standing and striding forward before grabbing the shovel.

"Stanley, I—"

"Are you happy now?" he snaps. "Now that I've entertained your insanity?"

"No."

"No? Seriously? What more could you possibly want from me?" he croaks, silent tears becoming sobs.

"I didn't mean... I'm satisfied. But I'm not happy. Not with myself."

Stanley sighs. "You're a good friend, Bridget. To Maisy, I mean. Now get the fuck off of my property."

My heart races as I stumble backward, almost tripping over the headstones that litter the perimeter of the cemetery. My mission to confront Stanley is finally coming to an end, but one last idea sparks in my mind—something I need to do before I can truly move on from him as a suspect. Fumbling with my phone, I quickly scroll through my contacts until I find the one labeled "Ben" based on the number I saw on Maisy's phone. With a trembling hand, I press call and hastily shove my phone into the padded pocket of my jacket to muffle the sound. The faint ringing on my end echoes around me, but Stanley's phone remains silent. And if it buzzes, he makes no impulsive move to answer it. It's not him. It was never him. It was always just Ben.

With a tremble in my voice, I utter the word "sorry" again, hoping it will somehow soften the blow of my actions. I then begin to run, my feet clumsily tripping over each other, tears streaming down my cheeks. I know that what I have done is unforgivable, and no amount of apologies can change that, and as I stumble back into my car, I know that I deserve whatever punishment is coming my way.

CHAPTER THIRTY-THREE

WHEN I STUMBLED INTO MY APARTMENT LAST NIGHT Noah was waiting for me in the kitchen, which, of course, scared the living daylights out of me. I laughed once I recovered from the shock, but he didn't. His disappointment was well-illuminated by the range hood light. I couldn't blame Buckaroo for tattling on me, but I had hoped Noah would sleep through the brief bout of barking. Alas, my sneaking skills, or lack thereof, had failed me two times in a row, and, I was a teenager all over again, caught in the act of sneaking out. Not that I ever did that as an actual teenager, but I've seen the movies to get the gist.

His distress now feels like a distant memory, as I sit across from Donna, baring the brunt of her displeasure and concern. Noah had quickly turned to comforting me, but if Donna's folded arms and tight expression are anything to go off of, I don't think I'll get any of that here.

She pinches the bridge of her nose. "Let me get this straight. You trespassed not once, but twice last night on Mr. Crawford's property."

"Yes."

"And you dug up a grave?"

"I did."

"Which, as I'm sure you're aware, is a criminal offense."

"Does it help that it belonged to a cat?" I ask meekly.

"Only a little bit. Mr. Crawford is distraught. He marched in here at eight in the morning and told the entire office about what you did. You're lucky that I managed to convince him not to press charges, though I expect your reputation might take a hit."

"Thank you," I say, hands clasped together.

"Don't thank me just yet. I'm still going to have to penalize you."

"Okay," I say, scrunching up my eyes, preparing for impact.

"You are officially no longer a part of this investigation."

I open my eyes wide, and my lips part, ready to protest. I stop myself at the last second, and deflate. "That's understandable."

"I hate to do this, Birdie. I really do. It would be an understatement to call you a major asset, but I can't risk a lawsuit. Or worse, an internal investigation. You're not supposed to have even half of the access to this case that you do. I could lose my job."

"I get it."

She sighs and shakes her head. "What on earth compelled you to do this?"

"I thought..." I trail off before groaning and bury my face in my hands.

"Go ahead, Birdie," Donna says, softening.

I peel my hands from my face, take a deep breath, and begin. "I know that Ben was talking to Maisy. I know that they had a prior relationship. I know that they met up. I also know that he knows Mia, that he's strong and capable, and that he was accused of killing his girlfriend. And there's the button."

"The button?" Donna asks, arching a brow.

I groan again, realizing I forgot to mention this crucial detail earlier. "Yeah. I found a shirt button at Lovebird's Nest on the day we first spoke. I found it by the tire tracks where the car was parked. I didn't think much of it at the time, but I pocketed it anyway, and when I went to confront him I noticed he was missing a button. So, I pulled it out of my pocket and it was a match."

"Meaning he was the one who took Mia to Lovebird's Nest," Donna continues.

"Yeah. It makes sense. It all adds up. He could've used the legal system to his advantage, turning people against Earl, using him as a cover for his own crimes."

"I feel like there's a but coming."

"*But* I have a bad feeling about the Crawfords. Or I did before last night. I spoke to Carrie Olson's grandfather, and he seemed convinced that Earl was a killer."

"Why?"

"I don't know. But Earl's own mother agrees. As you already know."

"Yes, the Bunny Sullivan case. I haven't found much on that I'm afraid, but there's a man who's currently in prison for a string of hitchhiker murders from around the same time period. He lived in this state. A lot of people think he killed Bunny."

"And I'm sure they're right," I say holding up my hands. "It's just that when I spoke to Ben—yes, before Maisy went missing—he was really convincing. He says that he was looking into Earl, so Earl retaliated and framed him for murder. And, he claimed, that Stanley had 'taken on the family business.'"

"That sounds far fetched," Donna says, though I notice her reach for her notepad all the same.

"Yeah, I thought so, too. Which is why I went to speak with Stanley the first time. I wanted to see what he knew. And it turns out that he knew basically nothing. Or, at least, that's what he said. For example, he said that he didn't know about his mom's body being missing. He didn't know that they buried an empty casket."

Donna stops scribbling. "*Birdie.*"

"What?" I ask, and then the penny drops. "Jane Doe."

"Could be," Donna says. "I'll get on that once we're done here. Go on," she insists.

"So, Stanley claimed complete ignorance, and I believed him to a point, but the whole time I'm looking at this freshly dug grave, thinking: what if Maisy is down there? It would be the perfect hiding place."

"Yes, it would."

"And then I asked him point blank if he murdered his dad."

Donna stares at me in shock, her pen pressed hard against the paper.

"I know. But it's what his grandma thought, so I had to ask."

"And I'm assuming he denied it?"

"Yeah, and he told us to get lost. But once I was home I couldn't stop thinking about that grave."

"You needed to know," Donna says in an understanding tone.

I swallow hard, the events of last night seared into my brain and all the feelings associated still burning hot in my nervous system. "Yeah. I couldn't just sit around waiting, not knowing."

Then I relate to Donna about calling the number associated with Ben from Maisy's phone. She listens intently and does a better job concealing her frustration than I would have thought.

"So you were wrong about Stanley?"

"I was," I state confidently.

"And you're sure?" Donna asks.

"Yeah. I was wrong about him. Which means it has to be Ben. All of it."

"Or someone else entirely," Donna mutters, her free hand wavering at her temple. "Christ."

"I know. And I'm so sorry. I've kept information to myself and acted irresponsibly."

"What's done is done. I'm just glad that you're not in a cell right now. Or worse."

"So, what happens now?"

"I will try to identify our Jane Doe and I will find Ben Ramsey."

"And what about me? I have to just… give up?"

"No. But you are no longer officially investigating. So, if you 'stumble' across any information, please call the tip line. But no more criminal activity, please. And for now, go home and sleep. I'll need your help in the future, I'm sure."

"Thank you," I whisper.

"I hope you aren't too disheartened. What you've done here is amazing. You are so good at what you do. I mean, the shirt button detail? That could turn a jury. Seriously. Not to mention everything else. And yeah, it's gotten messy and you've gotten too close, but that's serial killer cases for you. If I was to be any harder on you, I'd be a total hypocrite. And don't forget, I would've never even looked for those missing teenagers if it wasn't for you." She stands, rounds her desk, and puts a gentle hand on my shoulder. "What I'm saying is you've done a good job, Birdie. Let me take it from here."

I smile up at her. "You know, sleep doesn't sound like a bad idea."

"Yeah, those eyebags must weigh a pound a piece," she teases. I must look horrified because she laughs and adds, "Just kidding. You always look perfect."

I know she's just trying to boost my confidence. I must look like a disheveled disaster in comparison to her actual perfection. Her sleek bob that never has a hair out of place, frames her angular face perfect. Her short acrylic nails are both fashionable and practical, like everything else about her. Her brown skin is devoid of any flaws and her lashes and brows are beyond enviable. However, it's not just her appearance that's perfect. She's stunning on the inside, too. I can only hope that she really will find a use for my skills in the future.

"And I will find Maisy," she assures me.

"I know you will. I just—" The dam breaks and tears flow down my face in rivers. "I just want you to find her alive."

"I can't—"

I stop her before she can finish. "I know. I know you can't promise me that. I just hate this. I just... I can't lose anyone else. First Mia, then Keith, and now Maisy. It all feels so..."

"Personal," Donna concludes. "That's because it is. And that's why I still need you. Somehow, you are important in all of this. Beyond being an investigator." She pauses, moving to stand before me. "Hey. Look at me. I get it. But I need you sane and well-rested, okay?"

"Okay," I reply.

Donna gives my shoulder a little squeeze before putting her hand in her pocket. "You are a very brave woman, Bridget Hartley. I want you to remember that."

"I'll try."

Donna flashes me a warm smile. "You can do better than try."

CHAPTER THIRTY-FOUR

I'M LYING ON NOAH'S COUCH UNDER A PATCHWORK QUILT with my head on Buckaroo's warm back. My fingers knead his thick brown fur, and I don't care that I'm covered in the stuff or that he smells of wet dog after his walk. He's so comfortable and comforting; his heartbeat is almost hypnotic, causing me to fade in and out of consciousness. Admittedly, I'd rather cuddle Noah, but he's in the kitchen singing along to Johnny Cash while whipping up something that smells delightfully garlicky. So, I'll happily take his stand-in for now.

A piping hot cup of tea steams before me on the coffee table, but I don't have the energy to sit up and drink it. I can barely even keep my eyes open or speak. Between the guilt, defeat, and the sheer physical toll of recent events, I am completely spent. I want to sleep for a week. I want the couch to swallow me whole.

I groan as the events at Crawford Manor pop into my head for the millionth time, and Buckaroo grumbles and huffs. I apologize for spooking him with a kiss and a scratch, and he settles indignantly. I scoff. He's really the one who owes me an apology, considering his late-night howling got us kicked out of my apartment—not as in evicted, but Buckaroo is no longer welcome, according to the passive-aggressive text from my landlord.

Maybe it's better being at Noah's anyway. As I stare out of the windows, all I can see is inky blackness, and I pretend that we're floating through space, far away from Earth, uncontactable, and all alone together. I think if NASA or whoever announced the first flight to Mars tomorrow, to live out there under some sort of terraformed dome and never come back, I'd be the first one to sign up. Unfortunately, I'll probably just have to settle for a vacation abroad instead.

My family has, as expected, been blowing up my phone all day, and though I've replied and heart-reacted to Ada's ultrasound photos, I don't have the energy for lengthy texts, calls, or explanations. I am humiliated by what happened at Stanley's and mortified that it's become gossip. Admittedly, I think my suffering is completely justified, considering I dug up a grieving man's dead cat, but I still wish I could fast forward through this part of my life.

"I think I have to move!" I call out.

"Fine with me!" Noah replies, turning down the music. "This house is portable. All I need is land. What are you thinking: city, town, or off-grid?"

"Definitely off-grid."

I hear feet pad into the room and look up weakly at Noah. He's dressed in grey sweatpants and a baggy t-shirt, his hair freshly buzzed, and he smells like pine trees and cinnamon. This is nearly enough in and of itself to pull me out of my depression, but not quite. Still, it's a pleasant salve, and I manage to muster a smile as I stare at him sideways.

"I can do off-grid," he murmurs kindly as he approaches the couch. He tucks the hair in my face behind my ear and bends over to kiss my cheek. "It's always been a dream of mine. That's kind of what I came here to do, but I've ended up a lot closer to the action than intended."

I laugh miserably. "No kidding."

"You know none of this is your fault, right?"

"Mm," I grunt.

"Seriously, Birdie."

"So when can we leave?" I ask, changing the subject.

"After I've built your sister's house."

"Can't someone else do that?"

"Unfortunately, I'm a man of my word."

"Great," I say sarcastically. "So much for being a jerk."

"Hey now, I'm still a jerk," he protests.

"No, you're not. You're amazing." I sigh dramatically. "So, how long will it take to build the house?"

"Ten months."

"Seriously? I thought you'd be done before the baby was here."

"Yeah, you did mention that when you first came to look at the site, and I forgot to crush your hopes and dreams."

I snort into Buckaroo. "I guess I don't know much about building houses."

"Well, in your defense, most people don't. And if they did, I'd be out of a job."

"How did you get to be good at so many things?" I ask, gesturing vaguely to the kitchen. He can cook, clean, and build an entire house. He's the full package.

"I should be asking you the same question."

"What am I good at?" I ask, simpering, begging for a compliment.

He smirks that beautiful smirk, sits beside me, slips a hand up the back of my sweater, and begins to scratch gently. "You're good at investigating, bird-watching, and knitting. You're good with kids and dogs, and I know you'll be great at gardening. You're a pretty good driver and very good at picking out outfits and doing your hair and makeup. You're good at antiquing, eating Italian food, and asking questions while watching movies. You're good with people. You're good with me. And that's barely the tip of the iceberg. You're funny, sweet, intelligent, thoughtful, passionate, and loving. You are everything."

I pout, pretending as if I might cry, and I really might. "That's the nicest thing anyone has ever said to me."

"Well, I guess we can add compliments to my list of talents," he teases as he nuzzles my neck with his lips.

"I'm not sure that I am good with people anymore," I say.

"You are. You really, really are. Stanley's just... a really weird guy. And he brought something weird out of you, too."

"You can say that again."

"Stanley is a really weird guy," Noah states.

"Yeah, I don't know how I didn't notice sooner. When I first met him, it was like a dream come true." Noah stops scratching, and I turn to look at him and notice his expression has tightened. "God. I'm sorry. I shouldn't say stuff like that to you."

He shakes his head. "No, it's not that. I'm not jealous. I'm just mad that he let you down so badly. If I hadn't been around and you'd dated him instead, who knows what would've happened to you?" He resumes the physical affection, and I relax. "So, what's the deal? How did you two meet?"

"Are you sure you want to know?"

"Yeah, tell me everything. I can take it. I'm a big boy."

"Ugh. Fine. So, I met him at Notte Stellata, and we were both sitting on the balcony at separate tables with no one else around. We got to chatting, and then that turned to having dinner together. We clicked right away, partly because we liked all of the same things and mainly because I thought he was 'my type.' Which is something I'm now realizing I don't have."

"So we're judging books by their covers?" Noah teases.

"A little bit. And maybe skimming the blurb as well. But after that, I kept bumping into him, and then we started writing each other emails, and he met my parents at the wake. And, yeah. I was pursuing him, but I didn't really know him. Then I went to the manor with him after he saved me from some bloggers and a journalist. We had some wine and ended up kissing. It sucked, to put it lightly. It was like kissing a brother."

"How many brothers have you kissed?" Noah says, pretending to be aghast.

I slap his arm and roll my eyes. "Shut up. You know what I mean. There was no spark. And honestly, I couldn't stop thinking about you. When we'd hugged the day before, I don't know, it was like planets colliding."

"So you looked past my cover and blurb?"

"I never disliked your cover," I say, jokingly seductive and waggling my brows. "But your blurb was hit or miss."

"Hey!"

"I'm just glad I decided to start reading," I say, smiling coyly.

"Very poetic," Noah chuckles, blushing a little bit as he leans in to kiss me.

"It's a lame metaphor," I laugh as he pulls away. "But you get my point."

"I do. And I'm very glad you did end up giving me a chance because this is good. Isn't it?"

He almost sounds unsure, and I roll onto my back so I can look at him properly. "It is," I assure him. "It's really, really good. I don't do *this*. Not ever. I don't have sex right away, and I never start dating a guy and spend every waking moment with him. I like my space. I honestly hated living with my ex and ended up spending most of my time in the guest bedroom. But I just can't get enough of you."

"Same here. I thought I'd die a bachelor because my social battery is so short-lived. But being with you is as natural as breathing. Like you're a part of me."

"I feel like I've known you forever," I whisper.

"I want to know you forever."

I try to sound playful as I ask the question, "So... what exactly are we?" but then I cringe at how awkward I sound. It feels like I'm back in high school again.

"We're partners in solving crimes," Noah jokes with a wink.

"Come on, be serious," I plead.

He gives me a sincere look and replies, "I see you as my girlfriend and Buckaroo's stepmom."

"And I see you as my boyfriend," I admit, feeling the blood rush to my cheeks. "But that sounds so immature, doesn't it? Girlfriend and boyfriend."

"How about bae?"

"Ew."

"Boo? Beau? My love?" he suggests.

"Blah. No, I think girlfriend works just fine if those are the alternatives, *but* there's a certain *je ne sais quois* about partners."

"Agreed. It's like, are we cowboys? Are we cops? Are we criminal masterminds? Are we looooovers?"

"I like the idea of being both cowboys *and* lovers."

"Put 'em up," Noah says, putting on an Old West accent and pointing finger guns in my direction. I weakly lift my hands up to my face. "Bridget Hartley, there's a million-dollar bounty on your head."

"What's my crime?"

Noah looks self-satisfied as he answers, "You stole my heart."

I burst into tear-inducing laughter and fight him weakly. "You're so cheesy."

"You love it."

"I really do."

"Wanna come help me finish cooking, partner?"

"Yeah. Why not?"

I use a paper napkin to wipe the last remnants of puttanesca sauce from my mouth and sigh contentedly. "That was delicious."

Noah bows slightly in his seat. "Thank you, kindly. It's my mom's recipe."

"Is she Italian?" I ask, realizing I don't know much about Noah's family.

"Half. Her mother grew up in Sicily."

"Have you ever been?"

"No, never. Canada and Mexico are the furthest afield I've ever gone. What about you?"

I nod. "I was fortunate enough to travel to Europe a few times in my early twenties."

"Oh, to be a Hartley."

"We should go there together after the house is finished. It could be a reward for all our hard work. And who knows?

THE GIRL IN THE SPRINGS

Maybe we'll end up moving there and opening a restaurant slash detective agency."

"I like the sound of that. We could serve Sleuth's Spaghetti or Mystery Meatballs."

"And Columbo Calzones," I add.

Noah laughs loudly, even though I know it wasn't that funny. "I think we're onto something here."

"Yeah," I agree softly. "We definitely are."

Despite having red sauce all over his face, he leans across the table, kisses me, and then rubs his saucy lips all over my mouth and cheeks. I let him, laughing the entire time until my stomach hurts.

"I don't know how I'd do this without you," I gasp between bouts of hysterics.

"You'd manage."

"No. I don't think I would."

"Well, luckily for you, I'm not going anywhere."

"Good."

"Do you want to stay here for a while? We could swing by your place tomorrow and pack some bags."

"Yes, please. And I promise I'm a tidy house guest and a pretty decent cook."

"I believe it, but I wouldn't care if you were the messiest woman in Washington State. I just like having you around, and so does Buckaroo."

I smile as I wipe my face clean. "Well, I like being around."

"Good," he retorts.

"Good," I say back with a smirk. "How about a shower and a movie in bed?"

"You read my mind," he says, getting to his feet and extending his hand. I take it gladly, and he hauls me upright before wrapping his arms around me. "I'd offer to shower with you, but it's ridiculously small."

"That's fine, I like my showers molten hot anyway, and you strike me as a cold showers guy."

"You have guessed correctly. Okay, you go first, and then when I'm in there, you can pick a DVD from the shelf in my office."

"Perfect."

"Pajamas are in the top left drawer in the bedroom and—"

Noah's voice is abruptly cut off by an ungodly wailing that shatters the silence outside. Buckaroo is already thrashing against the door and barking furiously in response, and all I can do is freeze. I think I would fall if Noah wasn't still wrapped around me, and he must sense this because he sits me down on the dining room chair before pulling away.

"What the hell?" Noah mutters as he rushes to restrain the agitated dog. The noise sounds again, a deep and pained sound that sends shivers down my spine. It doesn't sound like any animal I've ever heard—it sounds human.

I shakily get to my feet and follow Noah, who has managed to wrangle Buckaroo. "It must be coming from Ben's hunting cabin," I say, my voice trembling.

Noah nods, his jaw set. He ushers Buckaroo away and rummages inside a storage crate used for muddy shoes by the front door before producing a gun. "I picked this up in town while you were talking to Donna," he explains. "I thought it would be a good idea, considering."

"Okay," I say warily, eyeing the weapon as if it might suddenly explode. "Do you know how to use it?"

"Yeah," Noah assures me, though I can sense a hint of uncertainty in his answer. "The guy at the store showed me how to handle it and let me fire a few rounds into a target. It's pretty straightforward." His words don't entirely convince me, but there's no time to argue as we pull our boots and clothes on and step out into the night.

"Don't worry, okay? The safety is on, and I'll ask questions before I shoot," Noah reassures me, whispering loudly as we trudge ahead.

"Yeah, it's fine," I say semi-convincingly.

Noah tucks his gun into his coat pocket, but I see him reach for it whenever the screaming happens again. The closer we get, the clearer it becomes—that is a man screaming. Something instinctual tells me to turn back, to call the cops, but we're already halfway there, my phone has no signal, and I refuse to let somebody else die on my watch.

Wanting to be on an even keel, I pick up a thick branch that is more of a wooden club and hold it by my side. I know it's silly, but

THE GIRL IN THE SPRINGS

Noah doesn't make fun of me. I don't even think he saw me grab it. His eyes are focused on the light ahead, and his ears perked for the sound. It comes again, and I flinch. It almost sounded as if someone was screaming right into my ear canal.

We follow the sound, and when the sound is at its loudest, we find ourselves not at a cabin in the woods but in a small, unassuming clearing that I've never seen before. Then I see it—a square in the ground, its edges made of light.

"Is that...?" Noah begins.

"A trapdoor," I finish.

CHAPTER THIRTY-FIVE

WE BOTH THROW CAUTION TO THE WIND, AND I RUSH forward and wrap my fingers around the handle of the seemingly heavy trapdoor. Meanwhile, Noah pulls his gun from his pocket and points it toward the door, ready to attack if necessary. We exchange a quick nod, one, two, three, and just as I start to lift the door, my gaze wanders, and I notice a large square patch of grass that has been carefully moved to the side. This is why no one has ever found this place on a search. It's usually completely hidden. You would have to know precisely where it is to find it. My stomach flips at the thought. Surely, whoever is inside is either a killer or a victim

THE GIRL IN THE SPRINGS

because what other purpose could such a secret hiding place in the middle of nowhere serve?

"Who's there?" Noah shouts, his tone commanding and his hardened expression illuminated by the golden light coming from below.

"Jesus!" comes a startled reply from whoever is inside. "Don't shoot."

The door is even heavier than it looked, and I groan as I open it all the way and lay it flat on the ground. Then I move to Noah's side and peer down into this underground enigma. Inside, I see Stanley, looking pale and petrified, his hands in the air. The heater is running inside, and he's wearing—unusually for him—a wife beater and tight sweatpants. He's not armed and looks far more afraid of us than we are of him. The gun certainly helps tip the scales, and as Noah keeps it trained on Stanley, I can take a quick look around.

From our vantage point, we see a large room below with wooden walls and floors that exude a cozy, rustic vibe. It resembles the other cabins scattered throughout this forest. The sturdy benches lining the walls are filled with tools and equipment commonly found in workshops, but they all appear to be brand new except for a layer of dust. And as with the other cabins, scattered lamps provide the only light source, while a low humming noise emanates from a generator in one corner.

Yet this cabin is unique. For one thing, it's situated underground and lacks windows as a result. Getting inside it, I imagine, is also not an easy task, and once you're in, there's no way to survey the surrounding area. Not that it's actually being used for hunting, it seems. There are no guns or stuffed animal trophies to be seen. Instead, it resembles a workshop, perhaps for building birdhouses or carving decoy ducks.

Stanley barks at us to come inside and stop letting the heat out, so we cautiously descend the ladder.

I turn to him, noting that Noah's gun is still raised. This doesn't seem to bother Stanley, whose gaze is fixed entirely on me. "Was it you who was screaming?" I ask.

"I'm afraid so," Stanley murmurs, cheeks reddening.

"Why?" I ask, bewildered. "Did you hurt yourself?"

"No, nothing like that. I'm fine. Really. I just... come out here to scream sometimes," he admits, lowering his gaze to the floor in shame. "I honestly thought it was soundproof," he chuckles dryly.

"It's definitely not, sorry," I say, trying to be kind. I can't exactly judge him for the noises he was making. If I, too, had an underground room that I thought was soundproof, I'd definitely use it for an occasional screaming session.

"You heard me all the way from Noah's house?" he asks.

"We did," Noah confirms, his brows growing close together.

"How do you know where I live?"

"Jealousy is a bitch," Stanley replies.

"You were stalking me."

Stanley tilts his head from side to side. "Only a little. Once or twice. I wanted to see what made you so special. Beautiful home, by the way."

"What is this place?" I ask, trying to detour from the stalking. After all, it's not as if Stanley is the only one here guilty of a bit of trespassing, and at least he didn't dig up any graves.

"It was my father's. He was one of those end-of-the-world preppers. The plan was we'd come down here in case of emergency."

"That explains the cans of beans."

Stanley nods, a flicker of amusement playing across his face. "Yes. And the cans of gas. He didn't really think it through, though. That door is a bit flimsy. I imagine it wouldn't keep nuclear radiation out."

"No. I imagine it would not," I laugh lightly, trying to find humor in an awkward situation.

"Is this all there is? This one room?" Noah questions, looking around.

"Yes."

"Where are the beds?" he pushes.

"Ah, yes. There are camping cots in the cupboard," Stanley explains, opening a door and revealing the folded cots, some sleeping bags, and a few pillows. As he stoops, I notice something that had been previously obscured by his body lying on a counter. It's a phone. Specifically an old flip phone, and clearly a burner.

Part of me tells me not to, and part of me needs to know. I pull my phone out as Stanley rummages in the cupboard, giving us a half-assed tour. I call the number associated with Ben Ramsey, the one I took from Maisy's phone, and the burner begins to buzz. Stanley quickly straightens, opens it, and then shuts it again, ending the call.

He looks at me and cocks his head. "Why are you calling me?"

"I wasn't. I was calling Ben."

"Ah," he says.

"Why do you have his phone?"

Stanley looks at me, smiling, his eyes dead. "It's not Ben's phone. It's mine."

"But... how?"

"Well, on my date with Maisy, she got a little sloppy and fell asleep on the couch. I then used her face to unlock her phone, changed my contact to Ben, and voila."

My heart rattles against my ribs, and I see Noah's thumb move to the safety release. "Why?" I ask. "Why would you do that?"

"Oh, Birdie. Don't play dumb. You know exactly what's going on here."

"You set up Ben. You took Maisy. You left that mysterious package on my doorstep."

"Yes, good job putting the pieces together. It's a shame, really. You're so intelligent and beautiful, something rare in this world. Most people aren't even worth their skin or oxygen intake, but not you. Yet you just couldn't resist interfering, could you? I had intentions of killing you initially but then decided against it. You weren't the right fit for my plans. You were lucky. Even tonight, you had the chance to leave, and I would have let you go unharmed. But then you had to go and make that phone call." He tuts, his expression manic.

"We can still leave," Noah says, looking back at the ladder. "You can't stop us."

"Are you going to shoot me, Noah? Really? Do you have what it takes to take a life?"

"I can shoot to wound," Noah counters. "Not kill."

"I find that hard to believe," Stanley says, taking a cautious step to the side.

"Stay right there."

"Alright," Stanley replies. "I'm still." He holds his hands up, and I am so focused on his face that I don't see what's in his hands until I hear the click of a button. Then we are falling. Neither of us bothered to look down, and now it feels like all there is is down—into the dark, into the black, hurtling towards God knows what. The entrance trapdoor wasn't the only one.

Thoughts of death rush around my brain, but it's hard to make heads or tails of what exactly I am feeling. Then I hit the ground hard, and I know immediately upon collision that the surface beneath me is concrete. It's unforgiving, and I cry out in pain as my shoulder crunches, probably fractured. Noah makes similar noises of agony, and despite the pain, I rush to his side.

"Noah, are you okay?" I ask, already crying, worried that I'll reach for his head and find a large, dented wound.

"Mm, okay," he mumbles through a mouthful of liquid. "Bit my tongue."

"Badly?" I ask, my hands on the sides of his face.

I feel him shake his head, scooch into his spread legs, and allow myself a moment of peace as he wraps himself around me. I feel him reach for the gun but with no success. It must've skittered far away in the fall. He pulls away from me to continue searching, and though I'm cold and afraid without his embrace, I don't cling.

Instead, I look around, my eyes adjusting to the darkness. When I start to make out shapes and objects, I begin to tremble like an earthquake, and my teeth are audibly clattering. We are surrounded by cages. Big ones, twice the size of the dog crate in Ben's hunting cabin, and with far thicker bars. I see movement in one and scramble backward, worried for a moment I might be about to be fed to a pet bear or wolf. At this point, it doesn't seem far-fetched.

The thing that is moving groans, and it sounds human. I take a swing in the dark and ask, "Ben?"

"Bridget?" he replies. "Holy shit, he got you, too."

"Was it you that was screaming?"

"Yeah," he begins, but his words are cut short as a door creaks open with a rusty groan. The hallway beyond is almost as dark as the room we're imprisoned in, illuminated only by a faint fluorescent light at the far end. In the dimness, the figure who opened the door is nothing more than a looming silhouette. Yet even so, his size and build are unmistakable: tall, broad, and beefy. This man is not Stanley, and as he turns his head toward Ben, I can see that he's wearing a gas mask. Before I can scream or beg, a soft hiss fills the air, and suddenly everything goes black.

CHAPTER THIRTY-SIX

WHEN I WAKE, I AM STARING AT BEN, WHO IS STARING at me. We're both lying on our sides, bathed in cold lighting, with bars separating us. He looks terrible; his face is a watercolor painting of bruises, and when he forces a smile, I see that he is missing one of his teeth.

"What did they do to you?" I ask, pressing a fingertip to my own teeth.

He tilts his head and props himself up, and I follow suit, seeing two people sitting in plastic chairs by the door of the concrete room. One of them is Stanley, pale and sweaty. And the other is a much older man with slicked-back silver hair and a large beard. He bears a striking resemblance to Stanley if you look past the extra

150 pounds and the excess of facial hair. Especially when it comes to the eyes and nose. I know who he is despite never having seen more than a dimly lit oil painting in the corner of a room. This man, the one who wore the gas mask, is Earl Crawford.

I glance to my right, checking on Noah, who is sitting up with one knee bent and his arm resting upon it. He looks worse for wear, bloodied, and bruised, but he's alive and cognizant. Which allows me to move on to priority number two.

"You're Earl," I state coldly, taking in every detail of his visage. He's well dressed, though his suit is a little tight.

"Very good, Miss Hartley," Earl booms, his voice deep and magnificent. In another world or circumstance, I might even think he's handsome or, at the very least, kind. However, I am in this world and this circumstance, and I find him disgusting.

"So, you faked your own death," I say, annoyed with myself for not seeing it before now.

"I did."

"Why?"

Earl extends a hand to me. "I could tell you, but why don't you give your best shot? Take a deep breath. I'm sure it'll come to you."

My head is swimming, memories blurring, but my tongue is sharp as I say. "In 1982, you murdered Bunny Sullivan, a hitchhiker. Your own parents were the only ones who suspected you, and they left you alone at the manor. Actually, they gave you the manor and a large sum of money, I assume. They probably felt guilty, or maybe even responsible."

"My mother certainly did," Earl agrees, and my eyes flick to Stanley. He still looks clammy, but something smug creeps onto his features. Is he proud of this?

"And I imagine, since Bunny's body was never found, that you dismembered her, buried her in the cemetery, or threw her into the river. At eighteen, you didn't know what you were doing yet."

"Ding, ding, ding. Very good, Miss Hartley. Yes. She, Bunny, was my first. A hippy, still riding the highs of the seventies. Quite literally."

"A hippy?" I ask myself. "Is that where the tarot cards came into play?"

Earl smiles fondly at me, and for a moment, I feel charmed by him. Apparently, he and his son have that ability in common. "Indeed," he answers, toying with his beard and relishing his exploits. "Bunny was a tarot reader, and that night, in my car, at Lovebird's Nest—yes, we oldies used it for hookups, too—she asked me to pull a card from her deck and tell her her fortune. I still remember her face as I pulled the card and showed it to her."

"Death," I say.

"Absolutely right. And before that, I was in two minds about killing her, but then I had a sign from the universe that it was time. She laughed it off initially, saying that it was merely a sign of things changing. But I could feel her fear, and when she asked me to drop her off or let her out, I struck."

"So Lovebird's Nest and tarot readings; that became a part of your ritual?"

"Yes."

"Even with your wife?"

Earl falters for the first time, and my eyes flick to Stanley as his smug expression is wiped from his face. Earl chokes on his own spit before spluttering, "Yes. Even Joanna."

"So she's the seventh body? The card on her grave was 'The Lovers.'"

"Ah, very good, Miss Hartley. You're just as smart as my son said you were."

"And why did you start to bury them? It seems a little counterintuitive, putting all of your victims together like that."

"I started to become more spiritual in my later years," he replies, scratching his hairy cheek. "You can blame Bunny and her fortune-telling and polytheistic beliefs for that. I wanted to honor the dead as one might honor a goat before slaughter."

"So," I continue. "You picked up hitchhikers and, I imagine, sex workers, and took them on dates before killing them. Then you disposed of them like trash because you probably thought they were. Then you wanted to graduate, wanted a 'higher tier' of prey. So you moved on to local teenagers, but instead of romancing them yourself, you killed couples."

"Yes, I was far too old by that point to go on dates. Plus, I was married at the time and couldn't risk upsetting my wife. Things change when you fall in love, Miss Hartley."

"So you want me to believe that you loved Joanna?"

"I did," he says solemnly, lowering his head but retaining eye contact.

"But she found out? So you had to kill her."

"Yes. Tragically. I believed, and believe, my work to be important, and I was not ready to be done. I wasn't scared of prison, mind you. But I was terrified that I'd never kill again."

"And then Ben found out. So you killed his girlfriend, left town, killed some more, and then came back. Except you weren't welcome here, so you had to fake your death to continue your 'work,'" I say, repulsed, my words dripping with bile.

"Yes. Though, mind you, I killed only once in California; it just didn't feel right. It felt cheap without the ritual. It lacked that magic, that higher power."

"Have you ever considered that God, or the gods, or whoever it is you believe in, were warning your victims rather than giving you the go-ahead?"

"Either way, it was a powerful way to garner some holy attention. And I haven't been smitten yet," he laughs ruefully.

I scowl at him. "So you're the ghost haunting Crawford Manor."

"I am," he confirms. "All those bumps in the night—it's all me."

"But you're not the only one. I saw your wife in the window," I tell him, maintaining unblinking eye contact. "Her spirit is trapped there because of you."

For the first time, Earl turns pale, and his hands drop into his lap. He looks between Stanley and me before focusing back on me. "What did you say?" His voice is low and threatening.

"I saw your wife's ghost in the window," I repeat confidently.

"That's impossible," Earl says before bursting into laughter. "You must have hit your head during the fall. Ghosts aren't real, Miss Hartley. Someone as smart as you should know that."

I smirk even though my cheek hurts. "So, when did you start using cages? After Gina and Carrie?"

"Correct."

"Wanted to play with your food?"

Earl looks at his Stanley, amused. "That's more my son's forte, but I enjoyed giving my prey a final meal, hearing their last words, absorbing what gave them and their lives meaning. It felt richer that way. Before, I was gulping down gruel just to sustain myself, but when I started to talk to them, it became a banquet. It gave them... flavor."

"You didn't."

"No. I'm no cannibal. This is more of a spiritual hunger."

I glance at Stanley, wondering what he's thinking about our current situation, but I can't get a read. Then my eyes shift to Noah, who looks like he may vomit at any moment. Finally, I turn to Ben, who is watching with wide-eyed fascination. All of the questions he's ever had are being answered bluntly and without persuasion. This is the closure he's been looking for, and I don't think he cares that we're facing certain death. He's just happy to have the truth revealed and is grateful that fellow innocents are here to witness it.

"Mia is a complicated story," Earl says sagely, returning to toying with his facial hair.

"I have plenty of time."

A smile graces his plush lips. "Not as much as you may think. Regardless, let's finish the story. I so rarely have the opportunity to tell it." He clears his throat before continuing. "Mia was a test for me. I caught sight of her running one day and couldn't help but be struck by her beauty. She radiated health and strength. A perfect specimen. So, I asked Stanley, who had shown interest in my work, to bring her to Lovebird's Nest under false pretenses. Then, while he played along, I 'captured' them and brought Mia here. I read her fortune—the Tower—and left her alone in this room to weaken. Finally, when she was vulnerable, I gave her her favorite meal before setting her 'free.' Stanley and I then chased after her through the woods competitively, and of course, he won. He graciously allowed me to finish the job," Earl says with pride, giving his son a pat on the back. "But it was clear to both of us that Mia would be my last."

"It was a passing of the torch," I say.

"It was."

"Which is why Maisy must be yours," I say, looking at Stanley now, his expression drawn. "The empty tarot box was a symbol of the new era. And you didn't go to Lovebird's Nest."

"No. I took Maisy home," Stanley replies. "Just like I did with you. It was easy with her. I didn't need to pay anyone to pretend to be a fake journalist to get her in my car. I didn't need to play hero."

The revelation is sickening. Those people at Notte Stellata were actors. Stanley set me up to murder me. "I could've died," I say aloud.

"You were very close. But then you turned down my advances. I have no interest in rape, but I do like to consummate with my kills."

I pull my knees into my body. "Maisy," I whimper. "Was she in the cemetery? Was that cat even yours?" I ask.

"No, and yes. Boudica was very much my beloved pet, and though your friend will eventually be buried next to her, for now, she's still very much alive, waiting in my bed for me to bring her champagne and chocolate-dipped strawberries."

"If she's alive, why hasn't she answered her phone?"

"Well, she's been rather drowsy lately, thanks to the morphine."

"So she was inside while I was—"

"Yes. And after I'm done with you three—collateral damage, I'm afraid—I'm going to plunge a knife into her heart."

My arms hang limply at my sides, palms turned up as if in surrender. My entire body feels numb, unsure of what to do in this moment or how to process the impending danger. Every fiber within me wants to scream, to lash out and beat against the bars of my cage, not caring if it breaks bones. Though I stay still, knowing it won't do any good. My prison is a solid one. Tears well up in my eyes, threatening to spill over as I think about my best friend's life hanging in the balance. Stanley is going to kill her, and there's nothing I can do about it. I wish he would kill me instead, but the reality of the matter is that he's going to kill us both.

"Did you pick her up because you saw Noah and me together?" I ask quietly, almost afraid to hear the answer.

"Yes," Stanley responds with a smug smile. "A little petty of me, I'll admit, but oh so satisfying. I'm sure she's a better lay anyway, and much less tempestuous."

The words hit me like a slap in the face, revealing just how callous and cruel he truly is. "And that day, that first day, in the restaurant," I continue, steeling myself for another painful revelation. "Did you know who I was and that I was looking into you?"

"Of course I did," Stanley laughs, sticking out his bottom lip, mocking me. "And I framed Archie and left Mia's body where you would stumble upon it. And when it comes to Keith, well, he actually broke out of your cage—quite impressively, I might add. But the door is thicker still, and after days of no food or water, he decided that the only logical option was a bullet to the head."

Tears of anger stream down my face as I struggle against the restraints, frustrated by my own weakness. Through gritted teeth, I hiss at him. My mouth is contorted in rage as I bare my teeth and let out a blood-curdling scream while kicking wildly. The men on either side of me join in, hoping to attract attention from anyone who might hear us.

Stanley and his father stand up, amused by our futile efforts. "Unfortunately for you all, this room is actually soundproof," Stanley mentions with a laugh. "I'll be back soon, but don't hold your breath for any last meals. None of you are special enough for that."

He picks up Noah's gun from a nearby shelf, examines it, and lets out a low whistle before putting it back in its spot. As he leaves the room, he flips a switch and plunges us into darkness again. Despite this, I am not subdued, and I scream until the others beg me to stop.

CHAPTER THIRTY-SEVEN

IT'S HARD TO GAUGE TIME IN THE DARKNESS AND QUIETNESS, but if I had to guess, I'd say at least two hours have passed when Stanley reappears. To my relief, Earl is not with him, and instead of turning on the blinding overhead lights, he presses on two wireless camping lanterns. They emit a similarly cold blue light but at a much lower intensity, allowing me to see without weeping or clutching my head. Of course, even if I did get a migraine, it would be over very quickly. I've heard a bullet to the head is something of a wonder cure when it comes to aches and pains.

"So what's it to be, Stanley?" I ask, far more cocky than I feel.

He doesn't look at me as he admires the gun on the bench, and after a few seconds, I realize that he isn't going to answer me either. My stomach twists as he puts the gun down and begins to rifle through a large box of what sounds like tools. I really hope he doesn't plan to get creative with our executions.

"So, I guess we'll be your first," I add. "You're a bit of a late bloomer."

"How so?" he asks, finally turning, a hacksaw dangling from his fingertips.

"Well, your dad was only eighteen when he killed Bunny. You're twenty-nine. That's an eleven-year gap."

"Never fear. I'll soon make up for it. Dad has never killed four people in one night."

"Hmm," I hum thoughtfully.

"What?" he snarls.

"It's just… Surely, if this was in your blood, you would've killed before now. I'm sure you've had plenty of opportunity, not to mention your dad would help you out of trouble."

"He didn't want me to. He wanted to hand me the reins when he was done. He didn't want competition."

"So you've just been waiting in the wings for your time in the sun?"

"I suppose."

"So, you've had the desire to kill all this time? It's been constantly on your mind?"

"Yes," he responds indignantly, his body stiffening and his back as straight as an ironing board. Yet I detect a slight tremor in his voice.

"Why do you want to kill? Is it a woman-hating thing? I know that there's a sexual aspect for you."

"What's with all the questions?"

"Come on, humor me. It's not every day an investigator like me gets to meet a serial killer in the making. And frankly, you kind of owe me, considering you're going to murder my boyfriend and my best friend."

"Fine," Stanley retorts, his voice clipped. "And no, I don't hate women. I prefer them, actually. None of this is about hate. It's about prey versus predator. It's about hunting something beautiful."

"And you inherited it from your father?"

"I believe so. And the way he tells it, his great-grandfather was similarly inclined. It's a family tradition."

"And where is Earl?"

"He left. It's all up to me now."

"I guess he'd be tempted to join in the fun," I say.

"It's not—"

"It's a bit like quitting smoking, isn't it, Noah?" I ask, twisting toward my partner. "Once you've stopped, you can't be around it anymore. Too tempting. Too sickening. Too nostalgic. And you know what they say about smoking," I add, ignoring Noah's bewildered look and focusing back on Stanley.

Stanley rolls his eyes. "That it kills?"

"No. That you should never start."

He makes a squeaking sound, his mouth hanging open in surprise. He quickly snaps it shut, transforming his face into a stoic mask, but I can still see the sadness in his eyes. "I want to start," he stubbornly insists, his tone almost childlike, and I half expect him to stomp his feet in frustration.

I speak softly, "Do you really want this? Or have you been groomed into wanting it? Your father is a killer, and he took your mother away from you and isolated you. He has brainwashed you into thinking this is what you want because it's all you've ever known. But it's not too late for you, Stanley. You're complicit, but you're not a murderer. You still have a chance to do the right thing. And let me make one thing clear—if Ben and I don't bring your father to justice, someone else will. My parents are influential, and I'm working with the police. What will they think when I suddenly disappear?"

"They're going to think your boyfriend murdered you," Stanley sneers. "Murder-suicide."

"Donna won't believe that."

"I guess we'll just have to wait and see," Stanley retorts.

"We'll back you up," I say, trying not to sound desperate. "We don't have to tell the cops about your participation. We can say that he's been holding you prisoner, abusing you, hurting—"

"He has!" Stanley cries. "For twenty-nine years, and I can't get rid of him. But if I do this, he'll stop. We'll be equals. He promised."

"Come on, Stanley. Do you honestly believe that? No matter what you do, it will never be enough for him. Even if he stops some forms of abuse, he'll just find new ways to hurt you. Do you really want to wait around for him to die? Wouldn't it be better if he was locked away in prison?"

"You don't know us!" he yells, regressing into a child before my eyes. "You don't know anything."

"I know that he killed your mom."

"I—" Stanley stops, swallowing hard. "He had no choice."

"Stop. You don't believe that. I know you don't. He has ruined your life, but it doesn't have to stay ruined. You can get rid of him and make something of yourself. Sell the house, be a librarian, and spend time with friends. It's all possible."

Stanley looks at me like I'm the dumbest person on the planet. "I'm not a librarian, and I don't have any friends."

"Oh," I reply quietly. I probably should have seen that one coming. "Well, I can be your friend. I can help you find a job. I can help you, Stanley, seriously. But I can't do anything if I'm dead. And you know that Maisy doesn't deserve this. You *know* that."

Stanley's shoulders sag in defeat, and his body trembles as he clenches and unclenches his jaw. Tears threaten to spill from his eyes, but he fights them back. "I don't want to kill her," he moans before sinking to the ground, his hands covering his face.

"Then don't," I urge.

"You don't understand. I have to. He'll kill me if I don't."

"You really think he'd do that to his own son?" I ask incredulously.

Stanley scoffs derisively, peeking through his fingers. "He did it to his own wife, and he liked her a lot more than he likes me."

He's got a point there, and I can understand his dilemma. "We can help you out of this. You just have to let us go. We'll go get Maisy together, and then we'll go to the police in your car. You'll be safe under their protection. And they will find your father, I promise you that."

Much to my astonishment, Stanley stands up and transforms back into the man I once knew. He reaches into his pocket and produces a glistening silver key before picking up the gun. "Don't try anything funny," he warns.

THE GIRL IN THE SPRINGS

We all raise our hands in a gesture of surrender, and he acknowledges this with a nod. He makes his way over to the cages and unlocks them one by one, starting with me and ending with the more formidable Noah. As promised, none of us make any sudden movements or attempt to harm him. What shocks me the most is when he hands the gun to Ben, who carefully secures it in his pocket with the safety on.

"I've never fired a gun," Stanley admits. "It'll be useless in my hands, and my dad is going to be waiting at the manor."

Even though I am still terrified of and disgusted by Stanley and his actions and his part in murdering Mia, I put a hand on his shoulder and whisper. "Thank you."

He shifts out of my grasp as if the unpleasant feeling is mutual and mutters, "Come on, let's go. The longer we take, the longer Maisy is alone with him."

I try not to think about what he's just said as we follow him along the concrete hallway, up the metal ladder, and into the warm cabin room. I let myself defrost for mere seconds before we press on up another ladder. Stanley struggles with the heavy trapdoor but manages at last, and I inhale freedom. Ben is ahead of me, Noah is behind, but it doesn't take long for us all to emerge into the forest. I bury my hands in the grass and soil as if I've been imprisoned for years. However, my joy is fleeting, and when I hear a tutting sound coming from the trees, I look up to see Earl ambling toward us, hands in his pockets, shaking his head.

"Dad!" Stanley exclaims. "I was just—"

"I should've known," Earl says, glaring down at his writhing son as the rest of us shakily get to our feet and back away. He places his boot atop Stanley's head and begins to apply pressure, causing Stanley to unleash a blood-curdling scream. I half expect his skull to explode like a watermelon, but it doesn't. Not yet.

"No!" I wail, lunging forward, ready to attack. Noah holds me back, and though I resent him at the moment—and I thrash and fight—I know I'll thank him someday.

"You are weak," Earl spits. "Just like your mother. I tried so hard to beat that weakness out of you, but it seems it was just a waste of a good belt. Your frailty runs all the way to the core. This was your chance, Stanley. And you blew it." Earl looks up at us and says, "So, I guess I'm coming out of retirement. I'll be damned if this oversized fetus ruins my empire. Who knows? Maybe your friend might give me a better son."

With a guttural, bestial roar that shocks us all, Stanley launches himself upwards, knocking Earl off balance and sending him stumbling backward. He lunges at his father with wild ferocity, his fists swinging in a frenzy as he scratches and claws at the man who has caused him so much pain. The man who killed his mother.

Stanley impressively lands three solid blows, and though blood gushes from Earl's broken nose, the larger man isn't fazed. In fact, Earl laughs callously at his son's futile attempts to hurt him, and in one swift motion, he levels a right cross to Stanley's stomach that sends him flying backward in a way I didn't think humanly possible. Yet, Earl is a huge man, a behemoth, somebody who managed to take down Keith. Stanley doesn't stand a chance, and after that hit to the gut, I'd be surprised if he wasn't bleeding internally.

As I look down at Stanley writhing on the ground, dark blood pouring from his open mouth, my heart races with fear and adrenaline, and I take a step forward. So does Ben, his gun aimed squarely at Earl's head, but Stanley's voice cuts clear through the chaos. "Don't!" he screams, and I realize that this is his fight. Even if it kills him. However, even though I retreat, Ben doesn't. He doesn't care about Stanley. He just wants Earl dead. With a slight smirk, he pulls the trigger.

Click.

I brace for the bang, but nothing happens.

Click.

Again, nothing.

Click.

Once more, the gun fails, and Earl is facing us now. He's a bull, and we're wearing red. "Shit," Ben mutters.

"Run!" Stanley yells. "Just go!"

I don't need to be told twice, so I take off running in the opposite direction, not even caring where I'm going. After about five minutes of sprinting blindly in the moonlit darkness, I figure out where I am. This is where I went birdwatching with Charlie.

That tree is where I saw an American Robin, which means we need to turn right.

"Follow me!" I say. "I know how to get to Crawford Manor!"

"We need to go to the police," Ben calls after me, winded by our mad dash.

"Do what you want, but I'm rescuing my best friend!" I call over my shoulder, the best runner in the group.

"But—" Ben begins.

"Listen to the lady," Noah interjects. "Or give me my gun back and piss off."

"Alright, alright. Jeez, everyone's so crabby today."

I can't help but laugh, even though we are fleeing from two crazed men through dangerous woods. "That's one way of putting it," I shout back. "Keep up if you can."

Ben grumbles quietly and drags his feet behind us, barely keeping up. Noah sticks close to my side as we make our way forward, and I gain confidence with every second. Confidence, which is not unfounded, as it turns out, as I duck beneath branches and jump over holes. As long as everyone copies me, we'll make it through unscathed. However, the terrain is not our only problem. After so many decades, Earl knows the way even better than I do, and just because Mia outran him doesn't mean I can.

CHAPTER THIRTY-EIGHT

AS WE FINALLY REACH THE EDGE OF THE FOREST, I AM out of breath, and Ben's heavy breathing suggests he may collapse at any moment. He tries to suppress his coughs, but it hardly matters. Our journey has been anything but quiet. We are not making an effort to hide ourselves either; Earl knows where we've gone and how to track us down. Mercifully, it seems like we've beaten him here.

"Jesus Christ. I'd forgotten how ostentatious this place is," Ben says, tonguing the word ostentatious in an unsavory manner. He clearly doesn't think much of the historical and enormous estate. I can't blame him. I love history, but I wouldn't shed a tear if they tore this piece of it down to the ground.

THE GIRL IN THE SPRINGS

"It certainly is *big*," Noah replies, saying the word with similar disdain.

I agree, though I thought it was majestic the first time I saw it; now all I see is a house of horrors, and what was once beautiful is oddly distorted. The windows on the side facing us aren't big; they're tall and thin like skeletal fingers. The red front door isn't an ode to Gothic architecture; it's a hungry, bloody maw. The hedgerows aren't perfect for privacy; they're perfect for hiding behind.

I shudder, and when I look closer, I gasp. The face—the same one I saw that day with Charlie, Joanna's face—is staring back at me from one of the windows. Her complexion is pale, her eyes dark and sunken.

I yelp and frantically point toward the window, exclaiming, "There she is! Joanna!"

Ben's jaw drops, and he curls up into himself, moaning in despair. "No, it's not."

"Then who is it?" I ask, wide-eyed, staring at the top of his thinning head of hair.

"It's Shelley."

Before I can say another word, and despite him being out of breath, he straightens and barrels toward the house at full speed, calling his ex-girlfriend's name at full volume. Of course, Noah and I pursue him, and as we do so, I look up and see that the woman has her hands pressed against the glass, and her panicked breath is leaving a condensation stain on the glass.

"Oh my god," I choke out as I stumble, not looking ahead. That is not a ghost. That's a woman. And she has been a prisoner for the past seven years.

I can hear Ben's voice echoing through the expansive green fields, shouting Shelley's name repeatedly. We rush towards the sound and pick up the pace as he reaches the front door. He hammers on it, he pulls, and he kicks, but it's futile. The door is too strong, and whoever is on the other side is clearly unable to reach it.

Frustrated, Noah curses and wraps his jacket around his fist and forearm. He punches the old, fragile window with all his might, causing most of it to shatter and fall away. He quickly clears out any remaining glass with a few more blows before jumping through the opening. He helps me climb through, making sure I don't step on any broken pieces. Then he extends a hand to Ben, who looks embarrassed for not coming up with this solution himself. However, his humiliation is soon forgotten, and without pause, Ben is screaming for Shelley once more as he races up the grand wooden stairs. I start to follow, but then I remember that I have someone else I need to save.

"Maisy!" I call out, but Ben's mournful hollering drowns out my voice. "Okay, everyone, be quiet for just a second!"

Thankfully, Ben silences himself long enough for me to hear the faint but audible response of "Birdie."

"Maisy," I whisper and throw open bedroom doors until I find the right one. And there she is, dressed in a vintage nightgown, in an enormous four-poster bed, weakly gripping an empty glass of champagne.

"Birdie. Where am I?" she murmurs, her eyes crossed from the drugs and drool pooling at the corners of her mouth.

"You're at Crawford Manor," I tell her, rushing to the bed and sitting down beside her, putting my hands on her arms. "Oh, God, did he hurt you? Did he do anything to you?"

"No," Maisy says. "No. We had sex, but I was only tipsy. He's left me alone since then." She turns to face me and gasps at the sight of my swollen cheek, her delicate fingers grazing over the bruise. "Oh, Birdie, what happened to you?"

"It's a long story—one I'll tell you later. For now, we need to get you out of here."

Maisy gives a slight nod of her head, and I quickly throw off the comforter and help her stand up. She stumbles and wobbles, but with my arm wrapped around hers and Noah's support on the other side, we manage to keep her upright. We make our way through the bedroom door onto the landing.

We pivot, and Maisy lets out an awful scream that is so unexpected I almost join her. However, I stop myself mid-intake of breath when I realize she's not screaming at Stanley or Earl; she's screaming at Shelley. And I can understand why. The poor woman looks like a ghost. She's pale, her dark hair is flat and greasy, and she must weigh eighty pounds at the most, which is far too little considering she must be at least five foot nine.

I can smell the stale sweat emanating from her clothes from here, but Ben doesn't seem to mind. He's wrapped around her, caressing her, gently peppering her with kisses that she seems to relish in. At the very least, she is appropriately dressed and wearing shoes, which is more than I can say for Maisy, but the years of torment are evident. She holds herself like a beaten shelter dog.

"He made me his pet," Shelley says, answering questions before they're asked. "Or more like his slave. It was just after he killed his wife. He took me from my home, intending to kill me, but then he changed his mind. He said I was special. He even took me to Northern California with him when he was chased out of town. He told everyone that I was his girlfriend even though he never touched me. Not like that anyway."

"And his parents?" I ask, bewildered that Wilma did not mention this crucial information.

"They were terrified of him. And they had no idea who I really was. But I could tell they pitied me. They even reached out to Stanley after Earl 'died' to check in on me, and he told them that I was free at last, severing my last lifeline."

I don't stop and tell her how sorry I am and don't ask more questions even though I'm dying to do so. Instead, I usher everyone to the stairs, and as a group of five, all down but not out, we descend and head toward our exit. As the four of us begin to climb through the broken window, Shelley lingers behind, insisting that she go last. Then, when her turn comes, and Ben reaches out a hand to her, a pained expression crosses her face, and she shakes her head in refusal.

"It's been too long," she insists, her voice trembling with fear. "I can't—I just can't."

"Please, Shelley," Ben begs.

After so many years in captivity with no sunlight, I understand her hesitation, but we don't have time for this. I wish we did. I wish this didn't have to be so hard. I wish I didn't have to choose between leaving her behind and saving my own skin.

Bang.

A deafening shot rings out, drowning out any other noise. I whip around to see Earl, illuminated eerily by the pale moonlight, standing fifty feet away. His finger is on the trigger of a rifle, the weapon aimed up at the sky. Then, before we can do anything, I'm staring down the barrel of it. The air feels thick and unbreathable. I don't know what to do or how to move. What I do know is that we were too slow.

"Here. Now!" he bellows, pointing at the ground before him.

I'm not in the habit of disobeying people holding guns, and apparently, neither is anyone else. The four of us move forward in a line and stand on our spots while Shelley sinks back into the darkness of the manor.

"Good," Earl says. "Now, on your knees. I'd like to make this quick."

It dawns on me that I'm about to get executed, and I freeze, unable to move. This is it. I'm really going to die. At thirty years old. In love for the first time. And worse, Noah and Maisy and Ben are going to die with me.

Earl eyes me with hatred. "I can do this standing if you'd prefer."

"Please don't kill us," Maisy whimpers. "We won't tell anyone anything. We'll move countries and change our names."

"I suppose you could do that, but this is so much cleaner, don't you think?" He looks back at me, and I resent the fact that he's too far away for me to grab the barrel. I'd never make it without getting shot first. "Now. Kneel."

Without a word, I slowly lower myself to the ground. I feel like a coward but don't know what else to do. I could run, but Maisy can't. I could try to attack and die in the process. Maybe that would be the best thing to do. Sacrifice myself for the other's survival. But I know they'd never leave me.

I can tell Noah is deliberating as I am as he joins Maisy and me in the grass. He looks spring-loaded, ready to leap, looking for opportunity. I don't think I can bear to watch him die, and when I catch his eye, I shake my head to tell him no. He softens, wilts, and looks at me long and hard with his emerald eyes. It makes me want to cry. His eyes are saying goodbye.

A startled gasp escapes Maisy's lips, drawing my attention back to the front. As I follow her gaze, a wave of exhilaration washes over me, and I dig my nails into her skin. She clamps her mouth shut, and we stare on in horror like sacrificial cows as Stanley emerges from the shadows with the same shovel I had used to dig Boudica's grave.

Earl gives us a peculiar look as he checks his gun. "Look at you. So still. Shaolin monks. I guess none of you are as weak as I thought. I appreciate that. The screaming is always tedious. It actually makes me respect you. It almost makes me not want to kill you, but alas," he says, cocking his gun, "I must."

Earl lines the gun up with my forehead, and as I squeeze my eyes shut, with Noah's hand in mine behind Maisy's back, a gunshot rings out. Yet I feel no pain. For a moment, I think this must be what death feels like—painless. But as seconds tick by, and I feel the elements battering my flesh, I open my eyes and look at the other three, who look back at me, and I see that all of us are unscathed.

Except for Earl. He is lying on his side, his eyes round and shocked, his rifle pointing far away from us, the barrel smoking. There is a wound on his forehead that is bleeding profusely, and Stanley holds the shovel above his head as it gushes. Earl moves thick fingers to the wound and gasps in horror as he brings the tips back down to eye level. He starts question after question but is never able to formulate a full sentence.

Screaming, Stanley brings the shovel down again, and blood splatters his face from the impact. Unable to tear my eyes away, I watch him hit his father's skull with force again and again and again until he stops moving. He's sobbing so hard there are clean streaks running through the cruor on his cheeks, but everything else is red as he falls to his knees.

We do the opposite of collapsing. Our bodies stiffen and extend, and our eyes widen in shock as we stand and stare at the scene before us. Then Stanley, with a face coated with pain and gore, reaches into his father's pockets. He doesn't even look my way, but I grab the keys all the same.

"Go," he says urgently. "Please, just go."

So we do, the fear, shock, and confusion chasing us like guard dogs as we flee to Earl's Jeep. We semi-patiently wait for Ben to coax Shelley out of the building, and this time he succeeds. So the five of us—Shelley sitting on the floor in the back, her head on Ben's knee—whiz away from Crawford Manor for the last time and make our way directly toward the police station.

CHAPTER THIRTY-NINE

I look at Noah as we pull up outside the restaurant and watch as he nervously adjusts his shirt collar. I lean back and fix it at the back before kissing him on the cheek. "It's fine. They already love you."

"Hmm," he says disbelievingly.

"Okay, they're close to loving you," I laugh. "The last time went well, didn't it?"

"Yeah," he mumbles, affecting a pseudo-pathetic voice and sticking his lower lip out.

I snort. "Come on. I'm their baby, and they want to make sure I don't make another decade-long mistake. Not to mention, everything is pretty weird right now."

"It's getting better, though," Noah says, squeezing my hand.

He's right. This month has been tough but also one of the most fulfilling of my life. I find joy and beauty in everything now and am determined to make the most of every second.

And it's not just me that's happy. Noah is back to working on the house project, Maisy has returned to Sproutville and sworn off dating, and Ben had his name cleared and now works for Donna. Shelley is still working through her trauma, but the family has been patiently, slowly re-integrating her into society after a tearful reunion. Archie is back to running Curio. And I have a new case to investigate.

It's not a murder this time, thank God. Instead, it's a very boring thievery case, but I've dubbed it 'The Porch Pirate Puzzle' to spice things up a bit. It's far from being my most exciting case, but I'll admit that I've been uncovering some intriguing information in my pursuit of the culprit. And I have a feeling there's more to this case than meets the eye.

As for Stanley, he's heading straight to prison. He pleaded guilty with a plea deal—twenty years with the possibility of parole. Typically, someone who's done what he's done would be locked away until the day they died, but his killing a serial killer—his abusive father, no less—and saving five lives in the process gave the judge a lot to think about. In a way, I'm happy with this outcome. Stanley has done terrible things, including murder, attempted murder, kidnapping, confinement, drugging, and assault, but I also pity him. I'm lucky I didn't grow up in such a horrible household. Who knows how I'd end up? And the only reason I'm here today, with Noah, about to walk into Notte Stellata to have dinner with my parents, is because of Stanley Crawford. I don't forgive him for Mia or Maisy—maybe I never will—but I am thankful to him, however hypocritical that may be.

"Ready?" I ask Noah.

"Ready," he confirms, kissing me quickly before exiting the car.

My parents pull up behind us, and they wave excitedly. My mom is basically jumping up and down in her towering Louboutins. I nudge Noah and glance upward at him. "See?" I mutter.

"It's actually your sister I'm worried about," he replies, even quieter.

"Oh, God, don't worry about Ada. She likes everyone, and her husband Patrick is..." I trail off, searching for the word.

"A jerk?" Noah inquires, almost hopefully.

"No. God, no. He's just not funny. He's super serious. He takes everything literally. It can be hard to make conversation with him."

"So that's the bar?"

"Yep, and you've already far surpassed it. You made my dad cry laugh. That never happens. Mind you, I have no idea why."

"You don't think my character was funny?"

"The bear from Chicago who's obsessed with deep dish 'pies'?" I question.

"Yeah, Jake."

"He's alright," I laugh.

"Birdie, darling!" Dad calls out. "And my good friend Noah."

I resist the urge to snort. One corny joke that would be more appropriate for a gaggle of easily amused children, and my dad and Noah are now 'good friends' apparently. Honestly, I'll take it in spades. It's better than Gavin ever got, and deservedly so.

Mom rushes forward and hugs us both, and Noah even gets an air kiss. He really must've made quite the impression at that last lunch. More so than I realized. It probably doesn't hurt that he's so great with Grandma June and volunteered to do the dishes, but whatever the reason, I couldn't be happier. I didn't tell him this, but I was just as nervous as he was. My parents can be a tad judgmental and were more than dismayed when I first announced that Noah and I were dating. His reputation—as unfair as it was—preceded him.

Noah looks very pleased with himself, and as my parents beam up at him, I suddenly feel like a bit of a fourth wheel. "Hey, is Ada still coming?" I ask, interjecting.

"Yes, of course," Mom confirms, peeling her eyes away from Noah as if by force. "At least as far as I know. Why?"

"She's just always five minutes early for everything."

"Pregnancy brain," Mom says confidently. "Poor thing. When I was pregnant with you, I forgot everything."

"She kept putting the TV remote in the fridge," Dad snickers.

"I did. I kept getting up, remote in hand, to get snacks—olives were the go-to—and then I'd take the olives and leave the remote behind. And on and on it would go. My God."

I laugh and relax. She's probably right. "Come on then," I say. "Before I lose my table."

"As if," Mom replies. "Your table is basically a permanent fixture."

"Not today," I say. "I got us a table on the ground floor."

My parents look shocked, but Noah looks proud. "Fresh start," he says, wrapping an arm around me.

I nod. "Yeah. Maybe one day I'll go back to it. But I want to try something new and be around people."

Ever since Stanley 'rescued' me on that fateful night, I can't bring myself to sit at my old table. It's become synonymous with him in my mind. Even though I miss it, it doesn't feel like my own anymore. I still have some healing to do before I'm ready to reclaim it.

We step inside, and Isabella quickly seats us at the second-best table in the house. Champagne on ice awaits us, and my stomach growls when I look at the updated menu. Dad pops the bottle before sitting, fills our glasses, and we chat while scouring the menu. I think I'll go for pizza. Noah talking about Chicago's 'pies' has got me craving them.

"Linguine alle Vongole sounds great," Noah says, nailing the pronunciation, which elicits approval from both of my parents.

As usual, those two go back and forth about what they want while we wait for our starters, and then ten, twenty minutes go by, and anxiety starts to roil inside, as well as hunger.

"Ada's really late," I say.

"Yes, she is," Dad replies, furrowing his brow. "I'll text her."

He does so, and I do, too. The message goes green. "Her phone is off," I say, holding up my phone to show everyone my screen.

"Surely not," Dad says and calls her, plugging one ear with his finger. It rings out. Then Mom tries to call her, and though I know it's hopeless, I do, too. Nothing and more nothing. So, I look up car accidents in the area, but there's none. Nothing on the traffic reports or in the news.

"God, I hope she's alright," Mom says, fiddling with her necklace while gulping down wine.

"They probably just forgot. My fault entirely," Dad says, trying to soothe us all. "I meant to remind them, but it totally slipped my mind. I haven't mentioned it to either of them in over two weeks."

"Yeah, me neither," I say.

"Patrick has been so busy," Mom adds, her high shoulders lowering. "And Ada has been so sick. Bless her heart."

"Well, there we go then," Dad says, enthused once again, as Noah reaches for my hand under the table. "I'm sure we'll hear from them soon."

We do. It happens on the sidewalk as we say our goodbyes. Dad's phone rings; it's an unknown number, but he's getting old and answers everything. He even talks to spam callers. Regardless, I wait to see who it's from.

"Hello?" he answers, and very quickly, the smile he's worn all evening is wiped from his face. "Yes. Okay. Yes. God. Okay. Okay. Yes. Okay." Then, after approximately four minutes, it's over, and he looks at us in horror.

"What?" Mom demands, tugging on her necklace so hard I'm worried it might cut into her skin.

Dad sighs, blinking rapidly. "That was Patrick. He's in jail. Ada is missing, and the police think he has something to do with it."

AUTHOR'S NOTE

To our insanely amazing readers, you have been on so many adventures with us. You cannot even fathom how much your love and support means to us. It has been our greatest joy to write for you and serve you with our writing. We are truly grateful for you taking your time to read our work and continuing this adventure together. If you're a new reader, welcome! We hope to hear from you as well.

We truly hope you loved this novel and enjoyed our newest series. Serenity Springs is a passion project for the both of us. We have read your emails and came up with this series as a response to honor our brilliant readers!

We are indie authors, and your wonderful reviews make a world of difference for us. We need your help to keep this series going. If you were enthralled by this novel and would love to see this series keep going and develop into something special, we would be truly grateful if you could leave us a review.

Just a few seconds of your time is all it takes!

By the way, if you find any typos or want to reach out to me, feel free to email me at egray@ellegraybooks.com

Yours truly,
Elle Gray

CONNECT WITH ELLE GRAY

Loved the book? Don't miss out on future reads! Join my newsletter and receive updates on my latest releases, insider content, and exclusive promos. Plus, as a thank you for joining, you'll get a FREE copy of my book Deadly Pursuit!

Deadly Pursuit follows the story of Paxton Arrington, a police officer in Seattle who uncovers corruption within his own precinct. With his career and reputation on the line, he enlists the help of his FBI friend Blake Wilder to bring down the corrupt Strike Team. But the stakes are high, and Paxton must decide whether he's willing to risk everything to do the right thing.

Claiming your freebie is easy! Visit
https://dl.bookfunnel.com/513mluk159
and sign up with your email!

Want more ways to stay connected? Follow me on Facebook and Instagram or sign up for text notifications by texting "blake" to 844-552-1368. Thanks for your support and happy reading!

ALSO BY
ELLE GRAY

Blake Wilder FBI Mystery Thrillers
Book One - The 7 She Saw
Book Two - A Perfect Wife
Book Three - Her Perfect Crime
Book Four - The Chosen Girls
Book Five - The Secret She Kept
Book Six - The Lost Girls
Book Seven - The Lost Sister
Book Eight - The Missing Woman
Book Nine - Night at the Asylum
Book Ten - A Time to Die
Book Eleven - The House on the Hill
Book Twelve - The Missing Girls
Book Thirteen - No More Lies
Book Fourteen - The Unlucky Girl
Book Fifteen - The Heist
Book Sixteen - The Hit List
Book Seventeen - The Missing Daughter
Book Eighteen - The Silent Threat
Book Nineteen - A Code to Kill
Book Twenty - Watching Her
Book Twenty-One - The Inmate's Secret
Book Twenty-Two - A Motive to Kill
Book Twenty-Three - The Kept Girls
Book Twenty-Four- Prison Break
Book Twenty-Five - The Perfect Crime
Book Twenty-Six - A Shot to Kill
Book Twenty-Seven - Double Cross
Book Twenty-Eight - The Silent Hunt
Book Twenty-Nine - The Hunter's Game

A Pax Arrington Mystery
Free Prequel - Deadly Pursuit
Book One - I See You
Book Two - Her Last Call
Book Three - Woman In The Water
Book Four - A Wife's Secret

Storyville FBI Mystery Thrillers
Book One - The Chosen Girl
Book Two - The Murder in the Mist
Book Three - Whispers of the Dead
Book Four - Secrets of the Unseen
Book Five - The Way Back Home

A Sweetwater Falls Mystery
Book One - New Girl in the Falls
Book Two - Missing in the Falls
Book Three - The Girls in the Falls
Book Four - Memories of the Falls
Book Five - Shadows of the Falls
Book Six - The Lies in the Falls
Book Seven - Forbidden in the Falls
Book Eight - Silenced in the Falls
Book Nine - Summer in the Falls
Book Ten - The Legend of the Falls
Book Eleven - Whispers in the Falls
Book Twelve - Sins of the Falls
Book Thirteen - Shades of the Falls
Book Fourteen - Revenge in the Falls

A Chesapeake Valley Mystery Series
Book One - The Girl in Town
Book Two - The Lost Children
Book Three - The Secrets We Bury
Book Four - The Secret Cabin

A Sapphire Valley Mystery
Book One - The Girl in the Valley

ALSO BY
ELLE GRAY | K.S. GRAY

Olivia Knight FBI Mystery Thrillers
Book One - New Girl in Town
Book Two - The Murders on Beacon Hill
Book Three - The Woman Behind the Door
Book Four - Love, Lies, and Suicide
Book Five - Murder on the Astoria
Book Six - The Locked Box
Book Seven - The Good Daughter
Book Eight - The Perfect Getaway
Book Nine - Behind Closed Doors
Book Ten - Fatal Games
Book Eleven - Into the Night
Book Twelve - The Housewife
Book Thirteen - Whispers at the Reunion
Book Fourteen - Fatal Lies
Book Fifteen - The Runaway Girls
Book Sixteen - The Woman Next Door
Book Seventeen - The Grand Heist

A Serenity Springs Mystery Series
Book One - The Girl in the Springs
Book Two - The Maid of Honor
Book Three - The Girl in the Cabin
Book Four - Fatal Obsession
Book Five - The Secret Packages
Book Six - The Hunting Ground

ALSO BY
ELLE GRAY | JAMES HOLT

The Florida Girl FBI Mystery Thrillers
Book One - The Florida Girl
Book Two - Resort to Kill
Book Three - The Runaway
Book Four - The Ransom
Book Five - The Unknown Woman

www.ingramcontent.com/pod-product-compliance
Ingram Content Group UK Ltd.
Pitfield, Milton Keynes, MK11 3LW, UK
UKHW021327140126
10102UKWH00023B/294